I0739087

LIV

VOL 1

ONCE UPON A TIME

ELEANOR "C-PASS" JONES

ISBN: 978-09976622-1-4

Library of Congress Control Number: 2016953386

Edited by: Ava Teherani

Cover Art Direction: Eleanor "C-PASS" Jones

Cover Design: Juan Roberts, Creative Lunacy, Inc.

Published by
Knowledge Power Books
Valencia, California 91355
www.knowledgepowerbooks.com

Printed in the United States of America

DEDICATION

I gratefully dedicate this book with all my love to the memory of my father and mother, Alvin McCoy Harrell, Sr., and Essiemae Lavetta Harrell, the sources of love, wisdom, encouragement, positive examples, inspiration, guidance, and support all my life.

Acknowledgements and Kudos

Above all, I acknowledge and thank God through my Lord and Savior, Jesus Christ, for His presence in my life and for all the good gifts given to me that can only come from above.

I thank Sunji Ali for casting me to play the part of "Liv" in his musical, "Sweet Water Blues" which was the impetus for this book in my endeavor to make the character come alive for me by creating a history for her, which took on a life of its own and grew into the story as told in "LIV: Once Upon a Time" and its continuation, "LIV: Happily Ever After."

I thank all of the people with whom I have come into contact over the years—family, friends, co-workers, supervisors, and even my enemies, for the roles they have played in giving me insights, inspiration, and the entire gamut of emotions from which I have drawn that I have endeavored to evoke through the words and stories depicted in "LIV."

To try to name all the supporters who have encouraged me through this process would be impossible; but I would be severely remiss if I didn't mention and thank my family members for their support, many of whom lent the use of their first names; my husband, F.B. (who remarked about Morgan, "Now everyone will know everything I'm not!"); my brother, Howard Harrell, for his consultation on some technical matters; and two of my very good friends who have been very involved, namely Charlene Moore and Diane Phillips. Thanks, everyone!

I would like to acknowledge three more very significant persons who were instrumental in bringing these works to fruition. Graphic artist Juan Roberts did a superb job in taking the scenes I envisioned in my mind's eye and bringing them to life. Editor Ava Teherani was quite competent and sensitive, effectively making suggestions and subtle changes while maintaining the integrity of my story and the characters. Willa Robinson, of Knowledge Power Books, was a source of encouragement and support, holding my hand throughout and has become a true friend and sister in Christ.

CHAPTER 1

I remember the first time I met her. How old was I? Four? Five? Three? I really don't know. I just know I was frightened. No, I was terrified! I wasn't crying, but I hurt . . . very badly. My throat was burning. I was confused and didn't know or understand what was happening to me.

I saw a light and I started running toward it through utter darkness. It was just a tiny speck of light in the far distance, but I kept running toward it. The closer I got to the light, the larger it appeared and the less frightened I felt.

Suddenly, I reached the light and found myself in an unbelievably beautiful place. The sky was the bluest of blue speckled with fluffy, white marshmallow clouds. There were many trees, and the plush, thick, cool grass was tall and very green with a rainbow bevy of fragrant wild flowers dispersed throughout. The sun was shining brightly, and the warmth and light were enveloping my entire being. I was no longer running, but walking, looking around and marveling at the beauty caressing my spirit and my body. I could hear the birds merrily tweeting an uplifting air. Everything was permeated with tranquility.

I heard the sound of gently running, flowing water, and I headed toward the sound. Soon I could see the sparkling clear blue water flowing a few feet away. There was a large, leafy olive tree looming head and shoulders above the other trees about an arm's length from the bank. It provided respite from the direct sunlight while maintaining the warmth mingled with a gentle, fragrant breeze.

I stopped short when I saw her, this little girl just about my age. She was sitting in the tall grass under the tree with her back against the trunk, legs bent Indian style. I stood motionless, watching her and wondering who she was, where she came from, and how she got there. She looked at me and smiled. Encouraged, I returned her smile, but said nothing. Still smiling, she held her arms out and beckoned me to come. I felt very relieved and safe to have someone else there with me. I sat down beside her under the tree.

"Hi, Olivia. I've been waiting for you. I knew you would come!" she said.

"Do you know me?"

"Of *course* I know you, Olivia!"

"What is *your* name?"

"What kind of fruit is on this tree?"

I looked up and saw the olives on the tree and said, "It's an olive tree. Those are olives that I see."

"Yes, they are olives. That's my name."

"Your name is Olives?"

"No, Silly. *Olive*! My name is *Olive*! I am your *best* friend. I knew you would find me one day. I've known you forever!"

Olive put her arms around me, and I held on to her. I don't know how long we were there under that tree, saying nothing, just holding on to each other for dear life. I felt safe and loved. I wanted to stay there with my new friend forever!

"Why haven't I seen you before now?"

"You never really *needed* me before now; but now it's time for you to go home."

"But, if I leave, how can I find you again? I don't want to go . . . ever!"

"Olivia, you *must* go. I'll *always* be with you; and you'll always find me whenever you need me, for as long as you need me. I *promised!*"

She was right, of course. We spent many a time together—singing, talking, sharing our hopes and fears (or *my* hopes and fears), my dreams . . .

CHAPTER 2

(5/10/2012) Her right front wheel bumping into the curb jolted Liv from her reverie. Her autopilot must not have been functioning up to par. No damage, however. She was just glad it wasn't another car, or worse yet, a person! She continued on toward her destination, making a mental note to pay more attention to her driving. Nevertheless, her mind was drifting back to the wonderful scene she had just left.

The car behind her was honking furiously before she even realized it was there, or that she had been creeping along at six miles per hour.

Liv was glad the temperature had fallen from its searing afternoon high to a pleasant degree which would require her to contend only with the heat she was sure would be generated by the situation she would be facing soon enough.

"Gee Whizzikcers! What have I gotten myself into this time?" she thought out loud. She knew she could still back out; Julia (that's Dr. Julia, her therapist) would not know. "Yeah, right!" she said, again out loud. "Who am I kidding? She *would* know. She seems to know *everything*!" Liv resigned herself to the fact that *she* would know, too; and she *did* make a commitment.

She reduced her speed even more and began looking for the address of her destination. There it was, 10887! Liv took her time parking. The meeting was to start at 7:00 p.m. It was 7:03. She was too early. She had to make sure things were well in progress so that she could slip in unnoticed. She had promised to come. She *didn't* promise to participate.

While killing time, she checked her appearance. She wondered if she should have downplayed it, not wanting to draw attention to herself. Her hair was shiny and black, hanging loosely in large waves past her shoulders. She scrutinized her face—her skin. She marveled that it had survived with no scars. Her body was well toned and agile. She was in perfect health. Like her mother, she had no problem with her weight. Her mother was very beautiful. All her friends said so. For as long as she could remember, people would comment about her looks and how much she looked like her mother.

"What an adorable little girl!"

"Will you look at those pretty little legs!"

"You're going to be a real heart-breaker, you know that?"

Liv didn't pay attention to them. Sometimes she wondered who they could possibly be talking about. She felt very uneasy. Dr. J would have a lot to say about that!

Liv had been seeing Dr. J for about six weeks, every Tuesday and Thursday afternoon, 2:00 o'clock. Thinking about it, Liv found it amazing how Dr. J could understand so much about her from all the things she did *not* say. It was almost like she could really *see* through the wall she claims Liv had erected between herself and the outside world.

Liv had become very indignant when Dr. J suggested she come to this meeting. What could she possibly do here that she couldn't do with Dr. J, just the two of them?

The 7:45 red LED numbers on the dash caught her eye. If she didn't hurry, she might just pop in during a comfort break. Heaven forbid *that* should happen! She climbed out of the car and put on her dark glasses. "Okay, Meeting, here I come!" she announced.

The sign in the entry directed her to room 206. As she climbed the stairs, Liv considered bailing out. The door to 206 was slightly ajar, and Liv could hear clapping as she approached. Hesitating, she peeked through the door. She was glad they were not on a break.

It was a large room with windows on the west wall. On the opposite wall a few feet from the door was a long table. One end contained all sorts of goodies and coffee and hot water for tea. The other end of the table contained various pamphlets and literature.

There was a smaller table, just big enough to accommodate the two people occupying the two chairs, flanked by chairs all around forming a large semicircle in the center of the room. One man was standing with his hands in his pockets, leaning his head apologetically to one side. He sounded as if he were about to cry.

"Oh, no!" she thought, realizing it was too late to bail. She thought no one noticed her slip in, but another man added a chair to the circle and gestured for her to sit. The older gentleman who was speaking seemed unfazed by her entrance. She definitely didn't want the focus to be shifted to *her*. Trying to take up as little room as possible, she squeezed into the circle and sat down. She kept her purse strap over her shoulder with the purse positioned in her lap and assumed the posture that said, "Do not disturb!" Nevertheless, everyone looked at her at least once and smiled.

The speaker obviously had not been attending the meetings very long. Liv didn't know his name and wasn't really listening to what he was saying. She focused on his body language. He looked disheveled, and he was playing with his fingers, probably out of nervousness, and his head was lowered and was still tilted, as if apologizing for being alive. She named him, "Mr. Apologetic."

Liv honestly tried to pay attention, or at least to not look so disinterested; but it was just too hard, especially since she hadn't slept much the night before and didn't want to be there. She focused on the other people, sizing them up, checking out their clothes, guessing their ages, anything, until she got bored with that just about the time Mr. Apologetic finished.

"We love you, Brian!" they all chorused and clapped as Mr. Apologetic, aka Brian, sat down. The woman next to him gave him a hug as the man on his other side patted his shoulder.

"Is there anyone else that would like to share before we go to our newcomers?" a gravelly voice sounded from across the circle behind the small table. A somewhat distinguished-looking gentleman readily stood up.

"Hello! My name is Bob, and I'm an alcoholic."

Then came the chorus again with, "Hi, Bob. We love you!"

"Yes, I'm an alcoholic," continued Bob, "and I have been clean and sober for two years."

The thunderous applause that erupted took Liv by surprise. She looked at these people who all seemed genuinely happy for Mr. Bob. She didn't know whether to unfold her arms and clap or not. By the time she decided to "do as the Romans do," everyone had stopped.

Mr. Bob began again. "It hasn't been easy. It's been a long, hard struggle. But with the help of my Higher Power and all of you here, it has been possible. I feel a little like Job in the Bible. You know? He had so much. He had everything, and then he lost everything, including his health. Only, Job didn't do anything to deserve what happened to him. But he was restored with even more than he had at first."

"Oh, for Pete's sake! Is this going to be a sermon? Please spare me!" Liv thought. But he continued, and she zoned out big time!

She thought about Olive, whom she had not seen since "That" day so long ago. Olive had promised that she would always be there if Liv needed her. Liv felt like she needed her now. Oh, well, she decided she would have to create the scene in her mind and imagine the peace and tranquility, which she did for a time.

Back in the present, she finds that "Job," aka Bob, is still talking.

"Finally, it all came to a head. When my wife left with the kids, I just started drinking more and more. It took several years for me to hit my bottom. I was so hopeless. But, thanks to the program and my sponsor, I have come a very long way. Although my wife, my ex-wife, moved on, I am looking forward to re-establishing relationships with my children. I have begun to try to bridge the gap, and I know it will happen. Thank you all for your love and support."

Amid the chorused "We love you, Bob!" and the applause, Mr. Boredom was calling loudly to Liv, so loudly that she just couldn't resist. But then she heard the gravelly voice from across the circle speaking to her, and she felt all eyes focused on her, probably the only "newcomer," she guessed.

"Miss, would you like to share with us?"

Of course she did . . . *NOT*. She felt like a rat caught in a trap with no escape. "Well," she thought, "since I have endured *this* much, I might as well grit my teeth and bear it." She rose to her feet reluctantly and began, "My name is Olivia Wa . . ." She had barely begun, and already, she was being interrupted.

"No last names, please!"

"Oh, I'm sorry. Okay. My name is *Olivia*," she said and paused.

"Hi, Olivia. Welcome! We love you!" came the chorus.

"You know, that's the first time I have said, 'My name is Olivia' since I was fifteen . . ."

Then came a voice from the circle, "You forgot to say, 'and I'm an alcoholic!' "

Liv found the face of the culprit and glared at her in silence while everyone waited for her to respond with the phrase of the evening. "Sorry! No can do!" she said to herself.

"I am *not* an alcoholic!" she said ardently. "I may have a *little* problem . . . *once* in a while; but an alcoholic? I don't think so!"

Liv took note of their smug reactions, looking at each other and shaking their heads as if they knew something she didn't, and should. She took a moment to collect her thoughts. She was peeved. "They want a show? I'll give them a show!" she thought.

CHAPTER 3

"I guess now I'm supposed to tell you my 'story.' " After a brief hesitation, she continued, "You want to hear about my childhood? My father died when I was little, maybe five or six. I killed him. I couldn't keep him as my father. When I went to school and the other girls would talk about their families, their fathers, I figured out for myself that the man I called 'Daddy' *couldn't* have been my *real* daddy. You see, I found out that *real* daddies didn't hurt their little girls, or make them do . . . I knew my *real* daddy had to be dead, or he would have come and taken me away!

"When there was no one around, he would make me drink from this little brown bottle. It smelled bad and tasted even worse. And it hurt when I swallowed. But somehow, when I drank it, he didn't *hurt* me so bad. I still felt awful, but not so hurt physically. I had two brothers, both bigger than me. *They* were just like my . . . just like *him*!

"One day, my mom and I were home all by ourselves. I was scared to death, but I forced myself to tell my mother about the things that he does to me. I had wanted to so many times, but I really believed it when he said he would cut my throat so that I couldn't sing any more. I wasn't worried about dying—that may have been a real blessing. But the thought of losing the only thing that made me happy—the ability to comfort myself by singing—was something I didn't want to risk.

"I knew she didn't know, because she would never have allowed it! My secret fantasy was that when I told her, she would take me in her arms, tell me she still loved me, and then she would take me away and the two of us would live happily ever after!

"I poured my heart out to my mother. I told her everything my six-year-old mind could comprehend. She looked at me the whole time, her expression never changing, never saying a word. After what seemed like a lifetime of silence, she held me by my shoulder, and I felt her palm land across my cheek with such force that I'm sure I would have flown through the wall if she had not been holding on to me.

"I couldn't believe it! By now she had both my shoulders in her firm grip, fingernails almost digging into my flesh, her cold, hard face two inches from mine. I could feel her brown eyes piercing deep into my core. Her words were seared into my brain!

" 'Listen to me *very carefully*,' she said unequivocally, accenting every word. 'You are *never* to speak of this again, *to anyone*! If you do, I hate to tell you what will happen to you! Now go to your room!' "

"I ran to my room crying my heart out. I tried to sing, but I just couldn't. I don't know why, but I went to where that little brown bottle was, and I drank some—without even being made to. It still tasted nasty. It still burned, but I did it myself . . . and I began to feel a little better—for a while. So you see, I *don't* have a problem with alcohol. I am *not* an alcoholic. I just drank some when I had real bad times, when I was feeling really bad. I knew I shouldn't let anyone know about that. No one told me to keep it a secret—I just wanted to.

"Everybody thought I was a good little girl. That is, everybody but my family. But then, they thought my whole family was good. Whenever we were in public, he became this loving, protective father, keeping us all close to him. He came with Mom to all of our school events—PTA meetings, parent conferences, back-to-school nights, open houses, doctor appointments—everything! Everyone thought he was the perfect father. But I knew the monster he was when no one else was around!

"I learned to be very good, very quiet. My brothers and I had to make sure we made no trouble. We didn't dare! I made all A's in school. I was even allowed to skip a couple of grades because I read and studied a lot. I even read my brother Randy's school books. My favorite non-school books to read were fairy tales. I loved Hans Christian Andersen and the Brothers Grimm. I think it was those stories that gave me some sort of hope that one day *I* would have a fairy tale ending and live happily ever after!

"I didn't have a TV in my room, and I seldom watched the TV in the den—only when no one else was there. My teacher, Miss Martin, told me I was a really smart little girl, I just needed to 'open up' more, not to be so shy. I loved going to school. I loved going *anyplace* where my family was not, especially *him*!

"I thought that when I grew older, it would be different . . . better. But I was wrong. I got bigger, and so did my body! I started noticing that the way my stepfather would look at me that made me feel so unclean, other men did, too. For a long time I felt so ashamed I did everything I could to hide my body and keep people from noticing me. I even started eating food that I didn't like just because I thought it was 'fattening.' I thought I could get so fat, and dress so frumpy that no man would even want to look at me. It didn't really help. Besides, often I felt so bad, I couldn't make myself eat. But I could still take a few sips from the little brown bottle!

"I vividly remember that night in particular when I was about ten years old. My stepfather had come in very late, and he was drunk as usual. He and my mother were arguing about something. I knew that was the prelude, and I knew what was coming next. I told myself, as I had so many times before, 'Olivia, you have to stop him. Don't let him do this to you again!'

"I thought back to the last time either of my brothers had tried to molest me. They knew about their father, but he didn't know about them. All I needed was to find out that *they* were as afraid of him as *I* was. How amazing it was to learn after all those years that the words, 'You touch me one more time, and I'll tell Daddy on both of you!' would immediately end the abuse at the hands of my brothers!

"I knew it would take much more than words to stop my stepfather. I quickly slipped into the kitchen and picked out the sharpest knife I could find. My heart was beating two hundred times a minute, and my hands were shaking so hard, I had to hold them under my arms. But I had come this far. I crept back to my room, put the knife under my pillow, climbed into bed pulling the covers over my head . . . and waited.

"The heavy, foul scent of stale alcohol, tobacco, and bad breath wafted in and announced his approach. My heart began to pound so loudly, I was sure it echoed throughout the house. I could hear him slurping down the last ounce from his famous brown bottle. I could picture the familiar sight of booze spilling out of his mouth, down his chin, and onto his hairy chest. (Oh, how I *hate* chest hair!) I don't know if it were a blessing in disguise or not that he didn't have anything left in his bottle for me.

"I thought about the knife resting just beneath the pillow under my head. I realized the mistake I had made in not having it in my hand. In an instant, this foul-smelling monster had yanked off my covers, turned me onto my back, and imprisoned me beneath 274 pounds of dead drunk weight.

"Wave after wave of nausea, loathing, and hatred swept through me as I endured for the millionth time the perverseness of this man who was supposed to have been my father. Mercifully, Olive was waiting for me in our haven, away from that awful little bed in that dreary little room in that terrible house with those dreadful people.

"All too soon, I was back. This time there was a difference. I knew I had to escape permanently. When I realized he was deep into his alcoholic stupor, I summonsed all the strength I could muster and heaved him off of me. He normally left me and went away; but tonight he was really out. I sat on the edge of the bed, every part of my body trembling, my brain in a heated battle between reason and the combined forces of all the emotions of fear, anger, self-loathing, shame, and hate.

"I reached under the pillow, my hand shaking until it touched the cold, steel blade. I found the handle and gently pulled out the knife. As I held it in my hand thinking about what I was going to do, I was so calm, it scared me. I was no longer shaking. My emotions seemed to have won the battle with my reason. I was going to kill him—and everything he stood for.

"I slipped off the bed and stood looking down at him, listening to him snoring loudly with his mouth open and thick, slimy drool slowly dripping out the corner. It literally turned my stomach to look at him. I realized I hated him so much more than I feared him.

"I held the knife with both hands as high as I could. I wanted to put the full force of my weight into the plunge. As I held the knife above my head, I contemplated where I could strike to inflict the most damage and do the job with a single blow. I didn't want to have to keep repeating it. The thought of a bloody sight sickened me so much so that I dropped the knife and barely made it to the bathroom. The time spent in retching and hugging the toilet bowl gave my brain the edge it needed to regain control over my emotions."

Liv was wrested back to the present hearing, "Miss, would you like to share with us?" the gravelly voice repeated as more heat began radiating from Liv's collar. She felt sweat popping out on her forehead. She felt everyone looking at her. She realized that she had been totally in her head, for how long she had no clue. She had no idea what had transpired or what she had missed while she was telling 'her story' in a flashback. It *may* have only been a second or two. At any rate, she was relieved that it hadn't happen. Still, she was caught off guard.

"I, um, don't think I'm ready just yet if you don't mind," she managed to say.

"Well that's perfectly all right. You don't have to say anything, Dear, until you are ready, whenever that time comes. We're glad you are here. You are free to just listen. Who would like to go next?" she asked.

Whew! That was close. Liv had dodged the bullet that time. She still had so many thoughts and memories crowding around in her head. A first-person account of her reflections reads like an autobiography, as follows.

I thought about my best friend, Elizabeth. We had been practically joined at the hip since the day she and I first enrolled in the same school and were assigned to the same class.

Since neither of us knew anyone, it was natural for us to stick together. Though our personalities and our lives were completely different, we did have a lot in common. We were both two years ahead in school, having been accelerated due to our scholastic achievements, rendering us "too young" to associate with our peers in the fifth grade, and "too old" for the third graders. We both were the only girls in our two-parent homes. I had two older brothers, while she had only one.

One big difference was that I was extremely shy and introverted while Elizabeth was totally bold and outgoing. It was because of her that I was not bullied. I was Elizabeth's friend, and everybody knew it!

Our major difference was in our home life. Elizabeth had to me what seemed like the *perfect* life. I loved to hear her talk about her family, the things they did together, the trips they took, and the games they played. I was not envious of her; as far as I knew at the time, *my* life was normal. I was able to enjoy life vicariously through her anecdotes.

I never talked to her about my life outside of school. When I only barely responded to her questions and never expounded on anything, she must have sensed my discomfort and did not press me, for which I was glad.

Elizabeth regularly went to church with her family and had been inviting me to come with her. I always made up excuses. I finally told her that my mom wouldn't let me. Her mom called to see if she could take me to Sunday school with her little girl. To my great surprise, my mom had consented. This was to be a one-time thing, I was sure.

The experience was all new to me. I felt very welcome and loved in this place of worship (as they called it). The people, even the men, were all so nice and kind. And I really liked what I heard about Jesus, how He loved *everyone*, no matter how bad they were. I remember thinking that maybe, just *maybe*, He could even love me, as bad as *I* was. I really *wanted* Him to. I wanted *somebody* to love me!

I knew that if I let her know how much I loved it there at Elizabeth's church and wanted to go back again, I wouldn't be allowed to. Everything that made me happy could be used as a tool against me, to punish me, or to control me. I pretended that it was no big deal. In fact, the next Saturday when Elizabeth's mom called, I said I didn't want to go. My mom looked almost disappointed. I could imagine Elizabeth's hurt. I had already told her how much I wanted to come again.

I was beginning to think I had made a mistake when a few weeks went by and they didn't invite me again. I tried to remember what I had learned. They talked about prayer. I wasn't sure what that was, or how it was supposed to work, but you were supposed to just ask Jesus—tell Him what you want—and because He loves you so much, He will give it to you. I wasn't sure if I really qualified for His love or even if I knew how to pray; but I figured it was worth a try. Besides, what did I have to lose?

I remembered seeing on TV little kids getting on their knees beside their beds at bedtime and saying things like, "God bless Mommy, and Daddy, and Grandma, etc. etc." I knew I didn't want to say, "God bless Daddy." If there were a chance that Jesus would answer my prayer, at least once, I sure didn't want to waste it on *him*. I wasn't even sure what "bless" meant. I just figured that if Jesus did it, and Jesus is loving and good, then "bless" would have to be something good, too. I wanted it for me.

I went to bed early that night, but I didn't say my "prayers" right away. I waited until everyone was asleep. I didn't want anyone to know. After all, I was almost eight years old. If we had never talked about prayer in our house before, it may be because they didn't want it, and they might be mad if *I* did. Besides, if they heard me ask Jesus to let me go back to Elizabeth's church, then they would know that I really *did* love going there. No, I couldn't let them know.

It took forever for the house to fall silent with lights out and everyone asleep. As soon as I was sure, I crept out of bed. I wasn't sure just how to do it, but I got down on my knees, put my elbows on the bed, my palms together with my fingers barely touching my chin, held my head up, and closed my eyes. Somehow I figured it had to be done just right. Besides, if I didn't get my wish, I could blame it on the fact that I didn't have the right position. Otherwise, it would mean that this kind and loving Jesus would be able to love everybody but *me*! Then I wouldn't have a chance at all!

Uncertainly, I began speaking, "Mr. Jesus, it's me, Olivia. I know You don't know me. Or, maybe You do. I don't know, but You probably know this is the first time I have ever prayed. So please excuse me if I don't do it right. I'm only eight, see? Well, anyway, my name is Olivia Louise Washington. I want to ask a favor of You. Will You please tell Elizabeth's mom to invite me to go to church again with them? I really loved it there. The people are so nice to me, and they sing songs all the time. I *love* to sing! They might even let *me* sing with them, too!

"I'm sorry for taking up so much of your time. There are probably other little girls who want to pray, too. But, please, before I go, if it's not too much, can I ask you for one more thing? Will you let my mother say 'Yes' when they ask? I will be so happy, and I promise I will be a very, very good girl from now on.

"Well, thank You, Mr. Jesus. Good night!"

I got off my knees and climbed into bed, but I couldn't sleep. I sat up in bed and went over and over in my mind the "prayer" I had just said to Jesus. Did I ask for too much? Did He really hear me? Did I do it right? What if He were too busy tonight? I knew I couldn't sleep until I figured out what to do.

I thought I'd ask Elizabeth tomorrow at school. I had a million questions. Then I thought, "If I tell her how I prayed, she might tell her mom, and her mom might ask my mother if I can come to church with them. Then my prayer would come true, but it will be because I told Elizabeth, and I'll never know if Jesus had anything to do with it. No, I decided to just keep practicing until something happened. Well, that was settled, so I went to sleep.

I prayed my prayer every night for the rest of the week. I just *knew* something would happen! Saturday afternoon I was singing to myself in my room when my mother opened the door. "Olivia Louise," she said holding the phone in her hand, "Your friend's mother wants to know if you want to go to church with them tomorrow. You can go if you want to."

If I *want* to!!! At that instant I thought I should become an actress instead of a singer. My performance was worthy of an Academy Award! In my heart I was jumping up and down yelling, "He answered my prayer! He really answered my prayer!" I don't know how I was able to contain myself so well, unless it was the ever-present need to hide my true feelings.

"My friend?" I asked with as much disinterest as I could muster. Is it Amber? Kamiah?"

"I don't know her name. It's the same one you went with the time before."

"Oh, that was Elizabeth. Well, okay," I said, nonchalantly.

Jesus had not only heard, but *answered* my prayer! I knew what that meant. He *did* love me! I knew I would not ask him for anything else soon, but that night, I got on my knees again.

"Mr. Jesus, it's me again—Olivia. Thank You for answering both parts of my prayer! I am *so* happy! I will remember my promise to be a very good girl from now on. And I won't keep bothering You all the time. In fact, I won't bother You at all for a while! Good night!"

I was up bright and early Sunday morning. I got my shower, dressed, and waited.

I had such a good time! The Sunday school teacher was very happy that I was so interested and that I was asking so many questions. I wanted to learn as much as I could about Jesus. I wasn't sure if or when I would ever be able to go back. The teacher, Miss Carter, gave me a little Bible to keep for myself. She said I could read it as much as I wanted, and anything I didn't understand, I could call her and ask her during the week. She had written her telephone number on the inside cover.

CHAPTER 4

A New Convert

I started going to church with Elizabeth and her family as often as I dared to. In between, I would question Elizabeth and make her repeat everything she had learned. She even began teaching me some of their songs so I was able to sing along with the congregation.

I read the Bible Miss Carter had given me every night before I said my prayers. I had learned so much more about Jesus since I had been going to church more often, reading my Bible, and following up with questions of Miss Carter.

One thing I prayed for was that Jesus would make my parents, especially my mother, love me like Elizabeth's mother and father obviously loved her. I was very careful to keep a low profile when it came to praying and reading my Bible. I questioned myself why, since I was learning that the Good News of Jesus' love was to be shared, and your whole family could be a part of it. But deep inside, I knew . . .

Inevitably, it happened. For several weeks I had been left alone at night. I dared to think that part of my life was now over. I became careless about my secret Bible reading and praying. On the eve of my 11th birthday, I was deep in thought about the passages I had been reading. I never heard my door open, and I was unaware of the presence of my stepfather standing over me, watching me with the open Bible in my hands.

"What 'cha readin,' Girl?" he shouted as he snatched the book from my hands. I was so totally taken by surprise I reacted instinctively.

"Give me back my Bible!" I demanded in a tone and volume to which he was not accustomed from me. Like a flash, his fist took me by even more of a surprise. I was sure my nose was broken. I didn't know what pain was until he lifted my eighty-nine pounds with his by then three hundred pounds and flung me like a rag doll into the wall. The force was so hard that the picture fell, and the window glass rattled.

I could feel the blood oozing from my nose and from a cut above my right eye. I felt the room spinning, and I could see my eyes growing dim, as if a dark shade were being pulled down over them. My last thought was that my mother surely heard the commotion and would come in and intervene. Sure!

I can only imagine that he proceeded to do what he had intended. I wasn't able to retreat to my haven, but I was thankful for the unconsciousness.

When I awoke the next morning, I had two black eyes and dried blood caked around my mouth and my nose. There was an extra-large grade AA egg-size lump on my head. My ripped nightclothes were discarded in a bloody heap on the floor. My nude body was sprawled, battered and bloody in my blood-soaked bed. My head felt like a rock, still spinning, and I ached from head to toe.

I dragged myself up and made my way to the shower. I would not have even left my room except that I didn't have my own bath. Even the gentle force of the water brought more pain. I stayed in the shower as long as I could; but with only one bathroom for my brothers' and my use, time was limited. Besides, I wanted to be out before anyone came. I didn't want to be seen. I didn't even want *me* to see me, but I forced myself to take a peek in the mirror.

Big mistake! I winced as I saw my right eye swollen shut; both eyes black and blue, a busted lip, my swollen nose. I didn't go any further. I grabbed my robe and headed down the hallway to my room. I heard my stepfather's voice talking into the telephone receiver, and I stopped dead in my tracks.

"... Yes, that's right ... No, I'm sure she will be out for at least a week ... No, there were no broken bones, but that truck hit us pretty hard. She wasn't wearing her seatbelt, as she knows she is supposed to, and she got banged up pretty good, more than any of us. My wife had only minor injuries. We were very fortunate ... No, that's really not necessary. I wouldn't want you to go to all that trouble. I'll just have her brother stop by and pick up her assignments. Yes, yes ... Thank you. Goodbye."

So that was it! I had been injured in an auto accident—with a truck, no less. I was happy to learn I had no broken bones! I quickly made my way to my room. I wondered why he said his wife had injuries, too, but I didn't dwell on it. I dressed, cleaned up the mess in my room, and changed and made my bed. I remained in my room all day. Although my feelings for my mother at this point were almost as hostile as those for my fa ... stepfather, I had hoped she would come in at least to see if I were still alive. She didn't.

I sat looking in my mirror at the horrible sight that was my face. I felt so ugly. It wasn't the black eyes, the swollen nose, the busted lip, or even the black and blue marks. I knew that in time they would return to normal. I pictured myself as I *normally* looked. I was still ugly. I *had* to be. Maybe my stepfather was right when he said I was good for nothing ... nothing else, that is. Did I cause him to treat me the way he did? Could I really blame my mother for not loving me?

But what about Elizabeth's mother? And Miss Martin? And Miss Carter? And all those nice people at Elizabeth's church? And what about Jesus, too? No, that didn't count. He's supposed to love me no matter how bad or ugly I am.

To Forgive or Not to Forgive

Jarred from her reflections by the sound of sobs, Liv looked up to see a woman about her age, maybe a little older, crying unashamedly. She wondered what she had been talking about, and she began to pay more attention. She looked around the circle to see how the others were responding to her. It seemed everyone was misty-eyed. Some were actually crying as well.

She was an attractive woman, casually dressed in baggy sweats. "All those years, I blamed myself," she was saying, "and it affected my whole life. But the hatred I harbored was turned inward and only hurt *me*, kept *me* from moving on with my life. I was a *very* angry person. I finally listened to those voices of reason from insightful friends who assured me that my hatred for him only impacted *my* life and had *no* effect on *him* whatsoever. *He* certainly wasn't hurting because I hated him; he was probably not even aware of my feelings.

"I sought and got help for myself. It was such a lightening of my burden to be able to tell my story to someone else, someone who really understood and was trained to help me. The most important thing I learned that *I* had to do was to *forgive* my father. I know how strange that may sound to some of you who may not yet have come to that realization. You see, I never *wanted* to forgive my father. Somehow, I felt that to forgive him was to excuse him for what he did, to absolve him of all responsibility. I *didn't* want to do that.

"I learned another important thing. I was not forgiving my father for *his* sake. It was for *mine*! My hatred for him was hurting *me*, not him. A counselor put it into perspective for me by telling me that hating him was like shooting *myself* in the foot and expecting *him* to limp!

"Actually, it was in letting go of the hatred and anger for my father and taking the steps *I* needed to take, and am still taking, to forgive him that I have been able to come to the level of wholeness that exists in my life today. It was and still is a process, I find, to forgive. At first it was just lip service. I had to learn to act as if, and I am finding that it is becoming. I've learned to fake it until I can make it completely.

"I've heard it said you must forgive and forget. There are some things you *can't* forget. If you cut off my right arm, I may find a way to forgive you; but every time I see my right stump, I will be reminded of what you did. So, no, you may *not* be able to forget. But forgiveness *is* possible."

By the end of her discourse, she was no longer crying. She smiled and took her seat amid the applause from all of her well-wishers. Liv had not heard her whole story, but what she *did* hear spoke volumes to her. She totally identified with this stranger. She felt a bond that both angered her and gave her some hope for the future. She was perplexed by her feelings.

"*Me*? Forgive *my* father? *Never!*" she thought. She had suffered too long and too much at his hands. She had no desire to forgive anyone! The hatred she harbored had fueled her anger and resolve, and she had *wanted* to keep it! It had been fueling a purpose she had determined for herself. Although that purpose had diminished substantially with the passage of time and her own evolution, she had held on to the hatred. Liv recalled the letter she had received from her brother, Kevin. She had been performing at her supper club for about two months. She took the week's accumulation of mail that had been placed in her dressing room home to read later. Once home, Liv sifted through the mail, and one letter stood out. She didn't recognize the handwriting or the return address but noticed that it was addressed to Olivia Washington c/o her Club. That really got her attention—her fans didn't know "Olivia!" She hurriedly opened the letter and began reading.

September 24, 2011

Dear Olivia,

I know you are probably wondering how I knew where to contact you, and I am probably the last person you would ever expect or want to hear from. I beg you, please, do not destroy this letter until you have read everything.

As you can see, I am in prison. I received a visit from an old friend who had gone to your club. He thought he recognized you, even though your name is different. He got an autographed picture of you to show me to verify if it were really you or not. I am truly happy that you are well.

You have every reason to hate me. I participated in making your life a living hell! I can only hope and pray that one day you can find it in your heart to forgive me. I am not offering any excuses for what I did. I only want to take full responsibility for my behavior and tell you how deeply sorry I am.

I've been here long enough to do plenty of soul-searching and reflecting on my life. I remembered the change in you when you started going to church with that African-American friend of yours, Elizabeth. (I bet you didn't even know I knew about that or even knew her name!) I could see there was a distinct difference in you.

Since I've been here, I understand it now. I have experienced what some call a "jail house conversion." Regardless, I now know God through my Lord and Savior Jesus Christ, and I fully embrace my new life. I have turned my life completely over to Him.

I am asking for your forgiveness because I am truly sorry; and also because I know that if you haven't forgiven me and won't, you will never be what you have the capacity to be or to enjoy the perfect peace and love that is there for you to embrace in Him.

Liv stopped reading. In anger, she flung the loose pages across the room and glared at them as they wafted to the floor.

"Who does he think he is?" she seethed to herself. She didn't know what upset her most—the fact that he was now asking for forgiveness, or that he was preaching to *her* about *her* need to be forgiving.

Though she was angry and stopped reading, for some reason she couldn't destroy the letter. She retrieved the scattered pages, crammed them back into the envelope and tossed it into her bureau drawer, where it remained, never to be consciously thought of again. No, she still had no desire to forgive.

Another circle member had begun sharing, and Liv could not make herself pay attention. She was still fixed on the thoughts prompted by the young lady who had talked about forgiving.

CHAPTER 5

The First Sleep-over

Liv was so caught up in her own reflections, she didn't realize that the last individual had finished his story. She didn't even know what it was. The clapping hadn't caught her attention, either. All at once she could feel the heat rising from her collar again, and she was acutely aware of the thundering silence and the unnerving sensation of many pairs of eyes all fixed on her. She looked from one to the other with a tinge of growing panic. Her attention was drawn to the sound of the gravelly voice from across the circle.

"Miss, you might find that it would help you if you would share with us. Don't be afraid. It's okay."

Liv found the pair of eyes that went with the gravelly voice. Suddenly, she was angry! "Who do they think they are? And what right do they have to pry into my personal life? Okay," she thought, "I'll give them a story they won't soon forget!"

She slowly stood up, surveying the group of strangers who were eagerly waiting with bated breaths for what was sure to be the highlight of the evening. She smoothed her skirt and flipped her hair. She stood there, her head held high, with an air of superiority, deliberately delaying to allow the suspense and curiosity of her captive audience to build before she would began "Her Story!"

It seemed that time stood still as her life began to flash before her eyes. Strangely enough, she focused on probably the most significant period of her young life. It was when she experienced the happiest time as well as the event that catapulted her into the person she was to become—at least for a while.

(4/12/2006) Olivia was excited at the prospect of "Youth Week" at Elizabeth's church. She had heard about the fun everyone had each year during the week of activities leading up to Easter Sunday morning, especially the three-day camping trip.

She wondered about one girl, Holly. They had become acquainted, but they were not close friends as she and Elizabeth were. She was a year older and usually very quiet. On Palm Sunday she approached Olivia, which was kind of unusual, because she usually kept to herself and did not initiate conversation.

"Are you going on the camping trip?" Holly asked.

"Of *course*!" Olivia replied. "Isn't everyone? Aren't you?"

Holly hesitated and finally answered, "No, I'm not."

Olivia could see there was more she wanted to say, so she waited. As Holly was about to continue, Elizabeth came running up, all excited, "Olivia! Come on! We have to go sign up! If we want to be tent partners, we'll have to get there right away! Come on!"

Olivia looked inquisitively at Holly, who responded, "Go on, Olivia. I have to go home now, anyway. Goodbye." Olivia watched as she turned and walked away, sensing that she had missed out on something important.

"Come on," urged Elizabeth, pulling her by the arm.

After they had registered, Olivia asked Elizabeth about Holly. "Why doesn't Holly want to go to camp? Everybody says it's such fun!"

"Yes, it is," she laughed. "I don't know about Holly. She used to go all the time, even last year. She has sort of changed . . . stopped saying or doing much kid stuff. She just comes to church on Sundays and leaves with her parents. She never comes to any of the youth activities anymore." She paused momentarily in reflection, then, "But come on! We've got to get ready for our trip!"

It was so exciting for Olivia, just thinking about the camping trip. Even more amazing was the fact that not only did her mother agree to let her go, she also let her spend Wednesday night at Elizabeth's house. Olivia was too happy to think about *why* it was allowed. She had never, ever spent the night away from her family before. She was going to make the most of it!

Elizabeth's mom and dad made her feel special. She helped Elizabeth set the table for dinner. She was a little embarrassed that she didn't know how to do it. They never sat down with everyone at the table together to eat at *her* house. Everyone just grabbed a plate, fixed it from the pots on the stove and went their separate ways, whenever they felt like eating.

Once she learned that it was good to give thanks before eating, Olivia was glad that she was usually alone. That way, in private she could give her thanks to God openly (but softly) without just having to say it in her head.

Elizabeth didn't make her feel uncomfortable about not knowing how to set the table properly. She patiently instructed Olivia to follow her example, which she did meticulously. She knew she would remember it exactly. Still, she didn't quite know how to behave with Elizabeth's family. Everyone seemed to have their own place, just for them. Mr. Randall sat at the end of the table in the chair with the two arms. Mrs. Randall sat at the other end. Roger, Elizabeth's older brother, sat across from her next to an empty chair, and Olivia sat next to Elizabeth in the other chair that would have been empty except for her.

Olivia was awed to witness and participate in a family "Grace" before eating. The food was so wonderfully delicious . . . and there was a marvelous apple cobbler for dessert! What was so amazing to her was that they actually *talked* to each other during dinner—and they included *her* in their conversation! After dinner, she helped

Elizabeth and her mom clean the kitchen. That was *her* job at home, so that was something she could do very well.

Olivia and Elizabeth were so excited that night, they couldn't sleep. They packed and repacked their bags. They had taken their baths, and Elizabeth's mom and dad listened to their prayers. They both kissed each of them goodnight on the forehead and tucked them into bed. Olivia didn't know what to think about that.

She was a bit nervous, but it felt very pleasant. (Elizabeth told her they had always done that for as long as she could remember, and they continued to do so even though she was a grown-up teenager of 15!) Olivia considered Elizabeth to be such a lucky girl.

The Camp

(4/13/2006) Camp was everything Olivia had imagined, and more. There were games, food, races, swimming, cooking out, storytelling, and even a talent show! Olivia couldn't swim, but she could cook, was very good at making up stories, and of course she could sing! She sang in the talent show, and everyone clapped and begged for more. It was no longer a talent show — it was an Olivian concert! She was elated! She must have sung every song she knew.

The youth minister, Pastor Jason, signaled an end of the first day with a call to prayer. It was sheer exhaustion fueled by excitement. Despite the group prayer, Olivia felt the need for her own personal prayer. She had so much to be thankful for, she wanted to make *sure* God knew.

The next day was even more exciting, if that were possible. There were more games, a spelling bee, a Bible quiz, word games, and more. Olivia participated in everything and did okay. She wasn't the best in anything, except the talent show, but it didn't matter. She was having a great time, and she felt like a normal person, doing normal things with normal people.

(4/15/2006) Olivia had heard about the activity everyone looked forward to the most. It had been instituted for the first time the previous year in which teams of two were paired off in a special version of "hide-and-seek." The "hiders" were given a 30-minute head start to find a hiding place. The "seekers" then had sixty minutes to find them. The "seeker" pair who found the most hiders won, and the hiders who were found last or not at all in the allotted time also won. Participants were restricted to ages ten and up. Other activities had been scheduled for the younger campers.

Olivia was disappointed that she could not be paired with Elizabeth. This would be the first time they would be on competing teams. Nevertheless, Olivia was excited. She felt lucky to have been paired up with Pastor Jason. He seemed so dedicated in serving the youth of the church, and he always prayed the most beautiful prayers! It didn't go unnoticed by Olivia that he was also kind of cute.

The boundaries had been established, about a half-mile in all directions from the camp. They all joined with their partners, synchronized their watches, and, following a brief prayer led by Olivia's new partner, they were off in all directions.

Olivia watched everyone scurrying off and was wondering which way to go. She didn't have to worry. Pastor Jason seemed to know exactly where to go. He took her hand and said, "This way!" with a confidence-inspiring voice of authority. As she followed him, she thought, "How wonderful it would be to have a kind, God-fearing man like him for a father!"

Olivia followed him exactly, in the footpath that his big walking boots trudged out for her. Instinctively, she began making mental notes of landmarks. She had a pretty good sense of direction, but part of her way of being was to be ever vigilant, another tool in her arsenal of defense mechanisms. It helped her to predict her level of safety in a given situation. In this instance, if something were to happen to separate her from her partner, she would be able to find her way back to the campsite. Her imaginative mind was always creating situations and ways to overcome them. In this instance, Pastor Jason could fall, or become trapped, or incapacitated in some way, and she would have to make her way back to get help.

The terrain grew thicker as they continued on up little mole hills and around huge boulders. There was a stream, which Pastor Jason found a portion where she could jump over without getting wet. They trudged over the terrain for about 15 minutes. Olivia was beginning to get a little winded keeping up with the pace. She saw several places she thought might make suitable hiding places, but Pastor Jason kept going.

About five minutes later they came to a secluded area that looked like a dead end. They had passed a few other such places, but this one was rockier and had thick brush and trees edging it. Olivia watched as Pastor Jason eyed the brush, seemingly looking for something in particular. Evidently, he found it, and took out a pair of thick gloves from his backpack.

Olivia watched as he carefully removed two large stones that were evidently holding the bushes in place. He then removed the trees and bushes to reveal a small opening in the side of the rocky mountain. It was just big and wide enough for them to slip in sideways.

"What a miracle," Olivia thought. "We will surely win. No one would possibly find us here!"

He carefully concealed the entrance by pulling on a cord that he tied around a few of the bushes and secured the rope inside the tiny cave. Olivia became frightened at the darkness. Pastor Jason struck a match and lit a hurricane lamp that materialized. Olivia was momentarily grateful for the dim light. As her eyes focused, she began to feel uneasy.

She could discern a crude pallet on the ground. She was puzzled. She turned to inquire of Pastor Jason, but the look on his face told it all! Her eyes closed in dread. "Oh, my God!" she thought. "This is not possible! Not him! Not here!"

But yes, it was happening. And she knew it would change her forever.

"Olivia," he said finally, "you are a very beautiful girl. Please don't be afraid of me. I won't hurt you. Please cooperate with me. Be nice to me. I won't hurt you."

He pulled her petrified body to him, her arms hanging limply at her sides. She could feel his hard body pressed up against hers, his warm, wet mouth on her neck. He was trembling, but his grip was firm. She didn't have a little brown bottle to dull her senses. She knew she could not overthrow this young, determined predator in minister's clothing. He would take her body, but she determined he would never break her!

She wanted Olive! She was trying fervently to find her! She didn't understand why she couldn't. Surely Olive would not desert her, not now when she needed her so desperately! She had promised!

There seemed to be no escape for her this time, no place of refuge. Once again, Olivia found her body under the control of someone other than herself, being used and abused for the purposes of some pervert. She tried to blank the on-going event from her mind. But it was difficult when she was so acutely aware that other hands were touching her body where only *her* hands should touch!

Olivia focused her thoughts and forced her mind to dwell on something far more important than what was happening to her body. That afternoon her entire world was being changed—changed forever! She became convinced that it was *her*. It *had* to be *her* fault! Her last spark of hope was being brutally, viciously, and irreparably trampled, much like a tender young flower under the booted foot of a menacing, giant ogre.

The thoughts prevailing in her mind included, "Why had I been given a glimpse of what a good life could be like, only to find that everything I had come to believe, to trust, was a lie? There are no good men in the world!" As far as Olivia was concerned, God wasn't real—He couldn't be. "Would a God who is supposed to be Love allow this to happen to me? To *me*? I, who had finally learned to trust in something with all my heart, who had taken great risks to pray and read my Bible?" she reasoned to herself. She determined it was all for nothing!

CHAPTER 6

Reinventing Olivia

Olivia had no idea how she came to the calm decision she had made. The thought, the idea had never entered her mind. She was faced with a situation, and she determined that she had a choice to make. *She had a choice!* For the first time in her life, Olivia realized that she had a choice. She determined that it was her against the world; her against her family; her against the church; her against *men*; her against God!

Her against *God*? She had to think about that a moment. She had learned many things about Him, and she still believed a lot of it was true. She believed He was all-powerful and could do anything. She didn't believe she could possibly prevail against Him, especially if He didn't like her. It was obvious to her that He *didn't love her*. How could He have betrayed her like this? Why was this happening to her . . . again?

No, she realized she could never get the best of God. She would just pretend He doesn't exist. She figured she could make it without His help since she had survived many years before she even knew He existed!

Now that she had stopped trying to escape to the comfort of Olive's arms, Olivia suddenly found herself in Olive's presence, in their haven. She didn't think about *why* she couldn't find her right away. She just wanted to be there with her. She didn't want to leave. She wanted to *never* leave there again! Olivia just allowed herself to bask in the love, the comfort, the peace and the tranquility that was the essence of their haven. As inevitably happened, Olive gently reminded her that it was time for her to go.

"Olivia, it is time for us to say 'Goodbye.' You must go, now."

Olivia was confused. Olive had never sent her on her way with those words. She would just say that it was time for her to go home. She didn't understand what it meant.

"Olive, why are you saying 'Goodbye?' I'll just say, 'bye for now!' "

Olive just looked at her silently and gave her a final embrace.

"I will see you again, won't I?" Olivia asked, afraid of the answer she might hear.

"Olivia, this is goodbye for a *long* time. We *will* see each other again, but not soon.

In a panic and on the verge of bawling like a baby, Olivia protested, "You *promised* me you would *always* be here for me as long as I *needed* you! Why are you breaking your promise? Why, Olive, why?" she wailed.

"Olivia, my love, I *have* always been here for you as long as you have needed me. You don't *need* me in the same way now. Not anymore. You are strong enough now. You can make it on your own. You *will* make it on your own, without me."

"No, Olive, *no*! I *do* need you! I am *not* strong enough!" she cried. "*Please* don't make me go. I won't go! I *won't*!"

Olive held her hands, looking her in the eye. "You are just a little afraid. You don't know your own strength. You have done many brave things. Have you forgotten how you confronted your brothers and ended their abuses? And how about that night you determined that you were going to kill your father with that kitchen knife? You didn't go through with it because that was not the way it was supposed to be. You bravely challenged your father when he snatched your Bible from your hands. These were not the acts of a person lacking in strength!

"You were wondering why you couldn't find me right away. You needed that time to do exactly what you did. You discovered that you can make choices and that you *do* have some control over what happens to you. You have made some decisions that will significantly impact your life. Are they the right choices? That's not for me to say, but for you to work out. You will.

"I am *not* abandoning you, Olivia. I will *never* abandon you. You are taking me with you. You won't see me, but you will know because I will be here, in your heart. You have only to think of me, to think of our haven. You must remember this, Olivia. You have made a significant discovery today; and as long as you remember that you can make choices, the answers you seek will lie within you."

Olivia found herself back in the cave. She realized the weight that had confined her was absent. She saw Jason's face in the dim light, and she stared blankly into his eyes. His expression had changed; and for a split second, Olivia thought she detected a trace of shame and/or remorse as he looked away from her empty stare. She said nothing and continued to look into the face of this man that she had respected and trusted, for whom she had held such high regard.

When he returned his gaze to her, there was no longer a sign of remorse or shame. There was at first puzzlement at her response. He eyed her suspiciously for a moment, and Olivia watched his eyes narrow and grow cold. She sensed he didn't quite know what to make of her reaction. She wasn't crying. She no longer showed fear. She only felt the rising hatred for this man, her father, and all men. Nevertheless, she was calm as she began to pull her disheveled clothes into place.

"Here, take this and clean yourself up," he ordered as he handed her a container of wipes. "We've got to get back to the camp." Olivia did as she was told. She followed him out through the narrow opening and watched as he concealed it again. She followed in silence as they headed back to the camp. About ten minutes into their trek, Jason paused to look at her. She supposed he was still trying to figure out what may have been going through her mind, what she might do.

Olivia went into that cave with much happiness, excitement, and hope for the future. She came out with a fierce determination and strength of conviction that she would *never* be put in that situation again—*ever*, by *anyone*!

"Of course, you know no one would believe you if you told them. You wouldn't be getting *me* in trouble, only *yourself*. You're not even a member of our church! Anyone who looks at you—the way you're developed—no one would believe you were not a willing party. Besides, Girlie, we both know you're a veteran. I was kind of disappointed, though. I like being the first!"

If Olivia had thought she couldn't hate him more, she was wrong. He was right, though. She was a "veteran." Being violated by her father and her brothers, as egregious as that was, she dealt with it all those years. She had come to know them as the evil people they were and had built up internal defenses. But today, totally caught off guard, she was dealt a severe blow! The betrayal of the trust, respect and high regard she had for this man by his heinous violation of her body was her ultimate bottom!

Olivia knew that they would be the last ones to return to camp. That meant they would be the winning hiders. It meant nothing to her. All she wanted was to be away from there, ironically, to go home. Never before had she *ever* desired to go home when she was *away* from home! At this point it was the lesser of two evils.

She devoted the rest of the hike to formulating a plan to leave. There was no way she could endure another moment there! In fact, she knew that she would never again go back to that church, or go to Elizabeth's house. Her life as she had known it to this point was over! She didn't want to be reminded of what she felt she could never have.

The shrieks, laughing, and happy sounds wafting from the camp was her signal that it was time to activate her plan. The small amount of water she had left was just enough to pat on her face and neck so that her skin would appear clammy when they reached the camp. She then began to concentrate on a subtext to sum up feelings that would bring tears to her eyes.

As they came in sight of the other campers, Olivia markedly slowed her pace and took on the mask of one in severe physical pain as she held her abdomen with both hands and doubled over. She took a few more steps to a grassy spot and slumped to the ground, still clutching her abdomen, moaning and writhing in the most severe feigned pain. The happy chatter turned to expressions of concern as the group nearest to them came hurrying to her. Pastor Jason was about twenty feet ahead of her and was unaware of her antics. By the time he turned around to see what the concern was, others had rushed passed him. Miss Carter reached her first.

"Olivia, what's the matter?"

"I feel really *terrible*. I want to go home," she cried.

"But what's the matter?" Miss Carter insisted. "Did you fall?"

Olivia was sorry for causing Miss Carter to worry so much. She wanted to ease her mind.

"Oh, Miss Carter," she whimpered, "It's nothing, really. I just have very, very bad cramps on my first day. I forgot my period was due; I was so excited about coming on the trip. I probably shouldn't have come. I'm always in bed the first day. My mother has my medicine.

"Ooooh," she moaned as another 'hard cramp' doubled her up again. That was necessary to reinforce to Miss Carter that she really needed to go home.

"Okay, you just take it easy. We'll get you home," she soothed.

By now everyone was standing around her. One of the counselors stepped forward for crowd control. "Okay, everyone, let's give them some room. Back to your places! We still have a few things to do before you get cleaned up for supper."

Gratefully, almost everyone left the area. Olivia caught a glimpse of Elizabeth's anxious face as she was herded away with the rest. Even though Pastor Jason was looking down at her with a threat disguised as concern, Olivia maintained her ploy. Another loud groan was necessitated by his concerned offer to take her home. Miss Carter had continued to hold her hand, and Olivia took that occasion to clutch her hand with both of her own hands, much as a woman travailing in labor.

"Oh, Miss Carter, will *you* take me home please? I'm really embarrassed. It would be even worse if a lady didn't take me. Please? Please?" she said as she cried, with genuine tears flowing down her face like a spigot.

"Of course I will. Don't you worry about a thing! Can you walk?"

"I think so," she said pitifully. As she was helped up, Olivia gave a veiled look to the good Pastor Jason that said, "Yes, I'm faking it, and, yes, I *am* in control, and there is *nothing* you can do about it!"

The Thrill of Victory

Olivia was relieved when they pulled up in front of her house, but that was only one battle over. Now a new battle was to begin. Lydia Washington opened the door with a look of surprise. She had not expected her daughter home until after church on Sunday.

"Good afternoon, Mrs. Washington. Olivia became ill, and I thought it best that she come home. She said you would have something to give her for her menstrual cramps."

Olivia saw her mother's eyebrow arch as she looked at her daughter suspiciously. When she passed her mother heading for her room, she heard her thanking Miss Carter for bringing her home. In her room she poised herself for her mom's inquisition. During the ride home she had decided how she would handle it. They both knew that she was lying about being on her period. Her mother kept a close watch on that aspect of her existence. She knew each month to the day and hour when Olivia was due, and she knew it wasn't today.

That's why Olivia had come to hate her mother probably as much as she did her father. Her mother was forced to face the truth and could no longer deny the fact that Olivia was being routinely sexually abused by her husband. Still, she did nothing to stop him or intervene. However, she was sure to prevent her daughter's getting pregnant again.

She had not said a word about anything as she drove Olivia, her 13-year-old daughter, to abort the embryo her husband was credited with fertilizing. Other than her calendar watching, it was as if nothing had ever happened.

"All right, Olivia. What is this lie all about?" she demanded. "I know you were faking."

"Yes, Mom, I was faking. But that was the only way I could get them to bring me home. Mom, I had a miserable time. I just wanted to come home. In fact, I don't ever want to go back to that church again!"

"What about your friend?"

"She's with them. And you know what else? I'm not even going back to school, either!"

Her mother was visibly relieved and, as Olivia expected, was all for it; that is, except the part about not going back to school. Her mother was relieved for reasons unknown to Olivia. Among other reasons, she would no longer have to figure out ways for Olivia to do things she knew Louis, her husband, would not approve or allow.

"Now, Olivia, you've *got* to go to school. You're all set to graduate!"

"No, I don't," Olivia heard herself say. She remembered all the promises she had made to herself in that cave and on the trek back to camp. "No, I don't!" she repeated with firm deliberation. "I will be sixteen years old in two weeks, and legally I can drop out! I will!" she said in finality, ending the dialogue.

Her mother looked at her for a moment, shrugged her shoulders, and left the room.

"Wow," Olivia thought, "Is that all it takes?"

She was encouraged immensely by the success of her first two exercises in self-determination. It felt fantastic! She had won the first real victories. She filled the tub with very warm water and her favorite bubble bath, removed her clothes, and sank into her frothy bath of renewal—a baptism. In with the old Olivia—weak victim supreme; out with the new Olivia—strong, determined, forevermore the victor!

As the soothing water reached her neck, she melted into oblivion as she released the old Olivia, washed away with the filth of her afternoon's ordeal. The one thing it couldn't wash away was the painful memory of her life to that point. She wasn't sure she *wanted* to forget the memories, for they would be the impetus and motivating fire to enforce and reinforce her determination in her newly defined undertaking as the controller of her own life and destiny. No longer would she be used and abused, forced into submission by fear, or pain, or any physical or emotional abuse. She would use those memories to make her strong—to insure her survival in a cold, cruel, unfair world!

Olivia knew her biggest challenge would be her father. She left the tub, dressed, and sat on her bed reflecting as she began to prepare herself mentally for the inevitable battle that would surely mean freedom . . . or death! She was determined that if she couldn't be free, she didn't want to live. She wanted desperately to live!

She thought about the knife incident a number of years ago. She knew she didn't want to do anything like that. But she knew she *must not lose!* She got up from the bed and went into her brothers' room. It was the weekend, and they were usually gone. She went into the closet and removed the steel baseball bat that her brothers had ceased to use. She held it with both hands, testing its weight. She assessed that it would be at least adequate, so she returned with it to her room. She surveyed the room and elected to stand it against the wall by her bed. Satisfied, she relaxed on the bed to wait for the inevitable return of her father.

The slam of the car door alerted her that the hour had come. She allotted time for his gruff greeting to his wife (merely a surly growl) and his daily trip to the bathroom before he would be briefed on the day's events, more specifically, her "new attitude!"

She started the countdown . . . five . . . four . . . three . . . two . . . Like clockwork, the door to her room was yanked open. With his voluminous frame filling the door-space, Louis stood glaring at her and then slammed the door behind him.

Olivia sat up and swerved her legs over the side of the bed, planting her feet firmly on the floor, her hands postured on the edge of the bed next to the waiting bat. She was ready for whatever was to come.

Her insides had turned to jelly, but her exterior was saying, "This is the *new* me! I am *strong*! I will *not* cringe! I will *not* be docile! I will *not* participate in my own victimization!"

It must have really gotten through to him as Olivia defiantly and unflinchingly returned his glare with her own. She watched his brow wrinkle momentarily as he blinked and looked down for a second or two. When he looked at her again, it was clear that he was uncomfortable. That only strengthened her resolve and gave her encouragement that she *could* really do this.

She relaxed slightly as he silently turned to leave. With his hand on the doorknob, he hesitated, then turned abruptly and started toward her. She repressed the instinct to retreat in submission and defiantly rose to her feet, her chin up, looking at him sideways. Seeing the bat in her firm grip, Louis stopped short with a disbelieving look of surprise. Never in her life had she ever defied him like that!

"What the hell ya doin' with that bat? What 'cha think ya gonna do with it?"

Ignoring her queasy knees, Olivia responded unequivocally, eyes flashing, "I will do *whatever* I have to do to protect myself from you, or die trying!"

Olivia barely recognized her own voice; it was so strong and determined. It must have had a profound effect on Louis, too, as he ceased to advance toward her. Encouraged, she continued, "I will no longer allow you, or *anyone* to use and abuse me, or intimidate me, in *any* way, for *any* reason. I will do *whatever* I have to do in order to protect myself from you and people like you!"

Olivia had gone too far now to wimp out. The fact that she was still standing gave her even more confidence. Anyway, what did she have to lose? So, she continued, "You have physically and sexually abused me for the *very last time*! And in case you still have a mind to, I'm telling you now, and you'd better believe it—if you *ever* abuse me again, you had better make sure you *kill* me, because the first opportunity I get, I will go directly to the police and charge you, *and* your wife with rape and child abuse!"

Louis stood looking at her with his mouth open and his narrowed eyes filled with anger. She saw his fists clenching and unclenching, the veins bulging in his neck. It seemed like an eternity before he finally responded. All the while, she remained fixed in her strong, defiant posture, never outwardly wavering.

His breathing began to slow to a more normal pace as he attempted to control himself. With a tight jaw, he said the very last words Olivia was to hear him say, "I'm leaving for exactly *one hour*. If I find you still here when I get back, Missy, I will *kill* you, just as surely as I would squash a pesky bug!"

With that, he turned and left her room, leaving the door wide open.

For a moment Olivia remained frozen as a statue, the bat still in her firm grip. Her brain struggled to comprehend what had just happened. The good news was that she was still standing. She had won probably the biggest battle she would surely ever have to face. But before she could glory in the thrill of her victory, she realized two things. First, she had now only 58 minutes to get out of Dodge before her father would come back to carry out his threat.

Second, she had not expected her independence—her *complete* independence—to come so soon. Thus, she had no plan on how to proceed from this point. Plan or no plan, she had no choice but to make haste. She knew her mother would be of no help. She had to think fast, one step at a time. She grabbed a duffle bag and began to fill it with essentials; a change or two of clothes, toiletries, and such. She pulled open the drawer in the stand next to her bed and took out her stash of all the money she had managed to gather over the last couple of years. It wasn't much, considering her new set of circumstances, but the $108.30 would afford her a few carefully planned meals until she could get a handle on things.

Her heart stopped when she saw the Bible that by now was worn and tattered from use. Hesitantly, she picked it up. As she held it, she thought about all the comfort it had brought her. Then, when she thought about her resolve earlier that day and her new direction, she dropped it back into the drawer and slammed it closed with no regrets.

One half hour later she had packed and was ready to go. She got her coat from the closet, put it on, and looked around for the last time at the room that had served as the location for a lifetime of pain as well as for the only peace and solitude she had been able to find. She walked through and closed the door and walked away.

Her mother watched her and said nothing as she walked to the front door. When she opened it and started to leave, her mother called to her.

"Olivia," she said as she approached her daughter and took her hand. "Here. You'll need this." She pressed a wad of rolled up bills into Olivia's hand. They looked into each other's eyes for a few seconds. Olivia saw something she had never seen before in her mother's eyes. It was as if she were trying to say what she had never in Olivia's life been able to express to her. It said, or Olivia *wanted* it to say, "I'm sorry; I love you; I'm hurting, too; and I wish you well."

Her mother also handed her a tightly sealed, clasp envelope. It was later that she saw it was addressed to her with the notation, "Please don't open until your twenty-first birthday."

Olivia was really at a loss. She was afraid and confused. Everything that had transpired from the time she entered that cave until the point she was fleeing for her life had her mind in turmoil. It all had happened so fast. She couldn't understand what she was feeling as her mother closed the door between them. She didn't have time at the moment to dwell on anything but getting herself away from there *post haste.*

Escape to New York

Pastor Jason began feeling increasingly uneasy when he realized something unplanned and unforeseen was unfolding right before his eyes. He had felt earlier that he had nothing to worry about. After all, his plan had worked successfully the year before. He knew that his first cave victim had been too traumatized and ashamed to ever tell anyone of his misdeed.

As for Olivia, because she had obviously not been a virgin, he felt secure that fact alone would impeach her credibility. He was a friend to all and had gained the trust and admiration of especially the youth of the church. Besides, except for her singing ability, quiet, shy Olivia was a newcomer and was relatively unknown to all but a very few members of the church.

Grasping an inkling of something that could potentially cause him grief, Jason had attempted to seize an opportunity to maneuver himself into a position of control by offering his services to take

Olivia home. His plan was thwarted by her heart-felt entreaty to Miss Carter to personally take her.

Jason realized and fully appreciated the precarious situation in which he found himself because of the unpredicted response of Olivia and her ability to stealthily remove herself from his control. It was then he made the determination that it was time for him to take his leave.

He struggled to finish out the day with some semblance of normalcy. The camp's activities culminated with the dinner and awards ceremony. As Olivia's best friend, Elizabeth, accepted her awards earned during the week and was eagerly looking forward to assuring herself that Olivia was all right when she delivered them to her, along with the personal belongings she had left behind.

Following the presentation of awards, Jason hastily made his way home and promptly began preparing for his departure. He was astute enough to realize that his sudden, unannounced disappearance would not bode well for him. He had begun to develop an exit strategy earlier and had finalized it on the drive home.

Two hours on the Internet had provided him with not only sources of potential employment, but also a dialogue with the director of a facility that was in dire need of a person with his skills and experience to reside in and supervise a residential boys group home. By the time they had finished chatting on Skype, Jason had accepted the job offered at the group home in New York. The job would provide him with an acceptable income plus room and board as well as a legitimate explanation for his hasty departure. If that were not enough, he was also provided with a boarding pass for a 3:00 a.m. flight to New York on Easter Sunday morning. He could not have talked his way into a more ideal situation.

When he had packed and had done everything he needed to do in tying up loose ends before leaving permanently, he prepared his letter of resignation in an e-mail to Senior Pastor Jeremiah Withers.

April 15, 2006

Dear Pastor Withers,

I deeply regret and apologize for this sudden letter of resignation without having had the opportunity to speak with you personally. We have had previous conversations in which I have shared my vision for my ministry.

Three-and-a-half years ago, I was led here where I was received with great love and enthusiasm. I feel the Lord has been able to use me to accomplish much in service to the youth of this congregation. Just as my path here was directed to fulfill a need at a place and at a time and for a season, I am again led clearly to another pasture where the harvest is truly great and the laborers are few. God has provided me with the way and the means to immediately embark upon this new commission, and I have no alternative but to heed the call. My plane leaves at 3:00 a.m. tomorrow morning.

I ask your blessing and continued prayers as I seek to follow God's will for my life. Please let everyone know of my love and hopes for them that they will continue to follow in the Lord's way.

Yours in Christ with love,
Youth Pastor Jason Winston

With that piece of business out of the way, Jason took the opportunity to pat himself on the back for his ingenuity and his glib tongue that has helped him to pull the wool over the eyes of so many of his devotees.

CHAPTER 7

The Entrance of Theo

(4/15/2006) On the eve of Easter Sunday, Olivia was sitting in the dark at a desolate bus stop, tired, cold, and hungry. She rode a bus to the end of the line, *where,* she didn't know, and walked and walked with the weight of her few possessions growing heavier with each step as she continued on to her destiny. She had failed to focus on her surroundings from the time she left home. Finding herself in a strange part of town so late at night, she realized just how lost she was. By now, tears were streaming down her face. For the first time, she felt afraid that she couldn't do this after all her resolve.

Her senses were alerted to another presence. Her defenses were immediately activated as she turned to the sound of a man's voice.

"Are you okay, Miss?"

At first startled, she relaxed a little when she saw an old man with a kind, gray bearded face portraying a look of genuine concern. She relaxed even more when she noted his frail frame and the walker he used. When she heard the noise it made as he moved it, she realized her "alertness radar" must have really been out of whack for her not to have heard his approach. She didn't know how long he witnessed her bitter sobbing.

When she stopped abruptly, he continued, "Oh, I'm sorry. I didn't mean to startle you. I thought for sure you had heard this rickety old contraption of mine."

Olivia couldn't speak yet, but she knew she had to say something. She had to reassert her *"in control-ness"* after he had witnessed her vulnerability.

"I wasn't startled . . . and there's nothing the matter! I was just . . . letting off steam." She wiped her eyes and checked the tears immediately. "Thank you, though, for your concern. Goodbye," she said, gathering her belongings to leave.

"My dear, you don't have to leave on *my* account. I'm just a harmless old man out for a little walk. It's not too often that I feel well enough to venture out, even though it's late.

"Speaking of late, what are *you* doing out alone at this late hour? How old are you, anyway—fourteen, fifteen maybe? From the looks of things, I'd say you're running away." Olivia didn't respond.

"I'm just a little tired," he continued. "Do you mind if I share your bench for a moment or two?" He didn't wait for a response; he just maneuvered his walker around and positioned himself a respectful distance from her. She didn't know why she didn't get up and leave, even though she had gathered and was hugging her gear. Where was she to go? She hadn't made any plans. She hadn't even finished crying yet! They sat there in silence for a few moments.

"Do you want to talk about it? I'm a good listener. I don't have many visitors," he continued, not concerned that she had not responded. "My relatives never visit. They are just waiting for me to die so they can collect my money and take over my property." He chuckled to himself. "They certainly have a surprise in store.

"They even tried to get conservatorship over me . . . But I fooled them all. I even had the judge feeling stupid." He paused. "Yes, I got a real chuckle out of that!

"How old do you think I am, young lady?" he asked. "You never told me how old you are. I guess I'm doing all the talking, haven't given you a chance.

"That's okay if you don't want to talk. I've lived on God's earth going on 88 years! Yessiree! You can be sure in all that time I've lived many things to talk about. Don't have much opportunity to talk, though. Nobody to talk to.

"The housekeeper comes in five days a week and cooks and cleans. But she doesn't speak much English, and I speak even less Spanish. I just let her do what she wants. I was married to a mighty fine woman for 57 years. Yes, a mighty fine woman!"

He continued to talk and talk . . . about everything, about nothing. Finally, he looked at Olivia and said, "You know, I've told you my life's story, and I don't even know your name. Will you tell me your name?"

"My name is O . . ."

Olivia stopped herself. She was beginning a new life. She figured she should have a new name, as well.

"My name is 'Liv,'" she said. From now on she decided her name would be "Liv."

"Liv? That's interesting. What is your full name?"

"My name is Liv—just Liv."

"Okay, Liv Just Liv. I am very pleased to meet you. But you know, Liv, I'm an old man, and I'm getting tired, and I still have a few blocks to walk before I'll be home, so I'd better get started. I think maybe you should be getting on home, too."

Liv continued to sit there with her arms tightly holding onto her meager belongings, beginning to feel frightened again as he stood up to leave. Following a span of awkward silence, he inquired, "What are you going to do, Liv? Do you *have* anyplace to go?"

Liv answered, "No" with her silence.

"Well, since you're not in any hurry to go anywhere, would you mind walking me part of the way? I could use the company. Maybe by then you might decide what you want to do."

Liv stood up and silently followed behind him. He was so slow with his walker that after three steps she was almost passed him. Instinctively, she matched her step to his gait. They inched on in silence for about five minutes, which equaled about 25 feet. Liv had to admit to herself that she was glad not to be alone.

"You didn't tell me *your* name," she said, tentatively.

"You know, you're right. I thought I had. That's what happens when you get as old as I am. You think you've done something when you haven't, and you don't remember doing what you did do." He chuckled to himself again. "My name is Theodore McCoy Henry. Most people call me 'Ted,' or 'Teddy,' which I don't like. I'm too old to be a 'Teddy.' I prefer 'Theo,' but some people call me 'Henry.'

"Do you believe in God?" he asked, interrupting Liv's thoughts.

The question caught her off guard and evoked feelings of ambivalence as she remembered her earlier resolve about God.

"Why do you ask?"

"No reason, really. You don't have to answer. It's really a personal matter. Forgive my intrusion."

Liv was relieved that she was off the hook. Still, she felt the need to say something to strengthen her new position about God. At the same time, she didn't want to say anything that might offend Theo. He was just a harmless, lonely old man who seemed sincere.

Liv listened to herself reasoning and realized she was relying on one of her defenses—planning to say something to placate *him*. She ended up compromising.

"Yes, I believe God exists." She allowed him to make his own interpretation.

"Well, that's fine," he said. They continued on in silence.

By now Liv had become unmindful of the rickety walker and the snail's pace they had maintained. It was the sudden quiet that alerted her to the fact that Theo had stopped. She looked inquisitively at him.

"Well, Liv, this is where I live."

He laughed, obviously pleased at the ring of his statement.

Liv turned in the direction of a beautiful house, with a well-manicured lawn, and flowers. It was a *very* nice house.

"You have a beautiful home!" she exclaimed.

"Oh, it's just a house. A building doesn't make a home. People make a home. And right now, this is not a home, just a house.

"By the way, Liv, have you decided what you will do?"

"I have a few options," she lied.

"I'd like to give you another one."

"What do you mean?" Liv asked.

"I know you have no place to go. I don't want to get into your business. Whether you've run away, or are in some kind of trouble, I don't know; but I'd like to help you, at least for tonight."

"I'll be okay, thank you!"

"Where will you go? Do you even know where you are?"

"No, but I'll figure it out. I'll get by okay."

"Yes, I believe you will, young lady; but will you do an old man a favor for some peace of mind?"

Liv looked at him suspiciously as he continued.

"Please allow me to give you a place to stay for tonight. That way, after a good meal, you'll have all night to figure out what it is you want to do." Liv was tired, and hungry, and really had no idea what to do or where to go. With a mixture of relief, gratitude, and still the suspicion, she accepted the offer.

It *was* a really nice house, but it seemed too big for one little old man to be living in alone. Knowing that he had a housekeeper, Liv was surprised at the unkempt appearance. It wasn't *dirty*; it just looked like an old man lived there alone.

Theo offered her a seat and disappeared into another room while Liv scrutinized her new temporary surroundings. There were pictures of a woman at various ages from about 20 to maybe 70 or 80. She was very beautiful, even in the latter years. Liv was curious about her and why hers were the only pictures.

Theo came back into the room to find her looking at the picture of his wife she had picked up from the table beside her.

"That's Eleanor. She's beautiful, isn't she?"

"I'm sorry. I didn't mean to disturb anything," Liv said, replacing the picture."

"No harm, Liv. Eleanor was my wife of 57 years . . . the one and only love of my life." He walked up to the fireplace and stood looking up at the large portrait of his wife. On the mantel beneath the portrait was a beautiful, solid gold urn. Liv felt a tinge of sadness from the sense of what she felt was his pain as he cleared his throat.

"Yes, she is very beautiful," Liv responded. She was overcome by a feeling of love that filled the room.

"Well, Liv, you must be hungry. When did you last eat?"

Liv had forgotten about food from the time she left that cave.

"It must have been early this morning when I was at . . . Early this morning."

"I'm sorry I don't have a home-cooked meal for you. My housekeeper, as you can probably tell, hasn't been here at all this week. She's having a few problems. I hope she can make it back soon, or I'll have to go to a hotel!

"Let me see. I bet you like pizza."

"Yes, I do. I like pizza."

"Good! I ordered one for you. It should be here very shortly. I bet I got just what you like. Want to see? Tell me what you like, and we'll see how close I came. Okay?"

"Okay. I like vegetarian pizza with plenty of tomatoes, onions, all colors of bell peppers, mushrooms, and if possible, garlic, too. No olives, please! No meat, no anchovies, no pineapple!"

"You're very specific. You know what you want, don't you!"

"I'm not used to getting what I want, so whatever you ordered will be fine. I appreciate it very much. I do have some money. I can pay for it."

"Oh, that hurt!" Theo said, placing his hand to his heart as if in pain. "You are a guest in my humble abode tonight. I will not hear of it!"

"The door chimes sounded, signaling that the pizza had arrived."

"Come with me, Liv," he said as he made his way to the door with his cane. He pulled out a bill and gave it to the deliveryman and handed the hot pizza to Liv, while he carried the drinks.

"The kitchen is this way.

"Help yourself to a paper plate. As you can see, the dishes are all dirty."

Liv looked around the kitchen with an urge to clean it. But first things first. She was anxious to see her pizza. She sat the box on the table and quickly opened it. Her eyes popped as she saw one large pizza with everything she liked, and nothing she didn't! Theo stood there watching her with a grin on his handsome old face.

"How . . . how did you know?"

Liv didn't wait for an answer. She sat down and prepared to dig in, forgetting that she hadn't washed her hands. She froze when she heard Theo's voice saying "Gracious Lord, we humbly thank Thee for the food we are about to receive for the nourishment of our bodies for Christ's sake. Amen."

Liv felt a pang of guilt as she repeated, "Amen."

"Here. Use this," Theo said as he handed her a baby wipe for her hands. "I always keep these handy as it is easier than trying to get to a bathroom every time I need to wash my hands."

Liv took the wipe and cleaned her hands. She could feel him watching her as she began eating the pizza. She avoided his eyes.

"Liv, I seem to have a sense about some people sometimes. I have a sense about you."

"You mean the pizza?"

"No, that was only a little thing. Let me tell you what I am sensing about you. No need to confirm or deny anything. I'm just sharing what I feel and why I'm glad you're here tonight.

"I'm feeling you have a passion for something very close to your heart. Something to do with the arts I'm thinking. Perhaps it's artistic ability—drawing or painting. No, that's not it."

He paused a moment and then said, "Of course! It's music. Singing! You are passionate about singing!"

Liv was taken aback. How could he know?

"You love to sing, and you're good at it. Am I right?"

"Yes, but how do you *know* that? How *could* you know?"

Liv thought to herself, "What *else* does he know about me?" She didn't want to know.

"Liv, I sense you are a very special person who will do great things in the future. You don't believe it, I know. You have had some very hard times in your young life, and you have been deeply hurt and betrayed. You are fearful."

"Please," Liv pleaded, "don't go on with this! I'm very tired. Can I be excused? I think I need to sleep."

"Of course, you do, child. Forgive me. I got carried away. Sometimes this 'ability' I have makes people uncomfortable—including me. I'll show you to the guest room. The door can be locked from the inside. Please lock it if it will make you feel more secure."

He waited as she took her belongings into the room.

"There is linen in the bathroom. Help yourself. Please don't leave in the morning without breakfast, if you will. Good night."

"All right. Thank you. Good night."

Liv turned the lock on the door and sat down on the bed to try to collect her thoughts. Her body was tired, but she wasn't ready for sleep. She didn't know what to think about Theo, about what he said, about her being in his house, this room. Not knowing when the opportunity would present itself again, Liv decided to take a long bath. Perhaps during that time she might come up with a plan. An hour later, she was very relaxed, but still had no plan.

Theo's Proposition

(4/16/2006) Liv had gone to bed and had quickly fallen asleep to wake up early Easter Sunday morning with still no plan. She put on some clothes, made the bed and tidied up the room before she unlocked the door. She peeked out into the hallway. All was quiet. She was sure Theo would still be sleeping for at least another hour or two.

Liv went into the kitchen where everything was as it had been left and decided to clean it. It was the least she could do. Although she didn't know why, Theo had been kind to her, and she could detect no ulterior motives, as yet anyway.

The kitchen wasn't nasty. It obviously had received care on a daily basis until very recently. In no time, Liv had everything sparkling clean. She looked in the refrigerator to see what she could cook for Theo. She had planned to eat the leftover pizza, or take it with her.

Liv wondered what old people ate for breakfast. She didn't know if he had his own teeth, or not. She had to laugh to herself about that. She decided to fix something soft. She decided on oatmeal, eggs, sausage links, and some soft toast.

Things were just about ready. She was beginning to wonder if Theo would be up in time when the telephone rang. It was answered, so she assumed Theo was up and would be down soon. She saw a coffee pot and made coffee. Looking in the cabinets, she found the cups with a note taped to one which said, "Liv, thanks for cleaning the kitchen and cooking breakfast. I appreciate it."

Liv was very surprised.

Shortly Theo entered with, "Good morning, Liv. Did you sleep well?"

"Good morning to you, too; and you should *know* how I slept," Liv responded, feeling somewhat vulnerable—a feeling she didn't like.

"Liv, I'm sorry. And no, it doesn't work like that. Come sit down, Liv. I want to talk to you. I don't know everything. I can't just look at anyone I want to and automatically know all about them. I don't know if such people exist. I just know that God has given me this gift, and it is He who decides who, what, when, where, why, and how. And in all my years, you are only the fourth person He has directed me to in this way.

"There are things in life that we have to discover for ourselves. Often it requires a span of living our lives. But believe me, Liv, our destinies are already established. You will reach yours, but you won't know it until you do. That's all I'm going to say about that."

"Theo, what are you talking about? I don't understand."

"I know you don't, child; but one day, when it's time, you will."

Liv was pondering his words while they both began to eat.

"This is a mighty fine breakfast, Liv. Very good—oatmeal and eggs just like I like them!"

"Thank you, Theo."

"Liv, have you decided what you're going to do? Where you're going to go?"

Liv's thoughts immediately shifted to her more immediate plight. No, she hadn't figured out a thing, and she was beginning to panic.

"Well, yes . . . and . . . no. I haven't yet."

"By the way, how old are you?"

"Sixteen. I'm sixteen years old, almost!"

"Do you have any ID? A social security card? A school ID?

"I quit school."

"Why did you do that? Didn't you like school?"

"I don't want to talk about it. I've got to get ready to leave," she said, rising.

"Liv, wait. I'm sorry. I didn't mean to pry. I just thought if you didn't have plans already, I might be able to help you. That's all. Please sit down."

Reluctantly, Liv sat down, not knowing what she was going to do. She thought about what her parents were doing at that moment, and it renewed her resolve.

"You know, Liv, the phone rang this morning. "It was Josafina, my housekeeper."

Liv looked at him curiously. "Will she be coming in to clean tomorrow?"

"No, she won't. In fact, she won't be able to come back. That's why she called."

"Oh, I'm sorry."

They sat a moment in silence. Then, "Liv, would you accept a job as my housekeeper?"

Liv looked at him in surprise, which soon turned to suspicion.

"What do I have to do exactly?"

"Well, you've already started doing it. You cleaned up the kitchen and fixed me an excellent breakfast!"

"Is that all?"

"No, there's shopping, doing the laundry, keeping the house clean, miscellaneous stuff."

"Miscellaneous *stuff*?"

"Oh, little things like running errands, nothing inappropriate, of course."

"What will you pay me?"

"Room and board and a small salary."

"How small?"

"Let's say to start, $175 a week."

"Whoa!" Liv thought, "$175! Calm down, Liv. Not so fast!"

Matter-of-factly, she probed, "What are the working hours?"

"Nine hours/day, including lunch."

"How about days off?"

"You can have any two days a week off you choose, as long as you allow for my dinner on those days."

It seemed perfect to Liv, but she didn't want to seem too anxious.

"Well," she said, "Since I haven't made any firm plans, I'll accept your job offer . . . on a trial basis."

Theo smiled and nodded in approval of her decision.

"But," Liv added, "I'll have to be free to come and go as I wish on my days off."

"Fine!"

"And our relationship is strictly as employer and employee?"

"Yes, but I hope we can be friends, too."

Theo reached in his pocket and pulled out four $100 bills. "Here," he said as he held out the bills in her direction.

"What is *this* for?" she asked, raising her guard.

"Well, Liv, I can't imagine the one duffle bag you have can hold very much. You are going to need clothes and other personal items."

"I'm sorry, but I can't take your money." Liv imagined all kinds of strings attached.

"This is not a gift, Liv; this is an advance of your first four weeks' salary. That means for the first four weeks, you will only receive $75 a week. In fact, you will receive even less because, after all, this is an up-front business proposition. Therefore, I will be deducting mandatory federal and state withholdings. You will be paying taxes.

"I am paying you in cash today only because I know you don't have a bank account and I'm guessing no ID. You may have trouble cashing a check. You probably don't know anything about all of this, but you are on your own, and you will have to up your game to adult standards. I will help you get things set up. I know you are a bright, quick learner. You won't need my help for long."

Relieved, Liv was able to relax. "Thank you, Theo," she said.

"Oh, yes, Liv, house rules that you will have to obey: no smoking, no drinking, and no drugs. As a fringe benefit, I will reduce your working hours to 4 a day Monday–Friday if you enroll in school. Will you finish school? Do we still have a deal?"

"Yes, we have a deal."

CHAPTER 8

Life on Her Own

(4/22/2006) Liv's first priority was to go shopping for school clothes with her salary advance. While shopping, she met an older gentleman, Walter La Salle. He didn't strike her as being a "dirty old man," and she was grateful that he had helped her out in a sticky situation there at the mall. But Liv had used up her allotment of trust on Theo and had none for anyone else. Besides, she was just beginning and was still high in her mode of "death and destruction to all men!" As Liv wanted first and foremost to finish her education, she leaned toward ignoring people in general, and males in particular.

Liv really put herself to work as Theo's housekeeper. She mostly saved her earnings because she needed little money. She had room and board and privacy. The work she did, cooking, cleaning, laundry, and errands mostly, was relatively easy.

Liv was happy to be able to return to school. She had always loved school and had always done very well. She met new people, but she did not get close to anyone. She still had no peers her age. She didn't participate in any of the school activities. She was focused on getting her diploma. She had only a couple of months to go when she quit at the end of the Easter week.

After almost three weeks, her transcripts had been received, and her counselor told her she had already fully met all the requirements for graduation. She could receive her diploma and participate in the commencement exercises in June without having to attend any more high school classes. She chose to immediately enroll in junior college to study music theory and other subjects, which she continued in the fall.

(May 22, 2006) Liv had been working for Theo for exactly six weeks when a TV news bulletin caught her ear. She was in the den writing a lyric that had been buzzing in her head.

"Man in drunken rage attacks family, bludgeoning his wife and shooting his two sons."

When she glanced at the screen, her heart jumped. She recognized the neighborhood and her family's house immediately. Her breath stopped at the image of her father being dragged out of the house, covered in blood.

She watched in horror as two gurneys were rolled out. She was in a state of shock. "Oh, my God! Oh, my God!" was all she could say. The craziest thoughts raced through her head—thoughts that made her feel ashamed, happy, and confused, all at once.

Liv was happy because she felt her biggest problem was solved —her father would never be in a position to hurt her again.

She felt ashamed for feeling happy about someone's death or misfortune; ashamed because she never wanted harm to or the death of her mother or her brothers; ashamed for thinking only about herself.

Liv was confused because she didn't know what or how she was supposed to feel or what she was supposed to do.

She had no idea how long she sat there staring at the screen, no longer seeing, no longer hearing, still in shock. She was not aware when Theo had entered the room, but she was relieved to know that she wasn't alone. Theo quietly walked over to the television and manually turned it off. Then he sat down beside her, taking her limp hand in his.

"That was about your family, wasn't it?" he said. It was more of a statement, not a question. He knew.

The tears that had been damned up in Liv's eyes the whole time burst through and flowed heavily. Theo continued to sit silently holding her hand. After several minutes, Theo patted her hand, stood and said, "Whenever you're ready, I'm here." And he left her, still as confused as before. Her body shifted into autopilot and took her from the den to her room upstairs and deposited her across her bed.

Liv avoided looking at the news, and she avoided reading the newspaper. She didn't want to be reminded of anything about her family. She didn't know the conditions of anyone, and she didn't want to deal with funerals, trials, anything. She seemed to have succeeded in erasing everything from her memory. She chose to stoke the hatred she felt for her father—that way, she couldn't grieve for her family, and she could feed on the horrible memories of her prior life to fuel her quest toward her new destiny. Liv never brought up the subject again, and neither did Theo.

Liv avoided any conversations with Theo about God and refused to go anywhere near a church. Somehow, she found herself running into Walter, who had a way of being in places she also found herself, and they did strike up a kind of relationship that she felt okay with. He seemed really interested in her as a person, and she found him to be very encouraging and helpful. He was respectful and obviously a generous person of means. In time, and for a significant period, theirs became the only close relationship she developed outside of her relationship with Theo.

Life went on, and the years seemed to pass quickly. Liv learned to dress to impress, to look and act more mature and sophisticated. She read prolifically to compensate for her naiveté. She had a natural, quick wit that had lain dormant but that was quickly growing to maturity. Soon, anyone looking at her would think she had always been a natural-born, classy, intelligent and sophisticated young lady! That was partially a result of Walter's influence.

Once she had enrolled in junior college, Liv was no longer around boys near her age. She had quickly grown tired of being hit on all the time and having her peace and energy drained by the constant activity of avoiding the unwanted attention and advances of her arch enemies, men! Constantly irritated, she began in earnest to retaliate in a passive-aggressive manner.

Liv quickly saw that men seemed to like her and wanted to be generous to her, no doubt in hopes of some sort of compensation for their generosity. She developed a very active, though superficial social life, one that she completely controlled. She preferred dealing with older men because they generally were more than satisfied just to be seen with her. Handling them was no problem. They would often take her to dinner, the theatre, concerts, museums, awards shows and other social events. Liv never sought to attract their attention; she seemed to have been an old-man magnet! She didn't really mind, because, in a way, it was like getting back at her father. Also, they were so much more generous and usually had more to give anyway.

She had to be more careful with the younger men. Although she never sought them out, they were always sniffing around her and would lie like dogs, coming on to her as if they were free. She was particularly annoyed when they went out of their way with their egregious behavior toward her. Liv would let them think they had a chance, and just when they thought they were about to score, she let them have it right between the eyes, employing very intriguing and imaginative ways that put them in positions they could do nothing about. Another thing Liv came to realize (or believed) was that *she* had the *real* power, that men were weak, primarily because they followed the dictates of the smaller of their two heads. She decided that she would take advantage of the stupidity of those men and use it to her advantage. She learned how to get whatever she wanted from them, giving nothing in return, making them pay for the privilege of the crumbs of her presence in their lives. Actually, she felt that *she* was the one who accounted for their abundance of blessings. She reasoned "The Good Book" says it is more blessed to give than to receive. Therefore, she let them give, and give, and give! After all, *she* had been giving (taken from) all her life. Now it was *her* time to *receive* the blessings for all of *her* giving!

All the while, Liv continued to work for Theo because it was easy work, and it provided a safe haven for her. Theo was an honorable man and never gave her a problem. She felt sorry sometimes, because she felt he knew more about her and her off-the-clock activities than she wanted him to. Yet, he respected her privacy and never pried. Since she had established that her off-the-clock hours were her own, she came and left—or stayed—as she chose.

Life for Liv went on, according to her dictates. At least, she chose to think so. She had everything she could ask for or want. Most of what she attained was through her own efforts through contacts with the many associates of Walter who allowed her to pick their brains and whose counsel she took. Anything she asked for (or demanded) was given with absolutely *no strings attached!*

She wasn't particularly proud of the life she had been living that involved what she considered "using" or "taking advantage of" instead of being used or taken advantage of. But she wasn't hurting anyone; at least she didn't think so. The men who chose to give her gifts could well afford to do so, and more.

Walter LaSalle

Her first attempted "victim" in her quest to use and not be used was Walter La Salle. She soon discovered that Walter was not to be used. He actually became her friend and bought her first car. After she had started college, he felt she was too vulnerable being at the mercy of public transportation. He helped her to get her permit and paid for professional driving lessons.

He also insisted that she take self-defense classes and was adamant that she learn to swim when he found out she couldn't. When he learned of her love for singing and her desire to sing professionally, he encouraged her further study of music theory and related subjects, which she increased. He arranged for her to have vocal coaching from some of the best; and in time he put together a band for her. She was very happy!

Walter eventually became very dear to her as a true friend. He asked nothing more of her than her occasional presence, stimulating conversation, and a song from her just for him. He never hesitated to give her anything, and he seemed to really take pleasure in giving her lavish gifts. His wife of 44 years had died, and they had no children. He had no one with whom to share his wealth, and he chose Liv! He was generous, almost to a fault. He was a dedicated philanthropist, and Liv was happy to be included among his projects.

(4/29/2011) Walter took Liv shopping for her twenty-first birthday early that Saturday morning. He wanted to take her to a special place for her birthday that evening, and he wanted her to look especially beautiful, he said, because he wanted every eye in the place to be on *her*. He took her to a super exclusive, high-end couture boutique on Rodeo Road in Beverly Hills. They were escorted to a private showing room where they were seated and were served refreshments. They waited for the parade of beautiful models wearing selections of the finest one-of-a-kind designer dresses from which Liv was to take her pick.

How could she possibly choose from so many wonderful gowns. Then she saw *The One*—it had her name on it! It had a black sequined sleeveless bodice and a form-fitting, ankle- length skirt with a mid-thigh high slit on the left side. The choker neckline was diamond studded with an oval opening directly below that exposed a tasteful amount of skin. A diaphanous, full-length overskirt completed the look.

In all, they viewed ten gowns, but Liv saw nothing after *The One*. She was escorted to a private dressing room where she was assisted in putting on the dream gown. It *was* a dream! It fit her as though it had been tailor-made for her. She couldn't believe her reflection in the full-length mirror. For the first time she saw herself as beautiful! She stood there looking at her image, not believing her eyes. Of course, she attributed it all to the dress.

A flood of emotion swept over her, overwhelming her to tears. She took off the dress and returned to the viewing room where Walter was waiting for her. Her eyes were still teary.

"What is it, Liv? What's the matter?" he asked.

"It's nothing, Walter, really," she said as she struggled to regain her composure. "The dress is so gorgeous! Thank you so much, Walter!"

Relieved, Walter's look of concern broadened into the beaming face of a man deriving pleasure from the joy his gift has brought to someone he loves.

The dress was presented to Liv in its permanent dress bag, and they left. As the limo pulled to a stop in front of her weekend condo, Liv leaned over and kissed Walter on the cheek.

"Thank you, again, Walter!"

"My pleasure, Liv," Walter said as he helped her out of the car and walked her to the door. "I will pick you up at eight sharp. Oh, yes. Don't wear any earrings, okay?"

"Okay. See you at eight!"

Liv floated through the lobby to the elevator and to her door. She took her new gown out of the bag and hung it on the door to stand back and admire it. She then laid out everything she would need once she got out of the shower to dress.

Liv felt like a Cinderella. She didn't know what was in store for her, but she was beating down the door of Heaven. At 8:00 o'clock the door chimes sounded. Liv took a deep breath and opened the door. She was carrying the mink that had been her 20th birthday present. "Hi, Walter. See, I'm ready!" she smiled, kissing him on the cheek and twirling around so he could see her in the gown.

"No, not quite," he said. "Here. He held up a pair of diamond studs that put the finishing touch on her exquisite appearance. She was literally bowled over as she put the earrings in her bare ears.

Liv's genuine fondness of Walter was not because of his generosity. He treated her with the utmost respect. He was very caring and never demanding or expecting anything in return. He had given her for her nineteenth birthday the four-bedroom condo that had become her weekend refuge. Walter was the only one who was able to come there as she usually met suitors at a designated meeting place. She never disrespected Theo by allowing anyone to come to see her in *his* home. Walter conversed with Liv. He talked and listened to her. He didn't treat her as an object or trophy. He was the only one that she ever felt sorry for trying to use initially. She came to understand that he genuinely wanted—even needed—to lavish attention on her. She did not mistreat him in any way or lead him to believe things were other than they were.

It was about a 40-minute drive in traffic, but it seemed like days. In fact, Liv thought they may have been driving in circles, perhaps to kill time. She wasn't even paying attention to where they were.

"Liv, will you sing a couple of songs for me while we are in traffic?" Walter asked.

"Why, Walter! I am *always* happy to sing for you. Anything in particular?"

"No, Sweetheart. Anything you choose is fine."

Liv began singing and continued until they finally stopped. A valet opened the door and Walter got out. Liv took his hand and couldn't help seeing the pleased look on his face. She didn't readily notice all the people standing around the door. She looked quizzically at Walter, who was grinning from ear to ear, motioning for her to look up.

She looked up and saw a giant picture poster of herself and the headline, "Debut Performance of Jazz Vocalist Ms. Liv!" Seeing her name in lights on the marquis left her speechless! In a daze, she looked at all the people as Walter led her into the plush Brentwood supper club. *Her* supper club! Her knees started to shake as she realized what was unfolding. The attendant took her coat and disappeared.

Her band was all set up on the raised floor and was beginning to play. They were led to their table right in front of the bandstand. Liv heard her name being announced. She now understood why Walter had her sing for him en route. She was warmed up and ready to sing!

She realized that her band was "in" on the surprise. She remembered the conversation with Billy, the leader, in which he suggested she start preparations for performing professionally.

"Liv, I think it's time for you to start preparing for public performances. You have a vast, eclectic repertoire, and your talent is just too great not to share it. Do you realize how you affect people when you sing? We are blown away just rehearsing with you! Each rehearsal is equivalent to an entire concert! Why do you think we are so happy to rehearse and never want to leave until you throw us out?"

"But Billy, I *love* rehearsing!

"We've been together so long, we know you, and we love you! You would be fantastic on the stage in the spotlight."

"Okay, Billy, you have convinced me. How do I get started?"

"For starters, let's just plan four sets. I would say when you first start out as an unknown, or before a new audience, open with a familiar song for them to relate to. If you can get that together in time, we can start on them at the next rehearsal!"

And they did.

Liv's Supper Club and Lounge

Liv had been on an unbelievable high the entire week following her debut performance and the official opening night performance the next evening. Working in her own club was a phenomenal experience! The impact was significant when she realized this was an ongoing, permanent situation. She didn't realize the privileged position she had since she had never sought "work" as a vocalist in a public venue.

Indeed, Liv was fortunate. She had her own high-end facility. She had excellent rapport with her band members, each of whom was highly skilled and versatile. As a band they were reliable, drug-free, and cohesive, working well together. Importantly, there was synergy and mutual respect. Liv also had a top-notch, well-trained staff, and a fantastic location. After her debut performance (which had been 'peopled' primarily by Walter's vast network of friends)

Liv had a growing, enthusiastic, appreciative and ongoing fan base. Not only did she not have to market herself as those showcasing themselves had to do, she received several hundred dollars a night in tips alone!

As her band members would attest, and her staff as well, she was a pleasure to work with and work for. She knew how to treat people and allowed her bandleader and the club's managers to do their jobs without micromanagement. In fact, the only thing Liv had to do was show up and sing!

The club was very successful and rated very high in every respect. Open for lunch and dinner Tuesday through Sunday, the club was at least ninety-five per cent of capacity for meals at any given time. On Friday and Saturday nights, the main dining room was usually filled to capacity, often with overflow diverted to one or more of the smaller, private rooms with closed circuit television viewing of the performance.

Later, after several years of operation, Liv opened up Sunday late afternoons and/or evenings for *paid* showcase performances by vocalists who had paid their dues and had received her personal stamp of approval. She determined that she did not want to subject her patrons to lest than exemplary performances by persons who were not yet at the level she required.

At rehearsal the following Monday, everyone was still on a fantastic high. There was a relaxed air as such a situation had already been anticipated by Billy and Liv, although Liv didn't know it would be coming so soon. Thus, there was no need for frantic scurrying to prepare for her next few performances. They continued to enjoy their rehearsals, routinely adding material.

Liv busied herself that week shopping and enhancing her wardrobe with appropriate performing attire. She had visited her club on Monday morning, particularly to become acquainted with her dressing room and to determine what, if anything, she would need other than her personal items and wardrobe. It was a very posh room with ample space. It contained a large wardrobe closet and a full bathroom complete with linen. There was also a small desk with a house phone, a trundle bed and coordinated armchair, microwave oven and a small refrigerator.

She sat at her dressing table and switched on the lights framing the mirror and studied her reflection. "Is that you, Liv? Is it *really* you? What did you do to deserve this?" she asked herself, examining her life to that point. She thought about Theo and Walter, the only men in her life who were kind to her and whom she felt really loved her. She wondered why they did what they did for her, why they loved her when practically all the men she had known, excluding her band members and staff, of course, were anathema to her. What did they see in her that she couldn't see? Liv only saw the lies she believed as her prior life had programmed her to believe. That surely could not be what they saw! She determined to discover what it was, to feel, to become—to *own* it.

Friday came, and Liv headed for her club, nervous with anticipation, but excited. She came in 90 minutes early to contemplate and relax. She knew she didn't want to be just another singer, doing the same songs the same way everybody else did. She was never an exhibitionist, and she didn't want to be a "performer." She had too much emotion bottled up inside of her and so many stories to tell! She wanted to be a storyteller, a communicator, an interpreter of lyrics!

As an interpreter of lyrics, her desire was to be able to literally perform for an audience of the visually impaired and be able to touch *them* on an emotional level with merely the emotion she wanted to communicate with her voice alone. That was something she could do only by opening herself up and making herself vulnerable to strangers. Liv had no problem doing so in her rehearsals, among those she had come to know and trust.

Her debut performance had been phenomenal. She had been excited, and she was so grateful to Walter, she envisioned herself singing for him alone, which she had done many times before. Now the game had changed. Liv questioned whether or not she was willing to do this. She knew she loved to sing. It made her happy. She wanted to make people as happy listening to her sing as she was singing. Billy had told her she was a professional already. He believed in her. Walter believed in her. Liv had to ask herself if she believed in herself as well. She chose to believe in herself and her inborn talent, which she eventually acknowledged as a gift from God.

Liv took out the dress she had chosen to wear. While showering, she did her vocal warm-ups. She donned her dress after doing her makeup and hair. She was ready in almost every respect. She had already determined how she would approach her performances. Her song list for each set had been distributed at the rehearsal, and she reviewed her copy.

In what came to be a routine, Liv avoided distractions prior to beginning her performances. Everyone knew that she was not to be disturbed short of a dire emergency the last forty-five minutes before her first set as she dressed and prepared herself. She took the last several minutes before stepping out on the floor to engage in what she dubbed "focus" time. While taking diaphragmatic breaths, she would center herself and focus on what she was about to do.

She knew what was transpiring on stage as it was piped in to her soundproof dressing room. The ending of the band's final instrumental was her cue. Hearing it, she took a final look in the full-length mirror on the dressing room door before opening it.

"Ladies and Gentlemen, please welcome to the stage MS. LIV!" Billy announced. Cordless microphone in hand, Liv stepped onto the floor to the intro of her opening song, and positioned herself as the eagerly awaiting audience applauded enthusiastically. On cue, Liv began to sing her opening number, an up-tempo standard well known to most of the audience. She knew she wanted to sing her own opening songs and had already begun writing them.

When Liv had completed the second song, she paused to address the audience for the first time, a pattern that she chose to follow in future performances. She did not want to spend a lot of time talking from the stage. When she spoke to her audience, she wanted it to be for a specific purpose and to have meaning, not just a lot of idle chatter!

When the applause died, Liv began, "Thank you, ladies and gentlemen, for coming to Liv's Supper Club." There is more applause as the band begins vamping the intro to her next song. "It is my privilege, my pleasure to perform for you. Please enjoy your dinner, relax, and have a good time!"

There was no doubt that the audience was thrilled as she took them on a journey with her in every song. She sang effortlessly with such feeling, passion, and skill. They laughed with her. They cried with her. They shared her joy and her pain, and they loved every minute of it!

As always, Liv was humbled by the response she received as a matter of course. Word-of-mouth advertising and reviews in trade publications catapulted Liv's Supper Club and Lounge into the forefront of places to go!

CHAPTER 9

Liv's performances at her club were always well received. Tips were fantastic, and she continued to expand her repertoire to accommodate the many requests she received. She was very glad that her style and the kinds of songs she chose and preferred to sing appealed particularly to the more mature, sophisticated and high-end audiences.

They really appreciated what she did and came to hear music that touched them personally and through which they could express themselves vicariously. That was fine with Liv. She continued to see herself, and was more effective, as an interpreter of lyrics. After all, she had a few lifetimes worth of emotions and experiences from which to draw.

Liv was able to interact, at least superficially, with the audience, which was her choice, even though she did become acquainted with many of the staunch fans who came regularly every weekend.

The years under the influence of Theo and Walter had continually brought about subtle changes in Liv. She felt less of a need to be on guard all the time, though she remained alert and cautious. She seemed to have become more sensitive to matters that were out of the norm. A case in point was the handsome young man that she dubbed "The Mysterious Stranger." He had been coming to the club for quite a while, almost since the club's opening, and had become a regular patron. Liv had taken passing note of him a month or so after she had begun performing at her club. She was struck by his eyes, not so much because of the unusual coloring—hazel rimmed in brown—but because they seemed to her to be . . . penetrating, for lack of a better description.

What caught her attention the most was the fact that he never approached her. He never spoke to her, although he had an appreciative facial expression and always managed to make his way to the tip bowl. At first, Liv had not given him much thought. She was busy doing her thing musically and thwarting the attempts of those bodacious men, young and old, who were always trying to smooth talk her or make a play for her.

Liv particularly noted he watched her intently when she performed, but she could never get a sense of what he might be thinking, what might have been on his mind. After a while, she began to curiously wonder about his behavior. She found it to be puzzling, fueling her curiosity and challenging her to satisfy it. Why did he never speak to her, or try to make a pass? He was always very serious-looking as he listened attentively and steadily watched her. It was almost as though he were looking at her knowing something he couldn't—or wasn't supposed to know.

Liv's curiosity finally got the better of her, and she decided to approach him. Of course, it had to be done in a sophisticated, classy way. She had the perfect opportunity the Saturday night of January 7, 2012, when the maître d' delivered a note to her from a couple at a table adjacent to where he regularly sat. They were out-of-towners visiting the club for the first time and wanted to meet Liv personally.

As soon as the set was over, Liv made her way through the tables, pausing here and there to exchange greetings and accept compliments. When she approached the table, a distinguished gentleman rose from his seat and offered his hand.

"Oh, your voice is *wonderful,* young lady! My wife and I were just blown away!"

"Thank you so much, Mr. . . ."

"Oh, forgive me. My name is Jerome Lawrence. This is my wife, Nora. Please, won't you join us for a moment?"

"Well, yes. Thank you."

It so happened Liv was positioned so that eye contact with the object of her curiosity was unavoidable. Liv focused her attention on the Lawrences, but she was acutely aware of the stranger's steady gaze.

"Ms. Liv, I can't tell you how refreshing it is to hear a young singer such as yourself singing the songs that tell a story and really *mean* something. You sing with such depth and clarity, and the emotion emitted brought tears to both of our eyes!" marveled Jerome. "I'll tell you, anyone who can make this old geezer cry has worked a miracle!"

"It's unheard of," added Nora, finally getting a word in.

"Oh, thank you. You're too kind," Liv managed.

"Nonsense!" said Jerome. "You are fantastic! Believe me; this will be the spot we come whenever we are in Southern California!"

"Oh, yes," added Nora. "It's as if you have maturity beyond your years. When you sing about pain, it's as if you've actually *lived* it and are reliving it again. And I actually *feel* the pain, or the fear, or the joy—whatever you are feeling and singing about!"

"Like I said," repeated Jerome, "Just fantastic!"

"Thank you so much. I enjoy singing, and it makes me very happy when my audience enjoys it. Thanks again," she said, rising to leave.

"Oh, before you go, can we please take a picture with you?"

"Um, yes, sure . . ."

"Excuse me, Sir," Nora said to Mr. Mysterious Stranger as she thrust her camera at him. "Would you mind taking a picture of us?" He smiled at her and took the camera.

"It will be my pleasure," he said.

In a flash, they were flanking Liv and cheesing for the camera. "Click!"

"Oh, please take one more just in case!" pleaded Nora.

"Click."

Eye contact with Mr. Stranger was spontaneous as Liv moved toward his table. Seizing the opportunity, she boldly extended her hand.

"Hi, and thank you. You made their night!" she said, trying very hard to sound casual.

"It was the least I could do."

"Well, I'm glad you are here again." Liv mentally kicked herself for saying that! "Now he knows that I have noticed him!" she thought to herself. Well, too late now. "Are you enjoying yourself, the show I mean?"

"Oh, darn!" she thought, "There I go again! Get a grip, Liv!"

"Immensely," he replied, taking her hand and kissing it. "You have a wonderful gift. But, of course, you know that."

Liv was taken aback by both his kissing her hand and his forthright expression of his opinion.

"You have me at a disadvantage. I have seen you here before, haven't I? You obviously know who I am. You are?"

"Pardon me. My name is Morgan, Morgan Avery Calais."

"It is a pleasure to meet you, Mr. Calais."

"Please, call me Morgan. I'd be honored if you could join me for a moment—if you can, if you still have a moment or two."

"I suppose I can take a moment more." Liv gracefully sat in the chair Morgan pulled out for her. "Are you a local, or are you on an extended visit?"

Morgan just looked steadily at her without answering, causing her to feel awkward.

"Sorry. I wasn't trying to pry. I was just trying to make small talk to break the awkward period of silence," Liv said.

She had become suspicious of his failure to respond and replied with more of a sense of irritation than she had intended. With an attempt at damage mitigation, Liv added, "I suppose I should allow *you* to lead the conversation since *you* invited *me* to join *you*."

Morgan shifted somewhat in his seat, averted his eyes for a split second, and then said as he stood, "I'm sorry I have taken up so much of your time. I know you have to get back, and I am anxious to hear your closing set. Thank you, Ms. Liv."

Liv was surprised and caught off guard again. Nevertheless, she was able to maintain her dignity and composure as she stood, nodded with a polite smile, and thanked him as she left for her dressing room.

CHAPTER 10

(3/5/2012) For a few weeks Theo had seemed to Liv to be slowing down; he seemed reflective, more contemplative. She came home the Monday morning of March 5 and was surprised to find Theo still in bed, not even dressed for breakfast when she called him. She knocked on his bedroom door. He responded after the second knock.

"Theo, why are you still in bed?" she asked with mock sternness. Your breakfast is getting cold!"

"Come in, Olivia."

Theo never called her "Olivia."

"Theo?"

"Come here, child. Sit down."

Liv walked the few steps to his bedside and sat down in the chair beside the bed.

"Please sit here," he said, patting the bed beside him.

With concern growing, Liv sat on the bed feeling his brow for signs of a fever.

"Are you okay?"

"Please arrange my pillows so I can sit up."

As she propped the pillows and helped him to sit up, Liv became acutely aware of his frailty. He cupped her hand in his.

"Olivia, Liv, I need to talk with you. I need to ask a favor and to explain some things."

He sensed her smidgen of panic as her heart started to beat faster.

"Don't look so worried, my child," he said, pressing a key into her palm. "This is the key to my lock box with my important documents. I want you to keep it. The box is in the den behind the facade cabinet. There is an envelope inside with instructions for you to follow. Everything is explicit and self-explanatory. Will you do that for me?"

"Of course, Theo."

"I have made changes to my will, and you are a major reason for that. I want you to handle my affairs."

"Theo, what are you not telling? Are you ill?"

"No, I'm not ill, really. It's just that my time here is just about up. You know, Liv, we all have a job or two to do on this earth. When everything's done, you're done! You, young lady, have a *lot* to do yet. *You* have a destiny to fulfill.

"I was there for you when you needed help. I can't help you anymore. I know you, Liv, more than you know yourself. You have much to learn, much to live through. We both know you have already lived through more than many people would live in *two* lifetimes.

"I know your pain, your anger, your resolve, your determination. I also know your vulnerability. I know the love you have hidden in your heart, even from yourself, for God and His way. I'm not going to preach to you. I am leaving, probably today. For a long time I have longed to join my beloved wife. Now I am free to do so."

Liv felt the tears pooling in her eyes and spilling down her cheeks. She could barely utter a sound over the lump in her throat.

"Don't cry, child," Theo said tenderly, "and don't be sad. I've had a *wonderful* life, and I was ready to go when Eleanor left me. But I had to wait until I got *you* straight or until my replacement showed up. I feel he has."

Barely able to speak, Liv pleaded, "But, Theo, I'm *not* straight! I *won't* be straight for a long, long time! You *can't* go!"

"Liv," he said patiently, "You are right. You're not straight, not completely straight—yet! But, believe me, you will be!"

"But how, without you, Theo? I *need* you!" The tears were flowing freely now.

"Liv, I need *you* now. I need *you* to help *me*. *I* need you to be *strong*—as strong as we both know you are. I need your reserves of resolve, determination, and will to do whatever it takes!"

Liv felt a pang of guilt for thinking only of herself. Theo had done so much for her, and she was repaying him with selfishness. Theo had never asked anything of her. He was her friend. Making the supreme effort to check her tears and concern for herself, she ventured, "What do you mean, Theo? What can *I* do?"

"Okay, Liv, here's the deal. How many times have any of my family members come to see about me? How many have you met in all the years you've been taking care of me?"

"I've never seen anyone that I know of, Theo."

"No, you haven't—yet. But you will. Believe me, you undoubtedly will!

"I have made you the executor of my will—if you will accept that job. Will you do that for me, Liv?"

"But, Theo, I don't know anything about legal matters like that!"

"You don't need to, Liv. My trusted friend and attorney will help you. All you need to do is follow the instructions that are very specific—that, and stand up to the wolves, also known as my blood-sucking relatives. I have practically cut them out completely. I am leaving almost everything to you."

"To me? But, Theo, why? I don't need anything, and your family won't like it!"

"Oh, I have no doubt they will try to contest my will. I would be disappointed in them if they didn't! But I've made provisions for that. I'm leaving each of them $50,000 on the condition that they accept my will as is *and* do not contest it. In the event it is contested, the amount will be reduced to $1 for each contestant."

"What if they say you were incompetent?"

"I'm sure they'll say anything they think might work. They have tried and failed before. My attorney and I have taken care of that as well," he said as he was overtaken by a spell of coughing.

Liv stood by, helplessly, trying to do what she could to ease his discomfort. She thought of the prospect of losing him then and there, and her concern turned to panic.

"Theo! I'm going to call 911!"

"No! No!" he protested between coughs. "I'm not ready yet. I have more to tell you. Just hold on a minute while I get my breath."

After a moment he continued, "Now. Another thing I want you to promise me. Don't let *anyone* do *anything* to prolong the life of this old body! I have an advance directive to that effect."

"But Theo . . ."

"Promise me, Liv. *Promise* me!"

"Okay, Theo, I . . . I promise," she said as fresh tears began to trickle.

"Now, listen to me, Liv. I know you don't understand a lot of things now, and I know you have questions. Believe me, Liv; they *will* be answered—in time.

"You said you don't need my money, my property. I know you have done well for yourself; and I am sure you will continue to do so. It's not about what *you* need or don't need. Sometimes, it is more about what you can *do* with your wealth for someone *else*! You will find that you will have a need for all the money you can get your hands on! It will help you to fulfill your destiny.

"You will need help, Liv, I know. I am asking you to trust my friend Murphy. That's what I call him. You will probably feel more comfortable calling him Mr. Murphy. You should do whatever he advises you to do."

"But, Theo, I don't know him. I can't just trust people like that, especially men!"

"I know you have a big problem with trust. You have learned that you *can* trust *some* people; but you know, too, that some people are not trustworthy. Your challenge is in learning to tell the difference.

"I remember how defensive and untrusting you were when I first met you. And I must admit it took you quite a while to learn to trust me."

"Yes, I do trust you, Theo, completely," Liv interrupted.

"Yes, I know you do. That's why you can trust what I say when I tell you that you can trust Murphy as you trust me."

"Is Mr. Murphy the 'replacement' that you spoke of earlier?"

"No, he's not. But in the meantime, he will be your friend and will help to guide you, especially in matters that you don't have the knowledge or experience to handle. I will give you a hint. My 'replacement' you will love and marry. You will have the same dream, the same passion. Together the two of you will fulfill your destinies!"

"But how will I *know* him? How will I *find* him?"

"Don't worry. *He* will find *you.* Just listen to your heart and take note of the signs, the clues—both subtle and overt! You'll know. Just listen and remember everything you have been told from the various sources besides me. Trust your heart. Always listen to you heart, child!

"Speaking of friends, everyone needs at least one friend, Liv. I'm glad that you have found a friend who cares for you."

"I know you're my friend, Theo!"

"I'm not talking about myself. I'm talking about Walter."

"Walter?" Liv gasped in surprise. "How . . . what do you know about Walter? I have never introduced you to any of the people I associate with!"

"Liv, I have to confess I know more about you than you know. Walter is an honorable man, and you have brought great joy and happiness to him. I know how much he has done for you, how he encouraged your continuing education, music lessons, everything. Your life has been no secret from me, Liv."

Surprised at Theo's confessions, Liv felt a pang of shame, which showed on her face.

"Now, Liv, no need to fret. I didn't reveal this to you to make you feel bad. I want you to know that I am *proud* of you. I am *really* proud of the character you display, the beautiful spirited young woman you have become!

"I'll tell you something else you don't know. I was there for your big opening-night debut at Liv's Supper Club and Lounge!"

Liv was astonished!

"I've heard you singing around the house here on a regular basis. It has always made me happy and proud that I was privileged to have so many private concerts right here in my own home. Like I said, you have been a source of pure joy to me. I must admit, seeing you in all of your glamour on stage with the full band, spotlights and all was an unparalleled, true highlight. I could not have enjoyed it more or been more proud of you. You made, and are making so many people happy with your music."

"Oh, Theo, you were there! Why didn't you let me know? Why didn't you come and sit with me?"

"I knew it was a surprise, and I didn't want to spoil it. Now, child, please go and fix me something to eat—nothing elaborate, mind you, just a little oatmeal, and a piece of toast."

Liv had already fixed him a breakfast of pancakes, which was now cold. She knew he had not forgotten, that he just wanted her to leave the room. She didn't want to leave his side. He took her hand again and squeezed it. Liv could see the sparkle in his eye as he winked at her and said, "Liv, child, you are the second great love of my life! The Lord will surely bless you as you will bless others."

Liv felt a lift in her heart as she saw the love and peace on his face. "I love you, Theo," she said as she smiled with all the love and tenderness she felt for him. "I'll get your breakfast before you starve to death!" She kissed him on the forehead and left the room, somewhat calmer as she prepared what was to be the last meal for Theo. In no time, she was bringing the breakfast tray to his room. She propped the pillows higher so he could eat more comfortably. He looked relaxed and happy as he began to eat.

"Liv, you know how to make oatmeal better than anyone I know. Not even Eleanor could bring herself to make it lumpy the way you and I like it. Thanks for that! Now, you run along and get the papers out of the lock box. I'll be fine, so no need to check on me. I don't want to take any calls or be disturbed until Murphy gets here, okay?"

"Yes, Theo." Reluctantly, Liv obeyed. She walked into the den where the security box had been left easily assessable to her. There was a small, white envelope attached to the large manila envelope with her name on it in bold letters and the equally bold words, "please open immediately."

With shaky fingers, Liv carefully unsealed the envelope and removed the content, a single page. Silently she read,

"Dearest Liv,

Since you are reading this note, we have already had our little talk, and you have made a few promises that I know you will keep.

I ask you now to remember and believe everything I have told you. In case I didn't tell you earlier, you have been the second great joy of my life, and the only joy since the night I first saw you crying your eyes out at that bus stop! You've come a long way, but you have a ways yet to go. You will have help, so no need to fear.

First, call the attorney whose name and number are enclosed in the manila envelope. Tell him who you are and that I asked you to call.

Please follow any instructions he gives you.

Secondly, dear Liv, you have the letter that your mother gave you the day you left home. You were supposed to open it when you turned twenty-one. I know you didn't open it. It is time for you to open it. You may find that you and I have more in common than you know.

Your mother loved you very much, and you never knew it. She did the best she could, mistakes and all. Everything she did was out of love for you and to protect you in the only way she knew.

Liv, what you are about to undertake will be your greatest step in becoming the person you are meant to become. Trust me.
Love, Theo."

Though her heart was beating furiously and her mind was racing with a myriad of thoughts, Liv immediately retrieved the number of the attorney from the manila envelope and was waiting for a response on the other end before she even knew she had done so.

"Murphy here!"

"Mr. Murphy?" Liv began hesitantly.

"Yes?"

"My name is Liv Washington. Theo Henry asked me to call you. He said you would know what to do."

"Yes, I understand. Can I speak with him?" he asked.

"I . . . I . . . He said that he was not to be disturbed for any reason until you got here."

"Well, if that's what he said, then we'd better not disturb him. I'll be there in 45 minutes. Goodbye."

"Goodbye," Liv said long after the disconnect. In a quandary, she sat down in Theo's favorite chair and waited. She could think of nothing else to do. She shut out all thoughts and just waited.

It seemed as though she had just sat down when she became aware of the door chimes. She hurried to the door, unaware of how long the chimes had been sounding. She opened the door to find two gentlemen standing there, each with an attaché or satchel in hand.

"Liv?" the taller man asked.

"Yes, I'm . . . I'm Liv."

"Liv, I am Attorney Howard Murphy," he said extending his hand. Liv couldn't move to respond. She knew her hands were shaky and sweating.

"This is Dr. Joshua Levine." Dr. Levine merely nodded. "May we come in?"

"Yes, of course. I'll take you to Theo's room."

Liv silently led them up the stairs. She gently knocked and then opened the door. Theo was sleeping peacefully, still propped up on the pillows she had fluffed for him. His half-eaten breakfast had been neatly placed aside.

Liv had never seen him looking so happy and peaceful. He seemed to be smiling in his sleep.

"Theo," she said softly so not to startle him. "Mr. Murphy is here."

Mr. Murphy and the doctor exchanged glances, and the doctor placed his fingers on Theo's carotid artery. He looked at Mr. Murphy and shook his head. Liv knew what that meant. Theo was not asleep, he had transitioned. He was happy because he had finally joined his beloved wife, Eleanor.

"Liv," Mr. Murphy said as he touched her shoulder. "Let's go out and leave Theo with the doctor."

"Please, can I have a moment alone to say goodbye? It won't take long."

"We'll be right outside,"

Liv approached the bed as they exited. The tears that had started to flow subsided, and she felt a sense of strength and resolution like never before. She sat on the bed beside the lifeless shell that once exuded the epitome of love and kindness that was Theo.

"Theo, it's me, Liv . . . Olivia." She could not help but smile as she realized the blessing he had been in her life. She didn't, couldn't focus on the loss she first perceived. She was focused on what Theo had given her that still remained.

"I know you can hear me, my guardian angel! You're not here on this bed. You are up there, where you have wanted to be for so long. I love you, Theo, and I will never forget what you have given me, what you have taught me about love and life. Oh, I'll really miss you, Theo; but I'm happy for you. And I will make you proud. I will keep my promises to you, or die trying.

"I don't know how things will all play out, but I believe you, Theo. If you said it, it's true; and it will come to pass. I won't say 'goodbye.' I know we'll meet again. You can bet on it!

"Well, Theo, I'm off to face the world and my destiny. See you later."

Liv leaned over and kissed his forehead, and left the room.

CHAPTER 11

Though she knew she would be all right, Liv felt the need to be away from Theo's house. She didn't want to talk to anyone, least of all any of Theo's relatives. She also did not want to be there while whatever they would need to do was being done. She didn't want to see Theo's body being handled, wrapped in a blanket, put on a gurney, or whatever they would do. She just wanted to keep the memory of his peaceful face as he slept propped up on the pillows.

Liv dreaded the encounter that was inevitable with Theo's relatives. Actually, they were Eleanor's family that Theo acquired when he married her. Because he loved her, he loved her family. They were his only living relatives.

There were at least two or three generations worth of them, but all Liv really had to deal with were the principal relatives—four nieces and three nephews. Liv chose to forget about them for the time being.

Once in her condo, Liv called Billy to apprise him of the situation and cancel the rehearsal. Billy made himself available for anything she might need. She thanked him and let him know that all she needed at that point was for him to follow through notifying all of the band members of the cancelled rehearsal.

She put on a few choice music CDs and sat quietly for hours listening to the healing music, reflecting on her life with Theo, and trying to imagine life without him. Finally, she filled the bathtub with very warm water laced with fragrant bath salts and bubbles and sank into it. She could feel all her worries and tension being eased as she allowed the water to work its magic. The liberating bath had the effect of rejuvenating her and giving her a surge of power and confidence. She felt fearless of whatever was to come.

Liv believed Theo. Nevertheless, she had a nagging thought that it was more than Theo. She sensed that subconsciously through Theo she was trusting in the God Theo believed in but consciously chose not to acknowledge. That thought made her uncomfortable, and she chose to dismiss it, or at least not to think about it then. The long, relaxing bath was instrumental in helping to clear her mind and prepare her for the next few weeks.

Enter the Leeches

(3/6/2012) Liv woke up early the next morning to meet Mr. Murphy at Theo's as planned. She had planned to arrive much earlier than agreed. She was surprised to see strange vehicles including a pickup truck parked in the driveway. She realized when she had left, the house was open, and there had been no discussion about the alarm. Hoping all of the doors were closed at that instant, she quickly armed the alarm remotely. In thirty seconds the motion sensors triggered the alarm.

Liv's first instinct was to go in and confront whom she knew would be relatives of Theo. However, she wisely waited for the armed response, which came within four minutes. She identified herself to the responders and briefed them.

"You are surrounded! Come out with your hands up!" ordered one of the officers through a voice-amplifying device. By now backup had arrived, and all exits were covered. Liv had no reason to believe there might be violence; nevertheless, the police insisted she stay back. She was willing to delay the inevitable encounter with Theo's kin.

"Put your hands up and turn around." was the order given to the first individual to come out, a woman of about 35.

"Back up until I tell you to stop!

"Stop! Down on your knees, and then flat on the ground with your arms stretched out, like a cross!"

One by one, they came out; three more women, a teenaged boy, and two men.

"Is there anyone else in the house?" the officer demanded.

"No, this is all of us," said the last man to emerge. "This is our uncle's house. He died yesterday. We're not criminals! We're just here cleaning up the place!"

Two officers entered with guns drawn and came out shortly to announce that all was clear. Liv was given the okay to enter.

She had arrived about 7:00 a.m. They had obviously arrived much earlier and had begun filling boxes and setting out the larger items they planned to pile into their vehicles. The first thing Liv noted missing was the 24-karat-gold urn that had graced the mantel beneath Eleanor's portrait, which had also been removed. Theo's jewelry boxes, and hers as well, were lined up for transport with so many other items of value. She didn't see the urn or the portrait anywhere.

Liv went back outside to see that all seven had been handcuffed, and were sitting on the steps. Mr. Murphy had arrived and was talking to one of the officers. Liv was glad he was there. She was livid, and she wanted him to prevent her from doing something she might later regret. These were Theo's relatives, and despite their despicable behavior, Theo had love for them, and she wanted to respect that. It was clear to her that Theo would not want them thrown in jail, even guilty as they were.

Liv conferred with Mr. Murphy, and he agreed that they didn't want to press charges. Nevertheless, Liv didn't want them to get off so easily; she wanted them to squirm. She wanted to express to them just what she thought of them!

As Liv neared the non-repentant contingent, it was apparent they saw her as the "infamous gold digger" who had been sharing their uncle's home. Composed, she patiently held her ground as they proceeded to angrily harangue her. She allowed them to vent, even at her expense. *She* knew the *truth*.

Their decision was communicated to the lead officer, who then addressed the detainees.

"You people are subject to arrest on a myriad of charges including attempted burglary, unlawful entry, trespassing, and whatever other charges we can get away with. It would behoove you to curtail your wagging tongues and listen to what this young lady has to say. Your fates are entirely in *her* hands at this time."

There was immediate silence. Liv deliberately paraded herself before them with a significant pause before each to execute a piercing stare to portray her loathing of them and what they had attempted to do. She wanted to make them feel uncomfortable and ashamed. When she paused before the younger woman who appeared to be about her age, the silence was broken.

"I *told* them this was wrong, not to do this," she wailed.

The first woman to exit the house scornfully said, "And yet, here *you* are, *too!*"

"Yes, here I am, too, to my shame," the young woman said sadly.

Liv appreciated the humility she sensed in the young woman, but she continued her scrutiny of the sorry bunch. When she felt the tension and discomfort had been sufficiently raised, she said what she had to say to them, attempting to allow the contempt and repulsion she felt to saturate each word.

"*You* have the nerve to call *me* names, to judge *me* without even knowing me! And *why* don't you know me, seeing that I have been living here and taking care of *your* Uncle Theo since I was sixteen years old? Is it because *you* in all those years didn't think enough of him to come and check up on him, to see if *he* needed anything? Just to visit and keep him company?

"His body is not even *cold* yet and here you leeches are, helping yourselves to whatever you want! You were 'cleaning up?' No, you are *thieves* . . . *thieves* and *hypocrites*!" Her sarcasm was not lost on them.

"Despite your lack of love and concern, you were still family to Theo, and he loved you regardless! That's unconditional love. You never hesitated to call and ask to 'borrow' money—$5,000 to get caught up on you mortgage; $1,500 to fix your car so you could get the kids back and forth to school; $750 for a dental bill. The list goes on and on.

"You asked for 'loans,' but you never intended to pay back *one red cent*! And you know what? Theo could discern the bogus needs from the genuine emergencies; but he gave you the money anyway, knowing fully that you had no intentions to repay any of those loans. I cannot conceive of the *audacity* you must have had to continue to borrow thousands of dollars knowing you hadn't repaid any of the thousands previously borrowed!

"Theo knew that you were all just waiting for him to die so you could do just what you tried to do this morning. Shame on you! *Shame on you*!" she said, punctuating each word.

"Yes, I loved Theo, with all my heart. Theo loved me, too, just as he loved all of you, unconditionally. Because you are Theo's family, I know he would not want to see you go to jail. Theo trusted *me* to do the right thing. Because I can't betray his trust, I am *not* going to press charges against any of you. Not for *you*. I don't even *know* you, and you have violated *me* as well as Theo! This I do for *Theo* and *only* Theo. Just know this for sure. I may be young; but you don't want me for an enemy! I can, and *will*, be a ruthless and formidable foe!"

When she had had her say, the lead officer asked, "Ms. Washington, are you saying you don't want any charges brought against any of these individuals?"

"Yes, Officer," she replied with Mr. Murphy's approval.

"I want to make sure you realize that this matter will be dropped with prejudice. You won't be able to change your mind."

"I will not change my mind. I am not pressing charges."

"As you wish," he replied. "Okay, everyone. We'll remove the cuffs, and you will be free to go. You should be grateful, apologize, and thank Ms. Washington for her generosity. Jail is not a pleasant place to be."

The handcuffs were removed, and six angry people went mumbling to themselves as they got into their vehicles and departed. Only the young woman related her apology and thanks. Liv removed a gold ring from her finger and pressed it into the young woman's hand.

"Mr. Murphy," she said as they entered the house to survey the damage, I may have acted too hastily. I forgot to find out what they did with Theo's gold urn. I didn't see it anywhere."

"Don't worry about that, Liv. I took it when I left yesterday, as well as Eleanor's portrait. Theo left instructions that I will be seeing to."

Relieved, Liv began to look around, wondering where to start.

"There's quite a bit of work that needs to be done here, Liv," Murphy said. "Do you have anyone to help, or would you like for me to arrange help for you?"

"Thank you, Mr. Murphy, but I have a crew I can enlist," she said, remembering her conversation with Billy. "You have done so much already."

"Now, Liv, I think it's about time you cut out the 'Mr. Murphy' business. My name is Howard. Theo was my friend. I know how much you meant to him and how much he meant to you, Liv. I don't assume that I can take on his role, but I *am* your friend. Please call me 'Howard.' "

"I'm perfectly okay with having you as a friend, Howard. Thank you."

"Now I think I should let you begin to deal with this mess. We can meet tomorrow to sign some papers you need to sign and go over everything that needs to be done at this point. The rest is a matter of bringing you up to speed on what is happening and what to expect, for instance, the reading of the will. Notices have been sent to all concerned. I was going to give you your notice today. The date for the reading of the will is this Friday in my office, and the memorial is Monday. All arrangements have been made according to Theo's wishes.

"Is tomorrow after lunch a good time for you, maybe here about 2:00 p.m.?"

"Yes, that will be fine. I will see you then."

Liv called Billy to let him know she needed his help.

"Hello, Liv. How are you holding up?"

"Hi, Billy. I'm doing okay, but I have run into a problem that I need a lot of help with. When I got home this morning, there were burglars in the house. The alarm had not been armed. The police were able to keep them from getting away with anything, but the house is a mess with things pulled out everywhere. I could really use some help in putting things back in place. Can you help me?"

"Of course, Liv. I let everyone know about Theo when I canceled the rehearsal. You know we all love you, Liv. I know everyone will be glad to help. Besides, we don't want you all tuckered out to the point that you won't be able to sing this week.

"I'm sorry, Liv. I'm being presumptuous in assuming you won't be taking off because of Theo's death. I just know what a consummate professional you are. Besides, you have never missed a performance. But we'll understand if . . ."

"Billy, it's okay. You are right. Theo would not want me to use his home-going as a reason not to sing. To him, my continuing to sing would be the most fitting thing I could do. His memorial service is Monday, March 12, so we may have to rehearse later than normally, or maybe move it to Tuesday morning."

"I'm glad you will not miss this week's performances, Liv. As for rehearsing, we can play it by ear. It's not like we can't skip a few! I'll round up the gang. See you soon, Liv."

Theo's Memorial Service

Liv met with Howard on Wednesday, and the will was read on Friday afternoon. Everything Theo had predicted was on key, and Howard guided her every steps. Theo had been thorough in planning everything to the most minute detail—even his own memorial service program. Liv didn't have to notify anyone or handle any details.

The reading of the will had gone about the way she had expected. Theo had not overstated the reaction of his "family" as the provisions of his will were made known. Theo's nieces and nephews felt free to protest their meager shares of Theo's vast fortune since they knew the threat of arrest was no longer present.

Anyone else would have cracked under the pressure. It was hard; but with Liv's history and everything she had survived and overcome, the leeches didn't have a chance! Besides, she wasn't alone. Howard was there advising and supporting her. The leeches kept it up as long as they could, trying and spewing threats and insults. The more abominable their behavior, the tougher and more resolute Liv became! She turned a deaf ear to their ranting and raving. With Howard by her side, Liv had no problem maintaining her composure. Eventually, everything had played out the way Theo had predicted.

"Liv, Theo arranged for you to be taken to the service in the only limousine to be provided," Howard informed her. "I'll be the only one with you. However, there is one thing I have to ask you to do that Theo chose not to discuss with you."

"What is it, Howard?"

"Theo wanted a very simple service. He also wanted you particularly to sing his favorite song . . ."

"Amazing Grace," Liv finished the sentence for him.

"Are you up to it?"

"I would do anything for Theo!" she said sincerely.

"I'm glad, Liv. I know Theo would be happy. By the way," he continued, "here is a copy of the program."

Liv took the program and started to read through it. Of course, her eyes were drawn to her name printed there, "Solo . . . Amazing Grace by Olivia Louise Washington."

(3/12/2012) Liv shuddered at the thought of facing Theo's relatives again. As they had shown at the reading of the will, they had resorted to their despicable, normal selves, now spewing non-verbal venom in her direction.

Liv was acutely aware of the daggers being thrown in her directions throughout the service by some of Theo's relatives. Their purpose was to let her know their feelings that she wasn't welcome there, that she wasn't *family*, and that she had come into Theo's life in his old, declining days to take advantage of him and to confiscate their inheritance for which they had waited so long.

If they only knew how wrong they were! What Liv received from Theo was a million times more valuable than all the money, property, or valuables he possessed. If his family only knew that if they had availed themselves, they, too, could have shared in that wealth, each and every one of them, and no one's share would have been diminished by what was received by Liv or anyone else.

Liv was relieved and grateful that Theo had planned everything so well and had given her everything she needed to carry out his wishes in such detail. Howard Murphy had been a valued friend to Theo and was now invaluable to her. Liv was glad that *he* accompanied her to the memorial service. She was also glad that Theo had chosen cremation. She wanted to remember him as she knew and loved him best—his kind face, warm smile, and the twinkle in his eye. She thought about the way he would look at her knowingly, yet allowing her to maintain a semblance of dignity. She knew he had come into her life at the perfect time; and because he did, she was more than she ever dreamed she could be.

Liv was surprised at the many people who came to honor Theo. She had not realized the huge number of people he had positively impacted and helped in so many ways. She was pleasantly not surprised to see Walter there since Theo had spoken to her of him. She was happy to see his familiar face amid so many hostile and strange ones.

"Hello, Liv," he said as he held her hand. "You know you can count on me for anything you need or want. I know how much Theo meant to you. If you need to talk or a shoulder to cry on, whatever, you know I am here for you."

"Thank you, Walter," she managed to say as she allowed herself to be comforted for a few moments in his supportive embrace.

Though there was a huge sob in her throat, Liv determined she would not cry. She knew Theo would not want her to mourn for him in that way. He would want her to be happy for him that his job was done and he had finally joined the love of his life. She really *was* happy for him. She could reflect on the love and kindness that he bestowed on her and the many life's lessons he taught her. Reflecting on these things brought joy and a smile to her heart.

It was because of this joy she truly felt in her heart for having had Theo in her life for the time they had that she was able to honor his wish to sing his favorite song so flawlessly when the time came.

Liv glanced at the program and noted they were at the end of the service. The last item was simply, "A Special Taped Dedication." At that point, Theo's voice appeared over the speakers, strong and clear:

"To my friends and relatives. Thank you for coming today to attend my memorial service. Sorry I can't be with you; I had pressing business to attend to."

The chuckle in his voice was very evident to Liv and those who really knew him.

"Please know that each of you holds a special place in my heart—some good, and some, shall we say, a little less good."

Liv could see the uneasy shifting of certain of his relatives, and deservedly so.

"As my final goodbye to you, I leave this song that I heard by a young lady who came into my life one evening and became a source of pure joy to be seconded only to my beloved wife, Eleanor. I dedicate this song to each of you, but especially to you, Olivia Louise Washington."

Liv was taken by surprise at the mention of her name and was aware of the many pairs of eyes now focused on her. Her eyes teared as she recognized the introduction to one of her tracks, "Remember Me for Love," flowing from the speakers.

The sobs that Liv had managed to contain throughout the service prevailed in abundance as she heard her own recorded voice singing the lyric. She was even more grateful for Howard's comforting arm around her. She managed to curtail the audible evidence of her sobs, but she allowed the tears to flow uninhibited. There was only silence as the song ended with the phrase, ". . . remember me for love."

In her heart Liv was saying, "Yes, Theo, I will always remember you for the unconditional love you showed me, which I know literally saved my life. Thank you, Theo. I love you, and I miss you deeply. Nevertheless, you will always be with me, here in my heart."

As they sat there in silence, Liv wondered when and how Theo obtained that recording of her. She knew she had not made it for him. Then she remembered the afternoon she had been listening to tracks and singing through her chores as she often did. She was in the middle of that song when she realized Theo had entered the room. How long he had been there she did not know. She stopped singing, acknowledging his presence.

"Theo, I'm sorry. I didn't hear you come in."

"Oh, don't stop, Dear. That was beautiful," he said with obvious delight. "In fact, would you mind singing it again so I can hear all of it?"

"Of course, Theo," she replied. "As you must know by now, I'd rather sing than do *anything*!"

Looking back, she realized he must have recorded it then.

As the auditorium emptied, Liv lingered a while, deep in her own reflections of Theo. Without conscious will or any forethought, she whispered, "Thank you, God, for bringing Theo into my life."

The thought surprised her and caused her to question herself. She didn't know how to feel about it. She thought briefly about her last conversation with Olive, but she knew she wasn't ready or willing to further entertain those thoughts.

As Howard escorted her out the door, the young woman to whom Liv had given her gold ring approached her. "Ms. Washington, I am so sorry for the way my family has treated you. You don't deserve their behavior toward you. They are angry at themselves for the way they ignored Uncle Theo and used him. You were more right about them—about *us*—than you know. We were not as we should have been. Maybe one day they may come to their senses and be honest. I realize that Uncle Theo loved you, and I can see why. I can also see how much you loved him. Please forgive me for my part in all of this."

Liv responded, "What is your name?"

"I was named after my great Aunt Eleanor. My name is Eleanor, too."

"Eleanor, thank you. I forgave you when I gave you my ring. Goodbye."

CHAPTER 12

The thing that really kept her going, to be able to take everything in stride, was Liv's regular gig on Friday and Saturday nights. She continued to work on putting everything into perspective.

She couldn't say that her life took an immediate change after Theo's departure. She was still Liv, although Theo's imprint was indelible. After the memorial service and the ordeal of Theo's relatives were over, she settled into her former routine—with some major changes.

Thanks to Theo, her friend Walter, her own endeavors, and her occasional miscellaneous benefactors, she was in superb shape financially and could have gotten along very well with nothing else. She had long since proven what she needed to prove to herself and to the world—that she was in charge and was not to be used, abused, or victimized. As she had already mostly done, she completely cut off all of her admiring benefactors. She was more concerned about her music and where she wanted to go with it.

Her relationship with Walter had continued to grow stronger. He was a real friend to her and really good company. Their relationship had always been platonic, and he was like a father to her. Walter had befriended her and looked out for her. Out of concern for her reputation, he had always presented her as his ward. He did not want anyone to think that he was her sugar daddy or that she was a gold-digger, neither of which was true. As her "guardian" he was able to introduce her to his associates and other influential people who were willing to expose her to things to which she otherwise would not have been privy. It was through those contacts that she learned about investing, finances, property management, and more, and this accounted for her prosperity so much more than anything she may have received as a result of her original mission to "take from" rather than "being taken from."

(3/16/2012) Liv's first performance after Theo's memorial was very emotional. However, being the consummate professional she always strived to be, she performed at her usual high level. Yet, this performance was special.

After singing her third song of the first set, Liv deviated from her usual MO and addressed the audience. "Those of you who have seen me perform regularly know that I don't spend a lot of time talking. Tonight I have to make a major exception; and I hope that you will indulge me.

"I have recently lost a significant person from my life. He was like a father to me and had come into my life at a time when I was at a crossroads, during one of the lowest points in my life. He took me into his home and gave me a job as his housekeeper and caretaker. He also gave me moral support, guidance, and unconditional love.

"He had been married for 57 years to a beautiful woman by the name of Eleanor, whom he adored. There was an almost life-size portrait of her hanging prominently in his great room. I entered the room one afternoon to finish my dusting when I saw him standing before the portrait, as he often did.

"I don't believe he was aware that I had entered. As I came nearer, he turned, and I could see his quiet tears overflowing.

"'Liv,' he said, 'I miss her more and more every day. I miss her laughter; I miss waiting for her call to me at work just to say 'hello.' I miss the way she would lay her head on my chest as we drifted off to sleep at night, and how I would sometimes watch her sleeping and hear her soft breath as she inhaled and exhaled. Without her there is only silence—a deafening silence. It's just too loud to hear.'

"He composed himself with a long sigh and said to me, 'Liv, you are a very talented young lady. Your voice is like the voice of an angel. I would like for you to use your talents to do something special for me. You've heard me talk about Eleanor time and time again. You know how much I miss her. Will you write a song for me about my love for her and how much I miss her?'

"Well, I did write a song for him. A week later I sang it to him. Two weeks later, this dear man had gone to join his precious Eleanor. This song I sing for Theo. It's called, 'The Silence Is Too Loud.' "

Liv proceeded to sing the heart-wrenching song with all the feeling she dared to release. When she ended with the coda, *"Why keep holding on? The silence is too loud. The silence is much too loud,"* she remained still and waited for the audience to reach its collective end. Still caught up in the emotion, the audience remained still as well, as if waiting for permission to break the emotion-filled silence with its applause. Liv raised her head and could see the audience was "stuck." She said, "Thank you" and bowed her head again. The response, a standing ovation, was awe-inspiring.

For Liv, singing Theo's song was cathartic, and she felt a greater sense of peace and comfort, fully understanding, appreciating, and accepting the role she had been privileged to play in Theo's life and his last days. It added another level of comfort.

CHAPTER 13

Morgan Calais, aka The Mysterious Stranger, routinely came every night that Liv performed. Since they had officially met in January, they had only exchanged polite smiles and nods; but he still managed to always leave a hefty tip. On March 16, the Friday following Theo's memorial service, he sent word to Liv that he wanted to have an audience with her.

During the break before her last set, Liv made it a point to stop by his table. He immediately rose to his feet. "Please have a seat, Ms. Liv," he said. There was an imploring quality to his voice that prompted Liv to want to see what he had to say.

"Please let me offer my condolences to you. Your performance of that song was stellar as are all of your performances. I could really feel how significant this loss is to you. You were really close to him."

Liv appreciated the sentiment he expressed and sat down in the chair he pulled out for her. He sat down opposite her and continued, "Ms. Liv, I owe you my deepest, most heart-felt apology for the behavior I exhibited that night in January when I invited you to my table following the 'photo session' with that couple from out of state. I realize I put you in a very awkward and probably uncomfortable position. I'm *really* sorry, and I hope you will forgive me and allow me to make it up to you."

Recalling the incident vividly, Liv leaned forward slightly, tilted her head and raised an eyebrow as she looked him squarely in the eye, gesturing for him to continue with a more precise explanation saying, "Oh?"

"Well, yes, I do owe you more of an explanation, especially if I want your forgiveness!" He paused before continuing. "You see, Ms. Liv, I definitely had something I wanted to discuss with you. But then, something told me that was not the right time. Other thoughts were on my mind, and I hadn't had time to really think how to approach the subject."

"What did you think I would do if you had said whatever was on your mind?"

"I know you would have thought I was either crazy, or drunk, or both! You may have even thought I was trying to come on to you, like I have seen so many men do since I have been coming here, just to see and hear you sing. I have seen some of how you deal with those characters. Ouch! I certainly don't want to be another one of *them!*"

"Well, try me now," Liv ventured. "Let me clarify that," she added quickly. "*Tell* me whatever it was that you felt you couldn't tell me then."

"Let's say we take it in a different direction, Ms. Liv. There'll be time to elaborate on that later; but for now, let me show you what I would hope you will be willing to do for some very special, deserving people I know. I think when you meet them, hopefully you will have a better opinion of me, and I would feel more comfortable speaking to you from my heart. Please let me treat you to lunch Monday or Tuesday next week, if you are free, and afterwards I can take you to see my special friends." Ordinarily, such a conversation would have struck several negative chords in Liv; but she wasn't alarmed, and she was even more curious.

"I can pick you up, or meet you at a restaurant if you would prefer. What do you think?"

Really intrigued, Liv responded, "As it happens, I *will* be free Tuesday afternoon. Let's say we have lunch *here* Tuesday; then we can go and see your 'special friends.' "

"Excellent! Shall we say eleven-thirty?"

"Eleven-thirty it is," Liv agreed as she prepared to stand. Morgan suggested, "Casual attire would be appropriate, if you wish."

"Casual sounds good. See you Tuesday."

On the way to her dressing room to prepare for her closing set, Liv was mulling over their dialogue. She had to admit she was really enthralled, and her interest was again aroused about this "mysterious stranger" who was not so much a mystery since she had met and had now two up close and personal encounters with him.

(Tuesday, 4/20/2012) Liv arrived promptly at eleven-thirty to find Morgan already seated at her table. "Good afternoon, Ms. Liv. You look lovely," he said, rising to pull out her chair.

"Good afternoon to you. Thank you. You don't have to call me 'Ms. Liv.' 'Liv' will suffice. After all, we *are* here to have lunch together."

"Okay, 'Liv' it is.

"I have already ordered at the insistence of the server. He assured me he knew what you would want."

As if on cue, the server arrived with their meal—a Ruben sandwich with Cole slaw for Morgan, and a Caesar salad with the dressing on the side for Liv. In silence, each ostensibly concentrated on their lunch. In reality, they were trying to picture how the "talking" part of their meeting would fare.

Liv opened with, "Well, Mr. Calais, Morgan, I'm curious to hear about your friends and what makes them 'special.' More importantly, what is it that you think *I* can do for them?"

"My friends are a group of kids I might describe as part of the growing endangered segment of our society of all races living below or at the poverty line. What makes them special is that they have talent and ambition and are doing everything in their power to not fall victim to the trappings of their environment.

"I am trying to help them to reach their goals. I hope one day to be able to have a large facility with everything they will need to succeed. I know it sounds like a pipe dream, but it's *my* dream and passion, and it *will* happen!"

Morgan paused, obviously overtaken by his passion. "Sorry, I go overboard just talking about it.

"Now, for what *you* can do. There are quite a few aspiring performers with real talent in singing, dancing, and acting; but they need structure and direction. What I am hoping *you* will do today is to just come and *talk* to them, encourage them, and give them something to think about. Will you do that for me? I took the liberty . . . I have already told them you would. They are looking forward to seeing you today."

Liv was impressed with his passion. She wasn't even concerned that he had already committed her presence. She sensed his sincerity, and it softened her heart toward him.

"Of course," she said. I would be happy to do at least that much!"

"Thank you, Liv. You don't know how much this means to me, and especially how much it will mean to *them*."

They finished their lunch and were on their way in Morgan's car to South L.A. Liv changed her mind about following him in her car. She felt more comfortable after their lunch conversation and felt safe in lowering her guard at least that much. After all, she still had her own defenses if needed.

In a while, they pulled up in front of a modest building with traces of removed graffiti. Once inside, Morgan was flanked by a swarm of kids of all ages, sizes, and colors.

"Mr. Morgan! Mr. Morgan!" they shouted, each vying for his special attention. He was happily delivering hugs, high-fives, fist bumps, and pats on the head. It was clear they adored him and that it was mutual.

While Liv was taking in this lively scene, one little girl about four who had been standing apart from the swarm had slowly inched her way to within a few feet of Liv, where she remained, shyly watching her. Becoming aware of the girl's presence, Liv traversed the short distance and kneeled to her level and said, "Hi there! My name is Ms. Liv. What's your name?"

The little girl peered into Liv's eyes but did not respond. Liv tried again, "Can you tell me your name?"

At the second prompting, the little girl shyly said, "Alex" and put her arms around Liv's neck and held on tightly. The hug was unexpected, but Liv instinctively put her arms around the little girl in return and held her in the embrace for quite a while. She felt the little body relax. She felt a need in the child, and there seemed to be a tacit dialogue between them. Liv gently removed the girl's arms from around her neck and stood up. Alex latched onto her hand and would not let go. The unspoken dialogue seemed to continue. Liv became aware that Morgan was watching them in amazement. "Liv, this is incredible! What did you do?" Liv was puzzled and questioned him with her eyes.

"Alex has never spoken since I have known her! I don't think she has uttered a word in almost a year! And she has *never* even let anyone get near to her. I am the only one she will let hold her hand. She actually *spoke* to you! Liv, you are truly the miracle I was promised would come into my life!"

He watched the two of them together, and suddenly he knew what it was. The love that he allowed to be revealed in his eyes was not lost on Liv, whose feelings toward him had begun to change even more in his favor upon seeing his interaction with the children. The look in his eyes was a look she had only seen in two men in her lifetime, the two men that she knew truly loved her.

She immediately thought of Theo and what he had told her the day he passed. She couldn't help but ask herself, "Is this the man Theo spoke of who would be my guardian angel that I would love and marry?"

"Liv, the children are all seated and waiting for you. They remembered I told them you would be coming and talking to them, so they are on their very best behavior. Are you ready?"

With Alex still clutching her hand, Liv nodded and followed Morgan. The kids were also surprised to see Alex so comfortably holding Liv's hand. It gave them all an even more receptive attitude toward Liv. When she sat in the chair Morgan had placed in front for her, Alex climbed onto her lap.

"Hey, guys, this is Ms. Liv," Morgan said, to which they chorused, "Good afternoon, Ms. Liv. Welcome!"

With one arm wrapped around Alex, Liv began, "Hello, ladies and gentlemen. Thank you for allowing me to speak to you today. I have never talked to a group of people like this, so I'm a little nervous. I'm not sure exactly what you are expecting, but let me first say that you are all special. You are beautiful, and you are all *very* special.

"I know you have hopes and dreams, and you want to be the very best you can be and successful in what you want to do in your lives. I understand some of you want to sing, some want to be actors, or artists, or athletes, or doctors, or dancers, or something else. What I want to tell you is that you can do or be whatever it is you *choose*. You just have to believe in yourself, be passionate in what you want to do or be, be willing to work hard to prepare yourself, and don't listen to anyone who tells you that you can't.

"When people say negative things to you, you have to be the one to tell yourself, 'No, that is not true. I am, I can, I will!' Be your *own* best friend, and be a friend to each other. Help each other to succeed. When you help others, you help yourselves.

"I am a performer; I sing. I have always loved to sing, and it makes me happy, and it makes other people happy. But I had to go to school. I still have to practice every day. To be successful takes determination, belief in yourself, and hard work. There are no short cuts, and you can't wait for someone to hand your dreams to you on a silver platter. But you know what? *You can do it!*"

"I want to be a singer like you, Ms. Liv," said Athene, a fourteen-year-old girl who had been listening intently. "No, I am *going* to be a singer!" she declared. Ms. Liv, will *you* help us? We like you!"

Liv was touched. She glanced questioningly at Morgan, who was waiting for her response as well. She looked down at the face of Alex, who was looking up at her with pleading eyes, and she surveyed the faces of her audience of about 50+ children and teens. She knew she would have to be involved in some way.

"What is your name, Sweetheart?" Liv asked.

"My name is Athene Baker. I'm 14 years old."

"Athene. What a beautiful name! Well, Athene, and all of you, I would *love* to help you. I don't know at this moment just how this can all work out. I will have to talk with Mr. Morgan. But I promise you, I will be back."

Her words were music to all of their ears, and to the heart of Morgan. They begin to cheer excitedly. "Okay, you guys. I've got to take Ms. Liv home. You can get back to your homework, your games, or whatever you were doing. And I don't want to receive any negative reports when I come back! But first, can we thank Ms. Liv for coming?" They all thanked her enthusiastically and went back to their various activities.

When Liv stood up, Alex continued to hold her hand. It was clear she wanted to stay with Liv. Liv held her hand until they reached the door. She turned to Alex, kneeled and gave her a goodbye hug. "Alex, honey, I've got to go, but I'll come back, I promise."

Morgan viewed the two of them together, and his earlier realization of the reason for their immediate bond crystallized in affirmation. The common thread they shared was their childhood sexual abuse! He wanted to embrace the two of them right then and there, but he restrained himself.

With Liv's assurance that she would return and Morgan's reassurance, Alex reluctantly released her grip on Liv's hand.

CHAPTER 14

MORGAN'S REVELATION

En route to Liv's Supper Club, each was deep in thought trying to sort and work things out mentally. Morgan was remembering the many things his grandmother had continually told him over the years about his "special gift," which he never really took seriously and had not appreciated, understood, or thought too much about—until this afternoon.

He had felt strongly from the beginning and knew in his heart that Liv was the one he was destined to spend his life with. It was easy for him to see her as his future wife. Any healthy young man would relish that thought. He had no idea how it came to be that in an instant he had come to know about her abusive history. He saw her entire childhood flash before him. The only thing that could explain it was that his grandmother's words must all be true!

Morgan was coming into the knowledge of what his gift really meant, and the responsibility imbedded within it. He knew he had to tell Liv the truth as he now understood it to be. He also knew how vulnerable and fragile she was, despite her confident, in-control facade. He was acutely aware of her deep-seated pain and fears.

Liv could not stop thinking about Alex. She felt responsible for her, to help and to protect her. It was like she was being given an opportunity to protect the vulnerable child that was within herself. Liv was also trying to figure out just how she could help all of those eager children in a meaningful, lasting way. She sincerely wanted to. She determined to delve into the possibilities with Morgan. And thinking of Morgan, Liv was unsure what to do about the feelings she was beginning to have toward him. On one level she was excited; but on the other hand, she was terrified—and she knew why.

Liv had loved Theo, and she loves and cares for Walter, both purely platonic relationships. She didn't see that kind of relationship with Morgan. She had never willingly or consciously participated in physical, sexual contact. She had never experienced the physiological effects, the pleasure that a loving touch, a gentle first kiss, a loving look from someone that she loved and who loved her could elicit.

The sensations that Liv was experiencing now in the close proximity to Morgan in his car were totally foreign to her. Her stomach was feeling queasy, her palms were sweaty, and her heart was beating so hard she was sure he could actually hear it. It was scary for her as she could only relate it to the fight or flight response with which she was so familiar. She felt herself to be in a precarious situation, and she was nervous.

With their thoughts running amok, both were silent throughout the drive.

After what seemed like an eternity, they pulled into Liv's. The valet opened Liv's door; and by the time she was completely out of the car, Morgan was at her side, still in a protective mode. He wasn't ready for their day to end, but he wasn't sure how to prolong it. He was relieved of that dilemma because Liv had her own agenda, which involved a dialogue with him.

"Morgan, if you don't mind, and if you have the time, can we go in and talk a bit? I just can't get those kids out of my mind, especially little Alex. I really want to help them. I'm not sure I know how."

Morgan said a silent 'Thank You, Lord' as he gingerly took her arm and led her toward the entrance.

"Good evening, Ms. Liv, Sir. Would you like to be seated for dinner?" the greeter asked.

"No, thank you, Aaron. We'll just have a seat in the lounge," Liv said as she led the way with Morgan close behind. She chose a small, two-person booth in a quiet spot away from foot traffic. As soon as they were seated, Liv began to regret her choice. Her "fight-or-flight" response revved up two notches, and her thoughts about the children suddenly seemed very remote. Her heart rate accelerated, and she began to feel uncomfortably warm.

"Liv, get a grip!" she told herself. "Take control!"

"Liv, are you okay? You look a little flushed," Morgan said as he summoned the server.

"Yes, Sir, what can I get you?"

"Two waters for now, please," Morgan suggested.

"I'll have a shot of bourbon, please, Ardis," Liv quickly added.

Surprised, Morgan asked, "Liv, is something the matter?"

Liv tried to slow her growing feeling of panic. She wanted to sound casual. "I guess it's just all the excitement of today. Let me just relax a moment."

Morgan waited until the server departed after delivering their water and Liv's shot before he began, "Liv, I told you that I would explain my egregious behavior when we first met."

Liv was abruptly reminded of that so uncomfortable, awkward first meeting the night they formally met when she unwittingly kept putting her foot in her mouth. It seemed to now be coming back to haunt her, and she wanted to kick herself again. She was anxious to know and waited for him to continue.

"I feel I should . . . I need to tell you now. I know it will sound crazy, but I have no other choice. You need to know."

"Well, of course, Morgan. If there is something I need to know, please tell me. I'm all ears."

"First, I want to thank you for speaking to the kids today. You can't know how much I appreciated it. The kids liked you, too.

"Now comes the hard part. You know that for a while I had been coming here to see and hear you perform. The first time I came I was invited by friends. But from the very first time I laid eyes on you, I knew."

"You knew *what*?"

"I *knew* you were the one I was destined to spend my life with; you are the one my grandmother told me I would know when I saw you."

Liv involuntarily gasped. The fight-or-flight response kicked into high gear immediately, causing her to react. She automatically picked up her shot glass and downed it so fast, Morgan could only look at her with surprise, and then with calm understanding. He had earlier experienced the epiphany that explained his grandmother's assertions and clarified all she had been telling him over the years. He chose not to dwell on her reaction at that point.

"When I saw you interacting with Alex, I knew for sure I had to tell you. You see, my grandmother has told me all my life that I am special, that I have a special gift. For years I just chucked it up to 'grandmother talk.'

"Now, don't laugh. One of the things she told me was that I would fall madly in love with *and marry* a beautiful, wonderful girl, and I would instantly know her when I saw her. I knew in my heart that *you* were that girl the first time I saw *you*!"

Liv's heart began to beat as though it had been jump-started, and the sensations that were racing through her body surged in intensity.

"Liv, I had to literally bite my tongue that night to keep from blurting out, 'Ms. Liv, I love you. You are going to be my wife!' After today, seeing you there with those children, with *Alex*, I was *never* more sure of *anything!*

"And Liv, that's not all she told me. I always just humored her by listening respectfully to her over and over again through the years. She said that *I* was special, that I *had* something *special*. I knew all parents and grandparents told that to their kids. That's what they are supposed to do."

"Not *all* parents," Liv thought bitterly to herself.

"She said I had a gift—a special gift that I would discover one day. She never told me just what it was. She said I would know, that I would discover it. I don't know what to call it. I don't fully understand it. This 'gift' has never manifested itself—until today! I never had an inkling. All I know at this moment is that I *love* you. I felt like my heart would burst if I didn't tell you.

"Seeing you with Alex today, how she bonded with you, watching you embrace her—it was incredible. I saw it all! I knew! Liv, I knew! I saw *you* as a child, just like Alex. I knew you were horribly abused. I wanted to take you in my arms and keep you safe forever. I don't expect you to understand all this. I'm not sure *I* do. I'll understand if you think I'm crazy."

Liv's heart was beating wildly as she listened to Morgan and remembered all the things Theo told her about his "replacement," that she would marry him. The fact that he also knew about her abuse took away most remaining crumbs of doubt, but she still held on to her reservations. She wondered what she was supposed to do now.

"Morgan, I believe you," she said with a calmness that belied the truth. The butterflies in her stomach were running amok.

"You . . . you *do?*" Morgan asked in pleasant surprise.

"Yes, I do."

Liv was now struggling to understand the terror and panic that she felt. The old demons that she had stifled and silenced on one level for so long, but not destroyed, emerged full force shouting to her how damaged, ugly, undeserving, unworthy, and unlovable she was.

The shot that she had just downed had no effect. Perhaps another might do the trick. She raised her hand to signal for another shot. Morgan reached for her hand, which, on contact, sent an electrifying bolt that surprised them both. Their eyes locked, and in that instant Morgan knew everything he was meant to see, to know, and to do. His epiphany was complete.

The shock wave that went pulsing through Liv's body was overwhelming. "I need another drink," she said and repeated with a painful pleading in her eyes. "You *can't* love me. You don't even *know* me, not the *real* me!"

"Liv—Olivia, I *do* love you, I *do* know you, and I *do love* you! *I* am here in this world for *you*! Just think about what Theo told you!"

The mention of her given name and Theo's name jolted Liv into focus. She was no longer wondering if he were the one. She now *knew* and truly believed. Still, she did not feel the way she expected she would feel when she found *the* one—or when he found *her* as Theo said he would. She was having strange feelings to which she could not relate. She removed her hand from contact with Morgan's hand and instinctively wrapped her arms around herself, rocking slightly.

"But you don't know my history!"

"Liv, I know everything I *need* to know about you. I knew that much when I saw you with Alex today. I knew why you were drawn to each other.

"Liv, I realize this is sudden and hard to digest all at once. You know what? It's new to me, too. Let's say we just make it easy on ourselves, and take it one day at a time as we learn and discover. I've waited all my life for you. Now that I have found you, I know I can wait another lifetime, as long as it takes!

"I hope you won't take offense if I am completely honest with you. We both have work to do. You have already begun, but I think it would be good for you to talk with someone who can help you sort through your deep-seated issues. It can only be a good thing. I know a lady who is very good at helping people with backgrounds similar to yours. Before we go any further with any kind of personal relationship beyond what we have already experienced, will you see her at least once? Then you can decide for yourself if you think it will be good for you to continue."

Morgan waited patiently for her to respond. He had reluctantly released her hand when she withdrew it, and now he watched her as she was obviously trying to sort things out. She was definitely calmer. She realized she needed more time.

"Okay, Morgan, I will call her. We'll see what happens. In the meantime," she said, changing the subject, "I made a promise to return to see Alex. I would like to do that. I think it is important to keep promises, especially to children."

"You are right, Liv. Shall we make it a week from today? We can meet for lunch and leave from here, if that's okay with you."

"Yes, that will be fine."

"And, Liv, can we meet again in about two weeks after we've both had a chance to think about all this that is happening to us? We may not be able to resolve everything we need to, but perhaps we can get a little insight, at least make a good start."

Liv was glad there was no immediate pressure on her. Two weeks was much better than two minutes! "Yes, that sounds good. I had better get going. Thank you for introducing me to your special friends."

Each was reluctant to make physical contact after the jolt they each received earlier.

"My pleasure, Liv," Morgan said as he stood to help her out of the booth. They walked out to retrieve their cars and did not speak as they waited for the valet. Liv's car arrived first, and their eyes met and locked briefly before she entered and drove away.

The Return Visit

Liv had an uneventful week except for trying to understand and make sense of recent events. Alex was heavy on her mind, and she wanted to give her something.

She saw a little doll that reminded her of the doll she had cherished as a child, which she named "Dolly." It had a cloth body as hers did, and it was dressed in a pretty, frilly pink dress. Its big, brown eyes reminded her of Alex. She chose that particular doll. Once home, she placed it in a prominent spot near her entry so that she would be sure to take it with her when she left for lunch with Morgan and the return trip to the Center.

Looking at the doll brought back bittersweet memories of her own childhood and her interaction with Dolly. She often would role-play with Dolly, who she pretended was herself, while she was the "mother" she longed to have. Dolly was her security blanket, which she held on to the way many children hold on to a blanket or favorite teddy. However, she never slept with the doll or put her in or on her bed. When she wasn't holding her, she always kept Dolly safely wrapped in a blanket and positioned in the chair in her room.

Liv often talked to the doll, telling her how much she loved her, how beautiful she was, what a good girl she was, and all the things they would do together "one day." After Liv had been going to church with Elizabeth, she decided to make up a song, a lullaby that she would sing to Dolly at night before bed. As she sang to Dolly the words to "Rock-a-by Lullaby," Liv would pretend that it was *she* being held, and her mother was holding *her* in her arms and singing to *her*.

(3/27/2012) The following week, Liv dressed casually for her lunch "date" with Morgan. She was careful to take the doll for Alex with her. As before, Morgan had arrived before she and had taken the liberty of ordering for her. He rose to greet her and pulled out her chair just as the server was bringing their lunch. Liv looked at the selection and was pleasantly surprised when she saw the vegetarian pizza with her favorite toppings. She was acutely reminded of that night years ago when Theo had taken her into his home and ordered pizza—just the way she liked it! Another point in Morgan's column!

"Is the pizza okay for you?" Morgan asked, curious of her reaction.

Liv did not want to go into all that. She just said, "Everything's fine. I have just never seen this pizza on the menu. It must be new."

"It's not on the menu, at least not yet. This is a special order I requested. Do you like it?" Liv didn't answer but picked up a slice of pizza and took a big bite, eyeing Morgan the whole time. She was keeping track in her mind all of the signs confirming that he is "*the*" one.

The reception Morgan had received at their previous week's visit was repeated; only, Liv found that she was included in the accolades. Alex ran to Liv and threw her arms around her waist. "You came back! You came back!" she exclaimed.

Morgan looked at Liv and smiled with pure joy that she was able to bring Alex to speech with just her presence. Liv had kept the doll concealed in the bag so that she could give it to Alex outside the presence of the other children. She decided she would wait until an opportune time. Alex would not let go of Liv's hand and was like a conjoined twin.

The day went pretty much like the previous week except Liv listened more and talked less. She was happy to answer the children's many questions and listen to and watch them perform, offering helpful suggestions. As the time drew near for them to leave, Liv had an opportunity to have quiet time with Alex after she had taken *her* position on Liv's lap.

Without warning, she climbed off and stood in front of Liv, putting her hands on Liv's knees. She looked up at her with her big, brown eyes and said, "Can I call you Mommy Liv?"

She was looking with such pleading, Liv's heart melted even more toward her. She could not prevent becoming misty-eyed. "Of course you can, Honey," Liv said as she enfolded her little body in an embrace.

"Will you take me home with you?" she asked.

"You know what, Sweetheart? One day, I will take you for a visit. I don't know when, but until then, I *will* come back and see you often."

Liv saw the hope in her eyes turn to sadness. She determined that would be a good time to give her the doll. "You know, you are my special little girl, and I want you to remember that. That's why I have a special present for you to keep. Every time you look at it, it will remind you that I love you and that I am thinking of you, and that I will come back! Is that okay?"

Still not convinced, Alex asked, "What is it?"

Liv took the doll out of its hiding place and handed it to Alex. Alex's big eyes got even bigger, and her face lit up with joy as she hugged and squeezed the doll. "What is her name?"

"What do *you* want to call her?"

"I want to call her 'Dolly Liv,' like you! Thank you, Mommy Liv! I love you!"

"I love you, too, Baby! It's time for me to go now. Just remember, whenever you feel lonely or afraid, just hug Dolly Liv and know that I am thinking of you."

"I will, Mommy Liv. I will!" Alex waived goodbye, still holding on to Dolly Liv instead of following them to the door as she had done the prior week.

Morgan, who had been watching, marveled that in just two visits from Liv, Alex was not only speaking, but conversing! "Liv, you are truly amazing! It's no wonder they all love you. It's no wonder that *I* love you."

Liv smiled at him and sensed the love that was evident in his gaze. Another point in the Morgan column!

Liv was instantly hooked by the kids. After a few weeks of working with them, she wrote a lively, spirited song titled, "A Day at the Fair," and taught it and others to them. Everyone participated in the group songs, and a few of the more talented kids performed solos in the concert, the first of many, that were performed for their family and friends and the community at large.

A Possible Site

At their meeting at Liv's on March 20, Morgan and Liv had agreed to talk again in about two weeks. It was hoped that would be enough time for both of them to at least begin the process of adjustments each would need to make.

Liv had so much to think about. She realized she probably could benefit from talking with a professional who could help her sort things out and give her some insight and tools for working through her issues. Liv was open, though somewhat skeptical. Nevertheless, she did make an appointment with Dr. Julian on Morgan's recommendation. She was anxious to let him know that she had been to four sessions with the therapist.

Since he had proclaimed his love for her, Morgan was trying to gage just where Liv might be emotionally when it came to physical contact with him. He remembered when they first met; he had kissed her hand with seemingly no adverse reaction. He decided the kiss on the hand would be his standard greeting for her for now.

(4/3/2012) Though Liv arrived before the designated meeting time, she found that Morgan had come even earlier and was waiting for her. Morgan stood when he saw her, and was aware that his heart, too, skipped a beat. It seemed that since he had professed his love for her, his love was growing stronger every day.

"Liv, you look amazing!" he said as he took her hand and kissed the back of it.

Liv smiled and was not unaware of the tingling sensation she felt when his lips touched her hand. She was also not alarmed. After all, he *had* kissed her hand before with no ill effect. Besides, she was anxious to let him know that she had met with Dr. J. She continued to smile broadly as she sat down. He looked at her with mock suspicion. "Why, Ms. Liv! You remind me of the grinning cat in that children's adventure story the way you are smiling. Just what are you up to?" he asked.

"I just can't wait to tell you what I've done! I think you will be pleased. It is a very big step for me, after all!"

Morgan knew that she had met with the therapist. Although his "gift" was not as far-reaching or developed as Theo's had been, he did have some revelations that seemed to relate only to Liv. He also had insight that kept him from robbing her of the joy of telling him herself.

"Well, My Love, are you going to tell me, or are you going to keep me in suspense? What have you done?"

"You will be happy to know that I have met four times with Dr. Julian!"

"You have? That's great! I'm so glad you followed through. I don't think you will regret it."

"I'm kind of looking forward to following through with her myself. I really want to get to a place where I feel . . . 'normal.' "

The server brought the appetizers Morgan had ordered, and they made their lunch selections. Liv was anxious to get to the subject that had remained on her mind since meeting the kids and visiting the Center twice.

"Morgan, we never really talked specifically about how I can work with the kids. I feel very strongly about helping them in a significant way. Why don't you tell me more about *your* vision for them and what *you* want to achieve. Perhaps I can see ways that I can support *you.*"

"That's a good thought. Where do I begin," Morgan said with a sigh. "I want them to have a place to go where many of their needs can be met. It has to be a neutral place where they can feel and be safe; where they can learn basic skills, develop their talents and special abilities, learn social skills . . . Oh, there is just so much I want for them!

"You may not remember him by name, DeShawn Hawkins. He is the tall young man with the braids who wants to be not just a teacher, but a university professor!"

"Oh, I know who you're talking about. He seemed so determined, as I remember."

"When he had been coming to the Center for a few weeks, he called me aside and said, 'Mr. M, I don't know when or if I'll ever be able to get out of the Ghetto, but I want *you* to help me to get the *Ghetto* out of *me!*' Liv, that had such a profound effect on me. It just made me more determined to help all of them.

"You know, Liv, I have given this so much thought, and it just keeps growing and growing. Actually, it's monumental, and I know one person can't do it all. I have tried to begin the process on a minute scale with the kids at the Center. They are simple things, but I believe they are essential. For instance, I try to get them to appreciate their own uniqueness and the uniqueness of others. I insist they respect themselves and others, to accept differences in others, to love themselves and their neighbors.

"I'm trying to have them understand that they need to communicate effectively, using correct English so that they can be perceived by society as the intelligent beings they are. I believe they need to have successes to know the feeling that comes from knowing you have done a great job. I expect them to take responsibility for themselves and the decisions they make and to show them how what they do today can affect them tomorrow, for good or for bad. We try to show them that they have a responsibility to help each other and not be selfish, only thinking of themselves.

"They are learning that helping others doesn't diminish, but enhances them. When they are successful, they won't take their success and abandon their roots. They will want to reach back and help someone else to achieve success.

"It will be starting off on a very small scale. It *has* started out on a small level. But, Liv, I *know* that it is just a matter of time . . . and money. I'm going to start a school and community center that will encompass everything a community needs—from childcare, pre-K through 12, adult education, and job training to colleges and universities—and everything in between."

Morgan paused, feeling exasperated that he was unable to take everything that was in his heart and articulate it adequately to Liv. What he didn't realize was that Liv was listening and heard his sincerity and passion. From the little contact she had experienced with the kids to this point, Liv was drawn in more than even she realized. She wanted to be a part of it!

"If you could have one wish that would enable you to begin to realize your dream, what would that be?"

"Well, omitting the obvious, which would be the financial basis to start and maintain this humongous undertaking, it would be *housing* . . . a facility. Real Estate. Permanent housing."

"That's a good start. Can you be more specific or detailed?"

"As a matter of fact, I can show you a place that I saw and inquired about that I believed would have been perfect. Everything about it, as far as I could see, would have been perfect—the location, the size, even the unimproved grounds!"

"I would love to see it. Where is it? Can we go there?" Liv asked.

It's about a 45 to 60-minute drive from here depending on traffic. If we can leave within the next hour, we can get there in plenty of time for enough daylight to see the outside of the structures and the grounds."

"Great! We should be finished here in time if we skip dessert."

"Are you sure you want to see it? I mean, it's not available. It is being developed by the owner, a law firm. I have no idea what they are planning to do with it. I just know it's definitely not for sale."

"I'd still like to see it. At least then I might get a better idea of what you're looking for and how I can help."

"Okay, Liv, let's do it!"

A half hour later they left for South Los Angeles. Conversation was superficial and haphazard, at best. Each was acutely aware of the nearness of the other, and neither wanted to do or say anything that might add to the tension.

Morgan, though possessing the patience of a saint, was still a man and could not help thinking about how it would be to hold Liv in his arms. He knew that for now he would have to be content with daydreams and kissing her hand. He also knew that she would one day be his wife; and he could wait.

Liv was comparing the two times Morgan had kissed her hand. There was definitely a difference. The first time she was curious about this "mysterious stranger." Even though his kiss had taken her by surprise, her focus was not on the physical contact. After all, it was just a harmless kiss on the hand. She was accustomed to shaking hands with her many fans, both male and female. There were always many people around, and she felt safe in her club.

The kiss today was decidedly different. Their relationship was not the same. She had spent time with him, and she definitely had feelings for him. He had confessed his love for her. She believed he was the one Theo had assured her would take his place in her life. Too many things had come into play to doubt.

"Well, here we are," Morgan announced as he pulled into a large, recently resurfaced parking lot.

Liv responded, "Please drive around the entire property so that I can get an idea of just what is encompassed."

Morgan started the trip around the perimeter. He found that it was even larger than he had realized. It was the equivalent of approximately three and a half city blocks. At one end there was a nice-sized, park-like picnic area that he had not noticed as being a part of the package. Next to the park were several structures of various sizes. There were other areas, one of which appeared to be a playground with tennis courts, a ball field, and so much more.

There was one large structure off to itself, and parking areas were sprinkled throughout. Included also were several bungalows at various locations and a two-story building that appeared to be the main building. Many of the structures appeared to be new, and others were under construction or being renovated.

Morgan lost some of his fire as he realized the enormity of the property, its suitability for what he envisioned, and the fact that it was not available. He was consoled by the fact that at least he had the opportunity to spend that time with Liv and had her interest. He was very aware that Liv had not mentioned or even given him a sign about how she felt about *him* after he had professed his love for her. He contented himself with the knowledge of what he knew. After all, there was no indication that Liv would automatically fall in love with *him* at first sight.

Liv was beginning to understand what Theo told her about the importance of having lots of money to be able to help others. She had never before felt that perhaps she may need even more than she had. She viewed the property with ideas of how it could be utilized for so many good causes. Whether *that* property or another, anything was possible to Liv.

CHAPTER 15

NEW REVELATIONS, A NEW BEGINNING

A New Revelation

While looking in her bureau for a particular item, Liv ran across the letter she had received from her brother. She remembered her displeasure when she had relegated it to the bureau drawer, but she felt a strong compulsion to read it. She continued reading where she had stopped.

I never dreamed it would be possible for me to forgive our father for what he did. I'm not trying to blame my actions on the fact that I was abused by him, as were each of us, including Mom, who probably suffered the most.

We were all terrified of him, for good reason. At first it was me that he abused regularly, until Randy was two or three.

From that time, we were both subjected to his perversion.

You were about two months old when mom discovered what Dad had been doing. At that time I was about six, and Randy was four. We were going to have a barbeque in the backyard and take a dip in the pool. We were really looking forward to swimming, waiting for Dad because we weren't allowed in the pool by ourselves.

Mom had been in the house trying to get you to go to sleep. After you went to sleep, she was bringing you outside to sleep in the shade in your playpen when she saw Dad molesting me. Mom was outraged. We were really afraid because she was yelling and screaming at him, holding you in one arm and hitting Dad with her fist.

She said she was going to call the police. That really made Dad mad. He grabbed you and hit Mom really hard in the face with his fist. Randy and I were scared to death. Mama fell and was bleeding badly. We didn't know what to do. We were just little kids, and we were scared stiff!

He threatened to kill you. Mom pleaded with him not to. She said she would do anything he said for the rest of her life. He told her what to tell the police, and he told us, too. The police and the paramedics came. We all did what we had been told. We knew how mean he was. He was a cruel, evil man. He wouldn't let Mom go to the hospital. She was really hurt. She was never the same after that day.

I used to hate him with profound passion and plotted with Randy on how we could get rid of him. We considered ways to kill him, but we never could go through with anything.

Olivia, I know you had a difficult life, and I think you may have blamed Mom for not protecting you from Dad—or me and Randy, for that matter. You may even have thought she didn't love you. But Olivia, she gave up her life for you, for us, and subjected herself to much suffering.

One night he beat her so bad, we thought he had killed her.

She had gone into your room earlier, but when she saw you were reading your Bible . . .

Liv stopped reading. She had just discovered that her mother knew about her Bible reading! Not taking time to digest that knowledge, she was compelled to continue reading.

. . . She didn't want to disturb you and quietly left. When Dad came home later that night drunk, everyone was in bed. Mom knew what he would want to do, and she tried to intervene. Even though she didn't scream out—she never did, thinking we wouldn't know—we did know. We always knew and had to suffer through it.

He always held up the threat of taking your life for anything she did to displease him. When he was dangling you over the edge of the pool threatening to drop you, Mom promised to always do whatever he told her to do forever in exchange for your life.

Sis, on the chance that one day I am blessed to be freed, I hope and pray that you will forgive me and that we may be able to establish a healthy relationship, if you are open to that. Even if not, please know that I love you.

Your brother, Kevin

Liv's head was reeling and she was blinded by tears. Liv read and reread that portion of the letter she had refused to entertain previously. So many things began to fall into place. She remembered the letter her mother had written to her and placed in her hand along with the money she had also given her that late afternoon as she was fleeing from the raging wrath of her father.

With the encouragement of Theo, Liv had opened the letter and read and reread its contents. It was only now that she realized and could appreciate the extent of the love her mother had for her and the sacrifices that she had made out of that love. She realized in her letter she could not bring herself to reveal all of the details lest her writings fell into her husband's hands before she was able to ensure our safety.

Her Mother's Letter

Liv had sat in her office and retrieved the letter from the desk drawer. She sat there with the envelope just staring at the writing. It hadn't changed since the last time she had picked it up to read it, only to put it back, or the time before that, or the time before that. Finally, she unsealed the envelope and removed the letter. Carefully placed within the folds of the letter was an old wallet-sized photo of a young interracial couple with a beautiful little girl about two or three years old. The woman was a beautiful African-American woman, and the man was a carrot-topped Caucasian.

Liv looked at the child for a moment before she realized how much it looked like it could have been a picture of *her* as a child. She turned it over to see if there were any indication of who they were, but it was blank. She put the picture aside and began to read the letter, which was dated September 7, 2002. She was only twelve years old when it was written, or at least when it was begun.

Dear Olivia,

I am writing this letter to you today, not knowing if or when you will ever receive it. If you are reading this, I don't know where I am or even if I am alive. I hope I am and that I will have an opportunity to hold you in my arms and tell you how very, very much I love you. I always have, and I always will.

There are things I want you to know that I am afraid to even put in writing. You are probably wondering about the enclosed picture. I am amazed how much you looked like me when you were a little girl! In fact, you have always looked like me at whatever age. The picture is of me and my parents, your biological grandparents.

I want you to know your heritage. I also want you to know that keeping secrets many times is not a good thing to do. I would advise never to promise to keep a secret until you know what it is you will have to keep silent about. Some secrets should never be kept!

As you may be able to tell, my mother, your grandmother, was a beautiful black woman, and my father loved her very much.

They loved each other, and they loved me. They were killed in an auto accident, leaving me an unwanted orphan. Neither set of my grandparents wanted me. They hated the fact that mom and dad wanted to be together, and neither family wanted to have anything to do with us. They disowned their own children and me because mom was black, and dad was white.

I was in foster care for a few years. No one wanted to adopt me. I didn't understand why until I was about seven, and I still didn't really understand. The agency worker in charge of my case told me that I could have a new family permanently if I never talked about my real parents. I wasn't to tell anyone that my mother was black. She said I could "pass." I didn't know what that meant. She made me promise. I wanted to belong to someone so I wouldn't have to keep moving all the time. I promised.

An older couple soon adopted me, and I know they loved me. They took good care of me and were God-fearing people. I was never concerned about having a black mother and a white father.

I never understood why it should be kept a secret. Nevertheless, I did, especially from my adoptive parents. I grew to love them. I was afraid they might change their minds and send me back. I didn't have to worry about that because somehow they knew, and they loved me anyway. I found out when they thought I was old enough to understand, and they gave me the picture that I am now giving to you.

I was only 17 when I met and fell in love with your father.

I didn't want to keep my secret from him. I didn't think it was right not to tell him before we got married. He didn't take the news very well. In fact, he was furious. He told me not to mention it again, not to tell anyone. He said he still wanted to marry me, but I had to obey him in this matter . . . in all matters.

I should have gotten a clue, seen his anger as a red flag, but I didn't. I married him anyway. That was the worst decision of my life that I have come to regret every day. I didn't realize how controlling he was, or how cruel! He took over my life so insidiously, I didn't realize it until it was too late. He moved me away from my family and friends and controlled almost every aspect of my life.

I loved to sing. He forbade me to sing! He said I sounded too "black." I was pregnant within six weeks. He wanted me barefoot and pregnant with no resources of my own.

I'm glad you found joy in singing. I'm also glad you sensed enough not to sing when he was around. I loved to hear you singing your made-up songs! I was so happy that you found a way to lift your own spirits.

I know you didn't know, but I was happy when you started going to church with your friend. Louis was an avowed atheist. I didn't know until after we were married.

Our wedding day was the last time I saw the inside of a church as well as saw my adoptive parents. But I always held hope and faith in my heart that one day it would be different. I was afraid to even write or try to call them!

You shared my womb with an identical twin sister who died in infancy. I won't go into details, but you were all I had left, and I vowed to do whatever I had to do to keep you. I did not make the best decisions.

I regret so much that I didn't have the nerve or resources to escape from Louis with your brothers and you. I can only pray that somehow, some way, someday I may get another chance to be a loving mother to you.

I know you have hated me, for good reason. I can't blame you. I can only hope and pray that I will find you again and attempt to let you know and show you how much I love you and how sorry I am for all the pain you have suffered.

With all my love, your mother

Liv was overcome with love for, and grief over the loss of the relationship she could have had, but never would have with her mother. Her mother *did* love her! Liv remembered the look in her mother's eyes as she was leaving. She realized now it was a look that tried to express everything her mother wanted her to know —that she loved her, that she was sorry for all Liv had to endure even as she herself was suffering, how she wished the best for her, and begged for understanding and forgiveness. Her mother's suffering included feeling the hatred of her own daughter towards her for the role she had felt obliged to play.

Liv could scarcely comprehend the depths of fear and terror her mother must have felt, and how she must have numbed herself, empowered only by the fiercely protective mother instinct, to endure life with her monstrous husband. One thing she did feel strongly was the desire to forgive her mother. She felt that despite the horrendous childhood she had experienced, it was her mother's sacrifices that allowed her to be alive. Her mother had given up her own life for her daughter! Liv found herself whispering, "Thank You, God, for my mother."

A New Beginning

"Miss," the gravelly voice repeated, "It's okay if you want to share. This is the time we usually end the meeting, but if you want to speak, we are all here for you."

Once again, Liv was jarred back to the present. The story of the young woman was still heavy on her mind. The replaying of her life had given her more food for thought, and she was beginning to see things more clearly. She had absorbed more than she had realized. She saw a common thread that bound all of them together. They were all alcoholics who *knew* they were alcoholics. They were trying to use alcohol to accomplish what "social drinking" could not do.

There was pain, loss, guilt, emptiness, fear, loneliness, shame, unhappiness—so many undesirable, unpleasant feelings that attempts had been made to numb with alcohol. Liv now allowed herself to recognize and own so many of these feelings as belonging to her. She could deny them, pretend they didn't exist. When her attempts at suppression failed, she turned to the cure that had been forced upon her initially, but that of her own volition she later sought and subconsciously embraced.

At some level she knew something was not right about it and kept it hidden. She was careful in public situations and could control the urges by controlling her circumstances, being in power as the determiner of her own destiny.

She thought of Theo. She thought of Morgan. She realized that both of them knew! Theo *had* to know. Morgan knew. That is why he suggested she go and see Dr. Julian. Of course, Dr. Julian knew! That's why she insisted Liv come to this meeting in which she was so loathe to participate.

Could all of these people be wrong? Liv knew the answer. She stood up with a humble spirit and announced, "My name is Olivia, and I *am* an alcoholic!"

CHAPTER 16

Truly, Pastor Jason Winston had the gift of gab. He was skilled in his ability to quote Scripture, and his mastery and use of Christian "jargon" evoked trust from the unlearned innocents as well as those non-discerning of wolves in sheep's clothing. (He could attribute his vast knowledge of Scripture to his parents who, for whatever their reasons, required him to read and memorize Scriptures.) With these abilities, his reprobate mind was forever formulating ways to further his most base inclinations.

Jason had a propensity for overpowering, controlling, degrading, and deflowering innocent young girls. It was not about sex. He was a very charming and handsome young man who could easily have had his pick of willing women *or* men. It was all about power and control. A glimpse into his childhood would reveal that it was fraught with evidence of his perpetual exposure to abuses over which he had no power or control, to his extreme detriment. What was totally lacking in his formative years, power and control, he sought to assert over those he perceived to be the most vulnerable, insuring his success.

He could easily have been successful were he to focus on deriving power and control by attaining great wealth via legitimate means. He had the skills, the looks, and the charisma to do so. As a person who could have persuaded the Old Woman Who Lived in a Shoe on the idea of adopting ten more children, he could have organized and built an unparalleled mega church with all of the perks, bells and whistles.

Jason Winston was resting easy due to his good fortune in successfully making his get-away from Los Angeles. He felt confident and reassured as he relaxed on the plane ride to New York City early Easter Sunday morning in 2006. He found his new situation to be palatable and kept a low profile over the first several months as he went about working his special charm to ingratiate himself into his immediate surroundings and in the community. He charmed his way into the church community by participating in outreach ministries, volunteerism, and active participation in several large congregations. However, a position such as the one he had abruptly left eluded him for too long, and he found no way to duplicate it in New York.

Unable to contain his perverted urges, Jason went out on the prowl in the seedy parts of communities some distance from his own stomping grounds. His preference was for picking up very young prostitutes and taking them to secluded locations where he would persuade them to allow him to "do it his way" for a lucrative fee. "His way" included restraining them and leaving them — without payment of promised compensation. He wasn't concerned about being reported to the police. He decided they were just prostitutes who themselves were breaking the law.

This he did on a regular basis. He only stopped in 2009 when one night he had acted a little too aggressively, and a thirteen-year-old neophyte was left lifeless. Though unintended, the deed was done, and he had to cover his tracks as best he could. He wrapped the small body in a dirty blanket and placed it in an alley dumpster.

His schmoozing in the Christian community for the first few years was paying off as he was gaining in recognition as a dedicated young man working to serve others in any capacity. He was involved with ministry to the homeless, working in soup kitchens feeding the poor, holding rap sessions with teens and young adults, counseling and working with drug addicts and kids in the system. He was especially interested in volunteering or working in facilities for special needs children and young adults.

He was elated when he landed a regular part-time position in a facility for Down syndrome youth in mid-September of 2012. He had dropped completely off the radar for some time since the unintentional death of the thirteen-year-old. By now it seemed to him that he was safe from any consequences.

In his new gig, Jason focused on a 14-year-old client whose physical appearance belied her diagnosis; her low-functioning cognitive level made her an excellent candidate for his purposes. He had only to wait for a suitable opportunity.

(10/29/2012) The opportunity came quite unexpectedly on the evening of October 29, when the facility's director summoned him moments before he was off the clock. "Jason, I know you're just about to leave, and I hate to impose on you. A serious emergency has occurred, and I must leave immediately. All of the clients have left except Kayla. We normally lock up at 6:30. Kayla's mother called to say she couldn't possibly pick her up until 7:30 at the earliest. Her car is being towed.

"Could you possibly stay with Kayla until her mother comes and then lock up?"

"Yes, I'd be happy to. Kayla is a sweet girl. She's no problem at all."

"Good. Thank you, Jason. Here's the key to the main door. All other doors are secure. I really appreciate this, Jason!"

Jason couldn't believe his good fortune! It was like being given the perfect gift—privacy, opportunity, control, and a warm, vulnerable victim. He had a good hour, plenty of time.

Kayla was playing with her favorite little ragdoll in the playroom. She looked up and smiled when Jason entered the room.

"See baby?" she said, innocently smiling and holding the doll up for him to see. She had the mentality of a young child who had outgrown the fear of strangers and trustingly interacted with everyone. Jason was not above the abomination of taking advantage of her. He had no shame for the pain and trauma he inflicted on her. He was not moved by her whimpering. When he was done to his satisfaction, he attempted to clean her up to cover his tracks. He was interrupted by the door buzzer. Kayla's mother had arrived sooner than she had anticipated, preventing him from completing his cleanup.

He did succeed in quieting her sufficiently. She was catatonic, but Jason couldn't worry about that. He grabbed her bag and put her coat on her and wiped her face with a wipe. He headed for the door, trying to compose himself as he went.

"Good evening, Mrs. Gentry," he greeted her. "I wasn't sure I heard the buzzer. I wasn't expecting you so soon. Come on in. I'll get Kayla. She's playing with her favorite doll. She likes it so much, I'll let her take it home if you promise to send it back with her tomorrow."

"Oh, thanks, Jason. I'll do that."

Jason left to get Kayla and the doll. He was right that having the doll to hold onto would help to keep her calm. Kayla had taken the doll and held on to it. All of her attention was focused on the doll, and her mother ushered her out and into the car.

Jason gave a sigh of relief, but there was a knowing in him that he had not done a sufficient cleanup job. The uneasy feeling that knowledge generated increased in intensity so much that before he arrived home, he was near panic. He hastily put his diabolical mind to work to forge a plan of escape that would not draw suspicion.

He arrived to find his employer, Simon Maynard, waiting for him. "Jason, I have something to tell you, and I'm afraid it's not good news. Have a seat, son."

Jason was surprised at this turn of events and could think of no possible bad news—unless his past had somehow come back to haunt him. He forced himself not to jump to conclusions.

"What's the problem?" he inquired as he sat on the couch.

"It's your parents. They were involved in a very bad vehicle accident. Your father was killed instantly. Your mom has survived, but she is in critical condition and may not survive. If she does, she will probably be incapacitated."

Jason lowered his head and raised his hands to cover his face. He was playing the role of grief-stricken son; he wanted to hide his face to cover his insincerity. When he thought he had taken the right amount of time, he said, "I've got to go! I've got to go home!"

"Of course, Jason! You've been a great help here. I hate to lose you, but you must go. I have already purchased a ticket for you. I hope you don't mind, but it's a red-eye flight that leaves at 1:43 a.m. tomorrow morning. I knew you would want to leave as soon as possible. This gives you enough time to pack. Anything you can't tie up tonight I will help with. Jason, I am deeply sorry for your loss."

"He hopes I don't mind that he has given me the reason, ways and means, once again, for escape!" thought Jason. "Thank you so much, Simon. I'd better get started."

Back to L.A.

(10/30/2012) Armed with the pertinent information of his mother's whereabouts, Jason was in no hurry to see her, the other half of the team that had caused him so much pain as a child.

Instead, he went straight to his old family home to see his inheritance. He went into his father's private space and poured himself a drink from his father's private stash. He then took a seat behind his father's capacious desk, crossing his feet atop.

"Well, Old Man, where are you now? And just look where *I* am!"

Before making his way to the hospital, Jason probed around and found documents he felt he would need to take control of his parents' possessions. In the process he chanced upon his parents' advance directives. He wasn't surprised that they each wanted every possible procedure or apparatus available to prolong their lives.

He proceeded to search through the desk drawers. An accordion file caught his eye, and he removed it to view its contents. What he found was a photographic record of the abuses he had suffered at the hands of his parents. There were dozens of photographs of him and his parents—and their friends. The first picture he saw was of his mother and father holding him down while he was being sodomized by one of their friends as others watched. It literally made him sick, and he threw up all over the desk. He had never seen those pictures and was loathed to see any more. He closed the file and determined to shred the contents.

The memories resurrected of the horrible young life he spent there stirred up his hatred of his parents so much that, had they been there, he would surely have killed them. He finally made his way to the hospital, once again donning the grief-stricken son role. He consulted with the doctors before actually going into the ICU. They apprised him of his mother's extremely critical condition and how they were treating her. They could make her comfortable, and she could be kept alive for years with no hope of recovery. She could not speak or move of her own volition. They were not sure if she had any awareness, but there was minimal brain activity—she wasn't completely brain dead.

His mother's attending physician wanted to speak with him before he saw her. He waited in the waiting room for the doctor as instructed. "Mr. Winston, I am Dr. Chung. I understand you have been told of your mother's condition. Is that right?"

"Yes, Doctor."

"They have told you that she can possibly live indefinitely in the state she is in? She is relatively young, only sixty-two. We could be looking at many, many years with no change. Her quality of life would be minimal at best. Tell me, Mr. Winston, does your mother have an advance directive?"

"I don't know," Jason lied, "but I know she and my dad always said they wanted to go together, they couldn't bear to be left alone. If my mother has any awareness of the situation, I know she wouldn't want to live."

"Mr. Winston, as painful as it is, I have to ask you to consider removing your mother from life support, especially in light of what you have told me about your parents' wishes."

"What would you recommend, Doctor? This is so heartbreaking for me."

"My medical recommendation would be to remove her from life support."

"When would you do that?"

"I'd say the sooner, the better. We could do it now, with your consent."

"Now? Oh, no! I haven't even seen her in a few years. I've been on the East Coast. I have to at least have time to say goodbye."

"Then why don't you go in now? I will have the consent papers brought in for you to sign when you're ready, and we will disconnect her."

"Thank you, Doctor."

Jason entered the room where his mother lay stationary. Her eyes were open, but her eyeballs didn't seem to move. Jason pulled up the chair as close to the bed as possible and leaned in even closer. Watching her eyes closely for any signs of recognition, he said, "Hello, Mother Dearest. This is your loving son, Jason. Remember me?" He immediately detected the distinct look of fear in her eyes, telling him not only that she could hear, but also understand him.

"Yes, Mother, you are right to be afraid. It's payback time! You see, I know how much you miss my dear old dad. You should have gone to Hell with him! But if you had, things may not have gone so well for me. So, I thank you for staying alive long enough to help me out. And so now, here we are.

"Are you sorry for how you treated me? You created a monster! Now this monster is going to destroy its maker. I am about to sign the papers for them to *pull–your–plug*! Guess what *I'll* be doing. I'll be watching as you struggle to breathe, just counting the minutes until you die, you old witch!"

Jason was satisfied his mother knew what he was doing and was afraid. It just made him relish his deeds even more. He continued to taunt her until he heard footsteps approaching. In the bat of an eye he had reverted back to the grief-stricken son the doctor had spoken with.

"Doctor, I can't bear to see her in this condition! I *know* she would not want to continue in this vegetative state. I'm ready to sign whatever I have to sign, do whatever I have to do. We can't prolong her suffering any longer!"

"I understand, Mr. Winston. I have the papers all ready for you."

Fifteen minutes later, Jason was on his way to his old home, now his home alone, to carry out his plans to eventually return to his old church.

Kayla Gentry, New York

(10/30/2012) New York Police Detectives Frank Garcia and Alvin Phillips arrived at the Albert Einstein College Hospital in response to a call from the hospital in accordance with required reporting procedures.

"Hello, officers. I am Dr. Landon Wallace. I called about a juvenile Down syndrome patient that has apparently been raped."

"I'm Detective Garcia. This is Detective Phillips." The doctor beckoned for them to follow him. "Do you have a rape kit for us?" Det. Garcia inquired.

"Yes, I do. The victim is 14 years old. She has the mentality of a two-year-old and can't really tell you anything. Her mother brought her in this morning when she noticed stains in her underwear. She advises that the girl has been pretty much non-communicative since she was picked up late yesterday evening from the facility where she attends weekdays. She is waiting for you in here."

The doctor opened the door to a small interview room where the victim's distraught mother was anxiously waiting. "Mrs. Gentry, these are Detectives Garcia and Phillips. They're here to talk to you about your daughter." Exiting the room, he said to the detectives, "I will see that you are provided with the rape kit."

"Mrs. Gentry, we are very sorry for what has happened, and we know how upset you must be. We have daughters ourselves. We want to find out who did this, and we must ask you certain questions. Is that okay?" Det. Garcia asked.

"Yes. I know you have a job to do. I need to know who hurt my daughter! Who could be so heartless!" she sobbed. What can I tell you?"

"Do you have any idea when the assault occurred?" Lead Det. Garcia continued.

"I believe it had to have been yesterday some time. The only place she has been is the facility. I had car trouble yesterday and notified them I would be picking her up late."

"What time did you take her there?"

"I didn't take her. My husband had a 7:15 a.m. flight. We took his car, and my son took Kayla to the facility in my car."

"Where is your son now?"

"I'm not sure. I haven't seen him since I left for the airport."

The detectives exchanged glances, and Det. Garcia asked, "Can you reach him by cell?"

Aware of their suspicious glances, she was quick to respond, "You are surely not suspecting *him*! Shawn would *never* do anything to harm his little sister! He *adores* her, and she *loves* him!"

"We're not jumping to any conclusions, Mrs. Gentry. We have to ask these hard questions and examine all possibilities before we can eliminate anyone. Is it like your son to just not come home? Where does he go?"

"He is eighteen years old. He comes and he goes. He doesn't have a curfew. He likes to hang out with his friends sometimes."

"We do need to question him. He is the last person to see her before going to the facility. He may have noticed something, or heard something that might be meaningful. Besides, it's the best way we can eliminate him as a suspect. Please call him, Mrs. Gentry."

Mrs. Gentry took out her phone and called her son, leaving a message. "Hi, Shawn, this is Mom. I need you to call me as soon as you get this message. It's urgent!"

"Thank you, Mrs. Gentry. We understand your daughter is not able to communicate."

"Before this, she could manage to make herself understood, to at least have her needs and desires met. Now she says nothing and just holds on to the doll they let her take when we left yesterday evening."

Her cell phone rang and she saw that it was Shawn. "Hi, Shawn . . . Yes, I'm all right. I'm at the hospital . . . No, Shawn, it's Kayla. I just need you to come here. Shawn . . . Calm down. She'll be all right. The police are here, and they want to question you, too. Okay, but drive carefully. I'll see you when you get here. Bye, son.

"He should be here in about twenty minutes. If you have no more questions for me, I would like to be with my daughter!"

"Mrs. Gentry, your daughter is being evaluated by an expert who is very competent dealing with situations like this. Please wait in the waiting room until she is done. Perhaps your son will be here by then."

Mrs. Gentry was about to go to the waiting area when the therapist entered the room. "Are you Kayla's mother?" she asked Mrs. Gentry.

"Yes, I am. Is Kayla all right?" she asked anxiously.

"I would like to talk to you about your daughter. Does she have any pets?"

"No, we don't have any animals. She has lots of stuffed animals, and she likes to play with dolls."

"I understand she has been traumatized. Nevertheless, she is responding very well when I show her pictures, and when she tries to draw. In fact, we were getting along very well until she saw a picture of a cartoon snake character. Has she been frightened by a snake at some time in her life?"

"Why, no. I don't think she has ever been afraid of anything! She is just like any ordinary exploring two-year-old."

"She took one look at the snake and went into hysterics. The doctor gave her a mild sedative. I can't account for her sudden reaction."

"Please, can I go and be with her?"

"Yes, of course. I think a familiar face is what she needs right now. Please follow me."

Mrs. Gentry followed the therapist and found Kayla curled up on the bed in the fetal position, holding on to the doll. Mrs. Gentry stayed with her and was there when Shawn arrived.

A very distraught young man came through the door where he had been directed. Seeing only the two detectives, he demanded, "Where is Kayla? Where is my little sister?"

"Shawn Gentry? I am Det. Garcia. This is Det. Phillips. We need to ask you a few questions about yesterday when you took your sister to the facility."

"Look, I'll be happy to answer any questions you may have, but first I want to see my sister! I understand she was molested, and I know she must be really upset. I *have* to see her!"

Deciding that more might be gained by observing the behaviors of the siblings at first sight, Det. Phillips suggested to his partner that they accompany him to his sister's room. As soon as Kayla saw her brother, she dropped her doll and held out her arms and cried to him, "Shawnee! Shawnee!"

She threw her arms around him tightly. He stroked her hair and spoke soothingly to her, calming her completely. She relaxed and fell asleep in his arms. The detectives realized that they had not found their suspect. They asked Shawn to come down to the station as soon as he could to make a complete statement, which he did. There was nothing helpful he could offer.

In the meantime, the detectives followed up with the facility's director. He recounted the events of that evening and identified Jason Winston as the employee who stayed until Kayla had been picked up. They made notes to follow up in California with Jason Winston. However, the sense of urgency regarding Jason was lost when the circumstances of his departure were known and in light of the glowing accolades and votes of confidence of both of his employers. Ultimately, the ball was dropped when his fingerprint results came back clean.

The rape kit had resulted in good samples of DNA, but there was no match in the national database. That is where the case stagnated.

His Good Luck Continues

Jason wasted no time in arranging for the disposal of his parents' remains. He had no intentions of giving them a proper service, or *any* service for that matter. He had their remains cremated, after which he did not deign to show any reverence. The ashes were presented to him in heavy-duty plastic bags, which he promptly deposited into a trash bag and illegally discarded in an alley dumpster.

Jason spent most of November taking care of things and getting himself set up in *his* home, taking care of all of the legalities involved. It wasn't until the last week in November that He contacted the Senior Pastor at his old church, and related the reason for his return from New York.

He did not inquire about an available position at the church. Instead, he continued to play the role of the grieving son, making a valiant effort to view their passing as the "will of God" and his duty to "accept God's will in his life." He knew just what to say—and what *not* to say.

(11/26/2012) "Jason, of course you know you have my most heart-felt condolences, and we are happy to do whatever we can to help you in your time of grief."

"Thank you, Pastor Withers. God has always blessed me in whatever test He has allowed. I am just waiting on God as I do what I need to do to settle my parents' affairs."

"Do you plan to return to New York when that is done?"

"I don't really know what God has in store for me. I came back expecting to care for my mother on a long-term basis. Her passing was so unexpected. Not knowing how things would work out, I resigned my positions in New York. I didn't think it was fair to ask them to put things on hold to wait for me indefinitely."

"Yes, that was a wise thing to do. As it turns out, our current youth pastor has given notice that he will be relocating with his family. His father has been called to pastor a large church in Dallas, and he has asked his son to come with him to help. Of course, he could not refuse. That leaves us with an opening for his position, your old position, which I am led to offer to you if you would consider accepting it. How about it, Jason? Will you?"

"Well, Pastor, I was considering just taking it one day at a time and trying to work things out. But perhaps getting involved again with my passion for working with the youth would be just what I need to keep from dwelling on my losses. I graciously accept your offer!"

"Very good, Jason. If you want to start right away, this coming Sunday will be Pastor Reid's last day. He will be saying his goodbyes. Perhaps you can come, too, and we will announce your return! I'm sure many will remember you, but time has brought about changes. There are many *new* members, and many of the 'youth' with whom you were working have families of their own. I'm sure they will be as happy for your return as I am. Will I see you Sunday?"

"Yes, of course. I'll be there!"

Jason Meets with the Senior Pastor

Following his warm reception, Jason was encouraged to ease back into his old ways. He had spoken with the Senior Pastor and indicated he had some ideas he wanted to institute based on successes he had experienced in New York working with troubled youth and unwed teen mothers. The Senior Pastor was interested in discussing his ideas further and scheduled a date for them to meet later.

(12/17/2012) "Come in," Jason hears Pastor Withers' voice. Jason entered. "Take a seat, Jason, and tell me about these ideas of yours! I'm anxious to hear them!"

Jason sat down and began, "First of all, Pastor, I want to thank you again, and the entire congregation for welcoming me back."

"We are happy to have you back. I am sorry for the tragedy that prompted your return. You have our deepest sympathy."

"Thank you, Pastor. I can't grieve too hard because I know they're in the arms of their maker." Jason thought to himself, "Yes, and they were made by the Devil himself. May they burn in Hell forever!"

"Now, Jason, tell me about your ideas."

"You see, Pastor, in New York I came in contact with conditions that were very hard for me see. There was such a great need there, and God used me in many ways. What I found most rewarding was working with the many young girls whose lifestyles had been very destructive. Preteens and teenaged girls were prostituting themselves on a regular basis, and teen pregnancy was epidemic.

The Spirit suggested to me that my role should be in trying to reach these girls as early as possible, before they became sexually active.

"I propose to start a series of workshops to help our young girls see their value and the need to preserve their bodies as the temples of God. I want them to understand the God-pleasing practice of abstinence, keeping themselves pure and undefiled. I want them to know that sex belongs in marriage according to God's plan and about the many dangers of prostitution and pre-marital sexual intercourse."

"Umm, I see. And who will teach these workshops?"

"I would do that. I obtained a lot of experience in New York, and I was quite successful."

"I must say I do like the concept, Jason. It seems to me that your plan would be akin to sex education . . . "

"With a Christian slant," Jason interrupted.

"Of course. Let us think this through. First of all, young girls—young women—do not participate in these activities or conceive babies by themselves. Addressing just half of the equation won't be sufficient. Young men also need to learn these values.

"Secondly, you must inform the parents of the scope and purpose of this endeavor and convince them to allow their children to participate. You will need to obtain their written consents.

"And lastly, in view of the climate in which we are living, I must insist that you obtain the services of a qualified female to teach the young women, while you address the young men. Perhaps someone from our own congregation may be qualified to do this. As a matter of fact, it may be even more appropriate to do this as a co-ed workshop with a team-teaching approach. How long do you anticipate it will take you to pull this all together to include a complete course description, consent forms, your presentation to parents, and the recruitment of a co-facilitator?"

"I don't think it will take me too long. I can revamp the program I used in New York to adapt it to young men and women. Selecting a partner should not be a problem. I'd say it could be pulled together in a few days."

"I would suggest you take a little more time. This is a sensitive area and deserves careful construction. Besides, this is a stressful time of year for most people. They are preoccupied with the holidays and various activities. Since I will want sufficient time to thoroughly review and approve of everything beforehand, I suggest a target date circa the second or third week of next year. That will also give you more time to promote your idea to the parents.

"I will require an orientation to be scheduled first for the parents so that you can make a formal presentation describing the program in detail and secure their written permission. I expect there will be questions for you as well."

"Thank you, Pastor. I'll get right on it."

Jason left, disappointed by the unexpected turn of events. He had expected to be given free reign; and he viewed the prospect of adding the young men and a female partner with dismay. Even so, he was sure he would find a way to further his own agenda unencumbered.

Ultimately, Jason enlisted Miss Carter to assist him with his plan. She had been involved with many of the members of the congregation as their children's Sunday school teacher, and she had their trust. This would be helpful in view of the new members added during his absence. Additionally, he felt confident he could effectively manipulate her to his advantage.

Jason decided to withdraw to get away and devote serious time to designing this program that he implied was already in place and only needed tweaking to adapt. He had to really research and come up with something that appeared thorough and legitimate. This he accomplished to his satisfaction within two weeks while staying at his family's, now *his* condo in Palm Springs.

Pastor Withers was satisfied with the documentation Jason presented. He approved the posting and distribution of the fliers and okayed the announcements to be made. Jason had the green light. He busied himself working his charm campaigning for his cause to culminate with the orientation scheduled for Saturday, January 12, 2013.

CHAPTER 17

(2/11/2012) Since May, Liv had been seeing Morgan almost daily, dining and visiting the Center as often as time would allow. Besides the fact that some day they would be married, she didn't know much about him—what he did for a living, his family, even where he lived. She decided to learn more. They were having lunch one afternoon when she broached the subject.

"Morgan, it has been a while since we have been seeing each other. Yet, I know so little about you, although you know just about everything there is to know about me. That is going to have to change! After all, if I'm supposed to become your wife, don't you think I should know more about you than your special friends and your dreams for them?"

"You're right, Liv. What do you want to know besides everything? Ask away!"

"It's as simple as that? Okay, then! First of all, your name is French, I believe. Are you French? You don't look the way I would imagine a Frenchman would look. I can't see you getting your tall, dark and handsome looks from just one source. You *don't* have a French accent."

"Oh? How is a Frenchman supposed to look?"

"*I'm* supposed to be asking the questions. *You're* supposed to be *answering* them!"

"Well then, my surname *is* French. The name has survived, but I don't know about the French heritage. I know there are a lot of other influences in the mix through the generations. My father was only part French, how much I don't know. His mother, my grandmother, was a mixture of Italian, Ethiopian, and Hawaiian—go figure! On my mother's side there is a hodgepodge of everything, but I would say predominantly Cherokee, Caucasian, and Hispanic from her mother, while my maternal grandfather was Caucasian with no other influences that I know of. Suffice it to say that I am the result of an ancestry of one big melting pot! I never paid much attention to that."

Morgan noticed Liv's demeanor had changed, as if she had retreated deep within herself. He asked, "What's going on in that busy head of yours? Was it something I said?"

Liv had indeed been wrestling with her thoughts as Morgan was describing his roots. She was remembering her mother's letter that she had read not that long ago. She felt it would not matter to Morgan, and she wanted to tell him.

"Morgan, I don't know just how comprehensive your knowledge of me and my past is in light of your special 'gift,' and you may already know this. If so, then you know that I only found out recently. If not, I'm putting it out now. My mother is of mixed ancestry. Her mother was black, and her father was white. That's it. How do you feel about that?"

Morgan looked at her with sensitive eyes and asked, "Liv, how do *you* feel about it?" Liv didn't have to think. "I am me. I am the same person I have been all my life. I don't feel any different knowing this after all these years of growing up as a white girl with a white mother and father and white brothers. I don't know if I am supposed to feel any difference, or what that difference would be."

Smiling, Morgan said, "Well, let me tell you what *I* think. Our children will have a whole lot more in their melting pot than either of us does! Are we finished with me?"

"No! We're just getting started! Tell me more about your grandmother, the one who told you how special you are!"

"She is my mother's mother and was probably the one who influenced me most growing up. I am her only grandchild, and my mother was *her* only child."

"Was?"

"Yes. She and my dad are both deceased."

"Oh, Morgan. I am so sorry!"

"Don't be sorry, Liv. They had a great life together. They didn't always agree on everything, especially concerning me, but they loved each other more than you could imagine. And I have to add here, that is how much I love you! I had a great example, Liv."

Liv could only smile as she waited for him to continue.

"Dad wanted me to be a man's man—tough—to do masculine things like fishing, sports, hunting, you name it. Mom was more practical and insisted that I learned how to take care of myself, and a woman, I might add. I had to learn how to cook and clean, do the laundry, sew, at least to sew on buttons and mend my own clothes as needed in an emergency. All these things Dad dismissed as 'women's work.'

"What they both agreed on was that I had to have a good education and the fact that they didn't want Birdie filling my head with all that tribal mumbo-jumbo, as they called it."

"Birdie?" Liv asked.

" 'Birdie' is what I call my grandmother. She was called 'Little Bird' as a child. She became 'Birdie.' It was Birdie that I went to for advice. She didn't say too much as she wasn't very talkative; but when she did speak, what she said was usually terse and profound.

"I learned my lessons well and succeeded in pleasing both my parents. I think my dad was a little disappointed that I chose tennis over basketball or football. I was very good at tennis and loved to play. I didn't think 6'4" was tall enough for a basketball player, and I didn't have the weight or the will to be successful at pro-football. Besides, I didn't have a desire to be a pro in *any* sport. He was okay with my wrestling. I was pretty good at it, too, and you might say I was the star of my high school and college wrestling teams! I enjoyed gymnastics as well.

"My dad worked very hard and was successful as an investment broker, financier, and entrepreneur. He was an avid investor in stocks, bonds, and real estate. He was a philanthropist and the consummate businessman, but he didn't take care of himself the way he took care of business. My mom went back to work part time as a paralegal when I started middle school. She never *had* to work, but it is what *she* needed and wanted to do for herself. I was a good kid, and she didn't have to worry about me. Besides, I had Birdie, and my parents always had time to spend with me.

"I wasn't raised as the typical rich kid. I didn't go to private schools although I did receive private tutoring when my parents determined that the local schools, and even the charter schools they investigated, were inadequate by their standards for a myriad of reasons.

"My parents were adamant that I know the value of being grateful and charitable. They always stressed 'giving back' and community service. Mom did a lot of volunteer work and was always helping someone out. I know my dad did a lot of things for the community and made large donations to various causes that benefitted many people. He supported various feeding programs and food banks, homeless shelters, and adopted a few elementary schools. Even today, I don't know the extent of his projects.

"Dad worked so hard being a Type A personality. Coupled with the fact that he did not take care of himself, he had a stroke working alone one night. He did not get medical care timely, which may have prevented the severity and permanency of the effects of the stroke and the irreversible damage he suffered. He was never able to recover.

"Mom quit her job to wait on him hand and foot. I did as much for him as she would allow, and I tried to encourage her to take time for herself. I wanted her to hire a nurse for him. She refused. She said her vows included 'in sickness and in health.' She said that taking care of him was a labor of love, and she was not going to let anyone take that away from her.

"Dad had always made provisions for the future and took care of business, be it life insurance, advance planning, and even long-term care insurance. Mom wouldn't hear of Dad's going to any of those facilities. She said she would have to work twice as hard with him *there* to insure that he would consistently get the proper care. She didn't have to leave to see to his care at home."

Liv felt such compassion as she saw Morgan dealing with the memories that were surfacing as he spoke, although he was making a conscious effort to keep the conversation light and his emotions in check.

"Mom really wore herself out. I told her for her birthday three days away I was treating her to an all-day spa session, and for her to refuse was not an option. I assured her I would personally see to dad. Mom was on the way home from visiting with Birdie when she was struck head-on by a drunk driver going the wrong way. She was killed instantly."

Liv instinctively reached for his hand and held it, feeling pain for this woman she did not know and for her son. Morgan looked at her and smiled, as if to say, "Thank you, Liv. I'm okay, and she's okay."

"As hard as it was, when I learned that my mom had been killed, I prepared to tell my dad. Although he was virtually an invalid, it was clear that he had sufficient comprehension even though he couldn't speak. It was as if he already knew. He was grief-stricken. With tears in his eyes, he just hung his head. He died in his sleep that night.

"My grandmother Birdie knew. I had planned to tell her in person the next morning. She called me early that morning before I was even awake. *She* told me that Dad had died during the night. 'It's ok, Baby,' she said. 'They are together now, and they are happy. You be happy for them, too. You just do what you have to do. You will be fine.' "

Liv understood the concept. She thought of Theo and Eleanor and smiled. She could not be sad.

"I see Birdie just about every week. When I told her I had finally found you, you can't guess what she said!"

Liv thought to herself, "I bet I *can*. She probably knew already! Nothing can surprise me anymore."

"She said she was thrilled that I finally decided to tell her! She wanted to know when I was going to bring you to meet her!"

"That's a good question, Morgan. I would love to meet her! When?"

"She left last month for her yearly retreat to 'get in touch with her roots.' I expect her to return in about a week. We can go when she returns if you want."

"Of course I want to. But first tell me a little more about her. How she influenced you, for instance."

"That could take hours to explain! Let me give you probably the most significant impact she had on my life that occurred when I was about six or seven years old. Birdie had so many interesting things that always attracted my attention. She had this curio cabinet in which she kept many cultural artifacts that were colorful and fun to handle. She always let me play with them, and there was never a problem. For some of them she would tell me about the legends behind them or some other fascinating story.

"One day she had a new item on the top shelf, front and center. I noticed it right away, but it was almost out of my reach. I asked Birdie to get it for me so I could play with it. It was far more interesting, colorful, and intriguing than any of them! Birdie looked at me strangely. I felt as if I had done something very wrong.

"She said, 'Son, this is a special artifact that you are *never ever* to touch! You may look at it all you want, but it is *very* delicate, and you *mustn't* ever *touch* it. Do you understand?'

"Of course, I understood the words she used, but I didn't understand why I could not touch it or play with it as I was able to do with all the others. She made me promise that I would obey her admonition. But, Liv, I was just a child. Sometimes, as an adult looking back on that incident, I believe she *knew* I would disobey her, and that is what she intended! She wanted to teach me a lesson that I may not have learned any other way."

Liv was listening to him with great interest. She was thinking there was a purpose that was to have far-reaching ramifications. She continued to listen, keeping her thoughts to herself.

"Being the normal kid that I was, as soon as Birdie had left me alone with that enticing artifact staring me in the face, I could hear it calling to me saying, 'Pick me up! Examine me!' I couldn't resist it! I stood on my toes and stretched as far as I could and was able to grasp it. I stood there holding it in the palms of my hands and was admiring its beauty. I was thinking that it wasn't so fragile after all when, right before my eyes, it disintegrated, leaving nothing but colorful dust in my hands! The most awful feeling I could ever imagine overtook me, the least of which was fear of what Birdie would do when she discovered that I had broken my promise and disobeyed her, both of which I saw as mortal sins. I was literally paralyzed!

"That is how Birdie found me. She had a plastic bag in one hand and a pouch of some kind in the other. She placed the pouch on the table and placed the opened plastic bag beneath my hands for me to empty the dust into it.

"I didn't think about it at the time, but when I turned my hands back over after shaking the dust off, there was not a trace of color left on my hands! You would think there *would* be, especially in view of the fact that I had begun to sweat knowing the trouble I was in, and my palms were wet.

"After she had sealed the bag and put it aside, Birdie was eying me hard. I felt her eyes, and I was afraid and ashamed to look at her. I just kept looking down at the floor. She ordered, 'Son, look at me!' She didn't sound mean or angry. I can't explain it.

"Reluctantly, I raised my eyes, afraid of what I might see in *her* eyes. 'Son,' she said, 'you know that I love you, and I always will. You are the only child of my only child. It is because I love you that I must do what I am about to do. You made a vow, a promise that you broke.

" 'You were disobedient when there was no reason for you not to obey. It is my duty to teach you a lesson that you will never forget. I want you to know that this hurts me far more than the pain you will feel, and you *will* feel pain! If you cry out or if you move or flinch, your pain will increase in severity and in duration. Take your punishment like a man, and it will be okay. It will cease. Do you understand?'

"Believe me, Liv, I understood! Birdie reached in her pouch and removed some kind of artifact that looked like a miniature whip to me. I had never seen it before, and I never saw or *wanted* to see it again. It had a carved wooden handle about six inches long, and there were four or five strands of what looked to me like flexible wires, or very thin leather strips coming out of one end. There appeared to be tiny feathers along the lengths of each strip. I held out my hands with palms up as instructed, and she proceeded to strike my palms five times with that whip. The pain was severe! It felt like my hands were on fire! I couldn't hold back my tears, but I didn't dare move or flinch. I forced my mouth closed so that not a sound escaped.

"Liv, it was the strangest thing! I felt the searing pain; boy, did I ever feel it! When I saw that there would be no more strikes, I looked at Birdie, and I saw her love for me and her pride in me. She put the whip down and she brushed my palms with her palms. The pain ceased immediately! She smiled at me! I knew I had learned my lesson, and so did she. We never spoke of that incident again.

"You know, Liv, I often have wondered if that whole incident was really real or not. Sometimes, more and more, I think she must have put me into some kind of hypnotic trance or spell so that everything I felt was in my head! I mean, it *felt* like the pain was in my hands, but I seriously wonder. She impressed upon me how much it would hurt, and I obviously believed her. I think one of these days I am going to ask her about it. One thing is for sure. I never disobeyed her again, or my parents either for that matter! Also, I don't make promises easily. If I make a promise to you, you can know that I intend to fulfill it, and I am committed to doing everything in my human power to make sure I do. Now you know something about me that I have never told anyone, not even my parents."

Liv had her own thoughts about that event. She felt he was right. She couldn't see Birdie inflicting such pain on a little boy!

"Well, Morgan, thanks for sharing that anecdote with me; but I'm not through with you yet. I don't know what you do for a living, where or when you were born, where you went to college, your major and degree, how many children you want, what your favorite color is, your favorite foods, your shoe size, if you prefer sleeved tees or wife-beaters, not even where you live!"

"Wow! So many questions! If we were speed dating, our time would be up before you were even half through asking your questions! I don't even know if I can remember them all. Let me see. Los Angeles; Sunday, March 10, 1985; USC; Masters in Economics/minor in Psychology; blue; four or five; lasagna; 10½ M; either; whew! What did I miss?"

"You missed where you live and what you do for a living."

"I will tell you what I do for a living. By that, I suppose you want to know my source of income; and I will show you where I live. Not only will I show you where I live, I will show you some of what I learned while I was growing up there!

"Actually, as you can probably tell by the amount of time I spend with you and with the kids, I don't have a nine-to-five. I don't have the time. Upon my parents' demise, I was the sole heir of their entire estates, that is, all that was not bequeathed to their pet causes. Likewise, I was the sole beneficiary of their life insurance policies. I took Birdie's advice and invested the proceeds from the insurance policies. As a result, I am comfortable. I learned well my father's lessons on remaining debt free, as he did, never buying anything on credit, never spending principal, living only on interest and profits. My only financial concern is that my dreams are far too extravagant for my present resources.

"And now, My Love, I think, at least I *hope* you have enough information to satisfy your quest for knowledge until we can continue this dialogue later. In the meantime, I want to make plans for visiting Birdie when she returns. We can kill two birds with one stone. I can take you to meet Birdie and to see where I live in the same day."

Meeting Birdie

(12/9/2012) Liv was excited about the prospect of meeting this woman who had been so instrumental in Morgan's life and who had made those predictions concerning her. Morgan picked her up at ten-thirty. "First, we are going to pick up Birdie. She tells me she has proof to show us that *you* are the *right* one. *I* don't *need* to see anything. I have proof right here," he said putting his hand over his heart. "I know *Birdie* knows as well. So I guess the proof is for *you*, Liv."

"I have my own sources of proof, Morgan. More proof I don't really need, but I am anxious to hear what she has to tell me. Perhaps she can tell me something, provide some input that can help me in other ways. Your grandmother sounds like a wise woman. How should I address her?"

"I call her 'Birdie.' You can, too. She will like that."

Liv was thinking that if Birdie *knew* so much, and was so wise, perhaps she could provide some insight that Liv might apply to her own *situation*. At least she could hope.

When they pulled up in front of Birdie's upscale senior living complex, Liv had a fleeting thought about perhaps providing such a place in a less affluent area for seniors. As it turned out, many years later, she did.

They entered the foyer to find that Birdie was waiting for them on one of the several plush couches. She immediately rose to greet them with her arms outstretched. She was a very petite woman who seemed to be well preserved, strong, and healthy for her age.

She had a steady gait and was sure-footed. Her long salt and pepper hair was pulled back into a tight bun at the base of her neck and would have made her to appear austere except for her warm smile.

It was with that very pleased, approving smile on her only slightly wrinkled face she embraced both of them simultaneously.

"My Morgy-Porgy and his bride-to-be!"

"Oh, Birdie!" Morgan said, obviously embarrassed. He had neglected to tell Liv of his grandmother's pet name for him.

"Morgy-Porgy?" Liv repeated, looking at Morgan.

"Please, don't ask!" Morgan said, hastening to present Liv to his grandmother. "Birdie, this is Liv. If you are ready to go, I will go and pull the car up front." He left the two women in each other's company, grateful for the opportunity to escape the "Morgy-Porgy fiasco, if only momentarily.

Amused, Liv flashed a broad smile at Birdie. "I am *so* pleased to meet you, Birdie. Morgan has told me so much about you! I am looking forward to spending time with you."

Morgan was right that for Liv to call her "Birdie" would make her happy. Her eyes lit up even more when Liv addressed her. "My child, it is *I* who am happy to finally meet the *real you.*"

Liv was puzzled at her choice of words, "the *real* you." "I have already learned something more about Morgan, his nick name! Why do you call him that? Does anyone else?"

Birdie laughed. "Oh, my! They had better not! He was such an adorable little boy, and he *loved* for me to read Mother Goose rhymes to him. That name I gave him because he always wanted me to read his favorite. I don't know why he liked that one so much, but Morgy-Porgy came from Georgy Porgy!"

Liv smiled to herself and put that little tidbit of personal information away for future use.

"Perhaps we should head outside. Morgan will be pulling up any moment. I don't want you young folks to be late for your lunch reservations."

They walked outside and down the steps just as Morgan pulled up. Morgan came around and opened up both passenger doors. Liv positioned herself to enter the rear seat in deference to Birdie. Morgan, who had intended to put Birdie in the rear, understood.

Birdie, too, was appreciative of the gesture but would not hear of it. "What makes you think I am going to sit up front while you take the back seat? You belong at Morgan's side, and don't you forget it, young lady! Now, in the front with you!"

At the restaurant, orders had been taken, and the trio was conversing and waiting for their selections to arrive. Liv was enjoying listening to Birdie talk about Morgan's childhood. It was obvious he was her pride and joy. Morgan didn't have too much to say. He didn't want Birdie to call him by her pet name for him again. "Birdie, you said you had some *proof* you wanted to show me," he stated.

"Yes, I did, and I do." She removed a 10"x12" manila envelope from her large bag. "It's in here. You open it," she said as she handed it to Morgan. He noticed it had been addressed to Birdie, and was postmarked April 10, 1985. There was a piece of tape over the seal with the date also hand-written under the tape and the post office stamp on top of it. It was clear the envelope had never been opened.

"This is addressed to you, Birdie. You never opened it! Why? Do you know what's in it?" Morgan asked.

"Of course I know what's in it! *I'm* the one who put it there and mailed it to myself!"

Morgan unsealed the envelope and removed the content as Liv watched, wondering, as was Morgan, what it could possibly be. He was blown away as he looked in amazement at what was on the single sheet of paper he held in his hand. Liv was scrutinizing his face, growing more and more curious with every passing second. Speechless, Morgan handed the sheet of drawing paper to Liv.

Liv had the same reaction as Morgan as she saw a sketch of a young woman that looked as if it had been sketched from a photograph of her! She looked at Morgan, and they each looked at Birdie for an explanation. Morgan looked again at the postmark and realized that Liv had not even been born. He was just a babe in arms at that time himself.

Birdie finally spoke, "Now you know why I never approved of any young lady you introduced to me. I knew none of them was the one."

"But Birdie," Morgan asked, "where did this come from? Who drew it?"

"*I* drew it, of course! I'm no artist. It came from wherever special gifts come from. I dreamed this face every night from the day you were born until I went and bought a sketchpad and tried to portray the face in my dream on the paper. Nothing happened. The next night I dreamed about the face again, and in my dream I picked up the paper and that is the result! I didn't question it. I knew that this was the face of the person that was meant for you. End of story! Was I right, or was I right?"

If there had been a shadow of a doubt in anyone's mind, it was totally and irrevocably eradicated.

"Morgan, Liv," Birdie continued, "You two have drawn this thing out far too long. It's time to set the date and start making plans. I'm not going to live forever, you know. I expect to see at least two of my great-grandchildren!"

"But Birdie, I haven't formally *asked* Liv to marry me, and she hasn't accepted!"

"So what is stopping you from asking her now?"

"Nothing, really, except I haven't gotten her a ring yet, either."

Birdie reached into her bag and brought out a little box. "Here!" she said, handing it to Morgan. He took the box and opened it. He immediately recognized his mother's wedding ring set that she *never* took off. He had suspected they had been taken from her finger by someone the night she was killed. In answer to his unasked question, Birdie explained, "When your mother visited me that night, she took off her rings and gave them to me. She said they were for you to give to the woman I had been telling you about all those years. We both knew that she would not be seeing you or your father again."

Morgan was deeply moved. He knew how much those rings had meant to his mother.

"She intended for those rings to be a comfort to you and inspire you to be as happy in love and marriage as she and your father had been. This is a joyous time. Don't spoil it, boy. Go ahead and seal the deal!"

Liv looked at him reassuringly as he removed the ring and got down on one knee beside her. "Liv," he began, "you know how long and how much I have loved you. I know how much you love me, although you have never said it in words, and I understand. Although some circumstances may not have changed, I am asking you now—will you marry me?"

Liv's heart melted. She did love him, and she knew in time she would tell him so, but not today. "Yes, Morgan, I will marry you."

There was a sense of finality in the air and a settling of the minds for Liv and Morgan.

"Now you just have to set the date. I think three months is enough time to plan a wedding, don't you?" Birdie asked. "Four, at the most!"

Morgan looked at Liv for an indication to find that she was nervously looking at him for the same thing.

"Four months?" he asked her. Liv hesitated a little too long to go unnoticed, looking at Birdie, and then at Morgan. She averted her eyes and lowered her head slightly, but not before Morgan detected a trace of panic in her eyes. She smiled faintly and nodded "Yes." Birdie also detected something amiss, a fleeting hint of cloudiness on Liv's face.

They settled down to enjoy their brunch. Birdie was reflecting on Liv's hesitation and noted she seemed to be in a pensive mood. Liv excused herself to go to the ladies room, and Birdie took that opportunity to speak confidentially to Morgan.

"Son, I sense unease in Liv. Is there a problem?"

"I know, Birdie. I think I understand how she feels. I believe she will be fine."

"I *know* she will. Your future together is bright. After all, it is fated to be!

"Now, to change the subject; Liv will be giving you, her husband, a fabulous gift for a wedding present. You must give *her* something that will give her as much joy as what she will give you. She will surprise you, and you must surprise her, as well."

"What will she give me, Birdie? What could she possibly give me that would mean more to me than just having her in my life, in my arms, as my wife?"

"If I told you, it would spoil the surprise. I can tell you only that you couldn't ask for more."

What could *I* possibly give *her*? She has just about everything a girl could ever need or want. The one thing we *both* want for her I can't give her; it's for *her* to obtain."

Birdie took note of his words.

"I will give you a hint. Every girl wants to have her mother with her on what is probably one of the most important days of her life!"

"But Liv doesn't know where her mother is, or even if she is alive!"

"She *is* alive, and you *will* find her!"

Morgan knew by now to accept whatever Birdie told him without question. He was curious about what Liv planned to give him, but he knew what he would give her. He made mental notes of what he would do to accomplish his mission.

Liv returned as the waiter was pushing dessert, which no one seemed to want right then. "I'll take a slice of apple pie to go," Birdie ordered. "That way, I can eat it with the ice cream that I plan to have for dessert tonight."

"Birdie, you have always had such a sweet tooth! I can't understand for a minute how you have never weighed more than ninety pounds!" Morgan teased.

"Ninety pounds indeed!" she said with mock indignation. "It's *98* pounds, I'll have you know! And I am as strong and healthy as I want to be, so never you mind! And remember, I can still handle *you*! I think it's time you took me home before I have to turn you over my knee in front of your fiancée, Mr. Morgy-Porgy!"

Birdie intended and was expecting an amused reaction from Liv to the mental picture she hoped her comment would generate as well as her use of her pet name for Morgan. It did not materialize.

They left the restaurant and were headed toward Birdie's home when she asked Morgan to stop for a moment at the drug store. "I think I ate something that is not sitting too well in my stomach. Will you run in, please, and get me some antacids?" Morgan thought it strange. He had never known her to complain of any ailments whatsoever. Nevertheless, he obeyed. Once he was out of the car, Birdie addressed Liv.

"Liv, I know you are worried. I'm not certain I know what it is, but I feel strongly that you are fearful of something. You are seeking answers, and you are confused. Am I right?"

Liv looked hopeful as she answered, "Yes, I *am* troubled about something. I have questions, and I am trying to come up with a definitive answer to my problem. Somehow, I was hoping that you might be able to help me."

"Child, I can only tell you this. The answers you seek lie within. You will discover them, but you must walk through the fire. You will prevail. Just believe and know that what I tell you is true."

That was not the answer Liv was looking for, but she accepted it.

"Now," Birdie added, "I have something to give you for Morgan. I didn't mention it earlier, but when my daughter gave me her wedding rings, she also gave me Morgan's father's wedding band. I want you to take it to give to Morgan during the ring portion of your ceremony. It will mean a lot to him. I'll leave it to you to decide when to let him know you have it."

"Thank you, Birdie. I can see how Morgan would want his dad's ring." Liv took the ring, noting it was definitely a match. She closed the small box and put it in her purse. She decided to keep it to herself for the moment.

CHAPTER 18

With Birdie safely back at home, the newly engaged couple headed toward Morgan's home. Liv was quiet as she pondered Birdie's cryptic words. She had been racking her brain ever since she accepted the fact that she and Morgan would inevitably be together. She could not seem to shake the consternation that seemed to overcome her whenever she thought about it.

"Well, my betrothed, on to my humble abode, where I shall dazzle you with my domestic prowess!"

"You are taking me to *your* home?"

"You still want to know where I live, don't you?"

"Yes, of course."

Liv began to pay more attention to her surroundings. They were exiting the 90 Freeway onto Slauson, past La Brea to Overhill. She was looking for hints when she saw "View Park" on a street sign on Mount Vernon. They traveled up and down hills and finally turned into a gated driveway at the end of a cul-de-sac. Morgan opened the gate remotely and drove down the winding driveway, which was flanked by well-manicured grounds and beautiful landscaping. It culminated in a circle around a large fountain in front of an impressive mansion.

"I'll just leave the car here. Are you ready to be wowed?"

"I'm already wowed! This is *beautiful*!"

"I'm glad you like it. Of course, I had nothing to do with it. It is almost practically the way my parents left it. Please come in! I will give you the grand tour!"

Morgan took her through the obviously well cared for home, room by room. The gourmet kitchen was spacious and had every imaginable gadget with a walk-in and a butler's pantry with a window that opened into the large family room. There was a half bath near the great room and the formal dining room. There was another adjacent to the family room. The main level included a library, and a utility-laundry room, which separated servants' quarters from the main living quarters.

"This is the sole bedroom suite on this level," Morgan said as he opened and quickly closed the door. Liv was only able to get a quick peek. "It is exactly like the ones upstairs, except for the master suite, so we'll just continue upstairs."

There were four other handsomely decorated suites, three of which had a sitting room and a balcony. All had full baths, dressing rooms, and walk-in closets. Morgan had been careful not to announce which suite was his, but Liv correctly deduced it was the one downstairs.

"This is the master bedroom suite, my parents' room. It is just as they left it," Morgan said. The suite was immaculate and featured a fireplace in the wall that separated the sitting room and the bedroom so that it was accessible to both. It included a wet bar, a mini kitchen, a sun porch, an office, and super-sized dual walk-in closets. There were his and her bathrooms separated by a huge circular bathtub with a whirlpool.

They returned downstairs where there was a large, subterranean area of about eighteen hundred sq. feet, which Morgan described as his domain growing up. It housed a regulation pool table, a table tennis, and a plethora of electronic equipment and devices, gym equipment, a small theatre, and everything a young man could desire.

The family room opened onto the large patio area overlooking a large, kidney bean-shaped swimming pool with a perpetual waterfall at one end. There was also a pool house with supplies, a shower, a utility room containing a washer and dryer, and other amenities. On one side were a rose garden and a vegetable garden with many different vegetables. There were four fruit trees—lemon, orange, apricot, and avocado. The outdoor patio was complete with a kitchen and outdoor furniture. The house was perfect for entertaining. A nice-sized, grassy play area and tennis and basketball courts completed the backyard.

Morgan pointed out a good-sized structure beyond the tennis court that he described as a mother-in-law's unit. It was actually a four-bedroom house complete with its own yard and attached double garage, which Liv saw later.

Liv was thoroughly impressed and marveled at how well cared for everything was. "You must have an army of hired help to keep this place up so wonderfully. Everything is so perfect!" she exclaimed.

"Yes, I do have *some* help, but I do most of it myself. I told you how my mother insisted I learn to take care of myself. That included my home. I do my own cooking and cleaning, and I find that working in the garden is good therapy for me. I have a gardener who keeps up the grounds and a pool service for the pool. I have a housekeeping service that comes in once a month. I find that's enough."

"Now I am *really* impressed!"

The tour was complete, and Morgan escorted Liv to the library, just past the great room. It contained an impressive desk, a large conference table, and some comfortable seating.

"Sit anywhere you like and make yourself comfortable. I have chosen the textbooks for your 'Introduction to Morgan 101' course. If you run out of material, feel free to go anyplace you like and do whatever you want. Just don't come into my kitchen until I say so, okay?"

"Okay, I won't," Liv said as she eyed the stack of photo albums on the desk. The first album opened was Morgan's baby book. The first page contained a printout of his ultrasound and his first photo as a newborn.

Everything she could have wanted to know about Morgan from pre-birth to age 24 was chronicled in photos, records, and notations. She browsed through all of the albums and got a very good sense of the loving home in which Morgan had grown up. She could not help but compare it to her own. Liv had become more aware of how dysfunctional her home life had been.

She stood to stretch and realized just how tired she was. She had not slept well the night before. She thought if she moved around a bit, she could shake off her sleepiness. When she passed by the downstairs bedroom that had been skipped on the tour, she succumbed to the temptation to go in for a closer look. Its layout was similar to the others, but it lacked the ornate décor. Yes, it was definitely a man's room—very masculine, but very *neat*!

Liv looked around the room, hoping to get a more intimate understanding of him than could be gleaned from albums. She saw a large volume on the stand beside the bed, which she found to be the King James Version of the Holy Bible. That did surprise her as religion had never come up in their many conversations. Liv presumed his knowledge of her past would have included her attitude toward God so that he would know to avoid that topic.

Her innate curiosity about all things Morgan compelled her to take an even closer look. She read the inscription on the cover, "To Morgan with Love, Mom and Dad." She thumbed through the pages and noted they were replete with underlining and highlighting of various passages, an indication that the Bible was handled frequently. She noticed a bookmark and turned to the marked passage. It was the Song of Solomon.

Liv returned the Bible to its original position. Standing next to Morgan's bed, being tired and sleepy, Liv found it was too alluring. She pulled back the comforter, seeking to just rest a moment or two. With her head resting on Morgan's pillow and his scent in her nostrils, Liv fell into an exhausted, troubled sleep. It was not long before she became agitated and began tossing and thrashing in her sleep, having broken out into a cold sweat. Her moaning soon escalated into cries. "No! No! Please, don't! Stop! Please, stop!"

Morgan had gone looking for her when he saw she was no longer in the library where he had left her three hours earlier. He thought he heard a sound coming from his room and opened the door to see Liv in the throes of a violent nightmare. Not wanting to make sudden physical contact to awaken her, he called out her name several times, with no effect. She continued to plead with her tormentor.

Not knowing what else to do, he sat on the bed beside her and made contact with her arm, softly calling her name. Still in the midst of her trauma, Liv began to struggle in earnest at his touch, screaming and kicking and striking out with her fists. She landed a hard right that caught Morgan's left eye. He had no choice but to grab her wrists to restrain her. "Liv! Wake up! You're having a nightmare! It's me, Sweetheart! Please wake up!"

Liv opened her eyes. She was not in her little room; she was not in a cave; she did not recognize her surroundings. She saw Morgan's distraught face. Remembering where she was, Liv stopped struggling. She could see the beginning of a bruise where she had just clobbered him. She was physically and emotionally spent.

"Liv, you were having a bad dream, a nightmare." He released her wrists, but continued to hold her hand, soothing her.

Liv, still shaken from her ordeal, her brow damp, and traces of fear still visible, looked pointedly at Morgan and said, "Morgan, I need to see your chest, all of it! *Now!*"

Morgan thought it was an unusually strange request, especially under the circumstances, but he did not hesitate to expose his full chest to her.

"Let me see your back!" she demanded. Morgan immediately completely removed his shirt and turned his back to her. Knowing that a beautiful woman was in his bed and had asked to see naked parts of Morgan's body, the Chairman of the Board immediately called to order an emergency meeting of the Hormonal Committee of the Whole (COW). Morgan was aware of their attempts to coerce him, but he ignored them. He had watched Liv as she scrutinized his chest and patiently waited while she surveyed his back, for what reason he had no idea.

"Thank you," was all she said, but he could see her immediate relief. It was puzzling to him, but he did not question her; he was happy that she was returning to her usual self. The emergency meeting of the COW was adjourned on a disappointed note.

"Even though it was the hard way, at least I have learned that you can defend yourself, and *well*, I might add! That's a good thing to know," Morgan said as his hand went to the spot where Liv's effective blow had landed.

"Oh, Morgan! Did I do that? Did I really *hit* you? I'm sorry! I don't know what happened! I'm so sorry!" Liv couldn't understand why after all these years she should have such an active, violent nightmare. And why *now* when she should be so happy? She looked with dismay at Morgan's eye, which was noticeably swelling and blackening. She started to cry.

She would never have thought that the self-defense classes Walter insisted she take would result in her using those skills on the man she loved and who loved and adored her as Morgan did! Seeing her distress, Morgan wanted to downplay his throbbing eye so they could get on with the evening he had planned.

"Hey, there! I can take a little punch from a *girl*! Come on. There are washcloths and towels in the bathroom. Why don't you go and freshen up while I put some ice on my eye." He helped her up and pointed her to the bathroom. "Come to the dining room when you are ready, Love. I'll be waiting."

Liv was penitent and docile as she made her way to the bathroom. Morgan went to the kitchen to ice his wound and prepare the finishing touches on the table setup and the meal he had lovingly prepared for Liv.

Refreshed, Liv appeared at the dining room entrance to find Morgan waiting for her. He had donned his blazer and offered her his arm to be escorted to her seat. The ambiance created was breathtaking, complete with soft music, fresh flowers, and lighted candles. Liv was so awed by it all, she almost forgot about the drama that had unfolded moments earlier.

"Oh, Morgan! This is absolutely amazing!"

"You can have your choice of glazed BBQ salmon with fresh spinach from my garden, and pineapple in BBQ sauce; or stuffed chicken breast with spinach, asiago cheese and dry apricot over spinach and vegetables, also from my garden, in shallots wine sauce; or both!"

"I don't want to be a pig, but I have to try some of *both*! They look so delicious! The fact that you went through so much trouble to impress me is really touching. You could have opened up a can of beans and I would have been thrilled! Oh, Morgan, I . . . I think you are amazing!" Liv caught herself. She wanted to tell him that she loved him, but she couldn't.

"No, I think *you* are amazing. I'm glad you are enjoying the meal I have prepared for you. Feel free to eat to your heart's content. But you have to save room for dessert!"

"What's for dessert?"

"Nothing fancy. It is peach cobbler with the flakiest, most delicious crust you ever tasted! If you like à la mode, I also have homemade ice cream!"

"Oh! That sounds decadent!"

Morgan served the warm cobbler with the ice cream, and Liv had to resist asking for seconds. He was proud of the meal he had prepared and was rewarded with the knowledge that Liv thoroughly savored it. Liv insisted on helping with the cleanup, but Morgan refused.

"This is *my* treat to *you*! Besides," he said, showing her the spotless kitchen, "I clean as I cook. That is something else my mother insisted I learn how to do. Now I think I had better get you home, young lady! You've had a full day, and I want you to have a good night's sleep!"

"Okay, Morgan, but would it be inappropriate if I ask for a doggie bag?"

"Not at all! I consider that a great compliment, My Love!"

Their day culminated with Morgan delivering Liv and her substantial doggie bag safely home.

CHAPTER 19

(12/10/2012) Following the events of the previous day, Liv wanted to talk with Walter, hoping she could gain something, *anything*, by confiding in him and seeking his sage advice. She vacillated for a time and finally called him about 11:00 a.m.

"Hi, Walter. It's me, Liv."

"Hi, Sweetheart."

"Walter, I need to talk to you. Since Theo has been gone, you've been the only person, the only friend that I have trusted and feel free to talk to about almost anything. I need to talk with you about some personal issues I'm having."

"You know you can always talk with me. When do you want to get together?"

"Is now too soon?"

"I've one hand on the doorknob as we speak. Do you want me to pick you up for lunch?"

"Can you come here? I'll fix lunch. This is not a conversation I want to have in public."

Very soon, Walter was at Liv's door.

"Come in, Walter." She greeted him warmly with an embrace.

"Liv, My Love, how are you? You look . . . different!"

"Different? Different good or different bad?"

"Just different. What's on your mind, Liv?"

"I hope you're not real hungry. I had to renege on fixing lunch. I have ordered lunch from your favorite Chinese restaurant. It should be here any minute."

"Never mind the food, Liv. What do you want to talk about?"

"Oh, I think the food is here," she said just as the chimes sounded.

"I'll get that," Walter said. Liv knew not to try to stop him from paying for lunch. It would have been tantamount to an insult.

Liv merely picked at her food while Walter began to eat in earnest as he waited for Liv. Finally, he asked, "Liv, what is troubling you? What are these 'issues' you are having?"

"I'm really not sure where to start, Walter."

"The beginning is usually a good starting point."

"I don't think I *can* start at the beginning. Things are happening so fast and on so many levels, it's getting muddled in my brain. I have found someone special, someone who wants to marry me. I told him I will. Only, that scares me very much."

"Well, Liv, being in love is enough to muddle anyone's brain! Marriage, on the other hand, is a serious step, and it *can* be scary. How serious it is? Do you *love* him?"

"I have already *promised* to marry Morgan." Liv was still reluctant to audibly affirm that she loved Morgan.

"Do you think *he* really loves *you?* Is he looking for something from you?"

"I know it sounds crazy. I *know* he loves me. He knows I have issues. He suggested that I see someone who could help me sort things out. I did take his advice and saw this therapist for almost three months. And, Walter, she helped me to see and understand that I . . . . It's hard for me to tell you this, Walter, but I am an alcoholic!"

Liv waited to see the shocked reaction she expected. All she saw was love.

"Liv, I'm happy that you can say that. Now you can get passed it and overcome it, if you haven't already! I have all the confidence in the world in you. It is very apparent to me that you were at least a highly functioning alcoholic or you could not have accomplished everything you have. Please notice that I used the term *'were'* "

"Walter, I know why I love you so! I know why I *'was'* an alcoholic. I only hope you are up to listening to my tale of woe!"

"Liv, you know I am here for you, just like any loving father would be." Liv proceeded to give Walter a truncated version of the saga of her life to the point that she met Theo. "You pretty much know everything from that point."

"Liv, I haven't been completely honest with you all these years. Our meeting back then was not by chance. I sought you out as a favor to Theo." It took Liv a moment, and she was uncertain how to take what he said. She just waited for him to continue.

"I am sorry, Liv. I don't want you to take it the wrong way. Theo was very concerned about you and just wanted you to be protected from yourself and anyone who might try to use or abuse you. I knew of your vulnerability from Theo. I didn't know specifics, but that didn't matter. I knew Theo; in fact, we were very good friends and distant relatives by marriage.

"Initially, my involvement was more of a favor to Theo; but I saw something in you back then that made me take to you like a father. I saw your naiveté through your hard-core façade. I saw your potential and passion, and I endeavored to support it. I didn't want anyone to judge you unfavorably by seeing you with me so frequently. That is the reason I asked you to play the part of my ward. I was able to expose you to so many things and introduce you to influential and knowledgeable people who were willing to share their knowledge and expertise with you in so many areas. That was my plan to help you develop into the accomplished young woman you have become and are growing into more day-by-day!

"Theo would be so proud of you, and I have him to thank for entrusting you to me. *You* have helped *me* more than you know."

Armed with this new knowledge, Walter was motivated to help her even more. "Liv, do you remember when we first met?"

"Of course, I do! I was shopping at the mall. I stopped to get a drink of water and sat my packages down. I didn't see that girl coming, but you did. You grabbed her arm and asked her why she had taken your daughter's property. She apologized and begged you not to turn her in, and you let her go. You offered to help me carry my bags to my car, which I didn't have. Of course, I didn't *know* you from Adam, and I wasn't about to get in *your* car for you to drive me home. But I did accept the taxi ride you provided."

"You remember that day very well! Liv, you have shared so much with me today. I want to share something with you. Remember how I pressured you into taking those self-defense classes and the swimming lessons?"

"Yes. And I'm so glad you did. The pool has done wonders for me mentally and physically."

"I want to tell you *why* I was so insistent about your learning to swim. You know I am a widower of many years and I have no children. I *had* a daughter. Her name was Kimberly. She was the child that we thought we would never have. She was just three when she drowned accidentally in our pool. We had not taught her to swim, though we were planning to.

"My wife put her down for a nap and dozed off herself. When she awoke a little while later, Kimmy was gone. My wife found her in the pool. She was never the same after that. She blamed and never could forgive herself. She died of guilt and a broken heart."

"Oh, Walter, I'm so sorry!"

"Don't worry about that, Liv. What is meant to be will be. I have been able to accept that. But from the day I met you, I found a purpose. Not that I was just floating through life. Not to pat myself on the back, I do many philanthropist things. That was true even before I lost my family. After all, what is money if it is not used for good, or to help others?

"To me you have taken the place of the daughter I once had. I want my daughter, you, to be successful and happy. I want you to have anything you want and everything you need, including a happy marriage in every respect. It's that simple.

"That being said, I want to get back to this young man of yours. Of course, I want to meet him. I think I am a pretty good judge of character. Now that I understand your misgivings as I think I do, it seems to me you might benefit more, gain more insight from a close girlfriend that you trust. Do you have anyone like that in mind?"

"I don't have any close women friends. In fact, now that Theo is gone, I only have you and Howard, Theo's attorney, to talk to. Most women that I meet regard me with suspicion."

"What about old school friends?"

Liv immediately thought of Elizabeth. "I did have a best friend, Elizabeth. I have often thought of contacting her, but I just never did. It's been so long, she may not even remember me—or still want to be my friend," Liv said sadly.

"Well, don't fret about it, Liv. It's not too late. If she really *were* your friend, she would be as happy to see you as you would be to see her. If not, then there is no loss.

"By the way, did you discuss this with the therapist you were seeing?"

"Yes, it came up, but . . ." Liv was reluctant to elaborate.

"But what? Did she give you any suggestions, any tools to help you?"

"Yes, she did, but I couldn't bring myself to . . . to do what she suggested. Can we change the subject?"

"As you wish, Honey. But just think about how much he loves you, and how much you love him."

"Walter, I *do* love him with all my heart!" There, she had said it out loud! She didn't have to worry, because she didn't say it to Morgan. She still didn't think she could yet.

"Don't you have a rehearsal tonight?" Walter asked.

"Oh, yes! I'd better start making plans to feed that hungry bunch! I'm not going to have enough time to go grocery shopping *and* cook!"

"Why don't you just relax. I haven't sat in on one of your rehearsals for quite a while. Let me take care of feeding them. I'll just call my caterer, and I can sit back and enjoy the private show!"

"Thank you, Walter. You know you are *always* welcome to sit in at *any* time. Besides, I have a couple of new songs to try out. You can give me your opinions!"

(12/11/2012) Liv took to heart many of the things Walter had shared with her and was feeling better. She knew and believed that she and Morgan would be a permanent force. She wanted to see how and what she could do to bring more to the table. She decided to call Howard for his advice.

"Hi, Howard! It's me, Liv."

"Hi there, Liv! Haven't heard from you lately. How've you been?"

"I've been kind of busy, but it's all good!"

"What's on your mind? Any problems I need to see about?"

"Oh, no. Everything's fine, I guess."

"You guess?"

"Well, yes. I've just been trying to figure some things out. I've gotten involved with some children that I'd like to help in a meaningful way. I'm finding that it may be financially out of my realm. I'm still in the idea stage."

"Why don't we get together in my office, and we can look at all the options. Let me help you. You know, you *do* have considerable assets. If you are feeling that it is out of your reach, it must be pretty grandiose!"

"But, Howard, I know this is what I was meant to do!"

"This indeed sounds important. I had cleared my calendar for this Thursday and Friday so that the wife and I could get away for some R & R. But why don't you come in first thing Thursday morning and we can talk. I can delay our mini vacation by a few hours or a day. Besides, I haven't seen you in a while. I promised Theo I would keep tabs on you!"

"Okay, Howard. Is nine o'clock too early?"

"No, that's perfect. See you then."

(12/13/2012) Almost two months had passed since Liv had seen Howard. She was anxious to meet with him and arrived early. Howard rose from his desk when the secretary announced her arrival and opened his door just as Liv reached it. They were both happy to see each other. "What's going on, Liv?" Howard asked.

"There are a couple of things, Howard. I should tell you that I am engaged!"

"Engaged? Now I *know* why I haven't heard much from you! Who is the lucky guy?"

"No, Howard, it's not like that. We have been working together with at-risk kids in South Los Angeles. They're really great kids, and they have so much potential. We are both passionate about helping them on so many levels!"

The excitement and passion in her voice caught Howard's attention. "Whoa, Liv! I can't tell what is exactly driving your excitement. Is it your fiancé, or these kids you also seem to be in love with?"

"It's both, I guess."

"Who are we talking about? What is the young man's name?"

"His name is Morgan Calais." Howard raised his eyebrows.

Liv continued, "He has been working with these kids for a while now. They adore him, and he really, really wants to help them succeed in life. Now that I have been working with them, too, I know this is what I am supposed to do. Together we share this dream of helping these children and young adults. They are so eager to learn and to listen to sound advice. They want to rise above their circumstances! We want to provide a place where they can come and the resources necessary for them to achieve their goals!"

"What kind of resources do you think you need? Do you have or are you working on a business plan? Have you done a cost analysis? Do you know how much seed money you will need for startup and for maintenance? Do you know what your housing needs will be? Do you want to operate a school? A private school? A charter school? Have you thought about incorporating? If so, profit or nonprofit? What will your human resource needs be? There are so many things you will need."

Liv's head was beginning to spin from the barrage of questions for which she had no answers. She was overwhelmed by the due diligence she sensed would be needed. What she had in her favor was her knowledge that this is what she and Morgan both wanted. She knew it would happen. She decided she would not dwell on the problems at that moment. After all, Howard was there to help her. He knew what would be needed. She was going to deal with only one aspect at this point.

"I can't possibly begin to answer your questions, Howard. Obviously, I haven't been thinking on those areas. I know I can trust you to guide me and offer your sage advice, as you have always done. What I want to focus on right now, today, is the housing.

"Morgan showed me a site in the perfect area that was large enough for now and for future expansion that would have been perfect in every respect. He looked into the ownership and found that it was owned by a law firm and was not on the market. Even so, we at least now have a sense of the scope of the site we want and know that the cost for it alone would be astronomical. That's why I am coming to you to find out the extent of my resources so I would have an idea of how much more I would need. I have made a quick summary of my resources and my assessment of the values in today's market of the properties I personally control. You know about everything I inherited from Theo. I am hoping that you and Abraham Goldman can give me a ball-park figure, not right now, of course, but reasonably soon, of my total assets."

"This property, the site you looked at, can you tell me exactly where it is? Do you know the address?"

"Yes. I have it right here," Liv said as she removed a note from her purse with the address printed on it. Howard took the note from her and read the address.

"Hmmm," he said, smiling. He went to his file room and came back with a rather large file and placed it on the desk in front of him as he sat back down. Liv was peering at him expectantly.

"Liv, I've got some okay news, some good news, and some even better news for you. The okay news is that you've got some work to do, and I will help you. The good news is that this file contains a significant remnant of Theo's estate that he did not will to you alone. The property address is the same as that written on this slip you gave me. It is *my* law firm that is controlling the site as instructed by Theo until such a time as you were ready to receive it, along with your husband. Title is to be vested in Olivia Louise Calais and Morgan Avery Calais as husband and wife."

Liv heard his words, but they weren't registering—it was too much for her to immediately comprehend. She had not given him Morgan's middle name. She questioned, "What are you saying, Howard? I don't understand."

"It is simple, Liv. The property you and Morgan Calais saw will be turned over to you when you are legally married. All of this is as dictated by Theo when he changed his will five years ago."

Liv was stunned! Five years ago, Theo knew she would marry a man named Morgan Avery Calais! He had left that property to them. It had to be worth millions! Liv was not thinking about the fact that *they* would be worth *millions* more. She was thinking about what it would mean to all those children they would be helping! She was thinking about how happy it would make Morgan because she knew how much he wanted it. She also was thinking that she would have to up her game and get her head together so that it could happen sooner, not later!

"I told you there was okay news, good news, and better news. You haven't heard the better news. Are you ready for it?"

"I don't know, Howard. I am still boggled." After a long, deep breath, she said "Okay!"

"Theo and Eleanor had established and funded a perpetual trust fund that is generating an average of $250,000 a month in interest. This amount has been steadily accumulating and is to be used to help fund the activities associated with the property."

Liv was astounded. Inheriting the perfect property was breathtaking news. But $250,000 per month on top of that was totally unfathomable!

"Are you *serious*? Oh, wow! This is just *incredible!*"

"It is true, Liv. Theo thought a lot of you and deservedly so. He knew you would be able to follow through and make him proud. I am proud of you, too. I know you have things to do, and now I have even more to do. But it will be a labor of love. I will be putting some things into place. By the way, when is the big day?"

"We haven't set the date yet, but it will be in three or four months. You will be among the first to know. Oh, and please, Howard. I would like to keep this a secret from Morgan and spring it on him as a surprise wedding present. Will that be possible?"

"Sure, we can work that out. I am very happy for you, Liv. Is there anything else I can help you with before you go?"

"Well, as a matter of fact, there is. I haven't discussed it with anyone yet, not even Morgan; but I would like your counsel. There is a little girl that I have fallen in love with. She has become very attached to me, and she loves Morgan, too. I want for us to adopt her as soon as we are married, or even before, if possible. I haven't mentioned it to him yet, but I know he would want to adopt her as well. Do you foresee any problem with that?"

"If she is adoptable, and both of you want to adopt her, I don't see why not. Is she in the system now?"

"Yes, she has been legally taken away from her biological father, who is in jail, I understand; and her mother is deceased. She is a beautiful, lovely spirited child, and I love her so much! She calls me Mommy Liv! Isn't that *cute*?"

"Liv, you deserve all of the happiness you will have. I can look into that next week. In the meantime, I want you to work on a cursory outline of what it is you would like to do with this property, the programs you want to run, startup plans . . . Do you get the idea? I would like a clearer, more detailed idea of what it is you have in mind."

"I think so, Howard. I will start putting it together."

"Why don't you take a week or two, then we'll meet again. You take care, now!"

Liv thanked him, gave him a hug, and floated out the door.

CHAPTER 20

Olivia had not been the first victim of Pastor Jason. He had always been hands on with the youth of the church and was well liked. When he first came into the position, there had already been an annual tradition of Easter week that culminated with a three-day, two-night camping trip. In his second year of service, Pastor Jason conceived and instituted what had become the highlight of the week of fun and games, the "Hide and Seek" competition on the third day of camp.

He had set his designs on 15-year-old Holly Albright. Everything went according to his designs and he carried out his heinous attack in much the same way he subsequently attacked Olivia. In Holly's case, he took her virginity and left her traumatized and shamed into silence.

Holly did not have an escape such as Olivia's. She consciously endured the pain, the shame, and the violation that she was forced to relive over and over. She stopped being the carefree, friendly young lady she had been and became withdrawn and distant, only coming to Sunday morning worship service with her parents. She no longer participated in any of the youth activities.

Holly had done much reading about rape and survival, but she never really internalized the truths she learned; she basically remained stuck. She also had never been able to confide in her parents. After a few years, she realized she needed to get professional help. She finally sought counseling at a rape crisis center and made great strides in the healing process. She was able to confide in her counselor, Megan Harper, who was also a rape survivor. An only child, Holly was a very gifted artist and returned to creating works of art, which she had suspended following her attack. She had begun helping many of the younger survivors at the counseling center, even engaging them in expressing themselves through art. With the several years of absence of her attacker, she was even able after a time to resume her former enthusiasm and participation in the church.

Her forward progress was suddenly stifled the Sunday morning of December 2, 2012, when she saw that Pastor Jason had returned from his long absence and was to resume an active involvement with the youth in place of the outgoing youth pastor.

Counselor Megan Harper was concerned when Holly turned up on her doorstep in hysterics that Sunday afternoon. She feared the worse, that Holly had again been attacked.

"Holly! What is it? What's the matter?" Megan asked, embracing Holly as she sobbed uncontrollably. Meg continued to hold her as her body heaved violently with each heart-wrenching sob.

"Holly, you are safe here. Try to calm down and tell me what's the matter!"

"H… he's back! He's back!" Holly managed between sobs. "That devil bastard . . . He's back!" She struggled to catch her breath and calm herself. "I thought I had gotten through all that." Somewhat calmer, she said, "I, I thought I had taken my power back and was living my life again! One look at him and I was back in that cave—physically, mentally, emotionally—and I am terrified! I, I just don't know what to do!

"I had envisioned seeing him again one day knowing that I was not that 15-year-old frightened child, but a strong, mature adult!"

"Holly," Megan said, taking her gently by the shoulders, "*Listen* to me! You *are* a strong, mature adult. You are *not* that terrified 15-year-old in that dreadful cave. You *have* come a long way."

The gentle, yet forceful way in which Megan redirected her focus began to have an effect, and Holly calmed down enough to try to focus on Megan's words.

"Why am I reacting this way? Why do I feel such dread, such fear?"

"Holly, I've wanted to have this conversation with you, but I have been waiting until the right time, when *you* were ready. Seeing him so unexpectedly has caught you off guard, and that child was awakened in you. I believe it is because that child needs closure that only you, the adult, can bring."

"What do you mean, Megan? How can I do that?"

"You have to confront your fear, this 'demon,' and end it!"

"But *how* can I do that? What can I do?"

"I believe you have to make him accountable for his actions. Press charges against him. Bring him to justice, or at least *try*. Only then can you permanently take back your power."

Holly's eyes darkened with doubt as she tried to grasp what was being suggested.

"But it's been so long. So *long*! I never told anyone but you, and you know how long that took! I didn't even tell my parents, I felt so ashamed. I thought if I just pushed it out of my mind, like it never happened, I could get by."

"And now, Holly, how well has that worked for you?"

"Obviously, it hasn't worked at all, since here I am!"

"Holly, I have been where you are. I know what I am asking you to do. I know how hard it will be. But I know that if I had it to do all over again, I would not hesitate! You see, it doesn't go away if you ignore it or pretend it didn't happen. It just goes deeper, manifesting itself in so many detrimental ways.

"Holly, if you decide you want to do this, you know I'll be there right by your side, holding your hand all the way. It is *your* choice to make."

Holly let out a deep sigh. "If I do this, what if it doesn't work? What if I go through this humiliation and shame for nothing? It may be too late. The statute of limitations could have passed!"

"It couldn't be for nothing, Holly. He will always wield power over you so long as he has the power to keep you silent. That is the power you give him and the power you have to take back. That will also remove the heavy cloud that is like an albatross around your neck, robbing you of the joy, peace of mind, lack of fear, and the sense of security you deserve and need. Besides, Holly, I don't know about the statute of limitation; but even if it has run out, he is still in a position to continue to abuse more unsuspecting victims! In any case, you can make your church community aware of his true nature and can keep him out of positions of trust."

Megan waited as Holly pondered, struggling within herself.

"So, what now?" she asked finally with a glimmer of hope.

"Holly, we don't want to rush into anything. We have to do our due diligence . . . our homework, and I know just where you can start! I have an uncle who is now an assistant DA. He is the one who plotted my course. I will arrange for you to meet with him, then we'll take it from there."

"All right, Meg."

Megan gave her a reassuring hug and said, "Now go home and get some rest. I'll call you tomorrow. In the meantime, I want you to write down as much detail as you can remember about everything, no matter how insignificant you may think it may be. I know it will be hard to do, but try to recount everything he did and said to you.

"Holly, you have no idea how much this will help you."

"Okay, Megan. I'll do my best. Good night."

Holly headed for home to the daunting task that awaited her. She had to admit to herself that she felt better and even dared to hope for an optimal end to it all.

True to her word, Megan called Holly the next day in the early evening.

"Holly, Hi! My uncle will meet with us this Wednesday morning, 9:00 a.m. If you like, we can get together before then and go over what you've written. You may recall additional details."

"Thanks, Meg. I still have two more nights to work on this, and I think I have some things to work out on my own."

"Okay, Holly, but if you need me, I'll be available. I will pick you up at 8:00 a.m. Wednesday morning. Bye now."

Holly worked well into the night on her task. She experienced many emotional twists and turns in the process. The gamut included fear, anger, shame, hatred, regret, doubt, and determination. When she awoke the next morning, she had a new outlook. She had finished writing, but she now had a fierce drive—to paint.

She got out her sketchpad and began to draw. The more she drew, the more driven she became. She set up her easel and began creating like a deranged person under hypnosis. By the end of the day, she had created frame after frame of scenes including landscapes, and several depictions of the cave's interior with its rudimentary contents, each one as if painstakingly copied from a photograph.

What Holly had been unable to relate adequately in her written words she translated in minute detail from the canvass in her mind to the canvass in her hands! Her pictures were truly worth thousands of words!

(12/5/2912) Megan arrived promptly at 8:00 a.m. Wednesday morning to pick up Holly and proceeded to her uncle's office. Though curious about the large portfolio Holly was bringing, she didn't inquire about it, and Holly offered no explanation.

Megan was pleased with Holly's calm demeanor—such a contrast from their last encounter. Holly only concentrated on getting to the meeting. When they entered the DA's office, Megan's uncle, Daniel Harper, was waiting to greet them.

"How's my favorite niece?" he said as he held out his arms to give Megan a hug.

"Hi, Uncle Dan!" She turned to Holly, taking her by the arm and nudging her forward.

"Uncle Dan, this is Holly."

"Dan Harper," he said, extending his hand to Holly.

Holly replied, "Hello, Mr. Harper. I'm very pleased to meet you. I'm Holly Albright. Please call me 'Holly' if you like."

"Well, Holly, I'm pleased to meet *you*! Ladies, please follow me to my office."

They followed him a short distance down a hall to the corner office at the end and were directed to a mini conference table in one corner.

"Can I get either of you anything? Coffee? Tea?"

"Nothing for me, Sir. Thank you," replied Holly.

"A cup of tea will be great for me, Unc!"

They made themselves comfortable as Dan secured the teacup, teabag, and hot water for Megan and a cup of coffee for himself. He also brought a few bottles of water.

"Now, Holly, Meg has told me a little about your situation. What we need to do is find out a couple of things. The statute of limitations for rape in California is six years. It may or may not have passed, but we can deal with that in time. We need to know if we have enough information, other than your statement alone, to secure a warrant.

"I must inform both of you that as an Assistant District Attorney, my involvement at this point would be a conflict of interest since I have a personal interest in the case because you are a friend of my niece, and she has discussed your situation with me. I don't want anything to jeopardize a successful outcome of your case. For that reason, I have requested a colleague to take over from here. I will be present, but only as an observer. My colleague's name is ADA Reginald Johnston. He should be in any moment. Oh, here he is now."

Dan stood as ADA Johnston entered. "Reginald, these are the ladies I spoke with you about—my niece, Megan Harper, and her friend, Holly Albright."

ADA Johnston greeted the ladies in turn thanking them for coming and began. "I will be recording your statement on videotape so that you may not have to repeat everything again when it is turned over to LAPD's Special Victims Unit, which will be done. Now, Miss Albright, do I have your consent to videotape your statement?"

"Yes. You may call me 'Holly,' if you like."

"Thank you, Holly. When I start the taping, I want you to state your name and the fact that you consent to having your statement videotaped. I know this may be difficult for you, but it is absolutely necessary. So just take all the time you need. I want you to state the name of the person or persons who committed a crime against you, the nature of the crime, when it was committed, and where it took place. Then, I just want you to tell me from your independent recollection everything you can remember in the order of occurrence, if possible. If you don't remember exact dates, that's okay. So, whenever you're ready, Holly."

Holly took a deep breath. Her mouth felt dry, so she took a few sips of water. After another deep breath, she indicated she was ready.

"All right, I'm starting the taping."

Holly began, "My name is Holly Albright, and I have given consent to have my statement videotaped.

"I was raped by Pastor Jason Winston. He was the Youth Pastor at my church. It happened on the Saturday before Easter Sunday in 2005 at a three-day camp out." Holly went on to relate the details.

About 25 minutes later Holly had come to the end. Her story was very much like Liv's. It was the same MO, same occasion, same perpetrator, same place, same tactic, same cave, same everything.

Reginald said, "Thank you, Holly. I am so sorry this happened to you, and we are going to do everything in our power to see that justice is served. I do need to ask you some more questions. You've done a great job in describing the events. I see you have brought notes and your portfolio. Do you want to refer to your material and see if there is anything more you can tell us?"

"I think I have told you all I have to tell, but I do have these."

Holly opened the portfolio and removed a rendering of a tattoo and several renderings of the interior of the cave. Reginald looked in amazement at the detailed paintings.

"Holly, this is the cave where it happened?" he asked.

Holly's eyes filled with tears as she slowly nodded.

"This is fantastic," he marveled with his hopes soaring. Everyone, even Meg, who was aware of Holly's talent as an artist, was in awe.

"This cave could possibly provide the physical evidence we will need to go full speed ahead! Holly, where is this place? Can you find it?"

"I know where the camp site is. We always went there."

Reginald stopped the tape and said to Dan, "Before involving the SVU, I want to be able to point them to the crime scene.

"Can you take us there, Holly?"

"I can get to the main camp site. Exactly where the cave is, I'll have to try to remember. I can try to find it, but I can't promise."

Reginald and Dan were both excited. It wasn't even noon, and there were still a few hours of daylight. "Holly, if you are up for it, will you show us now?" Holly nodded.

"In that case, let's go on a field trip!" Reginald said. "Ladies, do you want to go and change into some hiking clothes? Dan, I'm assuming you would like to observe?"

"For sure," Dan replied. I will need to change, too. Meg, I will pick the two of you up at your house."

"Okay, Uncle Dan. We'll hurry."

As the group left his office, Dan instructed his secretary, Ericka, to clear their calendars for the remainder of the day.

"This will be more like just an outing, ladies. Holly, if you find the spot, we won't disturb it. All I want you to do is point it out, if you can. I will map the location so that the detectives who will be assigned the case can arrange to have it checked out by forensic technicians," Reginald announced.

Slightly under two hours later they were entering the campgrounds at Sunny Creek Camp and Retreat Resort. Holly found the point she recognized as the site that was the beginning and ending point of the game. Following Holly's lead, they walked and walked—this direction, that direction, the other direction.

Everything looked the same to Holly. Not even the landscapes she had painted were helpful. It had been so many years since she had been there. There had even been a wild fire or two, which could have altered the terrain substantially. Besides, she had chosen to block everything from her memory for so long, it was difficult for her to recall many details.

Holly's hopes began to fade with each location investigated in vain. She realized it had been too long. As darkness began to fall, weariness and hunger began to rear their ugly heads, and the search was called off. There would be no CSI anytime soon.

All were silent on the trek back to the car until Holly broke it with, "I'm sorry to disappoint everyone. I really hoped I could find it."

"Don't worry about it, Holly," Dan assured her. "Let's just go and get a bite and relax."

"Uncle Dan, there's a pancake place nearby that we passed. Can we go there?"

"Sure. Is that all right, Holly?"

Still disappointed, Holly nodded her assent.

"You might as well come along with us, Reginald."

While the four waited for their orders to arrive, Reginald wanted to reassure Holly.

"Holly, "for your information, California law allows prosecution for this crime for up to six years after the crime was committed. The law removes the statute limitation in cases of aggravated rape that carry a lifetime sentence. It is a very brave thing you are doing in merely reporting the rape, regardless of what happens with your case. So many cases are never reported. Many times, the rapist is a serial rapist and will continue to violate other victims. Your testimony against him may help to convict him in a subsequent case that may not be successful without it.

"That brings me to my next question. Do you know if possibly there were any other victims in your church? Did anyone ever say anything to you, or did you hear any—gossip?"

"No, not actually."

"Not *actually*? Why do you say that?"

"I noticed there was a new girl that had started coming to our church. Her name was Olivia. She was really pretty, but kind of . . . awkward . . . very quiet and shy. She was only a year younger than me, but in some ways she seemed very naive, but in other ways, very . . . I don't know how to describe it . . . kind of mature?

"I noticed the youth pastor watching her the same way he watched me that made me feel so uncomfortable. When I saw how excited she was about going to camp that year, I felt I needed to talk to her—to warn her to be careful. I knew she liked him, as all of the kids did. It was like he wasn't an adult, but one of the kids. He was always doing fun things with them, giving them all hugs and praise, listening to their problems and their gripes against their parents, praying with them, even preaching to them about God. They all looked up to him and trusted him." She added regretfully, "I did, too, once.

"I really didn't get a chance to warn her. I never saw her again after that day. In fact, she never came back to church after that camping trip. I heard she went home early because she was sick, and she just never came back to church."

"Do you think you can find out where she is or get in touch with her?"

"I don't know. I can try. My church usually took the names and addresses of visitors, but I don't think her parents ever came. She always came with Elizabeth and *her* family."

"Does Elizabeth still go there?"

"Yes."

"Holly, it's very important for us to find another survivor. It sounds like Olivia may be the one."

"I will contact Elizabeth and try to find out if she knows how to get in touch. I'll see her the day after tomorrow at the 4th Friday church social for singles."

"Good, Holly. When you find her, it is *very* important that you don't discuss the details of your experience with her. As in your case, we need to hear her account of the events from her independent recall."

"I will remember that," Holly assured him.

"Oh, good! Here's our food—just in time!" exclaimed Meg.

CHAPTER 21

(12/10/2012) Morgan set out on his quest to find Liv's mother. He first contracted Frank Bynam, a private investigator who had done work for his father. He was extremely good at his job and was very successful years before the age of the Internet and Google.

Though older now, he was not averse to utilizing all available modern technology. Even though the information Morgan could provide was scant, it was sufficient for Frank. After only four days, he contacted Morgan.

"Good morning, Morgan. This is Frank."

"Hello, Frank! I wasn't expecting to hear from you so soon. I hope you have some good news for me."

"Yes, it is real good news! I followed up on the leads you gave me, and with the aid of the Internet plus some good, old-fashioned investigative instincts, I have gathered some very good information for you, probably all you will need! Not only have I been able to locate Mrs. Lydia Washington, but I also had a talk with a former neighbor who was very helpful. I can be available to meet with you any time today after 1:00 p.m. to provide you with my complete written report."

"Is 3:00 o'clock good?"

"You bet!"

Later in his office, Frank opened the file folder on his desk. He took out and handed Morgan the substantial written report. "Are you aware of any of Olivia's family history?" Frank asked.

"No, not her family's history." Morgan said as he felt the weight of the report. "I'm amazed at how much you were able to find out from the tidbit I was able to provide!"

"The Washington home was fraught with abuse and violence. The father was an alcoholic and had a real mean streak. The situation seemed to have escalated after the daughter left. Shortly thereafter, Lydia went to the neighbor indicating she was afraid for her life; but she was unable or unwilling to report him or go to a shelter.

"She gave her neighbor a rather large package that was addressed to her daughter. She asked her to take it for safekeeping should anything happen to her. She was not to give it to anyone but Olivia, unless she herself came to claim it. She didn't know what was in the tightly sealed package, and she never opened it. I had to at least try to get her to turn it over to me, but that was not going to happen.

"It was shortly after that when Mr. Washington attacked his wife. No one really knows what sparked the attack. The sons tried to protect their mother. He drew a gun and started shooting. The youngest son died at the scene. Both were shot. Lydia was very critical, not expected to survive. The other son suffered flesh wounds and recovered. He later shot and killed his father during his father's trial and is currently incarcerated.

"Lydia remained in a coma for a substantial period of time. Eventually, she was relocated to a facility in Kansas City, Kansas, where she has remained all these years. The summary page has all of the contact information.

"The only gaps have to do with her relocation and maintenance, how it came about, and who made the arrangements. Whoever was responsible obviously didn't want it known. If you want me to pursue that further, I will."

"Frank, you have done an amazing job, and I really appreciate it. If I find there is a further need, I will let you know. I want to make arrangements to see her immediately. I have your billing statement and will have a check delivered to you today, with a bonus!"

Morgan wasted no time in making the arrangements to leave at the crack of dawn the next morning. He made plane and hotel reservations, and was all packed before he went to bed.

He called Liv to let her know he had to leave.

"Good evening, Liv. Hope I'm not calling you too late."

"Hi, Morgan. No, I'm just getting ready for bed. I didn't expect to hear from you again until tomorrow!"

"I know, Sweetheart. I'm sorry, but I unexpectedly have to travel back east on urgent business. My plane leaves at 6:40 in the morning, so I won't be able to see you before I leave. I don't know how long I'll be gone—a week, maybe two or more. I don't know. I do know that I will miss not seeing you or being at the performances I will miss as your No. 1 fan! I may miss Christmas at the Center, too; but no matter what I have to do, I will be here to bring in the New Year with you!"

"Is anything wrong?"

"No, nothing's wrong. Tell me you will miss me as much as I will miss you while I am gone and that you will think of me every day."

His response eased her concern. "Of course I will miss you and I will think of you as well. But surely you don't plan to be traveling to a no-phone zone!"

"You know I will be calling you every day if you promise not to get tired of me. On second thought, I'd better just make it every few days. I've heard that absence makes the heart grow fonder. Hmmm . . . Maybe I won't call at all! That way, when I return, you'll be so much *more* fond of me, you just might say those three little words I've been waiting to hear!"

Liv was silent a moment. She was still trying to put everything into perspective. Some things she had come to terms with, but she still dreaded moving closer to a physical relationship. Even though her feelings for him continued to grow stronger, the thought of taking it to the next step still petrified her into inaction. Somehow she reasoned that as long as she didn't *tell* him she loved him, she wouldn't have to deal with the physical aspect of their relationship until she had gotten her head together.

"Is this pressure I feel coming from you, Mr. Calais?"

She tried to sound playful, but her true feelings were not lost on Morgan.

"Liv, I apologize . . . sincerely. I was kind of joking, but in all honesty, I have to admit that I meant it. I am truly sorry, and I will try *very* hard not to make you feel pressured in any way. Will you please forgive me?"

Liv was sorry she had made him feel pained. She *loved* him, and it wasn't *his* fault that she had her issues.

"Morgan, I'm sorry, too. Of course, I accept your apology. How can I *not* forgive my future husband?"

"Thank you, Liv. Consider your hand kissed! Remember, I promise to be back in time for us to bring in the New Year! I'll let you go now. I love you!"

Morgan's Visit with Lydia

Morgan arrived in Kansas, rented a car, and registered in the hotel. He was anxious to get to the facility to assess the situation with Liv's mother. After changing clothes and grabbing a bite to eat, he headed directly to the facility Frank had identified.

Upon entering, he approached the reception desk and inquired about Lydia Washington. He was asked to sign the visitor's log, and the receptionist checked the patient roster.

Glancing at his name on the log, she addressed him, "Mr. Calais, did you make an appointment or call in ahead to notify anyone of your planned visit?"

"No, I didn't. I was not aware it would be necessary. Is there a problem?"

"Well, no. Please have a seat." Morgan took a seat. The receptionist spoke briefly on the phone, glancing occasionally in Morgan's direction. A few minutes later, a gentleman came out of the door labeled "Administrator" and walked toward him.

"Mr. Calais, I am Dr. Leonard Brooks," he said. "Please come into my office." Morgan followed him and took a seat.

"I'm glad to see you. I understand you have come to visit Lydia Washington. May I ask what your relationship is to her? You are the first visitor she has had in all the years she has been here other than specialists and social workers."

"I will be her son-in-law in a few months."

"She has family? I didn't know. Mr. Calais, I'm sorry you didn't contact us before coming. Have you come a long distance?"

"I flew in from Los Angeles. Is there a problem?"

"Mrs. Washington is not here right now. She is being evaluated at another of our facilities out of state. She was just transported yesterday evening, and the evaluation will take 10 to 14 days, after which she will be returned here. Had I known of your visit, I could have made other arrangements; but there's nothing I can do at this point. When do you have to return to L. A.?"

"That is not an issue. I will return here as soon as I know she is back. In the meantime, Dr. Brooks, what can you tell me about the status of her health? I know you may be bound by privacy laws, but I would like some indication of her condition."

"Normally, I would not be able to tell you anything; but under the circumstances, I will make an exception."

"I understand that she suffered severe head trauma and was in a coma for some time."

"That is correct. When she came here, her physical problems had been resolved. However, she has not spoken or really interacted with anyone in a meaningful way the entire time she has been here. There appears to be normal brain activity, but we cannot accurately assess her mental state.

"All of our testing and evaluations indicate that there is no reason we can determine why she can't speak or that she has suffered permanent mental impairment."

"She is functional. She can obey commands and see to her own basic daily needs. She is physically active in walking around the grounds, sometimes jogging. She is in excellent *physical* condition. She has all the signs of life and comprehension, but she is totally non-communicative. There is just no real spark of life in her. We may never know her true status short of a miracle."

"I happen to believe in miracles. Here is my card. I will be back as soon as you notify me of her return."

"Certainly. I must tell you that her future here is uncertain. Her care is not without cost. Her residence has been fully funded; but we have been notified January's payment will be the last."

"Who has provided the funds?"

"I suppose it's the person who relocated her here directly from the hospital in California."

"Can you give me a name?"

"No, I don't have a name. We must make arrangements to have her transferred someplace else. That is the reason she is being evaluated at this time. Does her daughter have any plans to take her or provide funding for her to remain here?"

"I'll get back to you on that. How have the payments been made, and how were you notified about the termination?"

"She had already been here a couple of months when I first came. I have no idea what transpired before that. I just know that money has been wired directly into our bank every month. I can show you the correspondence we received indicating next month's payment will be the last."

"I'd like to see it and the envelope, if you have it."

"The file is still here on my desk." Dr. Brooks opened the file, removed an 8½x11-inch sheet with a No. 10 envelope stapled to it, and handed it to Morgan. "I'm afraid this won't be of much help. There is no letterhead, and the signature consists only of illegible initials."

Morgan took the sheet dated 12/10/2012, and read, "Please be advised that the final wire transfer for credit to the account of patient Lydia Washington will be December 31, 2012." The only return address on the envelope was a post office box in the 90291 zip code. At least Morgan had *something* to go on! "If you will, please give me a copy of the letter and the envelope. What would be the best time for me to see Mrs. Washington when she returns?"

"Visiting hours are from 10:00 a.m. to 7:00 p.m. I suggest you call before you come to make sure she is settled. Here is my card. I will have the receptionist make these copies for you."

Morgan drove back to his hotel. He telephoned Frank and gave him the new information, expecting that Frank would be able to find out who had been funding Lydia Washington's care, and perhaps who was responsible for relocating her. He faxed copies of the note and envelope to Frank.

Morgan now had almost two weeks of unanticipated time on his hands. He didn't want to return to L. A. only to have to leave again. He felt that would be harder on Liv as well as him. The delay would fit within the promised time frame. He made a call to a source in New York and was on his way there the next morning to fulfill a desire he had entertained for a while. This was a perfect opportunity. The trip was successful, and he was able to return to Kansas by the night before Lydia was due back. A telephone call from the facility indicated that Lydia would not return until Saturday evening, 12/29.

(Sunday, 12/30/2012) The next morning Morgan returned to see Lydia. Dr. Brooks came out of his office just as Morgan was signing the visitor's log. "Good morning, Mr. Calais!"

"Good morning, Doctor. I would like to see Mrs. Washington now."

"Of course! Please follow me."

Morgan followed the doctor the short distance to Lydia's room. After he had knocked and received no response, the doctor entered with Morgan following. Lydia was sitting in one of two chairs in the room that was facing the door. She was sitting sideways in the chair, and her head was turned completely toward the window as she blankly stared out.

"Lydia," Doctor Brooks called to her with no response. He walked to her and touched her on the shoulder, repeating her name. All Morgan could see was mostly the back of her head. He noted her long, black hair, which was hanging loosely down her back. At the touch of his hand, Lydia turned her head to reveal lifeless eyes—no spark of recognition, no obvious signs of awareness. The Doctor continued, "Lydia, you have a visitor. His name is Morgan Calais."

Morgan was now directly in her line of vision, but there was no change in her reaction. He was awed as he beheld the replica of the love of his life in an older version! There was no doubt she was Liv's mother!

"You see, Mr. Calais, this has been the extent of her response since she has been here. She goes through the motions; she robotically sees to her own needs and avails herself of the physical activity provided."

"If you don't mind, doctor, I would like to spend some time alone with her. I think if she sees something meaningful to her, she might respond."

"Well, it's definitely worth a try. God knows we've done everything we know how to do. I'll be in my office."

With the doctor out of the room, Morgan pulled the other chair closer facing Lydia and sat down. He removed the personalized headshot of Liv from the envelope and held it in front of Lydia. After a moment, he began to see signs of recognition as Lydia's eyes seemed to come alive. He became more hopeful when a trace of a tear appeared. When she reached and took the picture from his hand, he knew that all would be okay. When she spoke, he was elated!

"My baby! My beautiful Olivia!" she said as she closed her eyes and held the picture to her breast, her tears overflowing.

Morgan pulled the cord to summon staff and waited quietly as he watched his future mother-in-law. "Where is she?" Lydia asked, looking at Morgan for the first time with the spark of life in her eyes. "Does she still hate me?" she asked, her brow furrowing with a hint of sadness.

"Mrs. Washington, Olivia loves you *very* much."

"She's alive and well? Is she here? Oh, please! Can I see her? I want to see her!"

Dr. Brooks had entered the room in time to hear Lydia speaking. Astonished, he couldn't believe his ears!

"Lydia, you are *speaking*! You are speaking after all these *years*! Mr. Calais, what did you do? How did this happen? It's unbelievable!"

He looked from one to the other, not knowing who to say what to first. He was at a total loss. Finally, he addressed Morgan. "How did this *happen*? What did you *do*? What did you *say* to her?"

"I told you," Morgan replied, "I believe in miracles. I gave her a *reason* to speak. I showed her a picture of her daughter."

Lydia was looking at the picture, still in awe of the face looking back at her that was so much like her own. It was like looking in the mirror and seeing herself at a younger age.

"Lydia, do you know who that is?" the doctor asked. "Do you know who I am?"

"This is my beautiful daughter, Olivia," she said with the smile of a proud mother.

"Do you know who I am?" he repeated.

"Yes, I know who you are," she said rather irked at being asked a ridiculous question. "I know who *I* am. I know *where* I am. I also know that now I can *live* again!"

"Why have you never spoken in all these years?"

"I was dead and had no reason to talk, *or* live. Now, I do. I know my Olivia is alive, and I will see her again. I will, won't I?" she asked Morgan.

"You definitely will, Mrs. Washington," he replied. "We will need to work some things out, but you will see her soon. Can you be patient a little while longer?"

"Now that I know she's alive and well and that she doesn't hate me, I can wait . . . a *little* while longer."

"Mrs. Washington, I'm going now to see what kind of arrangements we can make for you. I have to go back to California, but I *will* come back, I promise. Okay?"

"Yes, Mr. . . . What was your name again?"

"You can call me 'Morgan.' "

"Thank you, Morgan, and please call me 'Lydia.' "

"Goodbye for now, Lydia."

Morgan returned with the doctor to his office. "I still can't believe what I have witnessed. I don't know what you or your fiancée plan to do. However, in the approximately five weeks she has remaining with us, we are going to be working aggressively with her now that she seems to be functioning normally. The assessments that have just been made are totally invalid, I *know*, even though we've received no reports yet. We will be evaluating and working with her to bring her up to speed on what has been happening in the world during her 'absence.' I trust that we will be hearing further from you."

"Yes, you will, Doctor. It may be that she will ask about other members of her family. I think that in her preparation it would be good if you could figure out how to bring her up to date on the status of the rest of her family—her husband and her two sons."

"She has more family?"

"Yes. I have your card. I will have information faxed to you so that you will know just what you need to do and figure out the best way to prepare her. I believe you have my card I left. Here is another with my contact information should you need to get in touch with me for any reason. Thank you."

Morgan returned to his hotel to find he had received a message from Frank to call him ASAP. He wondered if he had been able to get the information from the P.O. Box address.

"Morgan! Thanks for getting back so quickly. Have you seen Lydia Washington?"

"Yes, I just left her. What have you found out?"

"I have a line on the address but have not followed up yet. I have been working another angle. I did some old fashioned detective work on my own because for some reason I felt compelled to delve further to satisfy my own curiosity. I won't bore you with the mundane details, but here is the bottom line. I have found Lydia's adoptive parents. They are Arlan and Dionne Schwartz, and they live right there in Kansas!"

"Oh, really? I never even considered digging further. I wonder why they have not been in touch with their daughter. Liv has never mentioned having grandparents!"

"I would be surprised if she even knew about them. But that's not all. I kept following hunches and working backwards from bits and pieces and found that there were two sets of biological grandparents looking to find a granddaughter born to an interracial couple that was killed in a vehicle accident in Kansas City Kansas in 1970 who was subsequently adopted. Everything points to Lydia Washington.

"I took the liberty of contacting both sets of the biological grandparents and talked with them at length. They came to regret disowning their children because of the choices they made in marrying outside of their races and have spent the last sixteen years trying to locate their granddaughter. I told them that we would contact their granddaughter, and it would be her choice to contact them or not. I have the full report for you including all of the contact information.

There is one other item I'm following up on, but I won't go into that just yet."

"Frank, this is amazing! You are the best! Be sure to account for everything in your bill. I will take care of you when I pick up your reports."

"Morgan, you didn't commission all this. This is on me. You were too generous with the bonus tacked onto my last bill! Consider this an early wedding present! I take it I will be invited!"

"No doubt! I'm looking forward to your update."

Morgan called Liv and found himself very hard pressed to keep from telling her the good news. The sound of her voice was Heaven to his ears, especially when she told him how much she missed him! He assured her that he would definitely be back early morning New Year's Eve and would call her to let her know when his plane would land.

CHAPTER 22

Fellowship Hall

(12/7/2012) "Hi, Holly!" Elizabeth said, giving Holly a quick hug. "I'm glad you called me. I wasn't planning to come tonight. You said it was urgent."

"Hello, Elizabeth. Thanks. It *is* urgent. Where can we talk in private?"

"You know I teach the two-year-olds' Sunday school class. I have the key to the playroom. If you don't mind sitting in those teeny tiny chairs, I don't."

"Okay."

Finding as comfortable a position as possible in one of the small chair, Elizabeth asked, "What can I help you with, Holly?"

"Elizabeth, I need to find Olivia. It's *very* important."

"Holly, I've been trying to find her since she went home early from camp that year. They said she was sick, but she had been fine earlier. I don't know what could possibly have happened."

"I think I know what happened."

"What?"

"Liz, I have to tell you something only a very few other people and God know. Not even my parents know. But I have to tell you, and I hope you can help me find Olivia."

"I'll do whatever I can, Holly. This seems really serious. Let's pray first."

They held hands and bowed their heads in silent prayer.

Holly began, "I know people wondered about me when I stopped participating in the youth activities several years ago. I was not the same after the last camp I went to when I was 15. That was the year before Olivia went. I think what happened to me also happened to her."

"What happened, Holly?" Elizabeth asked with growing concern.

Holly was silent for a moment and then changed the subject. "Do you remember the hide-and-seek game?"

"Yes, of course. That was always the most fun part! Who can forget that?"

"Elizabeth, *I* wish I *could* forget."

"Why, Holly?"

Holly looked sadly at Elizabeth without answering. "Who was Olivia's partner that year?" she asked.

"Her partner? Oh, that was Pastor Jason. You know he's back now. He's the one that instituted the hide-and-seek game way back when. Now that he has returned from his missionary work, I hope he starts that activity up again. There are so many kids who have missed out on all of that fun! The kids are beginning to talk about it. Of course, it won't be the same for me since I am now one of the 'seniors' who will be paired with one of the young kids."

Realizing that Holly was not sharing her enthusiasm, Elizabeth became silent and waited for a response.

"He was my partner, too, the year before," Holly said in hardly more than a whisper.

Holly's sad gaze was fixed on Elizabeth, and she watched as Elizabeth showed signs of comprehending something untoward.

"Holly, what happened to you that you think happened to Olivia? Tell me, please!" Elizabeth pressed.

Holly was thinking about the high esteem in which everyone held Pastor Jason. She realized the risk she was taking in making this allegation and not being believed. But she knew what had happened to her, and she knew what she had to do.

"Elizabeth, he took me to a cave that he had obviously prepared in advance, and he raped me! I was a virgin, and he raped me! He *raped* me," Holly repeated emphatically with great control in a voice mixed with sadness and anger.

She didn't waiver or shift her eyes that were locked on Elizabeth's eyes. She maintained her gaze and watched for the reaction. Elizabeth was astonished.

Elizabeth had known Holly for years and knew that she would never create such a fabrication. She could also come up with no other possible reason for her best friend's strange behavior and her continued failure to communicate with her in any way.

Elizabeth let out a deep sigh and closed her eyes tightly, releasing the tears that refused to be contained. Wrapping her physical arms around Holly and her mental arms around Olivia, she said, "Holly, I am so, so sorry! How awful this must have been—must *be*—for you, for *both* of you!"

They remained locked in their tearful, healing embrace for a while. Holly was relieved to have confessed her rape in a precarious situation and have been validated with belief. Elizabeth's heart was broken with the knowledge of the ordeals of her friends. But at last she possibly, *probably,* had an answer for the abrupt departure of her best friend and renewed hope that they could rekindle that friendship.

"Holly, thank you for sharing your secret with me. I'll do whatever I can to help you find Olivia for *both* of us. I just wish she had confided in me like *you* just did. She should have *known* that I would understand as her best friend and *be* there for her!"

"Elizabeth, you can't know or understand what her state of mind was. It took me more than three years to tell anyone but my rape counselor. I'm sure Olivia did what she felt she had to do to protect herself and try to get to a safe place."

Elizabeth began to realize just how devastating the ordeal must have been for Olivia. That realization fueled her determination to find Olivia and help them bring the youth pastor to justice.

"We've got to do something fast. Have you been to the police?" Elizabeth asked.

"No. They really can't do anything about it right now.

"My counselor at the rape counseling center, Megan Harper, took me to see her uncle in the DA's office. I've talked with them, and we even went to the campgrounds Wednesday to find the cave. We searched for hours, but I couldn't find it. I was told we don't have enough evidence with just my word. Without the cave, or another victim to come forward, they can't really do anything. We can't let him go through with starting up those games again!" Holly proclaimed.

"Maybe if we go to the Senior Pastor, *he* can do something," suggested Elizabeth.

"No, we can't go to anyone else until we have more proof. We have a few months before any camp activity. We'll have to really pray and look for Olivia. In the meantime, I'm going to make my presence felt—let *him* know I'm watching *him*—and that I'm no longer afraid of him. I am *not*! I want to take *his* power. I want *him* to have the uncomfortable feeling of waiting for the other shoe to drop!"

"Now, knowing what you have told me, I can see how Olivia would be traumatized. Over the years I thought about her often and I keep her in my prayers. I refused to believe that she would not call or write to me without a really good reason."

"I understand exactly how she *might* have felt. Sometimes survivors block horrible things from their minds, or try to pretend they never happened. They blame themselves, God, anyone. Many undergo extreme personality and/or behavioral changes."

"Holly, I feel so badly for both of you, and I'm going to do everything I possibly can to help you get justice. I will start tomorrow by going by her parent's old house. Maybe someone in the neighborhood can tell me something that might help in our search.

"The last contact I had with anyone there was after Easter Sunday following the camp. When Olivia didn't come to school, I wanted to find out how she was, if she were okay. I wanted to get her awards and belongings to her."

"What happened?"

"When I called, her father said she wasn't talking to anyone and she wasn't coming back to our church and not to call again. I asked him to please let her know it was me calling. He said he didn't care if I were Jesus Christ Himself. He cursed, told me not to call again, and hung up."

"What did you do?"

"What *could* I do? I was very hurt."

The ladies ended their meeting with a quick prayer and a hug.

"Holly, I will keep in touch with you on my progress."

"I'll do the same. Good night."

Elizabeth left with a heavy, but hopeful heart. She had missed her friend very much. Her visit to Olivia's old house was fruitless.

(12/11/2012) Elizabeth received a call Tuesday evening from Kyra Merriweather, an old schoolmate.

"Hello?"

"Hi, Elizabeth. This is Kyra Merriweather!"

"Hi, Kyra! It's been quite a while. Good to hear your voice! How are you?"

"I'm just fine, fat, and sassy!" she joked. "Listen, Elizabeth, do you remember Yvonne?"

"Yvonne Jeffries? Sure, I remember her. You were best friends, *inseparable!*"

"Yes, we still are. We talk almost every week. The reason I called is that Yvonne asked about you. She remembers you and that you had a friend she vaguely remembered named Olivia. She saw an ad about a nightclub called Liv's Supper Club and Lounge. There was a picture of the singer who performs there. It is probably her club because she goes by the name 'Ms. Liv.' "

"She couldn't say for sure, but she thinks it's your friend Olivia. She said this Liv is very different from the Olivia we knew in school. That's why she can't say for sure. You know how quiet and shy Olivia was. Please excuse me for talking about your friend, but you also know how she dressed—real homely like, and wearing little girl clothes.

"Yvonne jotted down the information for me to give to you. I remember you were very upset when Olivia checked out of school so suddenly without a word or goodbye to anyone."

Elizabeth gasped in disbelief. "Are you serious? Are you really *serious?*"

"As serious as the plague," responded Kyra. "Got a pencil and paper?"

"Hold on a second . . . Okay."

Elizabeth wrote carefully as Kyra gave her the name, address, and telephone number, reciting the information back in verification.

"That's it," said Kyra. "Are you going to call and see?"

"I think I'm in shock! I am hoping with all my heart that it *is* her. Thank you, Kyra!"

"Anytime, Elizabeth. I've got to run now. Good luck."

"Thanks. Bye."

Elizabeth forced herself to breathe, taking several deep breaths to calm herself. She closed her eyes in silent prayer."

The next morning, with a plan of action in mind, Elizabeth dialed her brother's number.

"Hello?" answered Barbara, her sister-in-law.

"Hi, Sis. How are you? Haven't dropped your load yet I see!"

"I'm blessed. Yes, I'm still hanging in here, but soon, I hope!"

"Well, just take it easy. Is that brother of mine around?"

"Sure. Let me call him."

In a moment Roger was on the phone. "Hey, Lizard! How's my favorite little sis?" he said, genuinely happy to hear her voice.

"I'm your *only* sis, you know; but you can prove how much I'm your favorite. I need a *big* favor."

"A *big* favor?"

"Yes, a *very* big favor!"

"Shoot!"

"I need you to be my escort Friday or Saturday night to this supper club in Brentwood."

"Since when do you go to supper clubs, and why do you need to go to *this* particular club? Have you become a 'woman of the world' all of a sudden?" he joked.

"I'm serious, Roger. I *have* to go there. I can't tell you everything now, but I think I may have found my friend, Olivia! You remember her, don't you?"

"Quiet little Olivia with the big voice?"

"Yes! I've got to find out if this person who sings there and goes by the name of 'Liv' is her. I can't go unescorted."

"Yes, of course I'll go with you, Liz. I know what good friends you were and how much you missed her when she dropped out of sight. I would be interested myself to know what happened to her."

"Thanks, Roge; you're the best brother I have."

"Who are *you* kidding? I'm *your* only brother. What time shall I pick you up?"

"Let me make a few calls and get back to you tomorrow. Actually, I won't be alone. Holly Albright is coming with me."

"Holly from church? Are you corrupting her, too?" he teased.

"Roger! She has an interest in this, too. I'll call you tomorrow. Love you. Bye!"

"You, too. Bye."

CHAPTER 23

Elizabeth's fingers were shaking as she punched the number to the club on her keypad.

"Liv's Supper Club and Lounge. For reservations, please press one. For any other purpose, please press two."

Elizabeth breathed a sigh of relief and pressed one.

(12/13/2012) With confirmed reservation for three at Liv's Supper Club and Lounge for Saturday, December 15, Elizabeth excitedly telephoned Holly early Thursday morning.

"Oh, Holly! You'll never guess!"

"What is it, Elizabeth. Don't keep me in suspense!"

"I found Olivia! I couldn't believe it!"

"Where! Where is she?"

"Now, calm down! We can go and see her Saturday evening. Can you be ready at 6:30? I have made a reservation at a place called 'Liv's.' It's a supper club about fifty-five minutes from here according to Google maps. The reservation is for the 8:00 p.m. dinner show. I've got a few things to do now, but I'll tell you all about it. Be dressed to impress, and I'll pick you up at 6:30 sharp."

"I'll be ready with wings on! Oh, Elizabeth, I'm so excited! I never expected anything to happen so soon!"

"You know that God is mindful of His children!

"Yes! Praise God!"

(12/15/2012) At 6:25 Saturday evening, Elizabeth was pulling up to the Albright residence. She felt a little overdressed in the conservative, cream-colored chiffon after-five dress she had purchased for this special occasion. She didn't have to turn off the ignition. Holly was coming out the front door and heading down the walkway flushed with excitement.

Elizabeth no longer felt overdressed as she watched Holly coming toward her in a stunning black dress with a sequined bodice. It was classy and tastefully sexy, though showing little skin. The barely-above-the-knee hemline showed off her long, shapely legs.

Holly, too, had gone shopping that week. Never before would she have chosen such an attractive, figure-flattering dress. Her wardrobe contained only clothing carefully selected to conceal her curvaceous body—a defense mechanism she had adopted to hopefully deter unwanted and potentially harmful advances.

Although in her head she knew all of the facts that had been pounded into her which she easily parroted to those she counseled, deep in her psyche she harbored feelings and myths deeply rooted in many rape survivors. [If only I had not: a) been in the wrong place; b) been dressed as I was; c) put out the wrong signals; d) been so attractive; e) been careless, etc., etc.!]

Her conscious selection of that dress was a sign that she was taking back her power and putting the blame—and the shame—on the rapist, where it belonged. She knew and fully now accepted the fact that rape is not a crime of sex, but a crime of opportunity and violence meant only to exert power and control, to intimidate, to degrade, and to humiliate the victim! She knew the only thing rape and sex have in common is the anatomy involved.

Holly was proving to herself that she was in control. She was not fearful. She would no longer be intimidated!

"Holly, you look fantastic!" Elizabeth gushed as Holly slipped into the car.

"I *feel* fantastic! You're not too shabby yourself, girl! Where have you been hiding *that* dress?" Holly asked, fingering the material.

"Oh, it's just an old rag I happened to find—on the rack at Nordstrom's!"

"You, too?" Holly asked with a raised eyebrow. They both laughed as Elizabeth pulled away from the curb.

"Oh, Elizabeth, tell me what's going on. Where are we going? How do you know Olivia will be there?"

"Well, first of all, I'm driving home. Roger should be there by the time we get there."

"Roger?"

"Yes. He's going to be our escort for the night. We assuredly can't go to a place like this unescorted!" Elizabeth explained.

Once at Elizabeth's apartment, the ladies had just enough time to check their hair and makeup before Roger arrived.

"Lizard!" he exclaimed as he saw his sister all decked out and glamorous, makeup and all. "Is that *you*? No way!" he kidded.

"Oh, Roge, stop it!" Elizabeth scolded playfully.

"And who is your gorgeous friend?" he said, noticing, but not recognizing Holly.

"Come on, now, Roger. You know that's Holly!"

"Really? Wow! Wow to both of you! I'm gonna *really* have to work hard tonight to keep the wolves away! I see why you need an escort. We'd better go before I have to change my mind!"

In short time they were seated in Roger's car on the way to LIV's Supper Club and Lounge!" Once there, the trio exited the car, leaving it in the capable hands of the valet.

"Oh, my God! It's her! It *is* Olivia!" exclaimed Elizabeth as she stared at the poster on display at the main entrance. Holly joined in the jubilation. "My God, Elizabeth! I could just cry! Oh, Lord, thank You! Thank You!" Roger, who had first gone to check in with the host, looked at the picture and expressed, *"That* is shy little Olivia? No way! Look at *her*! Wow!"

"Randall party of three," the Host interrupted. "Your table is ready. Please follow me."

The party was seated at a choice table in the second row directly in front of the stage. The ladies were eagerly taking in the scene while Roger was really enjoying the band. He was a little more "worldly" as a jazz aficionado and immediately recognized the smooth instrumental rendition of "Let the Music Flow," a classic jazz standard.

"Now, *that's* music!" Roger beamed appreciatively, savoring every note. "I could listen to them all night!"

"Yes, that is nice," agreed Elizabeth, "but I want to hear Liv– Olivia – Liv . . . Oh, whatever! I am so *happy*!"

"Good evening, and welcome to LIV's! This is your first time?" the server almost stated as he handed them each menus.

"Yes, it is," replied Elizabeth. "We're really excited to be here!"

"Well, then, you're in for a real treat. My name is Aaron. I will be serving you this evening. I will give you a few minutes to review your menus. In the meantime, can I get you something to drink?"

Answering for everyone, Roger requested, "Yes. Please bring us three ocean cocktails on the rocks."

"With lemon on the side, please," Elizabeth added.

"Very well, three ocean cocktails on the rocks with lemon on the side coming up," Aaron said with a genuine smile.

"Roger, Elizabeth," Holly spoke up rather concerned, "I just want *water*. I don't drink. I didn't know that you did, Elizabeth, not that I'm trying to be judgmental."

"Relax, Holly," Roger said as they both laughed. "It's okay!"

Holly had to laugh herself and blushed with embarrassment when Aaron returned with three glasses of ice water and a small bowl of lemon wedges.

"If you are ready, I can take your orders now, unless you need more time."

"I'm ready," piped Roger. "How about you ladies?"

"You're always ready to eat, Roge. Everything looks good. If it's all right with you, Holly, let's allow Roger to order for us and surprise us. He usually has good taste," suggested Elizabeth. "Besides, he's paying for it!"

"That's fine with me," Holly agreed as the lights dimmed and the stage lit up. "It looks like the show is about to start," she said excitedly.

The ladies sat with their hearts pounding as they watched their long-lost friend walk on stage looking beautiful, confident, and so sophisticated. They melted into their plush seats as the smooth, melodic tones wafted from her lips and filled the large room.

"Oh my God!" marveled Elizabeth with pure adulation. "She's even better than before!"

"Yes, she is awesome!" agreed Holly. "What a precious gift."

"Well, she's certainly not the shy little Olivia *we* knew! Wow! I would never have believed it if I hadn't heard her voice! Excellent!" said Roger, evidently pleased to see her as well. Elizabeth was so happy to see Olivia alive and well, it was all she could do to keep from going immediately up to the stage and embracing her in a gigantic hug.

The server brought their dinner, but neither Elizabeth nor Holly was interested in food. They were too entranced by Olivia's performance and the joy of having found her.

"Is everything okay, ladies, sir?" Aaron asked as he topped off their cocktails.

"Perfect!" Roger responded.

"Yes, just perfect!" the ladies echoed.

The anticipation grew as the performance went on. Both ladies had issues weighing heavily on their minds about Olivia's reception of them. For Holly, it was concern that Olivia may not want to be reminded of her experience and would not want to get involved. Perhaps she had managed to put it out of her mind. She may not want to be pressured into dredging up the past. Additionally, what if her suspicion, her gut feeling about Olivia was wrong?

Elizabeth's troublesome issues were not only that they might be wrong about Olivia's reason for dropping out of sight, but also that she may not have *wanted* to be found. Maybe there was another reason Olivia didn't want to be associated with her anymore. After all, she appeared to be in good health, and Elizabeth could see no physical reason why Olivia could not have picked up a telephone and called *her*. Olivia undoubtedly knew where to find *her*.

While they were both allowing these thoughts to percolate in their minds, they chanced a glance at each other; and with that brief eye contact, they each seemed to sense the anxiety of the other. The same response was triggered in each: Quash those thoughts and have faith that everything will be as hoped. With the exchange of reassuring smiles, each returned her full attention to Olivia's performance.

They had not noticed that Roger had excused himself, and they did not question him when he returned in time to see the closing for that set. They rose to their feet to join the other fans in a standing ovation. When they were seated again, Roger asked, "Are you ladies ready for dessert, or are you worried about expanding your waistlines?"

"We've barely even touched our food as it is! We're so happy," Holly said.

"None for me," Elizabeth added. "We've got to figure out what we're going to do next. Do we just walk up to her when she finishes the last set? The server said that she would be back after a brief pause to finish out the night with a few more songs."

"Well, ladies," Roger interjected, "I think maybe you should just wait and see how it all pans out. It's not too late for you to eat your dinner. After all, you don't want to waste the good money *I'm* spending on you two.

"He's right, Elizabeth. If you're like me, you probably didn't eat anything today. Perhaps while we're eating, we'll think of something."

"Okay, Holly, let's dig in. The food is good, don't you agree?"

The ladies had begun to eat when the server returned to the table. He leaned over and spoke softly to Roger, who immediately got up and followed him. The girls found they were hungry after all and took no thought of Roger's departure.

The Reunion

There are no words to describe the scene that ensued shortly. Holly and Elizabeth were oblivious of Roger's return until they heard his voice saying, "Ladies, may I present to you Ms. Liv—also known as Olivia Louise Washington!"

They both looked up in unison to see their friend standing in front of them beside Roger! They were frozen in place, their mouths open, both speechless. There was Olivia standing there in the flesh with love and tears in her eyes!

"Olivia!" Elizabeth cried as she rose from her chair. In an instant they were locked in a tearful embrace. It was hard to tell who was happiest at the reunion. Holly rose to her feet, crying softly as she watched the two long-lost friends holding each other and weeping what she knew were tears of joy.

Although he would never have admitted it to anyone, and would vehemently deny it if accused, Roger himself was also crying—in a manly sort of way.

After a few moments, Liv acknowledged, "Holly? Is that you?"

"Yes, Olivia, it's me."

Liv removed one arm from around Elizabeth and reached out to Holly to draw her into the circle. Meanwhile, Roger was busy trying to conceal the tears in his eyes. He and Elizabeth had a great sibling relationship, and he was happy to have had a hand in making this happen for his little sister. He had staged this little reunion with the server.

Liv had returned to her dressing room following her set to find Aaron there with the message that a young man had requested a brief audience with her about something very important. She was leery about such things and asked Aaron to bring him personally and remain while she determined what he wanted.

"Hello, Olivia. I know you probably don't remember me," Roger began.

No, she didn't recognize him; but because he called her "Olivia," she tried hard to since it had to be from a long time ago.

"My name is Roger Randall. I'm Elizabeth Randall's brother."

"Elizabeth's brother? Oh, my God!" Liv exclaimed.

She had periodically thought about Elizabeth over the years and had thought of her more often since Theo's death. She had contemplated getting in touch with her since her talk with Walter, but had not taken action.

"Elizabeth and a friend are here," he continued. "My sister has been looking for you. She has been missing you all these years. She wasn't sure until tonight that she had found you. I hope you don't mind and that you will come out and speak to her."

Liv realized just how selfish she had been in cutting off ties with her best friend because of what one evil person had done to her. She felt joy at the thought of seeing her and possibly rekindling the friendship that they once had. Since Theo was gone, she only had Walter and Howard and she was grateful for them, but neither could take the place of a close girlfriend.

"Oh, my God! Yes! Yes! Where is she? Please take me to her!"

Now here they were, not only Elizabeth, but Holly as well. She hadn't thought of Holly, but now she did remember the almost conversation they had the day before she left for that fateful camping experience.

"Elizabeth! Holly! It is so great to see you! I can't stop crying, I'm so happy you've come! Can you wait until I finish here? It won't take long!"

"Olivia, we have been waiting all these years, surely a half hour, or two hours, whatever, can't matter that much! We have just loved hearing you sing again. You are better than ever! Oh, gosh! I'm going to start crying all over again," Elizabeth said as she tried to stop the tears.

"Yes, Olivia. You go ahead. We'll be right here! Won't we, guys," Holly assured her.

A few minutes later, Liv took the stage again for her closing set. Her regular fans were even more impressed with the extra special quality of her routine closing. They couldn't know that it was the happiness and joy of seeing her long-lost best friend that fueled the love and emotions that was embodied in her closing songs. The standing ovation was twice as long as the previous one and the bills that were appreciatively given overflowed the already substantially full tip jar!

Roger patiently, and the ladies not so patiently, waited for Liv to wade through the throng of adoring fans and make her way back to their table.

"Elizabeth, Holly, and you, too, Roger, "I can't begin to tell you what it means to see you again! I can't let you go right now!"

Glancing at his watch, Roger explained, "Olivia, I know the girls would love to stay longer; but I escorted them here, and my wife is expecting me home soon. Our third child is due in a few days, which means it could be any time now."

"Oh, congratulations, Roger. Of course you have to go."

Liv's disappointment disappeared in a flash as an idea came to her.

"I have a great idea! Roger, *I* can take them home! In fact," she said, still planning, "why don't you guys come and spend the *night* with me? We have so much catching up to do!"

"We would really love to, but we don't want you to go out of your way. Besides, we aren't really prepared to spend the night away from home," Elizabeth said, reluctantly.

"No need to worry about any of that. I can take care of whatever you need. Really! *Please* say you will! *Please!*" Liv entreated them. "You can even spend the whole day tomorrow, if you want."

Holly and Elizabeth looked at each other for confirmation of their no-brainer decision.

"Olivia, we would *love* to spend time with you!" Elizabeth exclaimed.

"Oh, God, Yes!" echoed Holly.

So the decision was made. Elizabeth thanked her brother heartily for all his help and gave him a kiss as he left them there in the care of Liv.

"I usually change before I leave, but I don't want to waste a single minute. Let's go!" Liv took their hands and led them out the door.

242

CHAPTER 24

The ladies stood outside the club waiting for the valet to bring Liv's car. Though they waited silently, each was thinking about what she wanted to happen once they were settled. Liv was overjoyed, thinking that this would be a time for her to rekindle the friendship she and Elizabeth had enjoyed, and even adding Holly to the mix. Two girlfriends might be twice as good as one! The only thing about which she was concerned was explaining her sudden departure. She didn't really want to go down that road.

Although Holly was grateful Olivia had received them so well, she still felt insecure about broaching the subject of the youth pastor and "The Cave." She decided to let Elizabeth make the first move.

Elizabeth was more concerned about why Olivia never contacted her and just effectively cut all ties. She had worried so much! She had to admit to herself that although she found Olivia well and obviously doing well, it would have been easier to understand and accept if her failure to communicate had been the result of some incapacity. Her joy at having found her at all, in any condition, overrode any negative thoughts she had.

Elizabeth sat in the front and started the dialogue. "Olivia, your car is just beautiful! I am so happy to find that you are so successful and doing so well pursuing your passion for music! I still can't get over how great you were tonight! I hope we will be able to hear you singing at your church tomorrow!"

Liv was caught off guard and wasn't sure how to respond. She didn't want to offend her old friend, but she wasn't ready to go there yet. She responded, "If you don't mind, Elizabeth, I would much rather spend the time with you and Holly, perhaps like a big-girl pajama party! I'm sure God won't mind. After all, it's been a million years since we've seen each other."

"Of course, you're right, Olivia."

Holly added, half joking, "Yes. Besides, I don't think these clothes we're wearing would be the most appropriate apparel for church!"

"Then it's settled. I can't wait to get started. It will be another ten minutes 'til we get to my place; but we don't have to wait. Elizabeth, tell me about that handsome brother of yours. He's got kids! Do I know his wife? Come on, drop the dime!" Liv urged.

Glad to have Olivia start the dialogue on a safe subject, Elizabeth was happy to bring her friend up to date on Roger. By the time she finished, they were pulling into Liv's parking structure. Moments later, Liv opened the door, disarmed the security sensors, and invited them in with, "Welcome to my home, Friends!"

As they entered the foyer, Holly gasped, "Oh, how *beautiful!*"

Echoing her sentiment, Elizabeth exclaimed, "Ditto!" as they scanned the area. "Can we please have a tour?"

The ladies marveled at the expertly decorated surroundings as Liv took them on the grand tour of her 3,800-square-foot home through the great room, the den (aka the music room), the dining and kitchen areas, the guest bathroom, the laundry room, the exercise room, her office space, the three large guest rooms and baths, the indoor pool, and finally the gigantic master bedroom, bath, and dressing rooms with all of the expected amenities.

As the ladies viewed Liv's home, they were aware of one significant lack, but neither dared to remark about it. Here it was, December 15, just ten days before Christmas, and there was no sign of the holiday, not even a greeting card!

They returned to the area of the guest bedrooms, each of which contained a king-sized bed and had a dressing room and full bath with an enclosed shower and a separate bathtub complete with a Jacuzzi. Everything they could possibly need was there at their disposal.

"You ladies can take your pick. In the meantime, I'll get you whatever I think you may need—toiletries, robes, PJs, even ear plugs," she added playfully. Anything you want and don't see, just ask. If I have it, so do you."

"I'll tell you what *I* want," said Holly. "I want to move in!"

"Not without *me*!" Elizabeth hastened to announce.

"Hey, girlfriends, you are welcome anytime—*anytime*," Liv was happy to offer.

Liv quickly removed her makeup, changed into PJs and a robe, and returned with supplies for her guests. "Now that you have chosen your rooms, I must tell you: at least for tonight, we will all party together in *my* room," Liv said. "So get out of those sexy clothes and get into some comfies! Meanwhile, I'll make sure we have everything we need if we get thirsty or the munchies. Just come to my room when you're done."

Before long the three ladies were relaxing before the fireplace in Liv's room on the most luxurious, thick, comfortable fuzzy, white throw rug either of her guests had ever seen. They spent a few moments enjoying the softness. Liv, to the relief of her guests, opened the dialogue in a casual tone.

"I'm sure you must have wondered all these years what happened to me and why I never made contact with anyone, especially you, Elizabeth.

"I have often thought of you," she continued, "and I have never been able to forget the worried look I saw on your face as all the kids were being ushered away that day. Elizabeth, I'm not the same person that you knew. I'm nothing like that almost 16-year-old girl!

I don't know that anyone can ever understand. It was just something I had to do."

Elizabeth and especially Holly felt a stab of pain at Liv's words. Holly was motivated to put her own fear aside and delve into the main reason for the compelling drive to find her.

"Olivia, we *will* understand. We *do* understand. Do you remember the day you signed up to be tent partners with Elizabeth?"

"Yes, I do, Holly. I felt that you wanted to tell me something I probably needed to know; but I didn't want to miss out on signing up so that Elizabeth and I could be tent partners! That was not only my first camping trip, it was the very first time in my life that I had been allowed to spend the night at a friend's house. I was just too excited to miss anything!

"Why do you ask, Holly? What did you want to tell me?"

Holly hesitated. "Olivia, I wanted to warn you about Pastor Jason," she said finally.

Liv looked at her in silence with the wheels turning inside her head, spinning a myriad of thoughts. "Why, or how would Holly know to warn me? Why didn't I listen to my gut instinct that said what she wanted to tell me was important? Did she *know* what would happen? How?" Then it dawned on her—it must have happened to Holly, too! That might explain why she had become so distant and no longer participated in the youth activities!

Those many thoughts became multiple emotions. Her heart went out to Holly for what she knew must have been so devastating for her. She somehow felt relieved to know that she was not the only one to fall victim to Pastor Jason, and she surmised that she was probably not the last. Her anger against him was rekindled to an even higher level.

It was evident to both her guests that a chord had been struck, and that Liv was trying to process things. They patiently waited for her response. Holly was no longer afraid of her reaction, and Elizabeth was ready to embrace her on cue. It seemed like an eternity, but Liv finally spoke.

"Holly, did Pastor Jason rape you, too?" she asked matter-of-factly.

Holly did not hang her head in shame. Her anger was also rekindled, and she was ready to do battle. "Yes, Olivia. The bastard raped me. He didn't just *rape* me. He took my *virginity* and left me with years of shame, self-loathing, mistrust, fear, feelings of powerlessness, and every negative thing you can think of!

"But you know what, Olivia? I am ready to do battle! All I need is *you* to help me do this for *both* of us. Are you willing to help me put him where he belongs while he's waiting to be sent to burn in Hell?"

Liv closed her eyes and took in a deep, calming breath. She felt such an incredible relief as the weight of what she had been holding in so deeply and so long was lifted.

"What do we need to do? Where do we start? I'm in. Boy, am I in!"

Elizabeth and Holly both let out big sighs of relief, and once again the three were locked in a cathartic embrace.

"Liv, we've already begun the process," said Holly, "but we came to a huge obstacle. I first need to ask you a question or two. We know for certain now that you were a victim too, right?"

Liv nodded.

"Can you tell us *where* it happened?"

"Yes. I realize I will never forget it as all of this 'stuff' is being resurrected. I have tried to eliminate that part of my life from my memory. There was this cave that . . . "

"That's all I need to know right now," Holly interrupted, "except…"

"Except what?" Liv asked.

"It may not be as much of a need now that we have found you, but do you think you could find that cave?"

Liv's face clouded as the thought of revisiting that place dredged up a plethora of painful memories. Nevertheless, the thought of helping to bring the youth pastor to justice made her know it was something she had to do.

"It's as though I have a road map to that cave engraved in my palm. I haven't even thought of it in all these years, but now it's like watching a horrible movie playing in Technicolor™ in my head. I could probably find it blindfolded," she said pragmatically.

"The uncle of my rape counselor is an assistant district attorney. I met with him, and the assistant district attorney that he brought in to handle it cautioned me that when I found you, we should not compare details. We need to go and talk to him as soon as possible. If a meeting can be set up for Monday morning, can you be available?"

"I will make sure I am. In fact, you can both stay here with me, and we can all go together Monday morning!"

"Oh, that would be great!" Elizabeth exclaimed. "Holly, can you see if Meg can call her uncle and set up the meeting?"

"I'll do it right now."

As Holly was busy calling Meg, Liv was reviewing her life from that day to now, and she could clearly see that there were things she could or would have done differently—if she had been the person she was now. She accepted that she did what she needed to do at the time.

Holly completed her call and announced, "Meg will make the call and let us know immediately. In the meantime, I'm getting the munchies! Can I dig into the onion dip with some of these veggies?"

Liv positioned the tray of goodies in their midst. "Here, help yourselves!"

They were subdued as they nibbled on the tidbits of their choice and waited for word from Meg, which came in about 15 minutes. Holly answered her phone and listened intently for a moment.

"Okay, Meg. That's great. Thanks . . . We will. Bye!" Holly showed signs of emotion, which she carefully controlled. The realization that things would soon be going forward stirred up some anxiety because of what she knew she would have to endure. Notwithstanding, she was driven to see it through.

"Ladies, we are on for Monday. We will meet downtown in the DA's office for Olivia to give her statement. They want us to be dressed appropriately for a trek in search of the cave."

"Then we will have to go home first to get the clothes we will need," Elizabeth noted.

"Remember, I told you that anything you need, you have right here," Liv reminded. "We are all about the same size. Clothing will not be a problem." Though it was very late, no one was craving sleep. There would be plenty of time for that. Seeing her friends, and remembering the past friendships, Liv had a complete reversal of her earlier feeling that she was not ready to talk about her life. She felt the need to unburden herself to her friends. Theo had made her come to see that she needed friends, that friends—true friends—have a purpose in your life, as you have in theirs.

"Elizabeth, Holly," she began, "I know I have a lot of explaining to do, especially to you, Elizabeth, as the one who was—and I hope is still—my best friend. I can only say that I did the very best thing I knew to do at the time.

"I ask you to please bear with me as this is so hard for me on so many levels. When I left the camp that day, I was not ill, as I wanted everyone to believe. I *had* to get away. I simply could not spend another moment there." Holly could immediately relate to that sentiment.

"Holly, he took your virginity. I'm not sure I can ever imagine how horrendous that must have been for you! When you hear my story, you may understand better when I say that I wish *he* had taken *mine,* too."

Shocked, Holly asked, "Olivia, how can you *say* that?"

Shocked at the statement as well, Elizabeth focused on the beginning of the sentence and decided that more information was needed before drawing any conclusions. "Holly, we don't have enough information to understand. I think we should let Liv tell us in her own way."

"Liv, please forgive me," Holly implored. "I allowed myself to sink back into that victim hole. I know better. It won't happen again, I promise. I need to put on my counselor's hat. I'm so sorry."

"Holly, I'm sorry, too. I should have been more sensitive. You see, I have *never* been a virgin—I don't know how it *feels* or what it *means.* For as early as I can remember . . ."

Liv began to recite the story of her life—the sexual abuse at the hands of her brothers; the sexual and physical abuse at the hands of her father; the perceived lack of love from her mother; the decisions she made on that fateful day about men; the betrayal she felt by God; her decision to eliminate Him from her life (and everything associated with Him, including the church and everyone associated with it); the ultimatum of her father; Theo; her new lifestyle; everything—except Morgan!

Throughout the discourse Elizabeth and Holly listened vicariously without interruption except for the many times tears and group hugs came into play. By the time Liv finished, daylight had made its presence known. All three were emotionally and physically drained, but the healing that took place was phenomenal.

"My dear Friends," Liv began, "I thank you so, so much from the bottom of my heart!"

"No, Olivia, we thank *you* for trusting us in sharing your painful history with us." (Holly was nodding in complete agreement.) "We feel your pain as if it were ours."

During that prior evening and that morning a bond was formed between the three of them that was to last a lifetime.

"I love you both so much!" Liv expressed with deep emotion. On a practical note she added, "I know you must be tired. I definitely am. This whole night has been draining. I think perhaps we should try to get at least a couple of hours of sleep."

CHAPTER 25

Elizabeth, though tired as the others, was troubled in her spirit and did not want to let it rest on that note. "Olivia, yes, we're all spent; but I would not be a true friend to you if I did not tell you what is in my heart, and I hope you will hear me."

"Of course, Elizabeth; if you think it is important, who am I not to listen?"

"Thank you, Olivia. You know I love you and always considered you the sister I always wanted. I listened to you very carefully, and I want to tell you the thing that was most painful for me. I clearly understand the sentiment you expressed earlier about your virginity. But, Olivia, what he took from you was far more precious than if he *had* taken your virginity. He took the beautiful, trusting relationship that you had with God!"

Olivia's first instinct was to harden herself, which she did whenever the subject of God came up, even if it were generated by her own subconscious mind. Even so, she attempted to be open to at least listen as she had said she would.

"I consider myself your first Sunday school teacher! I was happy to relate to you anything I knew and had learned about God. You were such an eager student!" Elizabeth smiled recalling some of their discourses.

"I think it is because of *you* that I am a teacher today. You inspired me! But, Olivia, I was a child, and *you* were a child. We thought and understood as *children*. You were so wounded, you reacted out of your pain and anger without the benefit of a mature knowledge of God and how it relates to our lives here in the real world. I don't know; I may have reacted the same way. The point is, Olivia, you were angry at *God* because you felt betrayed by *Him*.

"Many people become angry and distraught due to events that are common in life—an enormous tragedy, death of a loved one, debilitating health issues, many, many reasons. They blame God. What they don't realize is that God is not like us, and they want to ascribe to him humanity as *we* perceive it. If you do a friend wrong, that friend—who is not a *true* friend—will cut you off, period.

"That is *not* God. He is all knowing, and His love is *unconditional*! He knows the frailty of human beings *and* their emotions. *He* created them. He can handle our anger at Him. *He* doesn't leave *us*—*we* turn from *Him*. He just quietly goes about being the good God He is and continues to love and care for His own!

"Olivia, do you think that it was just a coincidence that you would come to rest at *that* particular bus stop? Or that an old man would just *happen* to be walking in that direction and want to rest at that same bus stop? That he would invite you to walk with him and invite you in for a meal and a warm bed for the night? Why do you think his housekeeper was not able to return? Look at the relationship of mutual love and care that the two of you shared! Oh, Olivia, I could go on and on! Your friend Walter, your club, this *beautiful* condominium! Do you think that all of this would have happened if that cave incident never happened, or if God truly did not *love* you?

"And consider this, Olivia: I had been trying to find you for *years*! Holly called me; we met, talked, and prayed. I got a call from someone I hadn't seen or heard from in years who gave me information that led us directly to you, and we *found* you—all in the space of *eight days*! Olivia, what are the odds? All of this is *completely* inexplicable except for application of Divine Intervention!

"We are *not* promised a carefree, fairytale life when we accept Jesus as our Lord and personal Savior. What we are promised is that if He allows adversity to come to us, He will see us through it. We are not given more than we can bear; we just have to continue to believe God in the good times *and* the bad times, and be thankful for both. Sometimes, when it seems God is farthest from us and we can't *feel* Him walking beside us, that is when He is *carrying* us in His bosom."

Holly was anxious to share her perspective as well. "Olivia, I know it can be hard to hear. As you may be able to imagine, *I* had a very difficult time dealing with what happened to *me*. In fact, it is only recently that I have begun to realize true healing. I am *still* in the process. I made some mistakes. I didn't confide in anyone for a long time, and I have yet to tell my parents. I will soon rectify that. I went through many of the typical emotions. I didn't exactly *turn* from God, but I completely lost my zeal.

"But because of my experience, I am able to help others facing the same issues. Just like a man cannot tell a woman what it feels like to carry a baby in her womb or travail in childbirth, neither can a person who has not been raped tell a person who has been raped how to feel or act, or be, or even assert that they *know* how it feels to be raped. I realized that I am able to make a big difference and promote healing and a return to normalcy that I never would have been able to do without my own personal experience. Helping, especially very young girls, has become a passion for me!

"I am able to use my God-given talent as an artist to aid in recovery, not only for myself, which I discovered recently, but also with those girls and ladies I counsel. I would *love* to be able to start an Art/Counseling Center, as crazy as that sounds! Excuse me, I'm getting away from the point, which is, Olivia, you have to find a way to turn all of this 'experience' into something that only *you* can do to benefit others. In so doing, you will be benefiting yourself!"

"Olivia, Holly is right," Elizabeth added. "And, Olivia, I *know* He is not through with you, with *us*! Oh, Olivia, can we pray about this, all of us?"

Liv had to admit to herself that there was reason in Elizabeth and Holly's statements. Though she hadn't fully opened herself to hear with her heart, she acquiesced. They were already still on the soft throw, and they rose to their knees and joined hands.

"Dear Heavenly Father," Elizabeth began, "we come to You in the name of Jesus with all praise, honor, and glory to You in all humbleness of heart and with earnest thanksgiving. We thank and praise You for Your presence in our lives, for Your unconditional love and grace, for giving to us Your beloved Son, Jesus Christ, who suffered, bled, and died on the cross for our sins and arose again on the third day and is seated at Your right hand continually making intercession for us. We thank You for the guardian angels you have provided that are encamped around us.

"We confess that we are sinners, saved by grace through faith in Jesus Christ, Whom we have accepted as our personal Savior. We thank You for the gift of the Comforter, the Holy Spirit, and for His indwelling in the receptacle of our bodies as holy temples.

"Lord, we know that all good gifts come from above, and we thank You for the gifts and talents You have bestowed upon us according to Your divine will, and we ask and pray that they be used for Your honor and glory.

"Lord, we ask a special blessing this morning in behalf of our friend and sister, Olivia. We ask You to renew her heart toward You. Help her to see and understand that You know her heart, even into the depths that she herself cannot measure. You see the love in her heart. We ask that You let it be revealed to her so that her peace and joy in You can be restored and renewed as it was when she first believed.

"Lord, we are eternally grateful and thank You for uniting us in this bond of mutual love. We know that You have a plan and purpose for us, and we ask that You reveal Your will for us so that we may be obedient and faithful servants."

Throughout the prayer, Liv was experiencing a chipping away of the hard core into which she had encased that part of her that was intrinsically connected to God. She could see the truth of Elizabeth's words as she reflected on the many aspects of her life and the words Theo had spoken to her about the love for God within her that she herself did not realize, and how she would learn many things in time. She thought of the many times she uttered without forethought the words, "Thank You, God!"

By the time Elizabeth had finished, and Holly had added her thanks and praise, Liv's heart was thoroughly softened and broken to the point that the healing well of tears from her heart swelled and overflowed her eyes as tears of joy. She lifted her hands and began to pray.

"Oh, Lord, it's me, Olivia. I thank and praise You for watching over me and keeping me during my period of . . . lostness. That's the only way I can describe it. I can see clearly now, Lord, that it was *I* who abandoned and broke fellowship with *You*. You said in Your Word that You would never leave me. I was so blinded by pain, fear, anger, and hatred; I couldn't see that You were there all the time, paving the way for me even in my ignorance. Oh Lord, please forgive me for my transgressions. Forgive my unbelief. I know that to be forgiven I must also be forgiving. I know so much more now than I did all those years ago. I realize that I can and must forgive my brothers. In my heart I have already forgiven my mother. But, Lord, I struggle with forgiving those I hold responsible for causing me so much anguish. I humbly ask Your continued patience and help in getting past the obstacles that especially keep me from wanting to forgive my father and Pastor Jason. I just can't let go yet. I think it may take a miracle that only You can bring to pass. My hardened heart has been pierced thanks to the fervent prayers of the friends that You have blessed me to have back in my life."

Liv was truly penitent and continued to praise and thank God for everything she could think of. Afterward, they were all totally spent, but extremely joyful.

"My friends, we have come to a new chapter in all of our lives," declared Elizabeth. "I believe we have formed a bond in love and sisterhood that is indissoluble. I know our destinies are tied to each other. I think we should seal that bond with a pinky link!"

"I agree," said Holly, "but I think we need a name!"

"I have an idea, guys," offered Elizabeth. We have been here for each other, all for one and one for all. So, how about "The 3Ms? You might think 'Three Musketeers,' but we know it's The Three Friends!"

"Sounds like a winner to me, Elizabeth. How about you, Olivia?"

"I think it's a fine idea!"

"Okay," said Elizabeth. "Let's do it!"

The three friends joined their pinky fingers and repeated in unison, 'Long Live the 3Ms!" They sank down into the soft rug and were almost instantly fast asleep.

(12/16/2012) Liv awoke first later that morning. She had never before entertained guests in her home overnight. After all of the excitement, pain, tears, rejuvenation, joy, camaraderie and more of the past fifteen hours, Liv felt better and more alive than she could ever remember. It was almost noon, and she was eager to prepare breakfast for her friends.

The aroma of sizzling bacon and freshly brewed coffee floating through the air aroused her two comrades from their peaceful sleep. "Get up, you sleepy heads!" Liv urged happily. "You don't need any more beauty rest. Your breakfast-brunch-lunch-pre-dinner is served. It is strictly come-as-you-are! You can shower, shave, and do whatever you need to do *after* you have breakfasted sufficiently!"

"What time is it, anyway?" Holly asked as she stretched and yawned.

"What *day* is it?" Elizabeth demanded sleepily.

The ladies donned slippers and robes and followed Liv to the dining room.

The table was beautifully adorned with fresh flowers, matching linen placemats and napkins in crystal napkin rings. The crystal juice glasses were filled with freshly squeezed orange juice.

They sat down to a scrumptious meal of bacon and eggs, pancakes, and home fries. After the meal, Liv refused their help in the cleanup. "Don't worry about this, you two. You see I am already dressed. You need to get showered and dressed. I will take care of this. Come with me and I'll help you pick out something to wear."

They followed Liv to browse through her closets.

A half hour later the kitchen was clean, and the ladies, had dressed and joined Liv on the enclosed patio by the pool. She had snacks and beverages, "just in case."

"Well, my fellow 3M's," she said, "I've been running down my life's story, so you know just about everything there is to know about me. Now it's your turns to confess. I want to know what you've been doing for the past several years. Holly, what's your story?"

"Nothing too exciting. Until very recently, I've been surviving, living life as best I can. As I've said, I've been working with rape survivors, especially the younger ones. I love the fact that I can use my passion for art to help them.

"Olivia, I know how much you love singing. I feel the same way about art. I can say through art what I have not been able to verbalize. Although they say I have a God-given gift, I have studied art as a minor in college. Something else I have a knack for is math, writing, and planning.

"I didn't know if I could make a sufficient living as an artist. The concept of the starving artist never appealed to me. I obtained my MBA, and I am doing nicely writing grants, proposals, business plans and consulting with small and medium-size businesses. I like that I can have more control of my life and time. I feel very blessed to do what I do."

Elizabeth spoke up, "Yes, she is good at all of that. She has helped Roger with several projects. He and Barbara think she is amazing!"

"Holly, that's great!" Liv exclaimed. If I'm not getting too personal—never mind. Even if it *is* too personal, I'm going to ask you anyway! What kind of bond do we have if we can't ask personal questions of each other?"

"You're right, Olivia! Besides, can we get any more personal than we already have? Ask away. I'm open to whatever questions you want to ask me!"

"I will. There is a very serious side to this question that I hope will give me some insight. Elizabeth, you can be getting prepared to answer the same question!

"Holly, what about men in your life? How do you handle them? Is there someone special?" Liv asked.

Holly was obviously discomforted by the questions. "That's at least three questions! But there was . . . is . . . was . . . a friend that I dated, but that is still something I find not easy to deal with."

"Who is he? Do I know him?" Elizabeth asked.

"No, you don't. We met in college. We were in a study group and dated only casually, more like friends—*without* benefits. I know, or at least I suspect he wants, or wanted, a more 'less platonic' relationship. He is a nice guy, and I really do like him. I'm just not ready, and he may have given up. I hope he hasn't. I feel that anyone I may want to have a relationship with, I would first have to reveal my past. I hope it is William. That's his name, William; but I'll just have to play it by ear. I'll have to trust and pray that when the time is right, it will happen. I know that is my own problem, one of the many issue that I still have to work on."

"Do you have any fear about having sexual intercourse, consensual intercourse, for the first time with him, or *anyone*?" Liv asked. That was what she really wanted to know.

"I probably do. I'm not sure. I really try not to let myself think about that. I can't imagine anything but how it feels to be raped. Have *you* thought about it, Olivia?"

"I never really had to think about it, until recently. I convinced myself I wanted nothing to do with men. But I think that may have changed. In fact, I know it has. I think we both probably need to talk with someone who has more experience."

They each looked to Elizabeth.

"What? You think *I* have all the answers?" she responded.

"You may not have *all* of the answers, but we think you can tell us *something* as someone who has *not* been 'involuntarily deflowered.' You *haven't*, have you?" Holly asked.

"All right. Okay. First, allow me to tell you about what *I've* been up to all these years. I would have to say my passion is teaching and molding young minds. I went to summer school and took college courses in high school. I accelerated my education and had my clear teaching credential at twenty. Besides teaching a primary Sunday school class, I teach second and third graders in public school.

"I especially like to help kids learn to read. They *really* need a good foundation in reading *and* math if they are going to be successful in school and in life. I have a *knack* for teaching remedial reading. I have even tutored adults privately who were too ashamed to go to adult school or have it known that as adults they can't read.

"I really love my students. I only wish I was not so limited by the system. There is so much I can do to help them. The system doesn't take into account the variables and differences in children—how each one learns individually, is motivated differently, has other issues that impact their ability to be successful. It is just so frustrating! Kids are not 'One-Size-Fits-All!' The system would have us standardize *everything*. It holds back those that are above the 'standards,' and perpetuates the downhill slide of those who are below the 'standards.'

"In a perfect world for me, I would have my own school or setting where each child is treated individually and given the opportunity to reach his or her full potential. I would educate the whole child including areas that have been almost completely eliminated in public schools."

Elizabeth's passion for her chosen vocation was becoming more and more evident as she was becoming more animated. Realizing that she was going further than she intended, Elizabeth checked herself before she completely climbed onto her soapbox. "You have to excuse me. I sometimes get emotional talking about my students."

"Elizabeth, I think that is so wonderful for each of us to be so passionate about something!" Holly said.

"Yes," Liv agreed as a seed was being planted in the back of her mind relative to her and Morgan's dream. She left that thought to get back to Elizabeth's response to the question of the day.

"How would you like to give your two newest pupils a much-needed lesson in sex education?"

"Sex education?" she responded. "When you put it that way, it makes a big difference. If you don't mind my getting technical, I may be able to provide some theoretical insight that may help."

"Theory is good, Elizabeth," Liv was quick to point out, "but theory and practice are not necessarily the same. We need the practical more than anything if we are to get any real understanding! Your *personal* experience would be the most valuable to *me*."

"Let me start out by saying this. People are unique. People experience things differently and react . . ."

"We get that," Holly interrupted. *We* want to know where the *sex* comes in!"

"I'm getting to that. Hold on! I first have to give you a mini lesson on the cave men."

"What do the cave men have to do with it?" Liv asked. "As far as we know, they probably just beat their women over the head with their clubs and dragged them into the caves and had their way with them." Liv immediately regretted her words, realizing how close to home they were hitting.

"I'm so sorry! I can't believe I said that!"

Holly was quick to respond. "Olivia, don't worry about it. Actually, it could be a really good sign that you thought it and felt free to express it."

Elizabeth interjected, "Let's talk about physiological responses, for example, the fight or flight response."

"That is all very interesting, Elizabeth. Are you saying that physiological responses have something to do with falling in love, or making love?" Holly asked.

"Well, yes, kind of. Let me just tell you . . ."

Elizabeth paused, realizing that she was rapidly losing her captive audience with TMI. She knew what they wanted from her, and it wasn't a textbook explanation of anything.

"I tell you what, guys, I'll just skip this boring lesson. Your assignment is to Google 'physiological responses,' or 'fight or flight responses,' or 'falling in love responses' and find out what you need to know. I know you want to hear about *my* personal experiences! You have called me to task. I can't delay the inevitable any longer."

Matter-of-factly, she said, "Look, guys, I'm sorry to disappoint you, but I haven't had a lot of experience. I was preoccupied with school and then with working with my students. "

Holly challenged her excuse saying, "But surely you dated at least *once* in a while. Hasn't there been someone that you met that you were attracted to and thought about going out with, or . . . kissing, or anything?"

"Well, yes," Liv added. "Did you go to your prom?"

"Of course, I did!"

"Well? How was it? Who did you go with? What did you do?" Liv quizzed.

"If you must know, I *wasn't* going to go. No one *asked* me. They all thought I was a nerd! I think they were afraid of being seen with a 'nerd,' even a 'cute' one as I had been called. They also thought I was too young. You remember how it was in school, don't you Olivia?"

"Well, did you go or not, and who did you go with?" Holly pressed.

"All right! I confess. Roger set me up with the younger brother of one of his friends. He was a charity case, just like I was. Only, at one point at the after party, he decided to press his luck and became a real jerk; so I gave him a knee in his 'tender.' He fell to his knees, and I took a cab home!

"And, yes, I've gone on a few dates, a *very* few, because I lay down the law from the start, and most would-be suitors back off. That tells me what they wanted in the first place, so there was never a loss for me. I haven't met that person that made my heart stop, or made me stammer, or daydream about or want to 'jump on.' I know the man for me is out there. I can wait.

CHAPTER 26

"Now I'm turning the tables on *you*, Olivia!" Elizabeth declared. "You said earlier that you never had to think about being with a man *until recently*. What does that mean? Have you met someone that has 'tickled your fancy?' "

Surprised by the sudden shift, Liv could only blush.

"Oh, ho!" Holly voiced triumphantly. "The blush on Olivia's face says you struck gold, Elizabeth! Come on, Olivia, fess up!"

"Yes, Olivia, fess up!" Elizabeth echoed.

Liv was relieved that she was now being forced to do what she wanted to do. "Okay, I have to admit there *is* someone. He says we are going to be married, that it is our destiny."

"Now *that's* a line I haven't heard before! You didn't fall for it, did you?" Holly asked.

They took her tacit reply as a "yes."

"You *fell* for it, Olivia?" Elizabeth asked.

"There is more to it than that! I met him about a year ago. I had noticed him in the club every week for a few months. He never approached me like so many of the men do. He has the most amazing, penetrating eyes! He would just *look* at me! It sort of made me feel . . . different, weird inside."

"Weird good, or weird bad?" Holly asked.

"I don't know exactly. It made me . . . wonder. I was curious because the way he acted was nothing like I had ever experienced in a man, especially when he never approached me. He would always leave a huge tip and just leave.

"My curiosity got the best of me, and I sort of forced a chance meeting with him one night—January 7 of this year, to be exact. He invited me to join him for a moment. In the sixty seconds I was there at his table, I managed to make a complete fool of myself, saying dumb things! Not only did I shoot myself in the foot, I also put my shot foot in my mouth!"

"If I may interject, it sounds to me like you found the one that made you 'stammer,' like I'm waiting for someone to make me do!" Elizabeth reminded her. "That's one out of four! Now, does he make your heart stop? Do you daydream about him? Do you want to . . . let me rephrase the 'jump on' to 'be intimate with' him?"

"Oh, my goodness, Elizabeth! You're not wasting any time, are you! In all honesty, I have to admit that it's more like four out of four."

"You have had *sex* with him?" Holly asked in disbelief.

"No! Of *course* not!" Liv exclaimed emphatically."

"But you said you have been *intimate* with him," Elizabeth pointed out.

"I didn't *say* that exactly, especially in the way *you* intimate—please excuse the pun—but we *have* been intimate—we *are* intimate. *Very* intimate!"

Liv understood their reactions; she realized how they had interpreted her words in the context of Elizabeth's paraphrasing. She enjoyed the opportunity to turn the tables on her.

"Please allow *me* to refer *you* to Google. Please look up the word '*intimate*.' You will find that it is *not* synonymous with sexual intercourse! We *have* been intimate in that we have shared details of our personal lives, our hopes and dreams, our goals, everything!

"But let me clarify things so you have a more accurate perspective. After our first official meeting in January, we never interacted again, except for a nod or greeting in passing, just as I do with all of my fans. It wasn't until after Theo's passing that we actually conversed again. It was toward the end of March."

"Does he know about your childhood and, you know . . .?" Holly inquired.

"He knows *everything*, and he swears he *loves* me. Regardless!"

"Do *you* love *him*?" Elizabeth asked. "Have you *told* him?"

"I haven't told him, but I *do* love him. I'm *afraid* to tell him. I'm afraid to *say* it. I feel that if I *say* it, I will have to *act* on it, and I don't know if I *can* yet. He says he has waited for me all his life; and now that he has found me, he can wait for as long as he has to!"

"Have you at least kissed him?" Holly was very interested.

"No, I haven't. He has only kissed my hand, as he did when we first met."

"Just how long is *this* going to go on? Do you *want* to be intimate with him in the physical way?" Elizabeth probed.

"Elizabeth, I just want to have a normal relationship and just live my life and raise a family in a normal, healthy way. Do I love him? That's an emphatic 'yes.' I'm just trying to figure out a way to allow myself to be held, to touch and be touched, to *physically* love him when the time comes. *That's* what I'm hoping you can help me with.

"When he is close to me, I feel panic. I can only relate it to how I felt when . . . when I was a child."

"Olivia," Elizabeth questioned, "When you were seeing that therapist, did you talk about this problem? Did she offer any advice?"

"Yes," Liv responded reluctantly. We *did* talk about it, but I couldn't—wouldn't do what she suggested." Liv was hoping that her response would be sufficient, although she knew she wouldn't get off so easily. Holly was really dying to find out what the recommended "cure" was. She wanted—needed to know for herself.

"But what did she advise you to do, Olivia? Why wouldn't you at least try it?" she asked.

"I . . . I just couldn't. I . . . Oh, it is just too embarrassing!"

Her friends wouldn't let her off the hook. She knew she would have to bite the bullet and put it all out there.

"Olivia, you *have* to tell me," Holly pressed. "*You* may not be able to do whatever it is, but please give *me* a chance to determine if it might work for *me!*"

"All right, Holly. I have told you everything else, so I might as well tell you this. To paraphrase, she said I should *'experiment with pleasuring myself!'* There! You have it!"

Holly looked quizzically at her, but Elizabeth just called it. "You mean she said you should *masturbate!*"

"Yes! Now can we just move on?"

"Okay, Olivia, listen up!" Elizabeth said, taking control. "Have you read the Song of Solomon?"

"Of Course! I read the Bible from cover to cover *several* times."

"What do you remember about Solomon and the Shulamite woman?" Elizabeth asked.

Liv thought for a minute and had to respond with, "I remember reading about them, but I have to admit I didn't *understand* much of it. I don't remember hearing anyone *talk* about it. As you pointed out, my understanding of many things I read was . . . infantile."

"Now that you are an intelligent, educated adult, I think you may want to reread it. It may help you to understand that men and women, humans, are sensual as well as spiritual beings. When they unite as one, it can be and is *supposed* to be a beautiful expression of their love from which they can mutually derive great pleasure. The Bible also says that the marriage bed is undefiled."

Liv determined she would reread the Scriptures, but she was not convinced that by merely doing so she could eliminate her reservations.

She asked "How can that alleviate my fears?"

Holly had been listening closely because she knew these were her issues as well. She determined to also reread the passages and take to heart any insight Elizabeth could give.

"Give me a moment or two," Elizabeth answered. She thoughtfully considered the question and came up with a possible solution.

"Olivia, I think you need to know, to be *reminded,* that you can face your worst fear and be triumphant. If I were to pick an event in your life when you may have been the *most* afraid, I would say it was the day you confronted your father! I bet if you allow yourself to relive that moment, you will actually *feel* that fear. Let's try. Think about it, Olivia."

Liv was intent on doing whatever she had to do to overcome what was now the biggest challenge in her life. She allowed herself to relive that pivotal moment. She saw her father looming large, darkening her bedroom doorway. She saw the veins bulging in his neck, the dark anger in his eyes. She saw his big, hairy fists clenching and unclenching.

Liv felt her fingers clutching her brothers' steel bat so hard the blood rushed from her knuckles, rendering them white. She felt her heart begin to beat frantically, and her breathing quickened. Her body began to shake involuntarily as she found herself back in that little room all those years ago.

Her tears prompted Elizabeth to end the exercise. Taking her by the hand to break the link, she said quietly, "Olivia, you did it. You see and remember *real* fear. You *survived!* That is as bad as it can be. You came through it in triumph! As an adult you are even *more* capable of facing fear of the unknown. Remember, Olivia, you are not without resources to combat any fear. Now that your faith has been restored, you have the greatest ally there is, and He did not give you a spirit of fear."

Still shaken, Liv could not answer immediately, though she was taking in Elizabeth's words. She was reminded of the blind faith she had demonstrated when she said her first prayer and how happy she was when it was answered. "Thank you, Elizabeth. I think that exercise is helping me. I know I will get it together."

Elizabeth had an idea that she felt would lighten the mood and bring some Christmas cheer to Liv's condo. "Ladies, let's say we go shopping!"

"Shopping? What do you need that I don't have?"

"It's not what *we* need; it's what *you* need—what this *condo* needs. What is the date?"

"It's December 16."

"Exactly! What is missing in this beautiful home of yours is a reminder that it is almost *Christmas*! As beautiful as it is, it could very well be the home of Scrooge! There is no sign of Christmas here! We have to go and get the holiday spirit. We have enough time to get what we need, stop for dinner while we're out, and come back here and decorate this place! By the time we do all that, it will be time for us to get some sleep so we can get up early in the morning and get to the DA's office!"

"Elizabeth, that's an excellent idea! I have to admit it's pretty drab for Christmas. Until you guys paved the way for me to reestablish my relationship with God, I never gave Christmas, or Easter for that matter, a thought all these years. That is now a thing of the past. I hope all the good stuff isn't all gone. Let's go!"

The 3Ms were in a light and festive mood as they shopped at the mall. They took their purchases to the car and returned to one of the mall restaurants for dinner. Afterwards, they shopped a little more and did a lot of sightseeing, taking in all of the spectacular displays.

At one point, Holly turned to say something to Elizabeth to find that she was nowhere in sight! "Where did Elizabeth go? I thought she was right here with us!" They both looked, but she was nowhere to be found. They even checked the nearest ladies' room.

"I don't know where she could have gone. Holly, will you call her? I haven't put her number in my phone yet. I'll have to do that for both of you."

Holly got Elizabeth on speakerphone. "Where *are* you? We've been looking for you everywhere!"

"I'm sorry! I thought you heard me say I was stopping in the stationery store and would catch up with you. I had one more gift to get and found the perfect one. It's being engraved now. It will be ready and wrapped in about five minutes. Keep looking at the sights as you make your way to the entrance of the parking structure. I will meet you there in ten minutes."

Once back at Liv's, they put up the fiber optic tree and adorned the condo with the decorations, transforming it into a Christmas wonderland!

"Olivia, you will need at least one present under the tree. Here. This is for you. You don't have to wait until Christmas to open it." She removed the beautifully wrapped package from the bag she retrieved and handed it to Liv.

"Oh, Elizabeth, you shouldn't have! I don't need anything. Besides, I don't have gifts for the two of you!"

"Olivia," Holly assured her, "You have been doing nothing but giving to us since we came. Speaking for myself, and probably Elizabeth as well, you have given us more than money can buy. You have given *me* something so valuable, I can't even begin to articulate!"

"I didn't get this for you because I expect you to reciprocate. This is from me to you because I know it is something you *don't* have. Please open it now," Elizabeth requested.

Liv graciously accepted the package and unwrapped it to expose the gift box. When she removed the lid and saw what the box contained, she was overcome with emotion. She looked at Elizabeth with such appreciation, she had to give her a giant hug. "I could not have asked for a more perfect gift! Thank you so much, Elizabeth! Thank you both! Group hug time!"

By ten o'clock that night, two tired guests were fast asleep in a tastefully decorated and Christmas-lighted condo. Liv was awake in bed thinking about her experience earlier in reliving her last encounter with her father. She had not gotten a definitive resolution. She was reminded, as Elizabeth mentioned, she was not alone in this dilemma. She had renewed faith in God, and her friends were absolutely doing what they could to assist. She felt that the pieces were trying to come together, but it seemed there were missing pieces still.

Perhaps if she could see Olive just once more, she could get some helpful advice. Though that had not happened in all those years that had passed, Liv often visited their haven in her thoughts. As she lay in bed picturing her haven and Olive, she remembered their last meeting, and it became clearer to her. She still had a choice! Just as she had chosen to no longer be a victim to anyone who would abuse her and changed her life radically as a result, she could make other choices just as profound! Here was another opportunity to make a life-altering choice. She could choose to no longer allow herself to be ruled by the fear that prevented her from being the woman she could be, free to touch and be touched, to love and be loved!

She remembered what Birdie had said to her, that she would have to walk through fire, and that she would prevail. She had not walked through fire yet, as far as she knew. There must be something more. But for now, she was content. She knew the outcome.

Liv got out of bed and picked up her newly engraved red-letter edition of the King James Version of the Holy Bible Elizabeth had just given her. She opened it up to the Song of Solomon and read it in its entirety.   She missed some of the symbolism, but it did much for her from   the standpoint of the answers she was seeking. She kneeled down to pray. When she climbed back into bed, she settled down to a peaceful sleep.

CHAPTER 27

(12/17/2012) ADAs Reginald Johnston and Daniel Harper had been eagerly awaiting the arrival of Dan's niece and the others. They were happy to learn a second survivor of the youth pastor had been located and was willing to come forward.

Dan met the group in the reception area and escorted them to the conference room where the SVU detectives were waiting along with Reginald Johnston.

"Ladies, I want you to meet ADA Reginald Johnston and Special Victims Unit Detectives Shar'ron Obriant and Ellen Rogers. They have been assigned to this case and will be handling the investigation. They have reviewed Holly's testimony and will take over from here.

Det. Obriant addressed Liv directly. "Miss Washington, is it okay if I address you as Olivia?"

"Yes, please."

"Thank you, Olivia. I want you to know how sorry we are for what you have experienced. We want to make this process as easy on you as possible. We don't want to pressure or rush you in any way. Any time you want to stop, or take a break, or even withdraw completely, just let us know. It will not be a problem.

"Do you agree to have your statement videotaped?"

"Yes."

"Thank you, Olivia. When I start the taping, please state first your name and the fact that you have agreed to the videotaping of your statement. Then, please state the crime of which you were a victim; the date, place and time; and the name or names of the person or persons who committed the crime against you. Do you understand?"

"Yes, Ma'am."

"Good. I need for you to tell us as completely and as detailed as you can what you experienced from your independent recollection. I am starting the taping now."

Liv began, "My name is Olivia Louise Washington, and I agree to have my statement videotaped. On Saturday afternoon, April 15, 2006, the Saturday before Easter Sunday at the Sunny Creek Camp and Retreat Resort, I was raped by the youth pastor of our church, Pastor Jason Winston."

Liv began describing the events as though she were watching a movie being played in her head, depicting orally what she was seeing. The details were specific and mimicked the events that had been described by Holly, even to the description of the cave and its contents, with the exception of the dialogue.

"Thank you, Olivia. I know it wasn't pleasant to relive that experience," Det. Obriant said. "I hope you don't mind if I ask you a few more questions. Holly was able to provide us with some excellent artwork describing the cave as well as some of the landscape. There was one important feature she described that you haven't mentioned. Did you notice any identifying marks on his body?"

Liv was silent, but it was clear she was visualizing something unpleasant for which she did not have to search her memory. She slowly nodded. Everyone waited patiently for her to elaborate.

"It was a tattoo under his left nipple, over his heart."

Liv was thinking about the position she was in when she was able to see it clearly, and it made her angry. As hard as she tried, she couldn't hold back the flood of painful memories associated with that tattoo. She likewise couldn't hold back the flood of tears that she had managed to hold back to this point.

Megan placed a box of tissues conveniently for Liv, who took a handful and composed herself as quickly as she could. Sufficiently composed, she continued.

"It was a tattoo of a snake coiled around a cross with a crown of thorns on its head!"

Elizabeth and Holly each took a handful of tissue from the box as Det. Obriant reached to stop the recorder. The mood was understandably somber.

"Olivia, do you think you can locate this cave after all these years?" Det. Rogers asked.

Liv had definitely worked through what she needed to, at least for the time being, and was now focused on the job ahead.

"*Finding* that cave after a *hundred* years would be easier for me than *entering* into it." Liv replied. "But I'm ready. I know the importance of finding it, and that's why we are dressed in our hiking gear. Let's just get this show on the road!"

"If it's all right with you, detectives, I would like to transport the ladies in my SUV for any moral support I can give and meet you there," Dan offered.

"That will be fine," Det. Obriant replied. "Ladies, I can't tell you how much we appreciate your courage and determination in following through. Thank you. We are going to get another predator off the streets!" There was little talk en route. Mostly there was only the sound of soothing music from the CD. Before they knew it, they were on the short side road leading to the camp entrance. Dan parked beside the detectives and the forensic team's van.

For Liv it was déjà vu. She looked around to get her bearings and led the group exactly to the starting point of the "game" where the participants were assigned partners. She then headed with determined purpose in the direction she had taken on the heels of Pastor Jason over six years before.

It wasn't a fluke that Liv remembered so vividly. She had been forced to depend on her own resources to protect herself all of her life. A major part of that was reading situations and being ever vigilant of her surroundings. Once she realized Pastor Jason was taking the lead, she didn't actively look for a likely hiding place but concentrated on the things she noted on the way.

She was always thinking of possible scenarios and determined that in the unlikely event that Pastor Jason became injured, or something happened and they were separated or lost, she wanted to be able to find her way back to safety. She also used her imagination to animate the shapes she encountered.

She was looking for two things in particular. The first was the stream they had crossed about fifteen minutes into the trek, which they followed toward the right until they came to the section they were able to jump across. She soon found the spot and easily jumped across, followed by the entourage.

The second major trail mark was the rock formation that she had named "The Three Bears." It consisted of what appeared to her as three rocks shaped like crude snowmen of three different sizes. To Liv they became the Mama Bear, the Papa Bear, and the Wee, Wee Baby Bear! After a few minutes more of walking at a steady pace, she saw the family of bears. At that point, she was able to walk directly to the narrow opening of the cave. Although there were no bushes covering it, and no boulders to pry away, the shudder that ran down Liv's spine told her that she had arrived. She turned around and waited for everyone, then she announced, "Welcome to 'The Cave.'"

The actual opening was not visible looking straight ahead. It was more like a crevice that could only be seen up close, looking behind and around what was visible.

Holly recognized it as well and had a similar reaction. She immediately decided she could not enter. "Oh, I can't! I can't go in there again!" she declared. She turned and walked several yards away where she sank to the ground, covering her face with her hands.

Megan went to comfort her. "It's okay, Holly. You don't have to actually go in."

Det. Obriant spoke up, "This may well be the crime scene, but I would prefer for at least one of the victims to actually go in for confirmation."

Liv initially was loathed to enter as well. Seeing Holly's reaction, she remembered much of their recent conversations about facing fear and taking back power. She thought of Morgan and knew she needed to see this through. She drew upon her own reserve of strength and power. Holly was now her sister, and what Liv wanted for herself, she also wanted for Holly.

It was suddenly clear to Liv. All the pieces were in place now, including Birdie's pronouncement that she would have to walk through the fire. Her walk through the fire, the final piece, was entering into that cave!

Liv went to Holly and compelled her to stand up. "Holly, this is the last step in both of our complete deliverance from the control of that monster. Seeing him rot in jail will be our putting the nails in his coffin! But it's more than just that, Holly. This is a chance for our *complete* healing.

"You see, I have been agonizing over my fear of closeness with the one I am bound to be with, the man that I *want* to be with. With all of our discussions and experiments and prayers, I think I have the answer. My imposing dilemma now is the same as yours. We have to choose—to *choose*—to overcome our debilitating fear by eradicating it completely! This we do by *facing* it head on. Until we do, Jason will continue to keep us trapped, limited, and afraid. *He* wins.

"Together we can do this. We can walk this walk through the fire together. Together we *will* do this! Come with me, Holly."

Holly drew courage from Liv as they embraced. "Thank you, Liv. Yes, we *can* do this." Hand in hand they walked back to the entrance of the cave.

An unforeseen obstacle presented itself as the entrance into the cave was surveyed. Pastor Jason was very physically fit and lean. Even so, he had to remove his gear and set it inside the cave before he could enter. On the other hand, most of the forensic team would be hard press to enter easily.

It was determined that the cameraman and two of the other technicians would be able to squeeze in if they first placed their equipment inside the cave piece by piece. The smallest member of the team, Kyoko Neason, went in first with a powerful lantern and determined that at the most, only two, possibly three people would be able to occupy the cave at any one time. Knowing that the complete procedure would be lengthy, and being sensitive to Holly and Liv's feelings, the detectives agreed they could go in once the photo and video documentation was completed. They were admonished not to touch anything. Once they had authenticated the cave as the crime scene, the forensic team could do its work.

Liv entered, quickly followed by Holly. The bright illumination enabled them to clearly see the surroundings in which they had been so callously violated. The feelings were extremely overwhelming; but supporting each other, they were able to endure the ordeal and emerged victoriously a few minutes later feeling strong, determined, and powerful!

In the interim, Elizabeth was anxiously awaiting and praying. When they emerged, she knew her prayers had been answered. Their transformation was evident. Once again, the 3M's united in a group hug.

Dan was ecstatic. "Ladies," he said, "I can't tell you what this means. I am so proud of you, and I promise we will do everything in our power to insure that justice is done as quickly as possible. What do you say to leaving the detectives and the forensic team to their work while we get something to eat before we head back? My treat, of course."

ADA Johnston, just as happy, declined the invitation, opting to return to the office.

They set out to make the trek back to the car and on to the pancake place that was again suggested. The mood this time around was definitely jubilant.

When they were leaving his office, Dan assured them the process would be painstaking and thorough. He told them, "Nothing will happen as far as arresting the suspect, or even letting him know that he is a suspect, until all of the ducks are in a row. I know you are anxious for this to be over, but please be patient a little longer. Except our processing, nothing will happen until after the holidays. Try not to worry and just concentrate on having happy holidays. Merry Christmas and Happy New Year!"

A New Plan

The ladies were spent from their day's activity. They showered and changed and were in a talkative, festive mood. A gigantic weight had been lifted, and they were basking in the freedom. The trio had been together from Saturday night to Monday, now late afternoon. So much had transpired, it was mind-boggling. Nevertheless, all were happy to be together.

"I have an idea, ladies. In fact, I have several ideas, and they involve you. Isn't school out for over two weeks, Elizabeth?" Liv asked.

"Yes, I am off until the fourteenth. Why do you ask?"

"Because I don't want you guys to go! We still have things to talk about, things to do, fun to have! I'll even let you go home for Christmas day and Christmas dinner. You are off, and Holly, you are your own boss. If you have anything that you have to do, you can do it here! *Please* stay with me," Liv implored.

"I am so tempted," Holly said with regret, "but we have already imposed on you so much. We're eating your food, wearing your clothes, enjoying the life of Riley! A girl could get real spoiled and would be hard to get rid of."

"Liv, I am also tempted. But I would have to go home at least to pick up a few things and check my mail. You could definitely twist my arm, though. I'm sure that Holly would be amenable to a little arm twisting as well, wouldn't you, Holly?"

Holly looked sheepishly at Elizabeth, and Liv took that as a cue. "Well then, consider your arms *broken*! You are staying!"

"I have a suggestion, Liv. I know my parents would love to see you. My mother *loves* to cook for people. Why don't both of you come and spend Christmas at *my* folks' house? I will call Mom later, but I need to stop by my apartment and pick up a few things."

"Can we go by my house, too, and . . ." Holly hesitated. She had something important to do that would be easier with her friends.

"And what, Holly?" Liv asked.

"As I told you, I never told my parents about Jason. Now I know I must. I feel it would be more assuring if the two of you were with me, especially you, Liv. I know they will feel badly. Seeing that we are okay, they might feel better. I know they love me and will be pained not having had the opportunity to be there for me."

"Of course we will go with you, Holly! We are sisters, and that is what sisters do. Don't give it a second thought!"

"Yes, Holly," Elizabeth agreed. "It is settled. Liv, what are these ideas you were talking about?"

"Well, before I get into that, today is Monday. I have band rehearsal here Monday evenings. I have two choices. I can cancel for tonight, or not cancel—and you guys will have to sit through it!"

"Are you *kidding*?" Elizabeth exclaimed. "We can actually sit in on your rehearsal? We would *kill* to be able to do that, wouldn't we, Holly!"

"Oh, you *know* it!"

"Well, then," Liv expressed. "It's done! I'm going to order food for them instead of fixing it myself. Tonight I'll just spend that time with you guys.

"Getting together with you this weekend has brought so much change to me, to the way I feel, to what I want to do. I feel like I have enough in me for another all-nighter, after the guys leave. I'll have to put them out on time and not let them hang around. I had better start making preparations. Everyone will be here by 6:00."

Liv ordered the food, and the ladies made their way to the music room and chatted while Liv was getting things set up for the rehearsal. As the band members arrived, Liv introduced them to her friends and indicated that the rehearsal would end promptly at nine. By six pm, the food had arrived as well as the band. After the feeding frenzy, they got down to the serious business of rehearsing, to the delight of Elizabeth and Holly.

By 9:15, the ladies had donned nighties and were positioned for another round of sharing. "Tonight I want to tell you all about Morgan," Liv announced. "I will try to be succinct, if I can. First, I want to wear this proudly." She pulled out her engagement ring that was on a chain concealed beneath her PJ's and put it on her finger. The diamonds sparkled brilliantly in the light.

"Oh, my God, Olivia. It's *beautiful!*" Elizabeth gawked.

"It must have cost a *fortune,*" Holly added. They ooohed and ahhhed in admiration while Liv thought lovingly of Morgan.

"Before this weekend, I was dreading my wedding day and the subsequent body contact. I wanted to delay it as long as possible and slip away when the time came to a quiet, no fanfare private ceremony before a judge. Now, everything has changed drastically! I want a fabulous church wedding with my two best friends as bridesmaids! You *will* do that, *won't* you?"

"You'd better believe it!" Elizabeth said.

"Not to rain on your parade, Olivia," Holly announced, "I have had a significant transformation as well. I keep telling myself, 'Call William! Call William!' I feel an urgent need to call him now. I think I will! I just hope it's not too late."

"Holly, I think you should. We want to meet him, too. Why don't you ask William to escort you to a dinner party with some friends of yours? I'm working this out as I speak. Morgan will be back sometime in the next week or so. He wasn't sure exactly when, but he promised he would be here for New Year's Eve. I know! I will throw a New Year's Eve Dinner Party at the club! I won't be working since it falls on a Monday, and normally the club is dark. On New Year's Eve we do something special at the club. This year will be exceptional! Morgan will be back. Everyone can meet everyone else!

"Elizabeth, you can invite an escort as well! Holly, can you call him right now?"

"Okay, I will!" Holly selected William's number, which she had kept from their days in college, and pressed "call." The call went directly to voice mail, which both disappointed and relieved Holly. She had called him before she had determined what to say. She had to wing it.

"Hello, William. This is Holly Albright. I hope you remember me." Already she was regretting that she had not prepared first. "I know we haven't spoken in a while, and I know it is short notice, "but I wanted to ask you, if you are not busy or not already tied up for New Year's Eve, if you would be available to . . . Um, please give me a call as soon as you can. Thank you. Goodbye."

Seeing her frustration, her friends encouraged her. "Way to go, Holly! The hardest part is over. And *of course* he remembers you! He probably has never stopped thinking about you, as gorgeous and as smart as you are!" Elizabeth said.

"Yes, Holly. Just have a little faith!" Liv had to laugh at herself. She would never have thought a week ago that *she* would be giving that advice to *anyone*. "If he has the smarts you attribute to him, he would be a fool not to drop an audience with the Pope to . . ." Her words were interrupted by Holly's cell ring. Holly looked to find that it was William calling. In a quandary, Holly gasped, "What should I say? What should I do?"

"First, calm down and answer the phone," Liv prompted. Holly swallowed hard and answered, "Hello, William, I . . . Really? I know . . . Oh, no! . . . I hope I didn't give you that impression. I'll have to explain some day. Yes, I'm sorry for that. New Year's Eve? Well, I am attending a dinner party with friends at this supper club in Brentwood, and I didn't want to go alone . . . You are the first, the only person I would even consider. That's why I called . . . You will?" Holly's spirit was visibly lifted as her whole tone changed. "The name of the club is Liv's Supper Club and Lounge, on . . . You do? . . . You *have?* Yes. She is my friend who is hosting the party! Okay, William, I will. Thanks. You, too. Bye!"

Liv and Elizabeth were waiting impatiently for Holly to give them the 411 on the other half of the conversation. Obviously, it was good news, but they wanted blow-by-blow details. Both were elated, but there was a hint of unease in Liv. She surmised from what she heard that William had been to her club before. She was wondering if he could have been one of the many young men who tried to come on to her.

"Well? What did he say?" Elizabeth insisted.

Still dazzled, Holly paraphrased the gist of his conversation. "He *had* been thinking about me. He was glad that I called him. He couldn't get up the nerve to ask me to go out with him again because he didn't think he could take another rejection. He doesn't have a stalker mentality.

"He didn't understand why we couldn't be a couple, especially since we had gotten along so well together, etc. He even thought it was because he is African-American."

"What about New Year's Eve and my club?" Liv asked anxiously.

"He said whatever was on his agenda is tossed. He knows about your club and has been there on several occasions with friends. He loves jazz, and he loves your performances!"

The response did not ease her mind, but Liv decided to take her own advice to "just have a little faith" that all would be well. "What about you, Elizabeth?" she asked. "Who will you bring?"

"That's a very good question! I'll have to let you know when *I* do. But what are the *ideas* you wanted to tell us about?"

Liv had been sidetracked with Holly's situation. Since that dilemma was resolved, she eagerly turned to the subject of the youth center. "Morgan and I had been looking at sites to house the school and community center we want to found. I have spoken to my attorney, and he has assured me of his help. He blew my mind with a plethora of question for which I had no answers. There is a lot of planning that has to be done.

"I have been so blessed to have the two of you back in my life. I think I know why this has happened, apart from the situation with Jason. Each of you has shared your passions with me, and I see a perfect synergy that can only be beneficial in just about every way for all of us!

"The scope is absolutely overwhelming to me if I look at the big picture all at once. I need to break it down so it seems more doable. Morgan introduced me to a great group of youngsters at a community center in South Los Angeles. He has a dream of helping them to overcome their circumstances to become self-sufficient, productive citizens. He asked me to come and speak to the kids to give some encouragement and feedback to especially those that were interested in the performing arts. I went and was immediately hooked! They are really wonderful kids and so eager to learn. I have been going there regularly ever since. I think his involvement with the kids is what first attracted me to him. The kids all love him, and soon, I found I did, too.

"I don't know what comes first. My attorney said we need a business plan. I'm thinking of you, Holly. Of course you will need to know what it is we want to do. Another part involves education. That is what I see for you, Elizabeth.

You will have an opportunity to design the kind of educational program you spoke of where the focus will be geared to the individual students' learning abilities. I see them learning about life in so many different aspects. I want to see a return to basics—math, science, and particularly English language skills, and old fashion discipline, etiquette, ethics, morals, life skills, economics, the arts, physical education, college prep, self-esteem building and nurturing, communication skills, common sense, parenting, nutrition, the list goes on. And, Elizabeth, there will be plenty of opportunity for teaching remedial reading. Foreign languages including signing are also needed."

"Sign language?" Elizabeth asked. "That's amazing! I was recently talking to a young lady who specializes in teaching signing to students and their parents. Her name is Charlene Carter. She was very passionate about the need for hearing impaired students and parents to be able to communicate effectively. I believe she would be very interested in the program."

"There is one little girl at the center, Alesha Olsen, who could really benefit from learning proper signing as well as her foster parent. Let's keep in touch with her!

"We intend to start off with the children that we already have, and build and add on as it evolves. We need a plan that can be initiated in stages, I think. As soon as possible, we want to reach out to teen parents. I envision a nursery and day-care facility on the premises that would offer services to working parents in the community and parent-students who would be caring for their own children as well as others as they learn and have childcare for their own when they are in classes.

"There would be the latest technology for students. We must have handpicked faculty and staff who embrace our vision and purpose. Which reminds me, we will need to define what our mission, purpose, and goals should be and commit them to print.

"Oh, there is just so much! I see eventually an adult education component as well as resources for the community at large. The major emphasis will be on everyone's being drug, gang and violence-free, and the requirement for parent involvement and personal responsibility for all persons. We will have to have security, which I would like to be subtle, but thorough and effective. We want to ensure the safety of everyone in our facilities and on our grounds."

Very interested, Holly and Elizabeth listened to Liv's discourse, particularly as it related to their fields of expertise. At Liv's pause for breath, Holly inquired about many areas including organizational structure and funding.

"Liv, there are a lot of questions that need to be answered. You have already thrown out a lot of food for thought. I do see great possibilities that might encompass counseling in various areas to include victims of violence and rape, perhaps?"

"Yes, definitely! We can include whatever is needed!"

"Liv," Elizabeth added, "I can see many areas in which I can help and be effective. I can develop curricula for one thing, and help with developing a mission statement along with a statement of the purpose and goals. I can even help with recruiting qualified teachers. There are at least two at my school who have feelings similar to mine. The only drawback is that they are entrenched in the system and are hooked on their salary scale, though nothing to brag about, and benefits. I can't see them settling for less than they have, especially without any kind of seniority."

"One thing I can assure each of you, this endeavor will be fully funded, and you will be compensated fully with both pay and perks."

"Perhaps one or both of you can explain something to me as far as schools are concerned. I know there are boards that govern the schools, some elected and some not. I don't know how the controlling power is structured. What we want is control from which we cannot be ousted by a board or other powers. I already know we don't want a charter school controlled by a board that is controlled by a higher government entity. I believe funds provided by government entities come with government-controlled strings attached.

"You are right about that," Elizabeth assured her.

"Liv, you may need an umbrella corporation for the different facets of the operation," Holly suggested. "Overhead may be substantial, particularly with regard to liability and other types of insurance. This really needs to be thought out and planned very carefully."

"You are right, of course. My attorney is putting together options. I would really love it if you can go with me next week when I see him. We don't have to have everything etched in stone, but I would like to have done much of the due diligence when Morgan returns."

"You will at least need officers for a corporation. Instead of a governing board, you can have an advisory board or committee, which your attorney will probably suggest if you are concerned about control. That way, your main concern is your officers."

"I don't think we have to worry about the officers. My thinking is the officers will consist of the three of us, if you are willing, and Morgan as president. Are you on board for this?"

Excited, Elizabeth exclaimed, "Absolutely!"

"Ditto!" Holly agreed. "I have so many ideas; I'm ready to get started right now!"

"Me, too, Liv! I will start working on everything in my area of expertise that I can!"

"Oh, you guys! What wonderful friends you are! I love you!" Liv was filled with emotion. She could see their dream becoming a reality.

"Liv, you have given *us* a dream, too. We can all realize our individual dreams as well as the shared dream of this colossal undertaking that can positively affect so many lives! You, Elizabeth and I are not 'The 3Ms' for nothing! We know that our futures are linked as our pinkies were. This endeavor is the epoxy that will bind us."

"For certain, Holly! Let's bless this venture with a prayer," said Elizabeth, the prayer warrior of the group." They joined hands and gave thanks and praise before asking for God's blessing. As always, their prayer culminated in a group hug.

"God is wonderful! His timing is perfect!" Elizabeth declared. As we were praying, the thought was given to me of one of the teachers I spoke of earlier. He is one of the two persons with whom I have had repeat dates. I think I will invite him to your dinner party, Liv. Isn't that something? We will all start the New Year with someone that we love or at least like a lot."

"You guys are great! My attorney is expecting me to bring him at least a tentative business plan. We can spend the time that you will be hanging out with me to work on it.

CHAPTER 28

A BUSY TIME

(12/18/2012) Conversation at breakfast was animated as the three continued to talk about their joint venture. Holly interrupted the flow. "I told my parents I wouldn't be home for Christmas. They will be working all day at the church preparing for the annual Christmas dinner for the needy and homeless again this year. I also told them I would be home tomorrow to discuss something with them and that I would have a couple of friends with me. They're expecting us after lunch. Are we still on?"

"Of course, Holly," Liv agreed for them both. We can go by your apartment first, Elizabeth, then to Holly's house.

(12/19/2012) When Holly let herself and her friends in, the pleasant aroma of freshly baked cookies said, "Welcome!" Mr. Albright was in his easy chair watching the news on TV, and Mrs. Albright was finishing up in the kitchen. "Hi, Daddy! Have you missed me?" she asked, kissing the top of his balding head.

"Hi, Hon. Were you gone?" he teased.

"Oh, Dad!" she said, accepting his teasing. "Where's Mom?"

"She's in the kitchen." Noticing the guests, but not recognizing Liv, he rose from his chair. "Well, well! Elizabeth! Good to see you! How's the family?"

"They're fine, Mr. Albright."

"That's good! And who is *this* young lady?" he asked regarding Liv.

"Don't you recognize her? It's been a long time, but I know if you hear her sing, you will remember Olivia Washington! She used to attend church with us!"

"Olivia! Yes, I remember you! It *has* been a long time . . . years! It's good to see you, Miss Washington. You are still singing, I hope!"

"Yes, I am. It is good to see you as well, Mr. Albright."

Mrs. Albright entered the room. "Oh, you're home! Hi, Honey. Elizabeth, how are you? Merry Christmas!"

"I'm well, thank you. Merry Christmas to you, too, Mrs. Albright!"

"Mom, do you remember Olivia?"

"Olivia? The shy little girl that could sing the devil to his knees?"

"Yes, Mom, that's her!"

Mrs. Albright embraced both of them. "Welcome to our home, ladies! You must have been having a really good time for Holly to have stayed away so long! That's a good thing. She has needed to be more active socially. Please, make yourselves at home!

"I've been baking, as you can probably tell by the aroma. The first batch of cookies is cool enough now. I'll bring them out. There is coffee or tea to drink, or milk, if you like. Holly always liked warm cookies and cold milk! It's amazing that she stays so trim!"

Mrs. Albright was nervous. It was not like Holly to request an audience for the specific purpose of discussing anything. It had seemed out of the ordinary and was disconcerting. Her reaction was to talk, anything to cause a delay.

"Mom!" Holly interjected. "TMI! Relax! We're fine."

"Don't you want some cookies?"

"Sure, Mom. Just bring out the cookies. I'll come and help you with the coffee."

They left and returned shortly with a platter of cookies, five mugs, and a carafe of coffee. During their absence, Elizabeth and Liv were making small talk with Mr. Albright. The group sat quietly a few moments munching cookies and sipping coffee. Finally, Holly got to the point of the visit.

"Mom, Dad, I want to tell you both about a problem I have had. First, I want to assure you that everything is *fine* now. *I* am fine, and we are looking forward to a complete resolution of the problem very soon. I regret that I didn't come to you in the beginning. I know you would have wanted to know and help, but I . . . I guess I was in denial and thought that by pretending it didn't exist, it would just go away.

"I am sorry if my silence until now will make you feel anything other than okay. Again, please be assured that *everything* is now totally fine, although there is still something that we must do to put the nails in the coffin."

"Holly, just tell us what you have to tell us! Don't prolong anything now," her father said. "Obviously, whatever it is, it has been resolved, and you seem to be all right. If you are worried about your mother and me, whatever it is, we love you unconditionally and will support you through whatever else is to be if you allow us, no matter what!"

"Yes, Holly," her mother added. "We love you and want nothing but to support you."

"Holly, you said '*we*.' What do you mean?" her father asked.

"That's why Elizabeth and Olivia are here. Elizabeth is for moral support. Olivia and I are victims."

"Victims? Victims of what?" he asked.

The 3Ms were seated on the sofa with Holly in the middle. Liv took Holly's hand and Elizabeth put her arm around her in support. "Olivia and I were both raped by Pastor Jason!" Her parents were stunned. Mrs. Albright covered her mouth with one hand as if to stifle a scream while the other clutched her chest. Her pain was reflected in her eyes as they brimmed with tears that spilled over and trailed down her cheeks. "Oh, my God!" she said repeatedly.

Mr. Albright's reaction was different, but equally as strong. He closed his eyes as if counting to ten to curtail the rising anger he felt that tightened his jaw and balled his shaking hands into tight fists, exposing blood-drained knuckles. He wanted to hit something! When he opened his eyes, his body relaxed, and he slowly shook his head as if willing it not to be so. "How . . . *when*? My God!" he said.

Mrs. Albright was more pained for what her daughter had endured *alone*. She tried to focus on her saying she was fine. She wanted to demonstrate her love and support for Holly especially, and Liv as well. She could see Holly's regret at not having told them initially and wanted to reassure her. "Come here, Honey. It's all right." She embraced her daughter as they both cried. Mr. Albright rose and put his arms around them both.

"I'm sorry you had to go through that alone. I believe you when you say you are all right now. If you want to talk about it now, or at any time, we're here," her mother assured her.

Holly realized that her parents were secondary victims and would be in need of help to deal with the problems inherent in that situation. Although uncalculated, not having been involved with the dynamics of dealing with the rape of their daughter at the time actually prevented them from experiencing some of the problems that often arise. Holly took this opportunity to help them.

"Mom, Dad, I *do* want to talk about it. I think it will help you to understand better and really see that it's okay. So, please, sit down, and we will explain everything to you." They spent the rest of the afternoon going over in sufficient detail the experience each had and how their lives had been impacted. They talked about their trips to the District Attorney's office, the search for Olivia, the trips to the site, and how they are waiting to be notified when Pastor Jason will be arrested.

"I tell you what I'm going to do! He has come back to our church, and I hear he is planning some kind of program to start next year. In fact, there's talk of an informational meeting at the beginning of the New Year. I'm going to put a *stop* to it!" Mr. Albright was fired up.

"Daddy, please!" Holly cautioned. "We're not supposed to do *anything*! If he finds out what we are doing, he may flee! The District Attorney and the police are handling it, and they will let us know."

"Mr. Albright," Elizabeth questioned, "do you know where and when this meeting will be?"

"No, I don't, but I imagine it will be at the church." Liv looked at Elizabeth, "Elizabeth, are you thinking what I am thinking?"

"Perhaps. What are *you* thinking?" Elizabeth asked.

"I'm thinking that this orientation would be the perfect place, in front of many witnesses, for Pastor Jason to be . . . 'defrocked!' "

"A public defrocksion! That's *much* better than what *I* was thinking," Elizabeth replied excitedly. "I *love* it!"

"Defrocksion? Is that a real word?" Holly asked.

"It is now!" Elizabeth announced. "I just coined it! We will all be witnesses! The whole gathering will be witnesses to his ignominy!"

"Holly, your father and I are glad you have come to us. We can't do anything about what has passed, but we feel much better now that you and Olivia have put it all out for us to know. If *you* are okay, *we* are okay. Rest assured, we will be right there with you ring side when the bum is arrested!"

"I will check with the church secretary and get all the information we will need as soon as it is available; and I'll let Megan know so she can tell her uncle. I know she will want to be there, too."

"Good idea, Holly! Don't you think so, Olivia?"

"Yes, that's perfect! Are we ready to go?"

"Give me a few minutes." Holly packed a few clothes and retrieved her laptop, which contained many of the programs that would facilitate her development of the business plan and other aspects under her purview.

"Well, Mom, Dad, we'd better get a move on. We have some work to do on a project the three of us working on. I will probably not be back until after Christmas. Do you need me for anything before I leave?"

"No, Honey," Mrs. Albright assured her. "You young ladies run along and enjoy yourselves!" Back at Liv's, the ladies began their tasks in earnest. While working on the vision statement, Elizabeth had an idea. "Olivia, can we actually visit with the children? I think it would help Holly and me with our projects and give us more of a sense of ownership. You know how I love kids!"

"Elizabeth, that's a *fantastic* idea. We can go tomorrow!"

Liv was anxious to tell Walter about her engagement. She hurried to call him.

"Hi, Walter. It's me, Liv!" she said excitedly. "Oh, Walter! Guess what!"

"Well, from the sound of things, I'm guessing you're excited about something!"

"Yes! It's official! I have a beautiful engagement ring on my finger, and I want to shout it to the world!"

"Liv, that's fantastic! I'm glad you got things worked out. Do you have the date yet? I still haven't met him!"

"Don't worry. I'm taking care of that. I have tentatively set a date, but I don't want to confirm it without Morgan's input. He is away on business, but he will return by New Year's Eve, and I am planning to have a party at the club.

I am expecting you to be there, and I want you to announce our engagement! Will you do that for me, Walter? You are the only one who can!"

"I wouldn't have it any other way! You know that before I do, I will have to give him the once over! I can't just let *anyone* walk away with the prize of a lifetime! What time do you want me there?"

"I would like for everyone to be in place by seven. I think 8:00 o'clock would be a good time for you to make the announcement! Everyone should have their orders by then. Oh, Walter, I'm so elated! I have to keep pinching myself to make sure this is really *me*!

"Liv, I am so happy that *you* are happy. Remember, I'm taking care of the wedding in every respect. I might as well take care of the engagement party. After all, isn't it the responsibility of the bride's family? All I need from you and your young man are the date and the guest list. You will have the *best* event planning team available!"

"Walter, you're the best! Love you!"

"Love you, too! 'Bye, Sweetheart!"

Liv rejoined her friends busy at work.

"I'm going to call Mom now before I forget to let her know we'll be having two extra guests for Christmas dinner! It will be more than just Roger and Barbara and the twins, that is, if she's not in the labor room. Mom will be *thrilled,* especially when she learns that it will be the two of you."

Liv and Holly continued working on the business plan and other items while Elizabeth made her call.

"Hi, Mom! . . . Yes, I've been having a *great* time . . . No, he didn't call me . . . Really? When . . . All right! I know Barbara is relieved! . . . Yes, of course . . . Have the twins seen their new little sister? Oh, how cute! That's great; they'll be settled by Christmas! Speaking of Christmas, that's why I called . . . Yes, of course I'll be there. I just wanted to make sure you set two extra places! . . . Yes, one for Holly Albright, and one for Olivia Washington! . . . Yes! I knew you would! What time is dinner? Great! Do you want me to bring anything? Okay. See you then. Love you much, Mom!"

"Barbara gave birth to her little girl! Mom and baby and dad are all fine. They will be home for Christmas!" Elizabeth happily told her friends.

"That's great! I've got to get something for the baby. While you guys are working, I'm going to order a few things online," Liv announced. She was not just thinking about the baby. She knew she would never go to the Randall's home for Christmas dinner without bringing lots of gifts for everyone, including her new partners. She proceeded to order thoughtful gifts for each person to be wrapped and delivered by Christmas Eve. She also ordered gifts for the Albrights, Howard and his wife, and Walter.

Liv thought about Morgan and the kids at the Center. She hadn't been involved with anything having to do with Christmas at the Center, although she did know they would be having a party with a Santa and gifts for all the kids. She made a few calls and made provisions for a gang of toys and gifts for everyone at the Center including the staff to be available and delivered by Christmas Eve as well. She wasn't quite sure what to get Morgan, but she knew she wanted it to be special and decided to take care of that after Christmas.

(12/25/2012) Christmas day was exciting for Liv. In a sense, it was her first Christmas, and she was alive with the spirit of it. They had planned to come early to the Randall home to spend quality time before dinner, assist Mrs. Randall, and visit with the new baby and the other children. When they arrived, the pleasant smell of Christmas was heartening. Liv was in a state of bliss just to be a part of it. The Randalls were happy to see Liv after so many years.

"Olivia Washington! What a wonderful surprise! How good it is to see you!" exclaimed Mrs. Randall, encircling her in a motherly embrace. "Come in! Come in, everyone! Holly, welcome. Glad you are joining us, too! How are your folks?"

"They're fine, Mrs. Randall. Merry Christmas!"

"Hi, Mom, hi Dad." Elizabeth greeted her parents with a kiss. "What can we help with?"

"Not a thing," Mr. Randall said. "Just come in and see the newest edition to the family."

"Liv, thank you for the gifts you sent. You shouldn't have! Your presence is probably the best gift ever, especially for Elizabeth!" Mrs. Randall said, "Make yourselves at home."

The 3½-year-old twins had already opened their gifts and were busy playing. Barbara was breast-feeding the baby. Proud papa Roger greeted his sister and her friends heartily and was anxious to introduce Liv to his family. Barbara smiled, "Olivia, I'm glad to finally meet you! I've heard so much about you from Roger and Elizabeth. I can't wait to visit your club and hear you sing! Oh, and thank you for the gifts. That was very thoughtful of you!"

"You are so very welcome, Barbara. I'm glad to meet you as well. You have a beautiful family. You are welcome to come to the club any time. As a matter of fact, I would love it if you can come on New Year's Eve. I'm having a dinner party. It will be a special night that I want to share with all of my friends. Roger, I would love for both of you to come!

"Well, then, it's settled! I'm afraid I won't be performing that night; maybe . . ."

"Dinner is served!" Mrs. Randall announced. Everyone scurried to the dining room for a delicious, traditional Christmas dinner with turkey, corn bread dressing, and all the trimmings.

CHAPTER 29

(12/26/2012) Frank Bynum aggressively pursued his quest to find answers and resolve all of the questions that had arisen since he took on the task of locating Lydia Washington. Armed with the copy of the letter Morgan had faxed to him, he found a private post office located on the first floor of a large office building on Wilshire Blvd. in Beverly Hills. He went there the day after Christmas.

He noted that the first opportunity to retrieve mail each morning, 9:30, had already passed. There were a variety of box sizes. He headed for the larger boxes and located the box number in question. It would be easy to see anyone entering that box because it was the last one on the first row. Surmising that the mail had already been picked up by that time, he decided to come back the next morning.

(12/27/2012) By 9:15 the next morning, Frank had established himself a safe distance away where he was sure to see anyone entering the target box. It wasn't long before a smartly dressed, middle-aged woman emerged from the elevator and headed directly for the boxes. When he was certain that she was the one to follow, Frank moved toward the elevators and ostensibly studied the building directory. By the time the target entered the elevator, four others had preceded her and had selected their floors. He stepped into the elevator right after her, but her floor had already been selected. He positioned himself toward the rear of the car and prepared to exit behind her, shifting his position as necessary.

She exited on the 17th floor, and he followed, pausing to look at the floor's directory as she went to the right. There were arrows pointing to the left for all of the offices except for the one office to the right, The Law Offices of Murphy, Garrison, and Workman. He thought the name had a familiar ring to it. He followed her at a respectable distance and a slower pace.

Frank entered the office and was prepared to make an appointment for another time when the phone rang. While the receptionist was handling the call, Frank was thumbing through his documents and saw the name he had recognized on the directory and the door. He realized that it was the same law firm he had determined owned and/or controlled the property Morgan had asked him to look into some months ago! He found it very curious that this same firm would have a connection with the property and Lydia Washington.

A gentleman entered the reception area from an interior office and was about to leave when he was addressed by the receptionist. "Mr. Murphy, your 10:00 o'clock is running very late due to a big-rig tie-up on the freeway and may have to reschedule."

"Well, I'll give him until 10:45. I will have to leave promptly at 11:00."

As he turned to leave, Frank spoke up, "Excuse me, Mr. Murphy. I was about to ask the receptionist for an appointment to see you. Would it be possible to have a few moments of your time? I couldn't help hearing about your ten o'clock appointment."

Howard turned, "And you are?"

"My name is Frank Bynum. I am a private investigator."

"Mr. Bynum, what is your client's name?"

"I don't know that his name is necessary for the information I am seeking."

"If you are not willing to reveal your client's name, I'm afraid I can't help you," Howard said, turning away.

"She is not my client, but it's regarding Lydia Washington."

Howard turned back, "Lydia Washington? I need to know who is interested in her."

Frank had come this close, and Howard's strong response added to his determination to find out everything there was to know.

"My client is Morgan Avery Calais, if that name means anything to you." Howard concealed his immediate interest but was decidedly eager to know what was up. "Mr. Bynum, please come into my office." Frank followed him into his office.

"Tell me, Mr. Bynum . . ."

"Please, call me 'Frank.'"

"Okay, Frank. I'm Howard. How do you know Lydia Washington? What do you know about her?"

"I don't know her personally. I only know that she has been in a facility in Kansas City, Kansas, for several years. She will be leaving there soon, sometime early next year, I believe."

"How does your client fit in?"

"Mr. Calais is engaged to marry Lydia's daughter, Olivia. Olivia hasn't seen her mother in years. I was hired to find her. He plans to bring her here in time for their wedding."

"Frank, you seem to know much more about the situation than I do. What can I add?"

"I was faxed a note and address that led me here. I'm hoping you can tell me who sent the note and who has been funding Lydia's stay at that facility. If you can, I suspect you may also be able to tell me who is responsible for relocating her to Kansas in the first place."

"Before I address your concerns, tell me, Frank. What do you know about Morgan and Olivia?"

"I have known Morgan since he was a little boy. I know he is crazy in love with Olivia. He was tenacious about finding her mother so that he could surprise her as a special wedding gift. He knows it will mean the world to her!

"Now I have a question for you. Prior to this assignment, Morgan asked me to look into a site in South L.A. I reported that it was owned or controlled by a law firm and was not on the market. Today I find out that yours must be the firm in question. Am I correct?"

"What about Olivia?"

"I have never met her personally. From all accounts, she loves him very much, too."

"Frank, I'm going to tell you what you need to know, but you must promise you won't reveal what I tell you until after they are married."

"I have to tell you, Howard, I don't know that I can make such a promise in advance."

"I appreciate that. I can see you are a man of integrity, and I feel you have a high regard for Morgan that I believe is extended to Olivia. I think that you will know what to reveal and when, so I will tell you."

Howard picked up the phone and dialed his secretary. "Ja'Sha, please call my 10:00 o'clock and reschedule and clear my calendar for the rest of the day. Thanks.

"Frank, I am going to fill in your gaps because I am impressed with your integrity and your tenacity in getting to this point. In fact, if you are amenable to it, I would like to retain you for assignments that arise regularly. What do you say to that?"

"Thank you, Howard, for your confidence. Of course I would be very grateful for any light you can shed. There is a possibility that I may be able to freelance for you in the future. Shall we address that at a later time?"

"Of course, Frank. What is your calendar like for today? Are you free to spend a little time with me, perhaps lunch and after?"

"I am as free as I need to be to complete this investigation to my client's satisfaction."

"Good! Your account provided insight for me. Liv worked as a live-in caregiver for a long-time friend and client of mine, Theodore Henry, where she remained for several years until his death earlier this year. That is when I personally met her. By then she had developed into the wonderful young woman she is today.

"Theo had a trusted friend and distant relative of his deceased wife by the name of Walter La Salle that he asked to befriend and look out for her where he couldn't, being physically challenged. Even so, he was mentally sharp as a tack and very insightful!

"Walter is a very wealthy man in his own right and is also an avid philanthropist. He had been working with Theo on his and his wife's dream project. The plan has virtually been put in place, waiting to be implemented when the principal players, Olivia and Morgan, are ready.

"Theo took me off the streets when I was just a snotty-nosed, pimply-faced, wannabe gangbanger and turned my life completely around. He kept me from going down the wrong path and saw that I finished school and got into college. He mentored and sponsored me financially, taking me under his wing. He saw me through my graduation from Harvard Law School and helped me get my practice up and running. He was my first client and became my most trusted friend. The only thing he ever required of me was to do for someone else what he had done for me. I learned so much from him about life, about respect and responsibility, about giving back.

What he did for me is the core of what his dream was—to have his modus operandi duplicated ad infinitum into a system that will benefit students, families, communities, businesses and corporations, cities, states, and the nation, all sprouting from the seed of the Calais Education and Community Center.

"Theo was a very unique, insightful, and gifted individual. He was disillusioned by the educational system in this country. He considered it to be ineffective, self-serving, stagnant, and discriminatory, relegating unfortunate members of society to perpetual failure and poverty. He realized that the perpetuation of the status quo would cause irreparable harm and be detrimental to the future of this country, putting it in severe jeopardy. He determined to use his influence and resources to do something about it, and he did.

"For the last 20 years of his life, Theo was busy networking and influencing other like-minded philanthropists to join him in his endeavor to reform the educational system, thereby causing an eventual paradigm shift in the national educational system and the nation. He established a vast network of influential individuals and companies in all areas that are dedicated to the project. The status quo will go down kicking and screaming, but it will eventually have to accede.

"The property you investigated is an inheritance to be turned over to Morgan Avery Calais and Olivia Louise Washington upon their marriage. When Liv came to me for advice, she told me about the young man she planned to marry and talked about the dream he had which she shared and about the property they had seen. When she gave me his name and the address of the property, I knew that everything was coming to fruition. I told Liv what Theo had done. She wanted to surprise Morgan with the news of the property as *her* wedding present to *him.* So, you see, that is why I hope you will not spoil the surprise for them."

"That is some story! I wouldn't think of spoiling it. Theirs sounds like a fairytale!

"If I may change the subject for a moment, I'd like to talk about Liv's brother, Kevin, who is incarcerated. I became aware that there is a group of law students that has been following his case. They determined there are questions of probable misconduct on the part of the prosecution that may enable him to be released, the sentence reduced to time served, or some other remedy. They have been working on it for a while, and I don't know where they are in the process.

"What is clear is that the prosecution withheld the results of its own expert witness's report that said Kevin was not in his right mind at the time he shot and killed his father. Had the report been entered into evidence, and/or had the expert witness been allowed to testify to his finding, the verdict may have been much different. I'm just wondering if there is anything that can be done to move this process along to a favorable outcome, namely, his release in time to attend his sister's wedding."

"Umm, it may be a possibility. It's worth a try. If you can get me all of the particulars—dates, court jurisdiction, case number, etc.—I can pass the information on to the appropriate person or persons in our network. It reaches even into the Governor's office, so an outright pardon is within the realm of possibility."

"That would be fantastic! Please tell me a little more about this network."

Howard looked at his watch. "We're about to miss lunch! Why don't we continue this conversation over lunch? My treat!"

"Sounds good to me! We're in your neck of the woods, so I'll follow your lead."

Howard drove to his favorite working lunch spot where he gave Frank an in-depth overview of "the Master Plan" epitomizing Theo and Eleanor's dream.

Over lunch and well into the evening, Howard described in detail the network and all the players. By the time he finished expounding on all the virtues of the network and its commitments he could think of, Frank was sold on becoming an integral part of the system. That meeting was the beginning of a long working relationship and a lasting friendship.

CHAPTER 30

Liv was working on her song lists when Morgan called.

"Hi, Morgan!" she said, rather animated.

"Hi, Sweetheart! You sure sound excited. Did you really miss me that much?"

"Of course I did! You have been gone more than two weeks!"

"I'm catching the first direct flight I can! I'll be home by tomorrow! I'll call you and let you know when I'll be landing! See you then, Love!"

Liv anxiously waited for Morgan's arrival. His plane would arrive at 6:40 a.m., and he wanted to come there directly from the airport.

It was almost 6:30, and she had just completed her morning workout. She hurriedly jumped in the shower. She busied herself visualizing how she would prove to herself and to Morgan that she was "cured," ready to be a real woman! Flinging herself into his arms and kissing him passionately on the lips was her first thought. No, she knew that wasn't her style. She had not suddenly become a wanton hussy. Liv realized she wasn't good at visualizing for herself something so foreign to her. She decided to wait and see.

Her heart started to flutter when she heard the chimes. She experienced a surge of nervousness—*not* driven by fear, but by excited anticipation. She wanted to appear cool and calm. She took a deep, slow breath and exhaled slowly through pursed lips. She opened the door and looked up into Morgan's eyes as she held the door open for him.

Morgan immediately noticed a difference in her. He wanted to pull her to him and just hold her close! Instead, he took her hand from the edge of the door and entered, still holding her hand as he closed the door behind him. Then he kissed her hand. Liv took his hand in her hands and raised it to her lips and kissed his palm, all the while steadily gazing into his eyes.

She wanted him to *see* what she wanted to say: "I missed you. I love you. I am no longer that fearful, abused child afraid to touch and be touched. I am ready to be the woman I long to be for you. I want to feel your arms around me. I want to be held. I am presenting my lips to you to be kissed. Kiss me now!"

The effect on Morgan was immediate and profound as she moved closer to him and embraced him. Morgan instinctively put his arms around her, searching her eyes. Liv tilted her head back, unmistakably indicating she wanted to be kissed on the lips. Morgan responded by gently brushing his lips lightly against hers. She closed her eyes and sighed, keeping her lips almost touching his, and tightened her arms around him. He answered by kissing her again with slightly more pressure.

Liv felt a surge of pleasurable warmness that sent a tremor throughout her body. She felt her knees weaken and threaten to buckle. It seemed that every nerve ending in her body exploded into fireworks of pleasurable sensations. She was putty in his hands as she consciously surrendered herself completely to him.

Morgan thought about Birdie's fragile artifact that he had desired to hold so badly which had disintegrated in his hands. He thought about Liv's vulnerability and her fragile inner child. He didn't want to do anything that might prove detrimental. He realized and was faithful to his responsibility in his charge to protect her from hurt and harm. Inherent was the obligation not to consummate their relationship outside of marriage. He knew that was something Liv would not want, and neither did he. He forced his head to overrule his heart and his surging hormones, aka the COW. Still, he had to hold her closer to him and prolong the moment as long as he dared.

Liv rested her head against his chest and seemed to go limp in his arms. He felt her melt into his arms as if their bodies were morphing into one. Their hearts were beating in sync, and Liv allowed herself to experience the sensations surging through every part of her being which she could never have imagined. Finally being held in the arms of the first and only man she had ever loved in this way, with his chin resting gingerly on the top of her head and intermittently kissing her hair, was so totally pleasurable, emotional, and overwhelming, Liv could only cry.

Morgan immediately loosened his grip. "Baby! Please don't cry. What is the matter? Tell me, Sweetheart. Should I stop?"

"Morgan, I *love* you! Oh, how I love you!" she said as she held him tighter. She had finally said those words Morgan had been waiting to hear! He kissed away her tears, closed his eyes and drew her close again. He was in a serious quandary. This was *not* the position he wanted to be in when those words were uttered! He did not want to break his contact with her body, not now! He knew he had to end it while his larger head was still in control. He decided to use levity as a distraction. He stepped back, holding her at arms' length and said, "Who *are* you, and what have you done with *Liv*?"

Liv took him by the hand and led him into the great room where she sat him down on the couch. She sat beside him at a right angle with one foot on the floor and her leg bent beneath her so that she was looking at him straight ahead.

"Morgan, love," she began, "so much has happened while you were away!"

"I can *see* that, but you haven't answered my question. Are you some kind of sensual alien being that has taken over my Liv's body?"

"Don't be silly! If that were the case, we wouldn't just be *sitting* here on my couch *talking*! Seriously, Morgan, there is just too much that has transpired. I hope you don't have to rush off right away. We'll have plenty of time to get ready for tonight. I have already made arrangements for everything. New Year's Eve is a special event at the club. This year it is even more special because, well, it just is. In the interim, I want to fill you in as much as I can on everything! And, by the way, Morgan, I've changed my mind about our wedding!"

"Whoa!" Morgan exclaimed. "What are you talking about? Surely you haven't changed your mind about *marrying* me!"

"I'm sorry, Morgan. I've gotten so ahead of myself. Never in a million years could I change my mind about marring *you*! I know you detected my near-panic reaction to the thought of setting a date within three or four months. To me it felt like a pronouncement of three or four months to *live*! I was so consumed with fear. That just didn't seem like enough time for me to come to this point in my existence! But because of everything that has happened, I don't *want* to wait, especially not now, not after today! I never *dreamed* I could feel so . . . I don't know *how* to describe how it feels to be in your arms, having your lips touching mine. I just know I *want* that! I *need* that! I want us to get married as soon as possible! And I want a *real* wedding, not just a low-key trip downtown to be married in a judge's chambers!"

Morgan was really perplexed. "Okay, I ask you again. Who *are* you?"

Liv had been so animated and talking a mile a minute, it was hard for Morgan to make sense of anything. Besides, he was still trying to recover his equilibrium from the effects of holding her so closely.

"I can't help myself, Morgan. I'm just so excited. Let me calm myself down. Are you hungry? I can fix you something to eat."

Food was the last thing on his mind. "No, thanks, Honey. Just tell me what's going on."

"Okay, but first I think I need to put more space between us. I don't seem to be able to function right so close to you. It's too hot, and I can't concentrate." Liv shifted to the ottoman and proceeded to give an overview of the events beginning with her reunion with Elizabeth and Holly. She recounted the trip to the DA's office, leading the way to "The Cave," her epiphany, the anticipated legal proceedings, her need to testify, everything. Everything that is, except anything having to do with the property and Holly and Elizabeth's involvement with their dream. She never intended it to be a secret. She just wanted him to meet them first.

Morgan tried very hard to give his undivided attention to what she was saying, but he found it difficult as the COW was aggressively trying to coerce him in another direction.

The Chairman of the Board put forth his best, most forceful plea. "What's the matter with you, man! Just *look* at her; she's beautiful, and she *wants* you! She *needs* you! You heard her say it. She told you that she *loves* you! What are you waiting for?"

"Look! I know what I'm doing. This is all new to her. She's like a child just tasting candy for the first time, and she wants more. *Of course*, she wants more! Children don't know what is best for them. That is why they have parents whose responsibility it is to make sure they are protected, even from themselves. Right now, I am in the role of parent, so back off!"

"Man, this is what we . . . what *you* have *wanted*! It is being handed to you on a silver platter! All you have to do is *go* for it. She is putty in your hands! Think about what you are passing up! You are a healthy, normal, red-blooded, virile man! This is *abnormal*!"

"Listen up! You will *not* persuade me. She is vulnerable, and I will *not* take advantage of her. In my eyes she is pure and undefiled. That is the way she will remain until our wedding day. So you had just better accept it. *I* am the brains of this operation! You stand down, *now*!"

With that business settled, Morgan was able to absorb the summation of events Liv was relating. He was especially pleased to know that she had renewed her unilaterally severed spiritual relationship with God. That was something he had wanted for her but knew better than to overtly promote.

When Liv had concluded her recount, Morgan drew her from her position on the ottoman, took her in his arms, and just held her benignly. "Liv, you have really been through a lot. I had no idea! Why didn't you let me know? I would have rushed to be here without a moment's hesitation!"

"I know you would have, Morgan, but this was a period that I had to go through alone. I had so many things to work out that only *I* could do. But I am *so* happy that you are here now!"

"I'm glad you had a nice Christmas with your friends. I didn't tell you about my plans for Christmas at the Center. I didn't want you to feel obligated or uneasy. They had a great party with a Santa and many helpers to distribute gifts to all. There also was a traditional turkey dinner with all the trimmings for them and their families. They took plenty of pictures!

"By the way, Liv, I have a present for you." He reached for his jacket and took out the beautifully foil-wrapped box that he obtained during his trip to New York and handed it to Liv. "If you want, you can consider it a belated Christmas gift."

Liv removed the foil and opened the box. She removed a small crystal bottle filled with liquid. Etched in calligraphy was simply, "LIV'S SCENT!" "Oh, it's perfume!" was her delighted response. Amused, Morgan watched her, waiting to see her reaction after smelling the scent. She removed the cap and sniffed. Her brow furrowed and she sniffed again.

Finally, Liv looked at Morgan with a mixture of questioning and of not wanting to hurt his feelings. "I don't smell *anything*!" she exclaimed. "Well, if *this* is my scent, I suppose not smelling like *anything* is better than smelling *stinky*! It's a *beautiful* bottle, though!"

Chuckling, Morgan let her off the hook. "I'm sorry, Sweetheart. I just wanted to see your reaction! You can't smell it that way. What releases the scent, and what makes it *your* scent is *you*! This becomes *your* scent when it interacts with *your* body chemistry! It won't smell the same on anyone else's body! Here!" He took the perfume from her and put a dab on each of her wrists. "It's very potent. It is your body heat that activates the reaction and releases the scent. Rub your wrists together, and *then* smell!"

Liv did so and was amazed at the subtle aroma that charmed her nostrils.

"Oh, my *goodness*! This is *heavenly*!" Liv was thoroughly pleased. "It is faint, not overpowering! I love it! No one else will ever smell like this?"

"No. Only you, my love." Morgan took an intoxicating breath, inhaling 'Liv's Scent." "Your scent is now forever recorded in my olfactory sensors!"

Now that Morgan had given her a gift, Liv thought now would be a good time to give him the special gift she had tailor made for him. "Wait, Morgan. I'll be right back." Liv exited the room and returned promptly with a gift-wrapped box. "I think now is a good time to give this to you," she said, placing the box in his hand.

Shaking the box and feeling the movement, he asked, "What is it?"

"Open it!" Morgan opened the box and removed the content. He held up the 3½-inch diameter key ring, which was made of tempered steel and coated in twenty-four carat gold. Permanently attached to the keychain was a heart-shaped gold charm, which was engraved with "MAC" on one side, and "Liv's Heart" on the other side.

Morgan looked at the key ring and knew that it had cost a pretty penny. He appreciated that Liv was "giving him her heart," but he didn't see a practical use for a key ring of that size and strength. "Liv, this is *beautiful*, but you shouldn't have spent this kind of money. I don't know if it would be possible to fill this chain even if I put every key we *both* have ever owned on it. Regardless, Sweetheart, I will always have your heart!" he said, and kissed her softly.

"Well, until you have enough keys, you can wear it like a bracelet on your wrist, if you dare!" she teased.

"In that case, I dare!" He put the key ring around his wrist.

"There's one more thing. Wait right here!" Liv went to her office and returned with a small envelope and handed it to him. He removed a set of keys, which he recognized as keys to her condo. He was moved as he saw the trust she demonstrated.

"I just can't believe my good fortune in having you in my life, Liv! You are a real blessing to me. And I can't tell you how proud I am of you for your bravery, your strength, and your commitment to obtain justice and to protect future would-be victims. I hope you know that although I know you will be able to handle the ordeal to its conclusion, I will not let you go through any more, any part of it, without me right there by your side. That's a promise!"

"Thank you, Morgan." Liv kissed him and rested her head on his chest for a moment, speaking only the tacit language of love.

Liv told him about how Walter wanted to meet him and also make all of the provisions for their wedding. She also felt secure enough to tell him about seeing Howard to have him look into the possibility of adopting Alex.

Morgan was moved that Liv had taken that step. He loved Alex and would love for them to adopt her. He knew how much Liv loved her, too; but he didn't want to suggest her adoption until they had a period of adjustment to marriage.

"Liv, would you really adopt Alex?"

"In a heartbeat! You *know* how much I love that little girl! I would adopt her today, if possible."

"By the way, when will I get a chance to meet all of these people who have been so instrumental in your evolution?"

"Oh, Morgan, I completely left out a critical bit of information! We're not just celebrating the New Year together. I am having a New Year's Eve *dinner* party tonight! I want you to meet my friends and the significant people in my life, and I want everyone to meet you! I've been so beside myself, I even asked Walter to announce our engagement tonight! I hope that's okay with you."

"Sweetheart, anything you do is okay with me. You *know* that. *Nothing* makes me happier than to know that you feel the way you do about me, about us, about Alex! I have wanted to shout to the world about our love from the night I first saw you!"

"Can you bring Birdie tonight? Do you think she will come?"

Morgan had envisioned bringing in the new year with just the two of them, but he wasn't disappointed that it was going to be a real party. He was interested in meeting the people who were important to Liv as they were very likely to become significant in his life as well.

"Knowing Birdie, she's probably already picked out what she will wear!"

"I will send a car for her so she won't have to stay for too many hours, and she can leave whenever she wants to."

"That's ideal. Birdie is a free spirit and doesn't like to be relegated to someone else's time frame. She was never one to intrude or interfere with young people having fun once she had a chance to assess them. By the way, who is on the guest list?"

"Let's see. There are Holly and Elizabeth and their dates, Elizabeth's brother and his wife, Walter, and Howard and his wife. Adding Birdie, that makes ten. You and I, of course, are the guests of honor! I want you also to personally meet the members of my band. Monday and Tuesday evenings are their off days. They all are my friends, too. It will be a treat for them to be included and have a chance to wine and dine and be waited on instead of providing the music. I've invited them all and their dates. There will be a DJ. It will be a real *party* party!

"Some of the guests *I* will be meeting for the first time. *You* will be meeting *all* of them for the *first* time, except Birdie, of course, so I want *you* to be on your *best behavior*!"

"You got it!"

"Oh, goodness, Morgan! In all my planning, I didn't even think that you might have friends you would want to be included, and it's so *late* now! Is it too late for you to invite anyone? I have only met a few of your friends, outside the Community Center, that is. I remember Kyle and Travis. Do you think they may want to come?"

"I will call Kyle and Travis. I'm sure they will want to come if they can. There were four of us at one time; but the other now former friend, Charles, is out of my circle. The guys say I have deserted them, first in favor of my friends at the Community Center, and now especially, *you*. I think they're jealous because they know they will never find anyone like you. There *is* none other like you! I am an *enviable* son of a gun!

"There's an old family friend I'd like to invite as well. His name is Frank Bynum. He will probably be coming alone, if he is available."

Seeing an opportunity to learn a little bit more about him, specifically, how a friend can be eliminated from his circle, Liv inquired. "What did Charles do to be eliminated from your circle of friends? It must have been something pretty awful!" Sensing his reluctance to address the issue, Liv quickly added, "Oh, never mind. Besides, you haven't been home yet. You probably have some things you need to catch up on before tonight.

"Oh, Morgan, I'm sorry! I've been so caught up in my own events, I didn't even ask you about your trip! How was it?"

"Don't worry a second about it, Honey. It was . . . dull, but successful. I will have to do a follow-up visit in a bit; but nothing will interfere with my being here for you when things get hairy.

"Liv, you asked me a question that has gone unanswered. You told me that you referred to me as the 'Mysterious Stranger.' I don't want there to be any mysteries about me where you are concerned. I want to answer your question.

"You know that it was Kyle who first brought me to your club. He had been there before with Travis, and they both had tried to hit on you.

They appreciated the fact that you didn't let on that you had had an encounter with them when I introduced you. Anyway, the four of us were there that night. Kyle thought that enough time had elapsed that you might not remember him. They were just behaving like the immature, hormone-driven boys they are. I just sat quietly, listening to you and keeping my own secret. They kept asking my opinion, what I thought about you."

"What did you say about me?"

"I simply told them that I was going to marry you!"

"You *didn't*! What did they say?"

"Of course they didn't take me seriously. Kyle just laughed and said, 'Ha! When pigs fly!'

"When your set was over, the two of them went up to try their luck. Charles was unmoved since you were not his cup of tea. He had never hidden the fact that he was gay. We all knew it, and it wasn't an issue for any of us, until that night. Maybe because I gave no outward sign that I was dealing with my own raging hormones, Charles decided I was in the closet and was reluctant to come out. I don't know how long he had felt that way. I suspect he was waiting for what he thought was a good opportunity. He started making inappropriate comments, subtle at first, but then increasingly bold.

"The four of us had been hanging out for several years, doing things guys do. His sexual preference had never entered the picture. It was understood that the four of us were just buddies. You know, Liv, I'm a pretty open-minded guy. I'm tolerant and patient. But when I tell a person something and am reasonably sure they understand the words I am saying, I expect them to accept what I say when it concerns me, or anything within my realm. He didn't.

"When he started his banter, I reminded him that I didn't swing that way and to knock it off. When I felt his hand on my knee, that was the last straw! Too bad for *him* he was sitting to my right. I may not have been so effective with my left hand. I was *thoroughly* peeved. I gave him a cold glare, reached down, and jerked his finger back so hard and fast, it snapped. I'm not proud that I broke his finger or at least dislocated it. That was not my intent. But I had told him to back off!"

"What did he do?"

"I *know* he was in pain! I had a similar dislocation wrestling, so I know how it feels. I'm glad he didn't make a scene in your club. He simply got up and left, nursing his finger and, I suspect, trying not to cry. What else was he going to do?

"I hope you don't think less of me, Liv. That was a knee-jerk reaction that took both of us by surprise."

"Believe me, Morgan. I have had to dislocate a few fingers, break a nose or two, and certainly exercise my knee joint by smashing it into the crotch of a few guys who didn't know what 'no' meant!"

"I bet you did!" Morgan said, remembering the shiner she gave him.

"When Kyle and Travis returned after their thorough humiliation at your hands, they asked about Charles. It turned out that he had pulled similar stunts with each of them. I had no plans to keep him out of *their* circles. It just eventually turned out that way.

"Well, I'd better get going. Would it be too presumptuous of me to ask for a goodbye kiss?"

"What makes you think I would let you go without one? And, by the way, just so you know, the day of the 'hand kiss' is definitely over!"

Morgan smiled, "Come here, you!" He cupped her chin in his hand and tilted her head back as he leaned in to place a series of kisses on her lips, her eyes, her nose, and returning to her lips as he pulled her closer to him and nuzzled her neck. With a final kiss, he reluctantly left, happy as a lark!

CHAPTER 31

Liv's head was still in the clouds as she gazed at the ring on her finger and entertained erotic thoughts of Morgan. She relived the time spent in his arms, and allowed herself to dwell on the sensations she experienced that were resurfacing as she reflected. "Liv, you *did* it! You *really did* it!" she said to herself. She couldn't erase the smile from her face.

She forced herself to go about doing what she needed to do to prepare for the big night ahead. She had laid out her clothes earlier and had selected the jewelry she would wear with the simply elegant, ankle-length sapphire dress she had ordered for the occasion. She was all ready when Morgan arrived.

The sight of her took his breath away. "Oh my God, Liv!" he said as he took her into his arms and kissed her passionately. "Do we really have to go?"

"Of course we do!" she replied breathlessly. "And I think we had better leave right now!"

"A penny for your thoughts," Morgan said, breaking the silence after Liv had been so quiet since they left. "You're not worried about anything, are you?"

"Oh, no, I'm not *worried* about anything. I just want you to like all of my friends. I know they will like you! I've told them all about you."

"You have, have you?" Liv smiled sheepishly and nodded. "What did you tell them about me?"

"I told them all they needed to know—that you love me, and I love you!"

"What? You told your *friends* you loved me before you told *me*? I'm crushed!"

Liv knew he was feigning his indignation. "Come off it, Morgan! You know you knew! You *always* knew! You *also* knew that I couldn't *tell* you until *I* was ready!"

"Yes, Honey," he said softly, "I knew. Besides, what else could you do but love me!" he jested. "Don't be concerned about your friends. If they are good enough for you to call them friends, then that's good enough for me!"

Liv had wanted for the two of them to arrive before any of their friends did so they could greet them together and handle the introductions up front. Walter was already there and was coming toward them. He greeted her with a bear hug and a kiss as Morgan waited.

"Honey, you smell wonderful!" he exclaimed. "What scent is that? I don't think I have ever smelled it before! And I have *never* seen you look more radiant!"

Liv looked at Morgan, who was beaming at her with a knowing smile. She blushed as she thought about their earlier encounter. She had been all aglow ever since.

"No, you haven't. It is a gift I received today from Morgan." Taking Morgan's hand and urging him closer, she said, "Morgan, this is my father, Walter La Salle! Walter, meet Morgan!"

They were surprised as they recognized each other.

"This is your father?" Morgan asked.

"Yes, my adopted dad! Do you two *know* each other?"

"Yes, we kind of do," Walter said. "I don't think I have been here a single time that I didn't see you here, too!" he said to Morgan. "Besides me, of course, you are probably her biggest fan!"

"I have to confess that is true," Morgan admitted. "You know, Walter, we even shared a table for a moment or two one *very* crowded night some time ago. I was with a couple of pals!'

"Why, yes, I think I do remember! I am happy to formally meet you. I just hope you know what a wonderful, precious prize you have in my daughter! I know you will honor her in the way she deserves. Anything less, young man, you will have *me* to contend with!"

"Walter, I value your daughter more than my own life! I will never dishonor her *or* you. Of course, these are only words. But time will prove them to be true, there is no doubt."

"I know, son. I know."

Shortly the guests began to arrive. Holly and Elizabeth with their escorts came first. The gentlemen had to stand by while the 3M's hugged and admired each other's attire. Holly and Elizabeth were both knockouts in their own rights.

"Morgan, these are my two best friends in the whole world! This is Elizabeth Randall, and this is Holly Albright! They are both as smart as they are beautiful inside and out! Ladies, this is *Morgan!*"

Ever the gentleman, Morgan took each of their hands in turn, and kissed the back of each, causing them to blush, secretly signaling their approvals to Liv. "It is so nice to finally meet you, Morgan," Holly said.

"Yes, Morgan," Elizabeth added. "Olivia has told us so many wonderful things about you. It's really nice to finally meet you."

"Ladies, the pleasure is all mine. As I told Liv—Olivia, any friend of hers is a friend of mine as well."

Holly took the arm of her escort to be introduced. Before introducing him, Holly winked at Liv and communicated silently a message that Liv received loud and clear as she recognized that Holly seemed to have worked out her problems with William.

"Olivia, Morgan, everyone, this is William Lacey." William was a very nice-looking, personable young man who seemed extremely taken with Holly. He had an air of confidence about him and despite his height, gave Liv the impression of a gentle giant. He was well spoken and had a charming smile. His dark chocolate skin made his teeth look like what one might expect to see in a toothpaste commercial. Liv remembered Holly's description of him as being somewhat "nerdy," but she saw no trace of it. More than anything, though, she was relieved that she had no recollection of any prior interaction with him. She was happy for Holly.

"Okay, it's *my* turn!" Elizabeth summoned her escort with a nod of her head and waited for him to come and stand beside her. She took his hand and said, "Everyone, I want you to meet Allan Reynolds." It was easy to see who was in control! It was also easy to see that Allan was happy to have effervescent Elizabeth take charge. "Allan is working on his doctorate and is probably the most intelligent teacher in the entire school district! He is especially good with the troublemakers! He speaks softly, but he carries a big, I mean *big* stick."

Allan was clearly uncomfortable with Elizabeth's introduction. He tactfully put an end to it when she came up for air. "Don't blame Elizabeth. I made her say all of those things! Hello, everyone. I'm really glad to meet all of you, and I'm looking forward to getting to know you better."

"Excuse me a moment," Morgan interrupted. "I see my grandmother is here!" As he left to escort Birdie, Liv directed everyone to follow her to their tables where Walter was already seated, looking over his planned announcement. By seven o'clock, all of the band members and their dates had arrived as well.

Morgan entered with Birdie, followed by Frank, who had come with Howard and his wife Kaye, and Roger and Barbara Randall.

The dining room had already filled almost to capacity by the time Liv's guests were all seated. Morgan and Liv had the prominent seats at the head of the main table with Walter to Liv's right and a place for Birdie to Morgan's left. Morgan escorted Birdie to the table and Liv rose to greet her. Birdie smiled and gave her a warm embrace.

"My child," she said for Liv's ears only, "I am happy to see you have worked out your problems!"

"Yes, Birdie, I have," Liv returned her smile. "Thank you!" To the crowd she announced, "Everyone, meet Birdie, Morgan's venerable grandmother. There were greetings all around. Walter took charge, clinking on his water glass to get the attention of the gathering.

"May I have your attention everyone," he said, and paused until everyone was still. At that point, Kyle and Travis entered with their dates and took their seats. "There are still some introductions to be made. Morgan, perhaps you and Liv can go around and introduce everyone."

Morgan took Liv's hand and together they proceeded to make the introductions, each one introducing their friends.

Liv began, "First of all, welcome! Thank you for coming to help us bring in the best New Year ever, 2013!" Everyone applauded.

"For those who may not know me, I am Olivia Washington to my old friends from back in the day," she said looking toward Holly and Elizabeth, "and Liv to my new friends. I will answer to either name! This mysterious stranger at my side is Morgan Avery Calais!

"And now, may I present the members of the greatest band ever to those of you who don't know them." Liv went around the table introducing each member of the band and the instruments they play. They, in turn, introduced their spouses and/or dates. After Liv had introduced all of her friends, Morgan introduced Birdie, Frank, Kyle, and Travis, who each introduced their dates.

All of the orders had been taken, and there was lively conversation throughout until the entrees began to be served. Everyone was enjoying the music, the meal, and the conversation. At approximately 8:00 o'clock, Walter again commanded the attention of the guests and addressed everyone in the club. At his cue, bottles of champagne had been delivered to every table, and the servers were pouring the champagne.

"Ladies and gentlemen, as you can see, there is champagne being poured for everyone with my compliments. It is my distinct pleasure to formally announce the engagement of my beloved surrogate daughter, our own Miss Olivia Louise Washington, whom most of you know as Ms. Liv . . ." (Liv and Morgan both stood and Walter took Liv's hand) ". . . to this extremely lucky young man . . ." (and took Morgan's hand and joined them) " . . . Mr. Morgan Avery Calais!"

The room exploded with applause as everyone expressed their sentiments. Many of the patrons were taken by surprise, and there was some disappointment on the part of some of the young men. They quieted down as Walter began his toast.

"I propose this toast to you, Liv, and to you, Morgan. May the light of love that shines so brightly in your eyes tonight continue to grow and glow brighter and brighter as you prepare to begin the New Year in a new journey to a bright and prosperous life as man and wife, bound together in love, one and inseparable, from this day forth! Okay, son, you have my permission to kiss her now!"

Morgan looked at Liv in that way that made her want to melt into him, and she blushed like a schoolgirl! "Why Ms. Liv! Are you blushing?" he teased. Not only was she blushing, she was praying, "Please, knees, don't buckle!" The crowd was anxiously waiting, especially Holly and Elizabeth! In a playful, teasing mood, Morgan put her hand to his lips and kissed it as he had done so many times before. Not about to be outdone, Liv grabbed a handful of his hair, pulled his head up, and kissed him passionately on the lips, putting her arms around his neck and shocking him to attention with a touch of tongue! He responded by wrapping his arms around her and holding her so tightly, they were both glad when Walter called, "Time out!"

The rest of the evening was filled with mirth. Billy had put together plenty of the best music for the DJ to play, and there was plenty of dancing, food, party favors, and fun, fun, fun!

About ten thirty, Birdie approached Liv. "Liv, I am so happy to see you and Morgan together like this. You have made him *and* me very happy. Is there someplace we can talk in private a moment?"

"Of course, Birdie. Come with me to my dressing room." Birdie followed Liv and took a seat immediately. "Is something wrong, Birdie? Are you all right?"

"Yes, I'm fine, child. I am getting ready to go home, so . . ."

"But Birdie!" Liv exclaimed, "It's barely ten-thirty. You will miss New Years!"

"No, I won't miss it. It will be New Year's at my place, too. Besides, I don't want to turn into a pumpkin!"

Liv smiled. She could see where Morgan got his joking from. "She *is* joking, I hope," Liv thought to herself.

"Liv, I wanted to give you *this*," she said as she handed Liv another sealed manila envelope. Liv took the envelope. She was almost afraid to ask, but she did anyway.

"What is this, Birdie?"

"You might say it's your future." Sensing Liv's worry, she quickly added, "Now don't give it a second thought. We'll just leave it here for now. You go back out there and have some fun. You haven't danced with Morgan, or *anyone*! Go and dance! You and Morgan can open this later when you go home. He will be able to explain it to you, you will be able to explain it to him, and there is something that neither of you will need to have explained!"

"Oh, Birdie, I can't dance! I haven't danced in anybody's arms ever before! I've never even *thought* about it. I wouldn't know what to do. I should have taken some kind of lessons! What am I going to do?" she said more to herself than to Birdie.

"Calm yourself, child! You and Morgan are spiritually, soon to be physically one. You are in perfect sync! Just hold on to him and he will lead you. Your breath is the same. Your rhythm is the same. Now get out there and dance!"

They left the dressing room and the envelope and found Morgan. "Morgan, Birdie is leaving now. Let's see her out."

"We're glad you came, Birdie. I didn't think you would stay this long, but I am glad you did. I told Liv you were a free spirit!"

"I don't need an escort! Here the driver is now. You two go back and join your guests." She hugged Liv fondly and gave Morgan a peck. "Go back in there and dance. Olivia wants to dance with you!" They waited until the driver took off and then went back to join the party. "Liv, I didn't know you wanted to dance. Come on, they're playing our song!"

"I didn't know we *had* a song."

"We do now." Morgan took her in his arms and they began to sway to a smooth rendition of "Forever Love." The contact with his body sent thrills through Liv and she found herself at one with him, basking in the wonder of it all. She could feel his heart beating faster as he tightened his grip. They were in a paradise of their own, oblivious to all others.

So went the rest of the night. The next thing they knew, the countdown to 2013 had begun, and everyone began activating their noisemakers and kissing in the New Year!

"Happy New Year, Liv!"

"Happy New Year, Morgan!"

Liv was exceptionally quiet as Morgan drove her home. Morgan attributed it to the excitement of the day and all of the activity at the Club. He was busy reliving his reception on his return and dancing with Liv, holding her so closely as they glided across the floor. He was extremely pleased with how the evening turned out and was glad Liv had taken it upon herself to put everything together so quickly. He really enjoyed meeting her friends. He could see including them all in his circle.

Liv's eyes were closed, and he thought she might have dozed off. "Wake up, Sleepyhead, you're home!"

Liv stirred. "I'm not asleep. I was just in my head, where I seem to be a lot these days."

"And just what is making that pretty head of yours do so much overtime thinking?"

Morgan unlocked the door and let them in, intending only to say good night and leave so she could get at least a few hours of quality sleep.

"Morgan, don't go," Liv surprised him. "I want you to stay with me tonight. Somehow, I don't want to be alone right now." Morgan was stunned! He had never spent the night with her, although he would gladly have done so. Now she was asking him to stay. He felt that something was wrong.

"Liv, what's wrong? Why do you want me to stay? I'll be back in a few hours, remember?"

"So what's the reason you are reluctant to stay with me, just a few more hours?" Liv was stalling for time, grabbing at straws. "Are you afraid I might seduce you or something?" Wrong choice of words, she realized!

"Liv, I'm not reluctant. It's just not *like* you. You have never asked me to spend the night before. And no, I'm not worried about your seducing me. I *know* that is not what you want to do. I just thought you might have a specific reason. Do you?"

Liv decided to level with him. "Morgan, I'm . . . concerned. Birdie wanted to talk with me in private earlier. We went to my dressing room."

"What did she say?"

"She told me that we were in perfect sync, that I should hold on to you and you would lead me, and that our breath and our rhythm are the same."

"But that's all *good* news, isn't it?"

"Yes, of course! But first she gave me this." Liv held out the manila envelope. "When I asked her what it was, she said it was our future. She said to wait until the two of us were together. She was cryptic and said you and I would each be able to explain a part of it, and that part of it needed no explanation."

"Well, then, let's open it!"

"No! Not just yet, please Morgan," Liv said pulling the envelope back. "I'm not ready. I'm not sure I want to know anything more about the future right now. Somehow, I have a feeling it is not all good news. Please give it a little more time. Besides, we still have a lot to talk about, now that you have met my friends!"

"All right, Sweetheart, let's open it later, say after breakfast. So you want to talk. Let's talk. Are you going to keep that dress on? I love the way you look in it, but it may not be the most suitable talking attire."

"I guess not. Give me your coat; I'll hang it up. Make yourself comfortable. I'll be right back." Morgan sent a cautionary warning to the Chairman of the Board to be cool, and sat down on the couch. He eyed the manila envelope on the table. He examined it more closely and noted that it was quite similar to the other envelope that had contained the drawing of Liv. It was addressed to Birdie and had a postmark of December 13, 2012, which was shortly after she had met Liv.

He contemplated opening it but knew he would not. He was anxious to know what it contained, but he was a man of great self-control. His thoughts went back to Liv. He could not even imagine life without her. What he wanted more than anything in the world was to ensure her happiness.

He was hoping that the impending events regarding the youth pastor would be resolved quickly. He wanted to bring Liv's mother, and potentially her grandparents, to Los Angeles as soon as possible. He knew that would make her happy.

Those thoughts were interrupted by Liv's return. He was relieved that the comfortable attire she chose was not night clothes, but sweats. She handed him a mug of coffee and sat down on the floor in front of him with her legs crossed. Her expression told him they were about to have a serious talk! He took a sip of the strong coffee and waited.

"Morgan, I know you have had a busy, busy couple of weeks, and I have monopolized your time since you returned. I made your coffee extra strong 'cause I need you to stay focused."

"Yes, it's strong, all right! Don't worry, Sweetheart, my mind is totally focused on you."

"You made me especially happy tonight. Of course, you *always* make me happy, but tonight was extra special to me. Thank you for being so charming to my friends. It was very important to me that you approve of them, because . . . well just let me tell you how it is. When we talked yesterday, or more correctly, when *I* talked about the events that took place while you were gone, I told you *almost* everything I had been up to."

"*Almost*?" Morgan questioned. "There's *more*?" Morgan's interest was heightened. The Chairman of the Board signaled the COW to turn in for the night. Their services would not be needed! Morgan wondered, in light of all that she *had* imparted to him, what more could she possibly say to top it.

"Morgan, I get carried away when I feel strongly about something, and I just go into action! I do things that seem right to me, and I didn't tell you everything because I wanted to make sure you would approve of my friends. I know they approve of you. They are happy for me, for us."

"Liv, come on, now. You are stalling! I've told you before. Anything you do is all right with me. You can tell me *anything*!" He got off the couch and sat down in front of her on the floor. He lifted her chin and kissed her on the forehead. "Okay, let it out!"

"I love you, Morgan."

"I love you, too, Sweetheart. Now talk!"

"I told them about our dream. I took them to meet the kids; they loved them and worked with them for several days. They each have experience and skills, and I put them to work. Their friends have special skills and want to be on board. They are ready and willing to drop what they are doing, leave their jobs and work on our dream! We have a name for our organization—The Calais Education and Community Center! We have a business plan, we met with Howard; he said everything looks good. He is handling the paperwork and legal things we will need in setting up everything . . ."

Liv was talking a mile a minute, skipping from one part to another, getting steps out of sequence, her enthusiasm and excitement growing with every word. Morgan's head was spinning. He was trying to grasp everything she was saying, disjointed as it was. What came through the loudest and clearest was her excitement about the dream they shared. She was so animated and invigorated, he found that it aroused him in a way he had not expected, catching him by surprised. He reached over and kissed her mid-sentence. Just as quickly, he released her before the COW knew what happened!

"Olivia, Baby! Slow down! We have what's left of the night and all tomorrow or all week, as long as you need!"

"Oh, Morgan, I just wanted you to know and be okay with everything. I know I must sound like a raving lunatic!"

"That's okay. You're *my* raving lunatic! I tell you what, why don't we go into the kitchen and let me watch you cook breakfast for us? You can continue this monologue there, if you still have more to say."

"Well, that's about all I have to say about *that* right now, but I *do* have some ideas about our *wedding*!" Morgan helped her up, and she led the way to the kitchen. They both realized that he had never seen her home other than the living room and the guest bathroom.

"Liv, not *now*, but one of these days you will have to give *me* a tour of *your* home."

"Oh, I will, of course, Morgan, as long as you promise not to get in my bed and fall asleep!" They both laughed.

"Believe me, Liv, if I am in *your* bed, I won't be alone, and I can promise you, I won't be sleeping!" Liv blushed and poured him some more coffee. They talked as they ate a light snack of Greek yogurt and berries. "You know, Morgan, I often feel like I grew up without a family, and working with you at the Center with the kids, I feel like part of a real family. It's even better now that my friends are back in my life. I want all of them to be a part of our wedding! The older kids can be included as bridesmaids and hostesses or groomsmen and ushers. Alex, of course, will have to be the flower girl! I would want all of them to attend the wedding and the reception! We can arrange for their transportation. We can have them all fitted for their clothes and/or take them shopping! We will have a rehearsal dinner for the wedding party, and . . . Oh, there I go again with my motor mouth running wild! You can stop me any time, Morgan!"

"Oh, but I love the way you are thinking, Motor Mouth!"

"Watch it, Mister! You are treading on dangerous territory! *I* can refer to *myself* as being a motor mouth, by *you* are not allowed to, Mr. Morgy Porgy!"

"All right, now we're even. Truce?"

"Okay, truce!

"How about that! Our first fight! We'll have to kiss and make up!"

"Our first and *last* fight! And be careful what you ask for. Now come here!" Liv looked bashfully at him as she came and sat on his lap. He kissed her once passionately. "Okay, no more distractions. Continue. I'm listening," he said, leaving her wanting more.

"Gee whiz, Morgan! Now I don't even remember *what* I was saying!"

"You were telling me what *we* want for our wedding. I like what I have heard! What else do you have, a date, perhaps?"

"As a matter of fact, yes. How does February 16 sound?"

"2013?"

"But of course! You're playing with me now! I'm trying to be serious!"

"I'm sorry, Baby. I think I was just trying to finagle another kiss! I'll be serious. That date sounds good to me. When do we tell the kids?"

"We can tell them this week! I think we should have all of the kids ten and up to take an active part as at least ushers and hostesses. Probably the groomsmen and bridesmaids can be the older teens. What do you think?"

"Sounds good to me. I think they will really be happy to be a part of something so formal. It will be a good social experience for some of them, and a good learning opportunity to see how things can work in the real world. I'd say we invite all the parents so that there won't be a babysitting problem with the younger ones. Of course, I know they will all be on their best behavior! They have been programmed to understand, at least as far as the Center is concerned, that less-than-exemplary behavior will result in consequences.

"There is one thing to consider, though. Some families may not want to participate because they may feel they won't be able to give appropriate wedding gifts. I wouldn't want anyone to feel obligated. I want them *all* involved!"

"That's a thought, Morgan. I have a plan in mind that might work, but I can't share with you just yet. Let me work it out. Okay?"

"I'm *really* curious now. But I trust when you have it all worked out, you'll let me know, and I'm sure I'll be pleased."

"You will be happy, I promise. My main mission in life now is to make you happy! Now, back to the wedding planning. I'm guessing you will want Kyle and Travis to be among your groomsmen. I'm guessing Kyle will be the Best Man?"

"Yes, he's my main man. How about you? I'm guessing Elizabeth and Holly for you with Elizabeth as your Maid of Honor."

"Yes! And what do you think about the ten oldest girls and boys to make a nice round number of attendants at twelve couples with the rest being ushers and hostesses? That way, we won't have to worry about trying to choose one over another. I'll let you choose the ring bearer. I think Athene would love the opportunity to actually *sing* at our wedding!"

"I *know* she would! She thinks the world of you and hangs on to your every word!"

"Oh, I am just so *excited*, Morgan!"

"I hate to bring this up while you are on such a high note, Liv. Getting back to our dream, I think all of your planning and ideas are terrific, and I can see our dream coming alive, at least in our hearts. I hope we are not getting ahead of ourselves. We still have a big hurdle to get over. We need an appropriate *facility*.

"Well *I* am not going to think about that right now, and I don't want you to, either. We have assurances that everything will work out, that we will be successful and happy. That's all *I* need to know! Come with me. I'm ready to open Birdie's envelope!"

They went back to the living room, and Liv picked up the envelope and handed it to Morgan to open. "You want *me* to open it? She gave it to *you*. *You* should open it, Liv."

"Are you *afraid* to open it?"

"No, I just thought that . . ."

"Open it, Morgan!" They sat down and Morgan opened the envelope and removed three separate sheets of sketch paper. The top picture was an unmistakable picture of Alex with her large brown eyes sparkling. Underneath was printed, "Alexandria Maria Calais." They looked at the picture and were amazed.

Morgan removed Alex's picture to reveal a portrait of a boy with jet-black hair and tanned complexion who looked exactly like Morgan, except for his eyes, which were decidedly Liv's. The name printed underneath was "Morgan Avery Calais, II."

Liv's breath caught in her throat and her eyes teared at the sight of the handsome little Morgan face that was peering back at her with her very own eyes! "Oh, Morgan!" she exclaimed, never removing her eyes from the picture. Finally, the third picture was revealed. It was a little face that looked a lot like Liv, but with Morgan's piercing brown-rimmed hazel eyes and a tuft of curly auburn hair. She was looking at the face of her brother, Randy, which was the name printed beneath the picture—Randy Alan Calais!

Liv looked at Morgan and sensed his mixed emotions. He obviously knew something or saw something that she did not. She remembered Birdie's words. She surmised the picture of Alex they both knew, and that the picture of Morgan II was self-explanatory. Only *she* knew that the third picture was a great likeness of her brother Randy, curly red hair and all. But what did Morgan see that she didn't?

"Morgan, what is it that I can't see? You seem troubled! I get the message that these are our children to be. Alex is about to be ours. I now know that we will have two sons. The first one will look like *you*, but he will have *my* eyes. Our second son will have *your* eyes, but he will look just like my brother, Randy. Tell me what I can't see, Morgan, please!"

Morgan checked his emotions; more correctly, he reassessed his emotions and put his arm around her to reassure her. "Liv, I'm sorry if I upset you. Everything is fine. I see what you see. I know what you know. The message that Birdie sent to me is that she is ready to move on. She told us that she would live to see at least two of her great-grandchildren."

"Well, that's okay isn't it? That won't be for a long time. We're not even married yet!"

"Yes, Baby, I know. But she *has* seen them, *all* of them! These pictures are the *proof*!"

"Do you mean she's . . ."

"No, Liv, she's still with us. She will dance at our wedding. She's just letting us know that it will be soon. Liv, do not fret! She is fine! She is ready. She is *happy* with a capital *H*!" He put the pictures down and held her in his arms. "Now let me see your beautiful smile." Liv smiled at him and laid her head on his chest. There they remained on the couch until daylight crept into the room.

CHAPTER 32

(1/1/2013) Liv awoke to find herself stretched out on the couch still wrapped in Morgan's arms. She extricated herself without awakening him. "Poor Baby," she thought. He looked so contented. Oh, how she loved him! She retrieved a fleece throw and lovingly covered him with it. She then jumped into the pool for a truncated workout and then into the shower. She was dressed and had a real breakfast well under way when the aroma of freshly brewed coffee and sizzling bacon found its way to Morgan's nostrils.

Fully awake now, Morgan stretched some of the kinks out of his body that resulted from the limiting confines of the couch. He looked at his watch. It was almost 10:30. He hadn't intended to sleep that long. He followed his nose and found Liv in the kitchen. "Good morning," he said as he put his arms around her and nuzzled the back of her neck.

"Good morning to you, Sleepy Head! Breakfast is almost ready. Give me five minutes."

"That's perfect, Sweetheart. I'm a crumpled mess. It's a good thing I took off my coat last night or my tux would have been jacked! I'll be right back." Morgan went to his car and returned with his toiletry pouch to freshen up in the guest bathroom. He returned to the kitchen just as Liv was setting out a plate of French toast, fresh fruit and crisp bacon for him.

"I hope breakfast is okay. I haven't done much grocery shopping lately."

"This is just fine. Aren't you going to have something to eat?

"I'm just having some fruit. I'm not feeling much like eating. I'm still hyper. I want to hurry and get to the Center and break the news to the kids! When you are finished with breakfast, we can go to your place, and I'll be working out some of the details while you are getting ready! Does that sound like a good plan?"

"Yes, that would be perfect except for one little detail."

"What's that? What did I forget?"

"Today is New Year's Day. It's a *holiday,* and the Center is closed!"

"Oh, no!" Liv exclaimed, her chagrin evident. "How dumb of me!" Morgan was quick to correct her.

"You? Dumb? Don't even *think* that! You are just anxious! I don't blame you. I feel the same way, Sweetheart! Come here," he said, embracing her and kissing her cheek. "Don't be disappointed. We can use this time to do a little more planning. We can go to the Center the first thing tomorrow."

"I'm just so disappointed! And now, I have no plan for today!"

"I still have to go home and change. Why don't you come with me, and then we can pick up Alex and spend some time with *her* today. You know she would love that!"

Liv perked up immediately. "Oh, yes! That's a great idea. She loves going to the park with us. Hurry and finish your breakfast!"

"Liv, you amaze me! I'm hurrying!"

On the ride to Morgan's, Liv had returned her focus to the wedding and the Center kids' roles. She was writing feverishly trying to keep up on paper with everything that was popping up in her head. She had accomplished a substantial amount of planning by the time they pulled in front of Morgan's estate. "Make yourself at home. I am going to shave, shower and get dressed. It shouldn't take too long, Hon."

"Okay, I'll be in the library." In high gear, she called Walter, who was still in bed. "Hi, Walter, it's me, Liv! I hope you're up. I want to tell you about the plans I'm making for the wedding. I have confirmed the date with Morgan. It is going to be Saturday afternoon, February 16. I hope that is enough time to . . ."

"Hey, Liv! Take it easy! Slow down, Sweetheart! Let me wake the old man up a bit. What time is it, anyway?"

"Oh, Walter, I'm sorry! Happy New Year! Do you want me to call you later, or do you want to call me back?"

"No, that's okay. I should have been up. Hold on a second while I switch on the coffee. Now. First let me tell you that your young man has passed my inspection with flying colors. I know the two of you will be very happy. I could see how much you love each other. He obviously adores you, and so he should; you have my blessing!"

"I'm glad, Walter! Your blessing is very important to me!"

"So you have the date, February 16. That's good. Start getting the invitation list together for you and Morgan. I've got a number of friends I want to invite, too.

I will activate the machinery, that is, get the planning team to work on the venue and the invitations. I have a great facility on standby in downtown L.A. It is convenient and large enough to hold everyone and have the reception there as well. I will be sending out several thousand invitations to my contacts who I know will not personally attend. But they are good resources for . . . oh, never mind."

"Walter, I have told you about our friends at the Center. We want all of them to be a part of our wedding. They are family to us. We want to provide everything for them, clothes, transportation, everything. You probably didn't anticipate so much, so we will take care of their expenses so . . ."

"Liv, don't do this!" Walter interrupted, gently admonishing her. "No expense is too great for me. I *told* you; as your father, *I* am taking care of *everything*! If you decide you want to fly everyone to the *moon* for your wedding, it's on *me*! Please don't forget that, Liv. Don't hold back on *anything* you think you might want."

Liv realized she had hurt his feelings. Despite that dark period in her life when it was her mission to use every man she could for her own gain, that was not the real Olivia. She had compassion and never wanted to be a burden to anyone, especially Walter. She remembered again Theo's words that it made Walter happy to do whatever he did for her.

"Walter, please forgive me! I am so, so sorry! I promise I will try very hard to never do that again!"

"Of course I forgive you, Sweetheart. I know you mean well. When you have all of the dates, events, ideas, whatever, just let me know as things progress. Give me the names of everyone at the center and their roles in your wedding, and a date when staff can come and take measurements. I will make it happen. Is that okay?"

"Yes, Walter. Thank you."

"And you don't have to always keep saying 'thank you.' Oh, Liv, what am I going to do with you?"

"Just keep being the loving father you are to me!

"About the kids at the Center, I want to send invitations to their families, but I foresee a problem in that they may feel obligated to give wedding gifts that they may not be able to afford. I thought perhaps they could get special invitations to specify no gifts, or a contribution to a favorite charity or their church in any amount they wish."

"The truth is, between Morgan and I, we don't *need* anything that would be in line with traditional wedding gifts. I don't plan to register for gifts. Can we do that?"

"We have been thinking along similar lines. My reason for sending invitations to my network is for the purpose of soliciting donations, in lieu of gifts, to the Calais Education and Community Center to be opening soon! I wasn't going to say anything just yet, because I didn't know whether or not Howard had talked to you about it."

"Walter, you *know* about that?"

"To tell you the truth, Liv, I've known about it a long time. It was not for me to divulge to you. I know about the site, the construction, everything. I know about the inheritances that you haven't yet received. I know you want the site to be a surprise for Morgan. Rest assured, I would never interfere with your plans. I've probably said too much already. Please don't ask any more questions about this. When you meet with Howard, he will fill both of you in on everything. Okay, Honey?"

Liv didn't know what to say or to think. She just didn't know how far-reaching their dream was, or who were involved or would have a hand in its realization. Between Theo and Birdie and her revelations, and now Walter, she did not want to even think about it then.

"Walter, I . . . I can't begin to process or even understand what is happening! I won't question you. I think my brain needs a good, long rest. Right now I will just think about breaking the news to the kids tomorrow and dealing with only issues surrounding *them* right now. I will leave the invitations and all of that to your discretion.

"Well, I'd better get a move on. We're about to go now, and I have a few more notes to make. Can the three of us meet for lunch or dinner soon?"

"You bet! Just say when. Bye, Sweetheart. Love you."

"I love you too, Walter. Bye!"

Liv had just finished completing her notes when Morgan appeared at the library door.

"Well, I'm all ready to go. I have spoken with Mrs. Dawson, and she will have Alex all ready to go when we get there. How about you?"

Liv looked up at him, taking in his clean-shaven face, his charming smile, and his lean, muscular body as he leaned against the doorframe. She thought about falling asleep on his chest last night on her couch. As so often happened when she looked at him, she felt a flutter in her heart as she thought smiling, "This hunk of man is mine, all mine!"

"I'm ready. Let's go," she said, picking up her notes and her purse. Hand in hand, they walked to his car and were on their way to get Alex. "I have worked out the problem of wedding gifts, Morgan. I just talked with Walter. He is arranging for a team to come to the Center on the day we decide and measure all of the kids and fit them for their outfits. I will meet with the designers to design the dresses for the wedding party as well as my bridal gown. Everyone will get an invitation, and it will be specified that there should be no wedding gifts. Don't you think that we have everything we need, anyway?"

"Yes, I know *I* do. I have *you!*"

"You know what I mean, Morgan. I won't register for gifts. In lieu of gifts, the invitations sent to families of our kids will suggest that a donation of any kind or amount be made to a charity of their choice, or to their church. All of the other invitations will request that a donation be made to the Calais Education and Community Center.

"Liv, you are a *genius*! That's an *excellent* idea! It will work perfectly. We won't even have to know if or what they gave. And the donations to our school, that is *fantastic*! I *knew* there was a good reason for me to marry you!"

"Morgan, you don't know the half of it.

"I helped myself to a couple of packages of index cards from your library. Everyone can fill out a card with their name and the names and addresses of their parents or guardians. The staff can do so as well, and we will be sure to get invitations to everyone."

"Good idea. You think of everything!"

"Morgan, do you think we should also let them know that we are adopting Alex? I have mixed feelings about that. We haven't even told Alex. I wouldn't want her to find out publicly!"

"You're right. We should tell her ourselves privately. I haven't wanted to mention anything to her until it's a done deal. We have no doubt that she would love to have a home with us! Let's not mention it just yet to anyone there."

Alex was waiting expectantly at the window watching for Morgan's car. As soon as she saw it, she ran to the door with Dolly Liv and was waiting on the porch. "Hi, Mommy Liv! Hi, Mr. Morgan! We're all ready to go!"

Morgan drove to Kenneth Hahn Park where the four of them had a fun-filled day.

(1/2/2013) Early the next morning Morgan and Liv pulled up to the Center.

Once they were inside, it seemed all activity stopped, and they were greeted by the children as usual, each one vying for individual attention. Morgan went to have a word with one of the leaders while Liv headed to where Alex was with Christiaan and Lavana, her favorite new playmates, playing with the building blocks.

Very soon, the signal to assemble for an announcement was heard, and everyone gravitated to the usual meeting place on the bleachers by the basketball court. Morgan was already in place, and Liv went to stand by him. Whenever Morgan and Liv had been in the presence of the kids, they had maintained a professional posture. As far as the kids knew, she was Ms. Liv, just another adult that came there on a regular basis to help them; and Morgan was just "Mr. Morgan," everyone's friend who cared about them and had been coming there for a long, long time. They felt the kids would be surprised, but happy to learn they were going to be married. They had not given them enough credit for being smart enough to have figured it out.

Everyone was quiet. They knew that whenever an impromptu assembly was called, there had to be an important reason. Sometimes it was positive tidings, and sometimes not. They were anxious to find out if the New Year were to be started out with bad news or good news.

"Hey, gang," Morgan began. "Thank you for gathering so quietly and quickly! I really appreciate it. We are here this second day of the New Year to make an important announcement that affects each of you; and don't worry, it's all good." There was a united sigh of relief and a few seconds of buzzing. "Listen up, now," Morgan quieted them. As the room fell pin-drop-fall-hearing silent, Morgan continued. "You all know that Ms. Liv has been coming and spending time with you for a while now. She has even gone with us on many of our outings. In the process, she has fallen in love with *all* of you!"

Everyone began to cheer. Morgan held up his hand for silence, which came almost instantaneously. "While she was falling in love with all of you, she was also falling in love with *me*!" More cheers ensued and subsided on Morgan's cue. "We are happy to announce that we have decided to get married!" The uproar was loud and jubilant as the kids jumped up from their seats and swarmed the two, cheering excitedly! Morgan and Liv were completely caught off guard by the reception of the news. It took several minutes to contain the bunch and get them back into their seats.

"Thanks, guys, for your enthusiastic reception of our good news!"

DeShawn stood up and yelled, "What took you so long Mr. M? We all knew you guys were in love from the get go! It was just a matter of time! Now you can relax. You don't have to be so formal. Go ahead! Take her hand! *Kiss* her!"

Then began the wild chant, "Kiss her! Kiss her! Kiss her!" Morgan knew the only way to quiet them down again would be to kiss Liv. She knew it, too. So, for the sake of quiet, Morgan put his arm around Liv and gave her a "G"-rated kiss on the lips.

"Okay, guys. Settle down. You haven't heard all of our news!" The gang quieted again, waiting for the next bit of news. "Not only are all of you and your families invited to the wedding, many of you will be a part of the wedding party!"

Subdued cheering commenced and was short lived. It was clear that many did not know the significance of being a part of a wedding party. Some were just looking in puzzlement. "If you will just stay with us a minute, Ms. Liv will explain to you what it means."

Liv didn't want to overwhelm them with details, but she did want to give them a sense of what to expect. She gave a brief overview of the various members of the party and the roles they played. She assured them that they would be given all the help they needed to do whatever jobs they would be assigned. She ended with, "This is what Mr. Morgan and I want you to help us with."

It was obviously clearer as the kids became very excited. They were smiling and talking happily. "Are there any questions?" Liv asked. Random statements and questions sprang up across the bleachers.

"Can I be the Maid of Honor?"

"I want to be the Best Man!"

"No, me!"

"I want to be a bridesmaid, too!"

Liv raised her hand for silence, but Morgan had to step in to quash the rambunctious crowd.

"Okay. Enough already! This is the kind of behavior that can get you eliminated! Now just simmer down. Relax! Ms. Liv will explain how the assignments will be made.

"They're all yours, Liv. You won't have any more trouble out of them!"

"Ladies and gentlemen, I know you are all excited. I'm excited, too! You know that Mr. Morgan and I love every one of you. We didn't want to have to pick and choose among you, so we have come up with a plan so *we* don't have to. *All* of you *and* your families are being invited. Every one of you age twelve and over will be included in one of the categories of hostess, usher, bridesmaid, or groomsman.

"We need ten young ladies and ten young men to be the bridesmaids and groomsmen.

The Maid of Honor will be my best friend, and another of my close adult friends will be a bridesmaid. Mr. Morgan's two best adult friends will be his best man and one of the groomsmen. The ten *oldest* young ladies and the ten *oldest* young men will make up the rest of the bridesmaids and groomsmen. The rest of you will be ushers and hostesses. Understand?"

The kids began trying to figure out among themselves where they fit in based on their ages. The older kids were more assured. The younger ones were not so sure, but they were hopeful. They *all* knew they would be included.

"When we get all of this sorted out after making sure we have all the right information, we will let you know exactly what you will be doing. One thing I want you to know. All of your clothes, shoes, and accessories will be provided for you. That includes *everyone*, not just the wedding party. When you get one of the index cards that are being passed out, I want you to print your name and date of birth, your complete address where your invitations are to be sent, and the names of your parents or guardians. Later you will be given a consent form to be completed, giving permission for you to participate in the wedding and to be transported when necessary. We need these cards returned as quickly as possible. We will be scheduling a session for you to be fitted for your clothes here at the Center."

Morgan decided that was enough information for one day. Besides, he wanted to spend some time with Alex. He wasn't sure just how much she actually understood. "Okay, guys, you know what you need to do, so let's get to it. I want those cards completed before you leave today. Understood?" Receiving their acknowledgement, Morgan left Liv and the other adults to help the younger kids while he sought out Alex. She had returned to the blocks with Christiaan.

"Hey, Baby Girl!" he called to her. She came running to him with Christiaan on her heels. "Hi, Mr. Morgan!" Christiaan said with a big smile. Morgan lowered himself and gave them each a hug. He noted Alex and Christiaan were a good match. Alex was coming more and more out of her shell, and Christiaan was quiet and shy. They got along very well.

"How about you two coming and talking with me a moment?" Without waiting for an answer, he held out a hand to each and walked over to the end of the bleachers and sat down. Alex quickly climbed onto his lap while Christiaan just sat down looking up expectantly at him.

"Do you know what our meeting earlier was about?" The kids looked at each other as they raised and lowered their shoulders, gesturing they did not. "No?" he questioned.

"I saw you kiss Ms. Liv," Christiaan blushed.

"Yes, me and Dolly Liv saw you kiss her, too," Alex added.

"Well, that's because we are in love!" Morgan explained. "We are going to get married, and we want all of you to be a part of our wedding! Would you like that?"

"What do we do?" Christiaan asked.

"You can be the ring bearer. Would you do that for me?"

"I guess so. What's a ring bear?"

"A ring bear*er* is the person who has the very important job of carrying the ring on a pillow and bringing it to the groom to put on the bride's finger. Do you think you can handle that very important job?"

"Sure! That's *easy*! May I go and finish playing with the blocks now?"

"Yes, you may go. Thank you!" Christiaan scurried off, and Alex remained, quietly sitting on Morgan's knee with a look that Morgan couldn't quite gauge. "What's the matter, Alex? Why are you so quiet all of a sudden? Do you know what we have been talking about?"

"You love Mommy Liv?"

"Yes, Alex. That's why we will be getting married!"

"What will happen when you get married?"

"We will live together in the same house, but nothing else will change much."

"You and Mommy Liv will live together like mommies and daddies?"

"Well, yes, Honey. It's kind of like that." Alex stopped talking, and Morgan could feel her body become tense. "What is it, Alex? What is the matter?"

Finally, she responded, her big eyes looking up at Morgan with a trace of fear, "When you and Mommy Liv are living together like mommies and daddies, will you hit Mommy Liv, or push her, or kick her?"

Morgan realized what was happening. Alex had done so well and had come so far out of her shell since he and Liv had been spending so much time with her away from the Center, he had almost forgotten what she had experienced. He lifted her from his lap and stood her in front of him and leaned down so that they were face-to-face, eye-to-eye.

"Alex, honey, I would *never, ever* hit, or push, or kick Mommy Liv or do *anything* to hurt her. I *love* her! You know that, don't you, Baby Girl?"

Alex stared into his eyes, probing for confirmation of the trust she had in him from the day he found her. Morgan saw the shine and sparkle begin to return to her eyes and blossom into her infectious smile. He knew that problem had been solved, and he was greatly relieved.

"Mr. Morgan, I'm glad you love Mommy Liv, and I know you will never hurt her. I'm glad you are getting married and will live together like mommies and daddies!"

"Thank you, Alex! I'm happy to hear you say that!" He saw her eyes grow very serious. He wondered, "What now?" He soon found out!

"Mr. Morgan, *I* love you. Do you love *me*, too?" Morgan was momentarily relieved.

"Yes, Sweetheart. I love you very, very much. I thought you *knew* that. You *do* know that, don't you?"

"Then will you marry *me* too, so that I can live with you and Mommy Liv?" Morgan was thrown for a loop! He felt unprepared to respond to her question, and wanted to involve Liv in whatever the response would be. They had not wanted to bring up her adoption just yet, but he knew she needed an answer right then. He had to say *something*!

"You know, Honey, that is a real good idea. Do you think we can talk about it later with Mommy Liv?"

"Okay, Mr. Morgan!" Just that simply, the crisis had been averted, or at least postponed.

"You said Christiaan could be the ring bear. What can *I* be?"

"The 'ring bear' is an important job, but *you* will have the *most* important job. *You* will be the *flower girl*!"

"The flower girl?" Alex asked happily. "Will I wear flowers in my hair? What does a flower girl do?"

"You will walk in front of Mommy Liv, and you will sprinkle flowers on the floor for her to walk on!"

"Oh! I will *love* to do that! I'll be the *best* flower girl in the world!" With that, she was off to tell Christiaan about her job!

Morgan was anxious to tell Liv about Alex's reservations about their "living together like mommies and daddies" and her wanting him to marry *her*, too. He knew she would be better able to speak with her about it. At the first opportunity, he pulled Liv aside. Liv understood Alex's concern and was happy with the way Morgan had handled it. He had been able to dodge the bullet and placate her for the time being.

"Morgan, I've been thinking about it, and I have an idea how we can kill two birds with one stone. I'll share it with you when I have it all worked out. In the meantime, we'll just have to assure her that we love her *and* each other, and she will always be in our lives."

"Great, Honey! That's a real relief to me."

When all the index cards had been completed and returned, information was verified and assignments noted on each card. Arrangements had been made for the wedding planning team responsible for dressing the wedding party and all of those involved to come to the Center on Tuesday, January 8, to begin their tasks by taking measurements, shoe sizes, and whatever else they needed to do for them to get the job done.

CHAPTER 33

A JOB FOR EVERYONE

(1/8/2013) The assignment cards had been provided to the planning team to extract the information they would need for the invitations and other purposes and returned to Liv. Before the team was scheduled to arrive, all of the kids had been assembled to receive their assignments. Morgan and Liv returned the cards with the assignments to the kids who, in term, would have to present them to the individual team members to record their notes and measurements.

Liv first announced alphabetically the names of the ten young ladies who would be bridesmaids. They were Ardis, Aleiya, Athaila, Guadalupe, J'Naye, Lourdes, Rochelle, Sabrina, Stephanie, and Vanessa. Morgan did likewise for the groomsmen. They were Christopher, Daniel, David, DeShawn, Erin, Gordon, Jose, Jonathan, Manuel, and Orlando.

All of the other young ladies and gentlemen twelve and up who weren't named knew they were hostesses and ushers, and they each were given their cards.

The last cards to be handed out were for the flower girl and the ring bearer, Alex and Christiaan, who were not among the group waiting to learn of their roles. Everyone was excited, especially the bridesmaids and the groomsmen. There was much activity and commotion as everyone was being measured or waiting to be measured.

Liv had one more card that had become separated and was missed initially. She looked around for Athene, whose card had been oversighted. She did not see her, so she began to inquire and search. No one had seen her; everyone was too excited to be focusing on anyone but themselves. Liv went to the little girls' room and saw Athene there, forlorn and crying.

"Athene, here you are! I've been looking for you! Why are you in here crying? What's the matter?" Liv said, putting her arm around Athene's shoulders.

Athene, now fifteen years old, replied tearfully, "I wanted to be a bridesmaid. I'm older than Aleiya and Lourdes, and *they're* both bridesmaids! You said the ten oldest girls would be bridesmaids! I'm not *anything*, not even a hostess! I'm not getting a new dress like everyone else!" she wailed, heartbroken.

"Oh, Honey! I'm so sorry! This is *my* mistake. I didn't forget you! I *couldn't* forget *you*! You are my shining star! I have your card and your assignment right here! I didn't want to mix it with the others because it is so special, one of a kind! Please! Don't cry anymore, Athene!" Athene checked her tears, taking the tissue Liv handed her.

"You *do* have something for me?" she asked hopefully. "It's special?"

"Yes, Athene, *very* special! You have worked so hard, and you impressed me so much the first time I came here, I never forgot. I want to offer you your first professional gig! Morgan and I want *you* to sing at our wedding!" Athene was at a loss for words.

"For *real*? Are you *serious*?"

"I am *very* serious! Will you accept the job?"

"Oh, yes! *Yes*! I can't *believe* it! What do you want me to sing?"

"Do you know 'The Lord's Prayer?' "

"Yes! I sing it at my church!"

"Good! The other song I want you to sing is one *I* wrote. It is called, 'This Is Love.' I will help you learn it. I have the lyric written for you." Liv removed the sheet from her folder and handed it to Athene.

"This will be my first singing job! I think I will be nervous! How many people will be in the audience? What if . . ." Seeing her anxiety, Liv interrupted her.

"Athene, it will be okay. Nerves are good. You can use that nervous energy; you just have to *channel* it."

"I *am* feeling nervous!" Athene admitted. "I wouldn't want to disappoint you and Mr. Morgan by messing up your wedding!"

"Don't worry about it. You won't mess up anything! I will help you so that you will be able to knock 'em dead! You will give a professional performance. That means you will *know* your lyric; you won't be looking at the words as you sing. You will know the melody as I wrote it. You will also have a subtext."

"What is that?"

"Well, think of it as what you will be *thinking* while you are singing to make people feel what you mean, feel your *emotion*, as they listen to you.

"That sounds very hard, Ms. Liv."

"It will be easy. You will see. First, I want you to memorize the lyric. This is all I want you to do for now. Can you do that?"

"Okay, Ms. Liv. I can do that. I will."

"That's my girl! Now, before you take your card and get fitted for your clothes, tell me. How much will you charge us?"

"*Charge* you?" Athene asked if that were unthinkable! "I *couldn't* charge you. I would do it for *nothing*!"

"Athene, you want to be a professional. Professionals get paid!"

"I don't know how much to ask for. If I ask for too much, you might say 'never mind,' and that would make me very sad," Athene answered matter-of-factly.

Liv smiled at her. "I'll tell you what. Since this is your first 'gig,' I will give you a deposit right now, and we can work out the final payment later when we determine your fee. We can have a conversation about this aspect of being a professional later. It's a business, Athene. I will write you a check now for $100 as a deposit. Does that sound reasonable?"

"One hundred dollars? Wow!" she exclaimed. But I don't have a bank account. I can't cash a check."

"Well, we'll have to do something about that. Right now, I want you to get your measurements taken. Then we can go and open up a bank account for you."

Athene took the lyric sheet and the card and hurried off to share her good news. Liv had her processing expedited, and then took Athene to the bank in Morgan's car.

CHAPTER 34

Because there was physical evidence placing Jason at the crime scene in addition to the statements of Holly and Olivia, a search warrant was obtained for his residence. The warrant was executed on 12/21/2012, while he was away working on materials for his workshop.

Authorities gained access and conducted a thorough search. Although mostly everything viewed appeared routine and/or innocuous with no probative value, there was an important discovery—an unlocked wall safe. On initial examination, it appeared to be empty. Upon further investigation, expert eyes detected a false bottom. When it was uncovered, what they discovered was implausible!

There were at least a dozen CD's, a few manila envelopes stuffed with negatives, and three ledger-type record books. A cursory review of a few of the negatives held up to the light revealed what looked to be a young child about four years old in the company of adult men and women in questionable positions. The journals appeared to be a record of transaction involving the leasing of a minor child to various individuals showing dates, times, and fees paid. One of the books had entire sections devoted to a particular, obviously regular, lessee. Also discovered was a master lease contract containing provisions such as, "return of merchandise in the same condition as when received with no evidence of abuse, i.e., bruises or marks." Payment was required in cash with an additional three-thousand-dollar cash security deposit "refundable upon return of property in good condition." Included were suggested ways to "compel compliance which would not result in visible evidence."

Although the references to the lessees were reduced to initials, investigators correctly theorized that after all of the negatives were developed, the individuals could be identified from their pictures and matched with the initials in the records.

"The victimization of innocent children is deplorable! Everyone involved should be held accountable! It looks like we will be working on this for a very long time. No matter how long it takes, heads will roll!" declared Detective O'Brien.

ADA Reginald was eagerly waiting for and received the results of the search. When he subsequently informed Dan of the evidence collected, Dan commented, "If my guess is right, I would say the child in those pictures is our suspect, Jason Winston. No wonder the poor bastard turned into the heinous monster he became."

"Nevertheless," Reginald said, "he made his choices as an adult; therefore, he gets no sympathy from me! *He* is going to pay for what *he* has done.

Though ancillary to the instant investigation, ultimately the roster of those subsequently identified and prosecuted included an impressive list of males and females who were prominent in government, law enforcement, politics, business, and the financial, medical, legal, judicial and educational institutions. When the dust had settled after several years, there were ninety-four arrests and convictions.

The majority plea-bargained when confronted with the clear and undeniable pictorial evidence. Those that chose to go to trial were dead in the water. The names of those perpetrators who had since met their makers, whether through natural attrition or by their own hands, were exposed. There had been other children included in some of the pictures, and as many as could be identified were sought out with positive results.

When advised of the impending arrest of Jason Winston, Dan notified everyone via his niece, Megan. The suggestion to make the arrest at the church during the orientation was passed on to the detectives, and they agreed to do so.

The Orientation

(1/12/2013) On the evening of the orientation, everything was in place. The auditorium began filling up as people streamed and then trickled in until the designated start time. Jason was delighted at the turnout. Promptly, the Senior Pastor opened with prayer and greeted everyone. After a brief description of the purpose of the orientation, he introduced Youth Pastor Jason Winston and Miss Carter and turned the mike over to Jason.

"Good evening, everyone. Thanks for coming. If you didn't get an info packet as you came in, Miss Carter will be happy to get one to you if you will raise your hand and keep it up until she gets to you.

"I am excited about the series of workshops we are starting . . ."

Jason continued to work his charm as the words glibly flowed from his lips like hot lava down a steep mountain. Holly's parents entered the auditorium and were standing at the back. Seeing them, Jason flashed his pearly whites in a toothy smile and motioned to them.

"There are still a few seats left up front. Welcome!"

He then continued to address the group and answered questions. The Albrights, still standing in the rear, were joined by Megan Harper and her uncle, ADA Daniel Harper. Jason acknowledged their entrance with a curious nod and continued his dialogue without pause. His flow was decidedly disrupted, though, when he saw that Elizabeth Randall had entered along with, of all people, Holly Albright! At this point they were all standing in the rear—the Albrights, the couple he did not recognize, Elizabeth, and Holly. Jason managed to recover somewhat, but he was not able to recapture his earlier flow.

It was the appearance of Olivia, who had entered and stood beside Holly holding the hand of a young man he did not know, that was his complete undoing, from which he was never able to recover. He turned white as a sheet as if he had just seen a ghost and was reduced to stuttering gibberish. As he stood there in disbelief, he was flanked by two uniformed police officers accompanied by the SVU detectives.

"Jason Winston, you are under arrest on two counts of aggravated rape," Det. Rogers announced. "You have the right to remain silent. If you give up that right, anything you say can and will be used against you in a court of law. You have the right to an attorney. If you cannot afford an attorney, one will be provided for you. Do you understand the rights I have just read to you?"

Jason, still reduced to the state of a blubbering idiot, could only stare incredulously at Olivia and Holly, oblivious to anything else as he was placed in handcuffs to be carted off. Collectively, members of the congregation were stunned and couldn't believe what they were witnessing.

At a loss, the Senior Pastor approached and addressed Det. Rogers. "Officer, is there any chance some terrible mistake has been made? Surely there has been a grave mistake! These charges are extremely serious!"

"Yes, they are serious, Reverend," she replied, "and we have highly reliable witnesses, the victims themselves, and forensic evidence that suggest he *is* the correct suspect. Sorry to interrupt your proceedings. We will remove the suspect now. Please excuse us."

Everyone watched in silence as Jason was practically dragged from the church, unable to stand on his own two feet.

Not knowing what else to do, the Senior Pastor addressed the congregation, "Let us bow our heads in prayer for Pastor Jason."

In response, Dan said in a loud voice as the group exited the building, "How about saying a prayer for the *victims* of Pastor Jason?"

www.ingramcontent.com/pod-product-compliance
Lightning Source LLC
Chambersburg PA
CBHW070802120726
47910CB00001B/262